Don't miss these

MW00935757

Vickie McKeehan

The Pelican Pointe Series
PROMISE COVE
HIDDEN MOON BAY
DANCING TIDES
LIGHTHOUSE REEF
STARLIGHT DUNES
LAST CHANCE HARBOR
SEA GLASS COTTAGE
LAVENDER BEACH
SANDCASTLES UNDER THE CHRISTMAS
MOON
BENEATH WINTER SAND
KEEPING CAPE SUMMER

The Evil Secrets Trilogy
JUST EVIL Book One
DEEPER EVIL Book Two
ENDING EVIL Book Three
EVIL SECRETS TRILOGY BOXED SET

The Skye Cree Novels
THE BONES OF OTHERS
THE BONES WILL TELL
THE BOX OF BONES
HIS GARDEN OF BONES
TRUTH IN THE BONES
SEA OF BONES (2018)

Keeping Cape Summer

By

VICKIE McKEEHAN

beachdevils
PRESS

Keeping Cape Summer
A Pelican Pointe Novel
Published by Beachdevils Press
Copyright © 2018 Vickie McKeehan
All rights reserved.

Keeping Cape Summer
A Pelican Pointe Novel
Copyright © 2018 Vickie McKeehan

This book is a work of fiction. Names, characters, incidents, locales, and dialogue are drawn from the author's imagination and are not to be construed as real. Any resemblance to actual events or persons, living or dead, businesses or companies, is entirely coincidental.

beachdevils
PRESS
ISBN-10: 1719449430
ISBN-13: 978-1719449434
Published by Beachdevils Press
Printed in the USA
Titles Available at Amazon
Cover design by Vanessa Mendozzi
Pelican Pointe map designed by Jess Johnson

You can visit the author at:
www.vickiemckeehan.com
www.facebook.com/VickieMcKeehan
http://vickiemckeehan.wordpress.com/
www.twitter.com/VickieMcKeehan

For Charlcie.

1905 - 1983

"Everything good, everything magical happens between the months of June and August."

~ JENNY HAN

Keeping Cape Summer

By

VICKIE McKEEHAN

beachdevils
PRESS

Welcome to Pelican Pointe

To see the complete **Cast of Characters** list go to my website:
www.vickiemckeehan.com
under the **Pelican Pointe Series** tab

Prologue

Two years earlier
Cape Cod, Massachusetts

The summer Simon Bremmer met Amelia Langston he'd been two months out of the Army and feeling freedom for the first time in a dozen years. His days dodging rocket-propelled grenades or ground fire or seeking out serious threats from the other side had run their course. He was done going on alert in places like Baghdad or Badakhshan or Kyrgyzstan or any of the other stans and was ready to get on with his life.

As an Army Ranger he'd spent enough time in dusty desert outposts and in Afghanistan's rugged provinces near the Pakistani border, that he'd almost forgotten what it was like to blow the better part of a day simply lounging around or sleeping late. He'd forgotten what it was like to have the time to do whatever he wanted. Even if all the downtime was making him slightly edgy, maybe even a little cabin-fever crazy.

Thanks to his mother and his aunt Lorraine, they'd let him transition and unwind at the family's summer home on Nauset Beach. His period of adjustment, of reconnecting, meant enjoying everything the Outer

Cape had to offer. Like beautiful, tanned, shapely females sunbathing in skimpy bikinis everywhere he looked.

So far, only one stood out from the rest. The one who always had a camera in her hand wherever she went. He'd seen her at the store, at the post office, and at several of the eateries in town. She was the one with rose-gold hair down to her waist, the one who took dozens of day trips around the Cape and always seemed more curious than the rest. The one who asked a million questions of the tour guides.

He knew because he'd decided to take in the Cape's scenery for himself. They kept bumping into each other wherever he went.

For three days he'd explored all the tourist spots before getting up the nerve to approach her. At the end of the third day, the alluring female took care of any awkward introductions herself. In the crowd of vacationers, she'd simply turned her body toward his, locked eyes, and struck up a conversation. "Are you as confused about upper, lower, and outer Cape Cod as I am? I've got this map, but it doesn't do much good."

Simon grinned. Maybe now would be a good time to admit he wasn't a typical tourist. "If you don't know your way around, it can befuddle the brain, and would be a problem if I hadn't spent every summer here as a kid since I was in diapers."

"But I've seen you on almost all the tours I've been on, sightseeing just like me."

"I haven't been here for at least a dozen years or more. I wanted to reconnect. Who am I kidding? I wanted to meet you for the past week. I thought this would be the best way. The name's Simon Bremmer."

She held out a delicate hand, silver jewelry on each slim finger. "Amelia Langston. If you're familiar with the area, then maybe you could be my personal tour guide."

"That'll work. I see you never go anywhere without your camera." He recognized the brand of expensive Nikon draped around her neck. "What brings you to Cape Cod?"

"I'm a travel photographer. I've already sold a few of my pictures to National Geographic. But I'm here mostly to document the lighthouses from the mainland to the tip of the Outer Cape. Oh, and I want to see all the historic houses in between, and the National Seashore. Then I want to see Woods Hole."

"That's a very aggressive agenda. With so much on your plate you'd benefit from a tour guide, certainly if you plan to be here for a while. Getting up close and personal with all the things to see and do will take a local."

She ran a hand through her thick bronze tresses. "Good thing I have the entire summer then. We might have to work extra hard and not leave anything out."

Simon may have been out of practice with females, but he caught the come-on, especially when it was accompanied by the look in her sultry green eyes. "Works for me. We could start tonight over dinner at the bistro on the main drag."

She twirled her finger around a lock of hair, part of the waterfall he could get lost in. And after that day, he often did. Spending time with her made him forget the dozen years he'd spent alone on foreign soil, sleeping on rock or anywhere else he could catch forty winks.

From that moment on, they rarely spent any time apart. They didn't want to. He took Amelia to all the places she wanted to see and more. He pointed out where the pilgrims landed before ever setting out for Plymouth. "Sorry to burst any historical bubble you've adhered to over the years, but it's true. Pilgrims reached Eastham first, long before heading off anywhere else. It's where they encountered the Nauset tribe."

She looped her arm through his. "Now see? That's why I need someone who knows the area. I'm lucky to have such a handsome guide."

Simon felt just as fortunate.

They explored every lighthouse from P-town to Bourne. They walked the beach where a German U-boat had once attacked the US by shelling tugboats and barges and, inadvertently, cottages along the Orleans and Chatham shorelines. The year was 1918. The U-boat, number 156.

He showed off the Woods Hole Aquarium, spending an entire day marveling at things like blue lobster and a wolfish with teeth like a canine.

When they weren't sightseeing on foot, they were biking around the spit of land like gawkers.

They perused art galleries and quirky antique shops. They went to wine tastings, enjoyed the local brewpubs, and dined on fresh crab. Wherever they ended up, Amelia's ever-present camera documented the fun and the scenery.

He loved the fact that she didn't want to sit in one spot and pour oil all over her body to soak up the sun. Not this stunner, who could put Aphrodite to shame.

After all the sightseeing, she had no problem lounging in bed until late in the morning, enjoying lazy brunches on the terrace with the sea air wafting over their meal. It was nothing compared to the bouts of lovemaking that might last all afternoon.

Simon found himself enthralled, caught up in the sex and the novelty. For a guy who hadn't experienced much domesticity up close in his lifetime, Amelia was a breath of fresh air. She never made demands, didn't seem to be high maintenance, and often seemed too good to be true. They discussed politics in a civil manner and didn't fight or argue about much of anything.

Their time spent together was centered on sultry days and nights where they never left the house. During those times, it was sheer bliss to wake up with her next to him.

To a military man who'd done four tours overseas, Amelia heated his blood like no one ever had.

Until one morning near the end of August, as Labor weekend approached, he woke to find the space beside him empty. When he got up to search for her, she was nowhere in the house. Sometime during the early hours, she'd packed up what little she had and was gone. Just like that, it was over. No messy breakup. No emotional blowup over their differences---there didn't seem to be any. No disappearing after an argument. She was simply…gone…and not in his life anymore.

It wasn't until later that morning that he found an envelope on the front porch with his name on it, the briefest of notes inside. Written in beautiful script, the sentiment seemed short and sweet, summing up their brief time together perfectly: "I hope you understand that I have to get back to Boston and to my life there. Please don't try to get in touch. We're on different paths, Simon, and it will always be that way."

Of course, he hadn't been able to let it go and tried calling the only phone number she'd ever given him. It was no longer a working number.

Amelia Langston was gone.
And he didn't even know how to find her.

One

Present Day
Pelican Pointe, California

Simon had adjusted to life as a civilian by shedding most everything that said military. He'd let his buzzcut grow to an acceptable length, somewhere between a crew cut and a messy windblown look. Over time, his brown mop of hair had turned a goldish color. Staying all day out in the sun could do that. He no longer wore camouflage and didn't want to look at green or tan uniforms ever again if he could help it.

He never referred to time as O-something. Never. He'd served his country with dignity and honor but now it was time to drop all the Army lingo he'd picked up during his twelve-year stint and move on.

He wasn't looking for thanks or accolades or recognition. He didn't want to bring attention to himself. At this stage of his life, he pretty much wanted to blend into society and be left alone, to go about his life and do what he wanted with it.

The only reminders of his time spent in the military were his tattoos. He still sported the black and red Army Ranger band designating his unit, capped off with a skull and crossbones emblem. The other arm showed off a badass, fire-breathing black dragon. He didn't try to hide them. He just didn't shove his service in anybody's face.

He'd ended up in this speck of a beach town because of connections. He'd stayed in touch with a few of his buddies over the years, namely Nick Harris and Cord Bennett. Both had moved to this place shortly after their Iraq experiences. Both had been messed up for reasons he now fully understood. He even knew Cord had once tried to end it all.

Simon never wanted to be that messed up for any reason.

That's why he stayed busy. Three jobs tended to curtail any spare time left over where he could get into trouble or feel sorry for himself. A ten-hour day of hard physical labor kept him from dwelling on anything he'd seen in the war. Thankfully, he spent his days outside in the fresh air and not sitting in some claustrophobic office cubicle behind a desk pushing paper. Nick did that. And Cord did it to some extent as the town veterinarian. But office work wasn't for him.

He'd rather help during planting season at Taggert Farms or spend time out on the water. He'd taken over the excursion business from Bree Dayton, ferrying tourists back and forth to a little strip of land known as Treasure Island.

If there were guests from the Bed and Breakfast who wanted to dive on an old shipwreck or fish from the deck of a forty-six-footer, Simon made it happen. If tourists wanted to take a three-hour sightseeing tour around Smuggler's Bay, they knew who to call. If they wanted to learn how to dive, Simon taught them the basics of safety and provided them with all the gear.

Now that Bree Dayton had started a family, Tours by Bree had morphed into Simon's own business he'd tagged Argonaut Tours. It was relatively successful enough and provided a satisfying way to earn a living, albeit seasonal. While summers were his bread and butter, when August came to an end, the hiking tours picked up. During fall, Simon could often be seen leading a group of guests along the cliffs, pointing out the best spots for snapping photos and making sure no one got lost, seeing to it that everyone made it back to home base alive and well.

Labor Day was usually the cutoff point. But this Tuesday in September, Simon had reservations to take out three fishermen who wanted to spend the day angling for lingcod, striped bass, rockfish, or albacore, if they could find it. The all-day event would net him seven hundred bucks. Not bad for a day's work doing what he loved.

It was a little after sunrise when Simon made his way past the apple-green sign that designated the only B&B nearby, a place called Promise Cove. Owned and operated by Nick and his wife, Jordan, the Bed and Breakfast had been around since 2009 and was responsible for most of his bookings. Since he practically lived next door, it was an easy commute.

Every time he drove down the long driveway, Simon recalled the man who'd started out here along the coast, in this Victorian arts-and-crafts-style house.

In those early days of the Iraq War, his unit had crossed paths with the National Guard soldiers from California, led by Scott Phillips, a charismatic captain who possessed a gift for gab. Simon remembered a guy who bragged about his hometown relentlessly, all over the desert and back again. Their paths had crossed for the final time when Simon's unit had moved in to back up a platoon of soldiers caught in a crossfire attack. Under fire and pinned down...

Simon blocked out the memory of the subsequent battle. As was his habit each time a scene like that popped into his head, he dismissed its power over him.

Instead of focusing on returning fire and desert engagements, Simon pulled up to the B&B on the Harley he rode and cut the engine. He kept his forty-six-foot cruiser, the *Sea Dragon*, moored off the jetty at Promise Cove instead of at the pier in town, because it was easier for guests to board directly from the B&B.

The trip down the long driveway through a copse of cypress trees always made his morning. The way the sun filtered down on the green stretch of lawn and the backdrop of the cliffs carving out the shoreline made him appreciate living here.

But it was opening the back door and stepping into Jordan's kitchen that made it seem like he belonged. It was always chaos. Or what Simon viewed as chaos---a family's rush to start their day. The scene came with a high-energy Jordan and an enterprising Nick setting out a buffet-style breakfast for guests and then serving pancakes to their own brood and doing whatever necessary to get them out the door for school. It meant simultaneously packing lunches for their two kids while taking care of the needs of up to eight demanding guests.

Simon wasn't sure how they got it all done.

"What's up, Harris family?" Simon yelled out over the racket, the noise of kids talking all at once.

Before he got two steps inside, little Scottie latched his arms around Simon's legs and wouldn't let go. "Did you bring Merlin with you today? I told Quake he could have a play date with Merlin."

Merlin was Simon's Newfoundland mix, a rescue that Cord had foisted off on him from day one. The pooch usually came along with Simon on most of his tours, but since this was an all-day excursion involving fish, Merlin could sometimes bark away the catch.

"Sorry, Scottie," Simon began. "Not today. Long day on the water for Merlin means boredom. I left him at home with Silas and Sammy, so he could run around the yard and play."

"Without Quake? Aww, man," Scottie lamented in his four-year-old voice. "Quake's gonna be soooo disappointed."

"David Scott Harris," Nick called out, using his son's full name. "Let go of Simon's legs and let him at least get in far enough to close the door."

Scottie dropped his grip and did as he was told. "I just wanted Quake to have someone to play with while I'm at school is all."

Simon ruffled the kid's hair. "And I promise we'll get them together this weekend. How's that sound?"

But Scottie had already gone on to something else. Pestering his older sister, Hutton, was his second-favorite pastime.

"Coffee's still hot," Jordan said to Simon. "And I fixed you a basket of food, mostly sandwiches, for the trip."

"I'd kiss you, but I figure your old man standing over there would get jealous."

"Is Simon gonna kiss Mommy?" Hutton piped up, her caramel-colored hair so much like her mother's, swinging with the bob of her little head.

"Simon is definitely not kissing Mommy or anyone else," Nick returned.

"Let's not rule out anyone else," Simon fired back. "I am unattached."

"Fine. But watch out who you call an old man."

After pouring coffee into a mug, Simon slapped Nick on the back. "Don't mind me. I'm preparing to spend the day on the water fishing and not stuffed into a suit. Like you."

Nick glanced down at his attire. "Makes me question why I ever decided to go back to banking. I was a lot happier helping Jordan run the inn."

"'Cause you help people get houses and cars and stuff," Hutton explained. "That's what Mommy said."

"The important stuff for sure," Simon agreed, lifting his cup. "Your dad gives people hope that they otherwise might not have."

"I shuffle paperwork around," Nick grumbled. "I used to have more time to spend with the kids and help out Jordan until someone talked me into sitting behind a desk for eight hours."

Jordan kissed her husband's cheek and patted his chest. "We've been over this. No one's chained you to the bank. Don't blame Murphy for talking you into it, either. You like helping people buy their first house or start a business. So don't pretend you're sick of it."

"Yeah, well, that's the only reason that makes it worthwhile."

Scottie stood tugging on his suit coat. He reached down to scoop the boy up in his arms. "Daddy's gotta go to work. Be a good boy today for your teacher, okay?"

Scottie bobbed his head. "I like Miss Neenah. She reads good stories. And she sings good."

Neenah Brewer, a grandmother and former teacher, had grown tired of retirement and decided she wanted to work with the pre-kindergarten kids at the Community Church. They adored her approach to story time and seemed to gravitate to the way she ran her classroom.

"Everybody loves Miss Neenah," Nick stated before kissing his son and setting him back down on his feet. "If you're done with breakfast, then grab your bag and head to the car."

The boy scooted to the corner of the kitchen where a desk had two backpacks on top, one a red canvas carrier sporting a likeness of Spiderman, and another light-pink tote with Hutton's name adorned across the back.

Scottie grabbed his bag and took off running through the house.

Nick swiped a kiss on his wife's face. "I'll see you tonight. Come on, gang, let's get moving. We don't want to be late. Hutton, don't forget your lunch box." He swung back to stare at Simon. "Nice day to spend on the water. Wish I was headed there myself."

"Want me to catch your supper?"

Nick finally cracked a grin. "The kids won't eat fish. But they love to toss a line in the water. We don't do that enough these days. I guess Scott's too young to clean one and Hutton thinks they're too slimy to touch."

"They may start out slimy but steam them over a smoky campfire with just the right amount of butter in the pan and they become a buffet. Where are my three anglers anyway?" Simon inquired. "The day's wasting."

"Dawdling over breakfast," Jordan stated. "I made the mistake of making Belgian waffles and they're lingering over their plates. Go on out and get acquainted," she urged. "Shoo them out of here so I can start cleaning up."

"Will do, boss," Simon answered with a mock salute, disappearing through the swinging door and into the dining room.

Simon took a seat across from three guys in their thirties who were still stuffing their faces with syrupy chunks of golden crust. After making introductions, he found out they were all from a little town in Nevada, on a sabbatical from their jobs and their wives. A trio of overworked buddies who'd gone to college together and needed a break from kids and their everyday routine.

Jason was a gym teacher. Locke was a computer nerd. And Jeff was a press operator for a printing company. Just working stiffs who needed some time off.

Simon was willing to do his part to make sure they could relax and enjoy themselves while they were on vacation. He grabbed a couple pieces of bacon off a platter and leaned back in his chair. "Are you guys ready to catch some fish or sit around all day? Because we're burning daylight and every minute counts."

Locke drained his orange juice. "This is what we came to the coast for, catching us a mess of striped bass for supper. The owners said we could use the firepit in the courtyard out back to cook whatever we bring in."

"We're hoping for at least one tuna," Jason chimed in.

"You won't catch anything sitting around the table," Simon pointed out. "Grab your gear or whatever you're bringing and let's hit the water."

"Don't we need to get bait?"

Simon smiled and took his sunglasses out of his pocket, slid them in place. "All taken care of. The cooler on board is stocked with everything you'll need. The innkeeper even provided your lunch."

Leading the way from the top of the cliff down to the sandy beach below, Simon came to a long pier he'd built himself. Two years earlier, this had been his first project. Born of sweat and pride in workmanship, this is where he'd left the dinghy tied up in the shallow water.

Jeff stared at the skiff. "Cool. Does that come with us?"

"It's what gets us to the *Sea Dragon* and back again. So, yeah." Simon hauled the basket of food onto the raft and directed the others to hop in. "Your fishing adventure awaits."

Locke cupped his hands over his face to peer out past the cove and into the horizon. "Nice boat. I gotta say I envy your lifestyle. Free to work like this, do whatever you want. I bet you aren't married."

Simon shook his head. "Nope. So far, I've managed to avoid the manacles of marital bliss."

"Not much bliss," Jeff grumbled. "Just a bunch of yelling and screaming when you don't follow orders."

"Tell me about it," Locke shouted over the surf. "Marriage is like a permanent stint in the Army."

That prompted the trio to go off on an in-depth discussion of their personal troubles, mostly about their wives. Simon only half listened to the analysis because he didn't share anything in common with these three. He had a great life sans marriage and he intended to keep it that way.

Pulling up next to the *Sea Dragon,* he motioned for the men to climb aboard and showed them where to sit and stow their gear. He handed out life jackets.

"Do we have to wear these?" Locke groaned. "I'm not a little kid."

Simon slipped his Wayfarers down on his nose and peered over the frame. "You didn't read the agreement you signed at the B&B, did you? The jackets aren't optional."

"Okay. Sure," Locke said, sliding his arms into one while tossing the others to his buddies.

After getting them seated, Simon revved the engine, guided the cruiser out of the cove, and headed for open water.

It took less than half an hour to get to the spot that Simon had discovered brought a good yield. Each time he'd taken a group here, it had produced enough of a catch to make the fishermen happy and willing to come back. Happy clients meant repeaters who would return again and again.

Even before the others baited their hooks and found a favored spot at the rail, Locke sought out the cooler that contained the beer and began to imbibe almost immediately.

They wagered, good-naturedly, who would bring back the most fish and the biggest.

The sun was warm on their faces and the group seemed to be having a good time. Every now and again one would feel a tug on his line and reel in a brightly-colored, but slightly puny, rockfish.

"Do these have a good flavor?" Jeff wanted to know.

Simon kept an eye on how much alcohol the guys kept consuming. The heat of the September day seemed to make them especially thirsty. "It's been my experience that Pacific flounder always fries up real nice. In fact, most anything you'll catch here does."

By noon, the guys were on their way to getting hammered. The more they drank, the mouthier they got. Between buddies, surly insults began to fly. Locke took out a bottle of bourbon and began to knock that back in between bottles of beer.

In the two years since Simon bought the business, he usually let these kinds of scenes play out without getting involved in the group's banter. It was, after all, why guys like this came hundreds of miles out of their way to fish along the coast---to let their hair down and have fun without consequences.

But when the name-calling grew intense, and the profanity turned toward Simon, it reminded him of another time and place. These guys were acting like a bunch of frat boys who weren't getting their way. When the insults came faster because they weren't catching anything big enough, they began chunking beer bottles into the water.

Simon had heard enough and cleared his throat. "You know, you might be better fishermen if you didn't scare the fish off. Maybe if you laid off the booze..."

"Hey, you can't tell us what to do," Locke challenged, swaying on his feet. "We're paying for this lousy trip."

"I've never thrown anyone off my boat before today, but with you, I'm willing to make an exception."

"You can try," Locke boasted. "But there's three of us and only one of you."

"Yeah, but I'm the one who's stone-cold sober *and* I've gone to the mat with guys like you before."

"Oh yeah. Says you," Locke retorted as he drew back his arm to throw a punch. "You're not that tough."

Simon would've had to be blind not to see it coming. He merely sidestepped the man, put his shoulder into his gut, and tossed him into the water. "Man overboard! I forgot to ask if you guys could swim. Which one of you wants to go next?"

Jeff put his hands in the air in surrender. "Whoa, not me. That was so cool."

"How about you, Jason?"

"No way. Locke's the one mouthing off. He's the ass."

"Locke!" Simon yelled from the deck. "Are you ready to fish or would you prefer to swim back to the hotel?"

"Get me out of here!" Locke screamed, bobbing up and down in the whitecaps, still wearing his life jacket.

"I don't know, have you sobered up yet?" Simon stated, throwing a buoyed rope into the water. He went to the helm and started the engine, maneuvering the bow into the wind so that Locke would drift toward the boat. He cut the motor and pulled the tow line up to the side, reaching out to help Locke up and over the railing.

"I guess I had that coming," Locke admitted as Jason handed him a towel.

"Next time, don't throw trash into the water," Simon cautioned. "And if you're unhappy about the catch, I'm always willing to move to try out another spot. All you need do is ask…nicely. Just don't go shooting off your mouth. I don't put up with that crap. Not on my boat. Are we clear?"

Simon waited for each man to acknowledge in his own way. "All right. Good. Now what is it you're unhappy about exactly?"

"We wanted to catch something really big."

"All right. I'll go out farther. But if you're serious, you gotta stop scaring off the fish."

After trying another location, the rest of the day proved fruitful. The gym teacher Jason caught the most at nine good-sized lingcod. But the real winner was Jeff, who reeled in a thirty-pound halibut.

Simon took pictures of the trio with their catch, so they could post it on whatever social media accounts they had.

"This'll prove to Katelyn that I'm with you guys," Locke said before all eyes turned on him.

Locke lifted a shoulder. "She got it in her head that I'm having an affair and thought you guys were covering for me. She was sure that I intended to go to Cancun with a coworker."

That statement brought another round of disgruntled talk about married life while Simon did his best to tune them out, silently counting down the minutes when he could unload these guys back at the B&B.

But he was surprised when Jordan grabbed him as soon as he entered the kitchen. "There's a woman in the living room who's been here for forty-five minutes waiting for you."

"What does she want?"

"She's from Boston."

Alarm jammed his throat. "Is it about my mom?"

"I don't think so. She brought a baby with her."

"A baby?"

Simon allowed Jordan to lead him into the other room where he spotted a rather stern-looking thirty-something woman sitting on the sofa holding a baby on her lap. When she saw Simon, she stood up, all business, prepared to do what she'd come to do.

Jordan made the introductions. "Simon, this is Margaret Tyler, an attorney…uh…from Boston, like I said. She's been appointed by the court as the guardian for Delaney Bremmer."

Still not worried, Simon nodded. "Okay. Who's Delaney Bremmer? Obviously one of my relatives, right?"

Margaret cleared her throat. "Temporary guardian for Delaney Amelia Bremmer, who is the minor child of Amelia Langston and Simon Bremmer."

He started to protest that she had the wrong Bremmer until the name Amelia sank in. "Amelia Langston? It doesn't mean it's the Amelia Langston I knew."

Undeterred, Margaret shoved onward. "I've been appointed to represent Delaney. I'm her temporary guardian and the conservator of her mother's estate. You obviously knew a woman by the name of Amelia Langston, address…"

The lawyer rattled off numbers and a street Simon recognized as the Allston section of Beantown.

"Uh. Sure. I know an Amelia Langston. I'm just not sure we're talking about the same Amelia, because the one I'm familiar with never said anything to me about a baby."

"I'm here as an officer of the court for the state of Massachusetts. Ms. Langston died ten days ago in a car accident."

"Whoa. Was the baby with her?"

"No. Fortunately the child was with a nanny. Ms. Langston's will, probated two days ago, left the bulk of her estate to you and named you legal guardian of her daughter, Delaney."

"To me? Why me?" Simon looked dumbfounded. He stared at the cute, very female bundle in the woman's arms, wearing a pink outfit with a rabbit on the bib. "I still don't understand what this has to do with me."

"You're named in the will as Delaney's legal guardian," Ms. Tyler repeated slowly as if she were speaking to a very dimwitted adult. "I'll need you to sign some paperwork."

"No way. This has to be some kind of a joke, right? Why would Amelia ever do that unless I was the father?" His own words hung in the air, suspended there in time, the implication sinking in. "Now wait just a minute. Amelia never told me I was a father. I haven't heard from her since…in two years. You obviously need to find this baby's real daddy. It's not me."

"It doesn't matter if you're the father or not. At all. Amelia Langston made you her daughter's legal guardian in the event anything should happen to her. It did. The court already approved you as Delaney's guardian after doing an extensive background check on you. That took an extra three days, by the way. So whether or not you're related to this child is immaterial. The court's found you suitable as her guardian and Ms. Langston's last will and testament, found to be valid, states that you are this child's legal guardian. How many ways must I say it? If you persist in this childish denial, you should also know, I brought all the documentation necessary with me that says, you, Simon Bremmer, were named on Delaney's birth certificate as her father. It's an official document."

Simon's knees wanted to buckle. "You can't leave that baby here with me. I don't know a thing about taking care of a baby, especially a girl baby, especially one that young."

"Toddler. Delaney's a toddler. She's fifteen-and-a-half months old. Everything you need to know about the child is in the folder I brought with me, including her medical records."

"Not everything," Simon muttered, combing his fingers through his hair. "You aren't listening to me. I don't know a thing about toddlers or kids in general. You can't do this. She obviously needs someone to take care of her who knows what they're doing. I'm telling you that isn't me."

"Look, Mr. Bremmer, the estate paid for this trip. I've fulfilled my obligation by getting your daughter here to be with her father. I'm delivering her to her next of kin. That's the end of it as far as I'm concerned."

"But I should be able to talk to an attorney to see if this is all legal. You're being so pushy about this it sounds fishy to me." Simon angled toward Jordan, his eyes pleading for help. "The lawyer in town who handled the sale of the tour business was Kinsey Donnelly. I need to talk to her about all this."

He turned back to the unyielding lawyer. "Let me at least get Kinsey on the phone, talk this out with her before I sign anything."

But Ms. Tyler ignored the plea. She slipped an oversized diaper bag onto the coffee table and cleverly shoved the toddler into Simon's arms. She pulled paperwork out of a leather purse-like portfolio. "Sign here, here, and here," the woman instructed. "And initial there."

"I don't feel I should accept...delivery...of another human like this. It isn't right," Simon protested.

"Look, Mr. Bremmer, I understand you're taken by surprise. I get it. Anyone would be. But I promised my kids I'd be back home tonight. I have a flight out of Santa Cruz at five-fifteen this afternoon and I plan to be on that plane. Alone. Without Delaney. She's a good baby, but she isn't mine. She belongs with her father, her family. That's you. Do not make me go get the local authorities on this. The police chief already knows I'm here. I stopped to apprise law enforcement of the situation. Who do you think gave me the directions to find you? Don't make me call him in here for back-up. Because as an officer of the court, I most certainly am authorized to get whatever help I need if you persist in this manner. The police will show up and simply read the court order I have, read it to you slowly, and instruct you to sign the paperwork I've provided."

With his hands shaking, Simon reluctantly scrawled his name as indicated.

"Thank you. Now, if I hustle out of here I can just make it through security and make my flight. I have the rest of your daughter's stuff in the car."

"I still don't understand what kind of court order dumps a baby on an unsuspecting person like this, a stranger, and calls that fair to the kid. That doesn't make any sense to me. I could be the worst person in the world and you just handed over an innocent baby to a...psychopath."

"Not according to the thorough background check done on you. You're a war hero, a former Army Ranger with a stellar career as a soldier. You're exactly what the court sees as acceptable, even a good fit as a guardian."

"I'm not that person anymore. I'm telling you…I'm not. Besides, I don't understand why anyone couldn't have given me a heads-up about this, a phone call, a telegram, an email, something."

But the hardline attorney had already reached the front door. "I wish you luck, Mr. Bremmer. I do. But my job here is finished. I'll be in touch with you later to settle the estate. It probably won't be much after Ms. Langston's final expenses are paid, maybe around twenty-five grand or so. If you ask me, you should set it all aside for the girl's college fund."

"I don't want Amelia's money," Simon shouted as the woman stepped outside onto the front porch. But he watched as the attorney dashed toward the driveway as if the house were on fire. Once she reached her rental car, she opened the trunk, reached in and pulled out a suitcase, which she set down on the gravel driveway.

"I can't believe this is really happening," Simon said as he whirled to look at Jordan and then dropped into the nearest chair. "What am I gonna do with a kid?"

He was so upset, so bewildered, Jordan didn't have the heart to crack a smile. "You'll learn as you go like every new father does that I've ever known. Nick included." Jordan sat down across from the two of them. "Do you think you're not the father? Is that it?"

"I'm not disputing anything yet. I could be. But this is warped."

"She's a cute little thing. Looks like you, too. And quiet. Delaney is a pretty name for a pretty girl," Jordan cooed as she tugged on the little girl's foot.

On instinct, he jostled his knee up and down. "No one's saying she isn't cute. Her mother was a real knockout. But I'm still trying to wrap my mind around the fact that Amelia never told me. Why would she name me as a legal guardian and not tell me I had a daughter?"

"Because no one actually thinks they'll ever die in a car accident. It's one thing to make it legal. It's still another to think it'll ever become a reality."

"And yet, here we sit. I can't believe she's gone. Although I never saw her after that summer we spent on the Cape. We had ninety days together. Less than ninety. I remember it was about this time two years ago that I first heard from Nick. He called me up out of the blue about moving here. By the end of September, I'd packed up everything I owned, which wasn't much, and made the trip out here to check it out. Nick made it sound like Utopia. I couldn't wait to get here. Up to now, it's been great. Do you realize I don't even own a car? I ride everywhere on my motorcycle. I can't strap a baby to a Harley."

"We'll work something out. You can use mine until you get one of your own."

"I don't have any baby food."

"She eats finger food, anything she can hold goes in her mouth anyway."

"You do realize this is the reason Bree gave up her tour business. She had a baby and didn't want to do this anymore. How will I make it work with a kid if she couldn't?"

"For one thing, Bree made a decision to stay home after she became a mother," Jordan pointed out. "You don't have to give up your business. There are these things called babysitters that working parents use all the time. And for several years now the Community Church has offered something called child care."

Simon heaved out a loud sigh. "Why are you being so reasonable about this when it's nuts?"

"It's bound to be frightening. And you've had all of ten minutes to get used to it."

"I think I'm numb. I'm not sure what to do next. So many things to decide." He sat there staring at the bundle in his arms. Never one to shirk responsibilities, not even for a brief respite, Simon stood up. He could've easily asked Jordan to watch her, or keep her overnight, or help him get her to the car. But Simon did none of those things. "What do I do without one of those car seat things to put her in? I have to get home to Merlin. Obviously riding the motorcycle is out."

"Like I said, you can take my car. And I have a car seat that's still in date that we used for Scott when he was about that age. It's in the garage. We'll put it in my Explorer for now."

"Thanks. You've picked up the kids from school already?"

It was like him to consider whether she needed the car. "I have. They're upstairs playing with Lilly's kids."

He blew out a breath. "Okay then, I guess I'll see you Wednesday when the next tour comes up. Those are three guys who want to see the shipwreck, right?"

"No. And the reservation is for Thursday. You're taking out a horticultural group who wants to document the flora on the little island."

"Right."

"Simon?"

"What?"

"Are you okay?"

"I'm not sure I'll ever be okay again."

Two

First, he paid attention to how Jordan switched out car seats, swapping out Scott's booster for a toddler seat that sat rear-facing. "How am I supposed to see what she's doing back there when she's facing the other way?" Simon grumbled, clearly flustered. "Use my imagination?"

Jordan chuckled. "Install a mirror. If she's unhappy, believe me, she'll let you know. In California, state law changed a couple of years ago. Newborn to age two faces rear. It offers more protection if you're involved in an accident."

Simon paled. "Oh jeez, I should make sure I don't speed then."

After adjusting the headrest, Jordan turned to Simon and stared at the baby resting her head on his shoulder. "Try that, because it looks like you have an exhausted little girl there."

"So I noticed. She's been yawning up a storm." Awkwardly, he settled her between the harness and strapped her in. Then he loaded up the back of Jordan's Ford Explorer with the stuff the lawyer had dumped on the driveway.

"Look, Simon, if you have any questions at all, call me. I'm more than happy to go over anything you need to know."

"You don't happen to have a manual I could read, do you? What about diapers? What kind does she use?"

Jordan went over all that, but when Delaney started to fuss for the first time since getting there, she stopped. "Go home and use whatever's in the diaper bag. I'll send Nick over later to check on you with a few items that might come in handy."

"Okay. You know where to find your car if you need it."

"I won't. Nick'll be home soon."

Simon's house was a five-minute drive away because he lived next door in the Taggert Farms caretaker's cottage—a box of a house painted bright red with white shutters.

It was once occupied by Gavin and Maggie Kendall and their two kids, who'd moved into the main farmhouse after Simon arrived. Since then, he'd renovated the inside by gutting the interior walls and changing the layout.

Now the place had an open great room and an island kitchen, a design that worked far better for him than the claustrophobic, caged feeling. He'd built bookshelves on one end of the living room. He'd added a second bathroom that separated two small guest rooms on one side while expanding the en-suite that belonged to the master bedroom and on the other.

As soon as he pulled up in the SUV, Merlin bounded off the porch to greet him. The Newfoundland mix had bronze fur and a short snout that made him look like an adorable bear cub in the face. Merlin had the best disposition of any pooch Simon had ever owned and swore the dog was the smartest canine he'd ever been around.

"Hey, boy, have I got a surprise for you. Look what we have. Don't go scaring her now, okay?"

Simon got out and opened the car door, and immediately realized Delaney had fallen asleep on the short ride home. He unfastened her seat belt and lifted her out doing his best not to wake her up. When he reached the front door, he realized he had a problem. He couldn't open it with his hands full.

"Merlin, get the door."

The dog responded by standing on his hind legs and using his front paws to repeatedly hit the lever until it finally cracked open an inch. Merlin stuck his nose in the space and nudged the gap wider.

"Good dog. Good boy. I'll get you a treat after I put her down." He glanced around the living room, looking for where that would be and decided on the sofa, that way if she woke up he'd be able to see it immediately.

Gently he placed her into the cushions before dropping down beside her on the couch. Leaning his head back, he closed his eyes and let the tension fall away before promptly falling asleep.

A light tap on the door had him bolting upright. Next to him on the sofa, Delaney was still zonked out, fast asleep. It was dark outside. He wasn't sure how long he'd been out, but the nap hadn't changed the fact that he was a father. Rubbing the sleep from his eyes, he stumbled to the door.

Nick stood on the porch carrying half of a crib. "Jordan thought you might need this. Cord's getting the other half out of his truck."

Simon tilted his head to study the piece of furniture that seemed so out of place in his house. "It's like a cage. You gonna help me put it together?"

"That's why I'm here. Jordan insisted on giving you Scott's high chair, too. And I put a call in to Kinsey. She'll be here later after she gets her kids down for the night to read over the paperwork you signed."

"Thanks. Be kind of quiet, okay. The girl's still…" The girl was now sitting upright. Her face puckered up as she started bawling her lungs out.

Totally out of his depth, Simon did the only thing he could. He went over and picked her up. "Oh, hey. You are totally soaked." He looked around for the diaper bag. "I forgot to bring it in. We'll go get it, okay? It'll be okay. Shhh, now. Shhh. It's okay."

All the way out to the car, he bounced and tried to soothe her by talking in his normal voice. But the more he talked the louder she cried.

Once back inside, he set her down on the floor, where she stood in one spot in the middle of the room and wailed.

Nick helped by digging through the bag until he found a Pampers and handed it off.

"Okay. Tell me how this works."

Cord found the instructions on his phone and handed it to Simon. "There's a video. You're good with how-tos, right? Piece of cake."

Simon watched the YouTube post and then began the process even though Delaney was still unhappy.

While Nick looked on, he offered his own expertise, leaning over Simon's shoulder. "Rip off the sticky tabs first."

Simon obliged and yanked off the wet diaper. He turned to grab the clean one, but Delaney used the opportunity to roll over on her stomach and scurry away faster than a cockroach.

Nick skillfully stopped her progress and brought her back to the starting line. "This is what they do. They try to escape. You gotta be quicker and a whole lot smoother. Kind of like when you handle a rifle, load it, and take it apart with precision without even thinking about the drill. Changing a diaper has to become second nature. Like this." With one hand, he held Delaney in place, slipped the clean diaper under her backside like a pro and with the other, wrapped the front part across her belly. "Now you secure the tabs. First one, then the other. Quick and fast. There. See. All done."

Simon breathed a sigh of relief like he'd just finished a marathon. "That wasn't so bad for my first time, right? At least it wasn't poop."

"Not yet," Cord muttered as he slapped Simon on the back. "That'll come later. I'm gonna carry in the rest of the stuff."

Simon nodded and scooped the baby up. Stunned that she'd stopped fussing, he jostled her in his arms. "There. She's fine now. Did you notice when I picked her up she stopped crying?"

Nick rolled his eyes. "Just because she's small, doesn't mean she's dumb. Getting you to pick her up is what makes her happy."

"She's probably hungry by now."

"Jordan thought of that. She sent over cold scrambled eggs and some applesauce. They eat food cold, not steaming hot, so don't try to make her eat hot foods," Nick offered. He held up a Tupperware container of finger foods and a sippy cup. "Use the bottles in the diaper bag at bedtime and naptime. The sippy cup is for during the day. There's enough food there to get you through a couple of days. Do you have any Cheerios? Cause they eat cereal by the handfuls when they won't eat anything else. Cheerios are always your go-to back-up at mealtime or snack time."

Cord reappeared in the doorway with the high chair. He rubbed his hands together. "I'll set this up while Nick brings in the rest. After you get her to eat, I'll go start putting the crib together. Which room?"

Simon pointed down the hallway. "Both are kinda small, but the first one is slightly larger."

"First one is the nursery. Got it," Cord said as he headed that way.

While Nick went outside to retrieve the other items Jordan had sent over, Simon strolled into the kitchen.

"Nursery? Good lord, doodle-bug. You have a nursery and I have a baby's room in my house. Keep your expectations very low and we should be fine. Don't expect too much right away."

After settling her into the high chair, Simon somehow managed to charm her into eating some of the egg and applesauce. For good measure, he poured a cupful of Cheerios in a plastic bowl, which she promptly dumped out on the tray and, one by one, stuck in her mouth.

Merlin hung around to lap up anything Delaney dropped on the floor. And toward the end of the meal, that was a lot.

"Kinsey just texted to say she's on her way," Nick announced. "What else can we do before we leave?"

"Leave?" Simon repeated in a panic. "Don't take off just yet. Take a look in the room...nursery...and see what else I might need. Make me a list."

"You'll need a diaper pail. I didn't bring one of those. You can use a wastebasket for now," Nick said as he went in search of one.

Before long Kinsey arrived, looking around and taking note of the situation. "Wow, what a way to find out you're a father. Am I right? No phone call ahead of time?"

"Nope. I'm not even sure how they tracked me down at work. You know, out at the Bed and Breakfast."

"Don't bite my head off," Cord began. "But is there any part of you that thinks she might not be yours?"

"Why would I bite your head off? It's a logical question. I mean, I spent a summer with Amelia Langston. The timing adds up. I'm not stupid, I did the math. Fifteen-and-a-half months would be about right."

"You could always get a DNA test," Kinsey suggested. "It's what I'd recommend to any of my clients in your situation. It wouldn't be a slap against you or the baby or the mother for that matter. It's a practical, easy and quick thing that verifies your responsibility, legally. If I ask, I bet Quentin could get you an answer by the end of the week, Monday at the latest."

"All right. Sure. Set up an appointment."

Kinsey eyed the folder and the documents spread out on the coffee table. "Have you gone through any of this stuff?"

"No," Simon said quietly. "It scares me a little."

Kinsey began to paw through the papers until she held up an envelope. "There's a letter here addressed to you. It's attached to the copy of the will. Give me the baby while you read over it. Could be important."

Simon stared at his name on the outside. It was written in script and probably in Amelia's handwriting.

Dear Simon,

If you're reading this the unthinkable has happened. I'm no longer around to take care of our daughter. You're probably pretty upset at this point, wondering why I didn't tell you about her from the beginning. The reason is simple. I didn't want to share her with anyone, not even you. We weren't together long enough to do any more than create this beautiful child, a child I discovered that I desperately wanted more than anything else, more than traveling the world as a photographer.

That summer we met was magical, but neither one of us was in a good enough place to make it last for longer than a summer fling on Cape Cod. We probably weren't the first two people in the world to spend a summer there like that and we won't be the last.

Surely you agree we weren't meant to remain together. It's a fact. What we had that summer wasn't a forever kind of thing and deep down you knew it, too. That's why when August ended we went our separate ways. It was the right thing to do. For both of us.

I hope you'll forgive me for not telling you I was pregnant. But after finally getting out of the Army, it seemed to me like you were just beginning to find yourself. Not a good time to embark on a different course like fatherhood. I think I did the right thing.

I wanted this baby. Girl or boy, it didn't much matter to me. It was unexpected, but not entirely a bad thing. At least not for me. I didn't need or want your help in this. But now, it seems fate has chosen a different path entirely for both of us. And now, for Delaney.

Please take care of our daughter. I hope you learn to love her as much as I do. Please don't hold hard feelings toward her for what I did. She's blameless. Delaney Amelia Bremmer is yours now.

Love, Amelia

Simon bit his lip and fought back the tears that formed in his eyes and tried to keep them from dripping down on the letter. He folded it back up and stuck it in the envelope.

"What did it say?" Kinsey asked.

Simon handed it back to the lawyer. "That Amelia was more warped than I remembered."

"I'm sorry," Kinsey said, resting a hand on his shoulder. "Is there anything you want me to do?"

"Is there any way you can get Delaney's birth records from the hospital?"

"I have the birth certificate right here. Your Amelia delivered a baby girl on May 28th at ten-seventeen in the morning, weighing seven pounds, one ounce."

"She was never my Amelia. Didn't you read the letter?"

"Simon, you shouldn't take this as a…"

"Stab in the heart? No way. What Amelia says about us not being right for each other is absolutely the truth. It wouldn't have worked out between us. We were too different. I knew that while we were together. But as a guy she slept with casually, even I deserved to know about a baby. I could've…I don't know…done something."

Nick stood up. "Well, I came over for moral support and to drop off a few things that should at least get you going. I'm headed home to help put my own two wildlings to bed. If you need anything, call."

"Thanks, Nick. You too, Cord. I'll be all right now. Go home where you belong."

"I have surgery in the morning," Cord explained. "Otherwise I'd play uncle for a little longer. But I'm better with animals than kids."

Kinsey let out a laugh. "That's probably why you make a great veterinarian." She turned to Simon. "Put him on the list to babysit down the road."

He managed a grin. "Don't worry, Cord. I don't expect you to take care of her unless it's a full-on emergency. Will Merlin be okay around her?"

"You need to ask? Merlin has one of the best temperaments I've ever seen in a rescue dog. I think it's the Newfoundland in him. Nothing to worry about on that score."

"Want me to set you up with an appointment at the Community Church for daycare?" Kinsey asked. "They're expecting a new pastor to take over any time now since Reverend Whitcomb had his stroke last month. Dottie's already moved out of the cottage and put him in a retirement home near Santa Cruz, a place Dr. Blackwood found. It specializes in stroke victims. She's there with him full time now. The reason I'm bringing it up tonight is because you might need to hold a spot open for a fifteen-month-old. The twins go there three times a week for five hours a day and it's getting crowded. They've been talking about hiring more help but so far without anyone at the top, it hasn't happened yet."

"Then do what you think is best. You guys get out of here now and go home to your families. I'll be okay. And if I'm not, I'll call out for help."

Outside as Kinsey got into her car, she turned to Nick and Cord. "You know him better than I do, but does it seem like he's in…"

"Shock?" Cord supplied. "I've never seen him so subdued."

"Neither have I," Nick offered. "I think we should all keep an eye on him and come by as often as possible. This is such a life-changing event for him."

Shortly after everyone left, Simon put his charge to bed. Nick had fixed the crib up with clean, crisp sheets and a soft, pale blue and buttery blanket. He stood over her, afraid to leave the room, watching her mouth move in a sucking motion in her sleep.

The scene was so surreal. He put another blanket around her just in case she got cold. He touched her forehead, thinking how hot she felt, but the movement woke her up. And she wasn't one bit happy about it.

Three

ER nurse Gilly Grant looked up from her post behind the reception area in time to see a man dash through the double doors into the lobby carrying a small screaming bundle.

"I need help. I think my baby is running a fever. She won't stop crying. She won't even keep her pacifier in her mouth, just keeps spitting it out. And I don't know what to do."

Calm and cool was Gilly's trademark. And she needed it now more than she had during the last seven hours. She liked to think she could size up a situation and get it under control in record time. Now was no different.

"Let's take a look at her. Let's move into Exam Room One at the corner."

The ER area was partitioned off using blue, floor-to-ceiling curtains, the only privacy that any emergency room afforded anyone.

Gilly directed him to one of these sections. "Park yourself in there and we'll get this show on the road." She trailed after the man with a clipboard in her hand. "I need you to fill out some papers for insurance purposes. So I'll trade ya. You take the clipboard, I'll take the baby. How's that sound?"

Simon's hands shook as he relinquished his hold, handing Delaney off to the slender blonde with ash-colored locks tied back in a no-fuss short ponytail. "I changed her diaper. Did a bit better than the first time, but she still won't settle down enough to go to sleep. It's almost like she's too wired to sleep. That's after she napped around five o'clock."

The nurse grimaced in disapproval. "This afternoon? That's really too late for a toddler to be napping unless they're sick. Next time, put her down earlier, like say around twelve-thirty or so after she's eaten lunch."

"I might've done that, but I didn't have her at one o'clock."

"I see." Gilly deftly placed a digital thermometer in Delaney's ear. "She's ninety-nine. But good lord, no wonder she's hot. You have her bundled up like it's two degrees outside. Way too much clothing."

"I put everything on her that was in her diaper bag. I thought…you know…it must be in there for a reason."

Gilly bit back her laughter as she peeled off each layer one by one until she got down to an adorable set of PJs dotted with little purple monkeys. "No. The pajamas will suffice. Next time, try to remember sometimes less is the way to go."

Simon was on his last nerve. So when he detected a hint of sarcasm, he lost it. "Could you, I don't know, cut me some slack here? I've been a dad for less than ten minutes so I'm trying my best. Be glad I got her to eat supper."

Gilly's heart softened. "Less than ten minutes, huh? New daddy jitters?"

"Brand new. I just found out…" He looked at his watch. "Seven hours ago, so I suppose there's a possibility she might be missing her mom."

At the word, Delaney hiccupped and said, "Mama."

"It breaks my heart," Simon revealed. "So far that's the only word out of her mouth that I recognize. Otherwise, it's just a bunch of babbling."

Gilly decided she'd sized up the situation and had it all figured out. It must be Dad's week to take care of the little munchkin. "Custody issues can be hard on a child this age."

"I wouldn't know about that."

Gilly continued to bounce the toddler on her hip, hoping to coax her temperature back down to ninety-eight now that she'd unlayered the little tyke. "Oh really? So, it isn't your week to…?"

"No. It seems this is a permanent deal."

"I see. Where is her mom then?"

Simon sucked in a nervous breath at the prospect this was all on him. "Gone. Dead. Car accident. Ten days ago. I just found out this afternoon."

Gilly's hand whipped out to rub his arm. "I'm so sorry."

Simon went into a detailed play by play of how the lawyer from Boston had all but dumped Delaney on his doorstep and taken off.

Gilly's hazel eyes sharpened into spears of disbelief. "That's how you found out? That seems incredibly unfair with no warning like that. Look, I'll take her temp again. With any luck it's dropped to within normal range and you can take her home."

This time, Gilly used the thermometer with infrared technology. It only took a few seconds to get a reading. She smiled and grabbed the clipboard out of his hands. "You don't need to fill this out. There's not a thing wrong with this baby that a good night's sleep won't fix. Your little traveler has had a very long day and she's tired and cranky. That's my opinion, for what it's worth. If she keeps fussing and won't settle down, you might want to make an appointment during regular business hours to see Dr. Blackwood. It wouldn't be a bad idea anyway since she's a new patient and you want to get her established."

"Thanks. How'd you get so smart about kids?"

Her lips curved. "I spent four years in nursing school. Plus, I have a toddler of my own."

"You're kidding? And you work nights? How on earth do you do all that? Nurse, mom, wife."

"Oh no. Not me. I'm not married. I had a boyfriend once who knocked me up and took off as soon as I mentioned the P word. I was in Texas at the time. Why? Because like the idiot I was I'd followed that lousy asshole right out of state just two months out of nursing school. But as soon as I learned I was pregnant and he didn't want to be part of it, I got myself back to Pelican Pointe faster than he could push me out the door. But hey, I'm lucky. My mom takes care of my three-year-old during the time I'm working."

"Working graveyard is tough."

She grinned again. "Three days a week I work my tail off, four p.m. to four a.m., thirty-six hours total and then I'm off four. The hours aren't for everyone, but it works for me."

"Your three-year-old, boy or girl?"

"Boy. Jayden. I'm Gillian Grant, but people call me Gilly."

"Simon Bremmer." Feeling better, he stood up and took Delaney out of her arms with slightly more confidence than he'd had walking in there. "I still have to call my mom and let her know she has a granddaughter."

"Will it be a good surprise or…?"

"No, she'll love it. I think. I hope."

"Then maybe she could come out and help you."

"She would if she could. But she takes care of her sister. They live together. My Aunt Lorraine suffers from Alzheimer's."

"I'm sorry. That's a horrible disease to have." Gilly caught a glimpse of the toddler's now sleeping face. "Looks like your little angel's finally given it up."

"I better get on the road then. Where do I check out? There's no one in here but you."

Gilly laughed. "This is a small hospital. I'll note it in the log that you brought Delaney in, but really, there's no charge. I just took her temperature and got all those layers off."

One-handed, Simon began to bundle up what he'd brought in, but Gilly did it for him, stuffing it all back down into the diaper bag.

"My to-do list is really long tomorrow. But maybe I'll see you around."

"Maybe. It's a small town. I'm here Sunday nights, Mondays, and Tuesdays into Wednesday morning."

"And off the other days."

"And off the others. Good luck, Simon Bremmer." She slipped the diaper bag onto his shoulder and walked him to the double doors. "Don't be so hard on yourself. You'll learn that kids are fairly resilient. Get the basics you need for her comfort and the rest will take care of itself. And try to relax. Get to know your daughter. Don't be so uptight. Delaney will sense that and react. Go with the flow."

Simon nodded. "Thanks. I'll try to remember all that."

He breathed in the fresh air on the way to Jordan's Explorer, feeling calmer than before. Merlin greeted him with a lick to the face.

He put his finger to his lips to make sure Merlin didn't wake up the baby and whispered, "Scoot over. Make room so I can fasten her in."

Merlin obliged by leaping into the front seat.

After getting Delaney secured and managing not to rouse her, he started the engine. His mind drifted to a new set of wheels, one more thing he needed to take care of tomorrow. Maybe not brand new but new enough that he could get around with the doodle-bug in tow. There were only two people in town who sold used cars. Wally Pierce at the gas station tended to buy and sell the classic cars he fixed up. But in this case, Simon didn't think a classic was the answer. He needed something a dad would drive, something that came with all the bells and whistles and safety features for kids.

For that, he headed to Tradewinds Drive and Pacific where Bradford Radcliff had taken an empty lot full of weeds and started buying up used cars from the surrounding towns until finally he'd put together enough vehicles to start selling off his inventory.

Simon slowed down at the corner to inspect what Brad had on hand. He spotted a few minivans, the kind he knew soccer moms drove. Those things had enough room for a slew of kids, but it wasn't his style at all. Nothing he saw on the lot caught his fancy so he headed for home. As he gunned the engine, he hoped to Christ he didn't have to waste money on an ugly box like that. He'd rather drive a station wagon. Did they even make them anymore? he wondered.

At home, he put Delaney in her crib and started unpacking the diaper bag, setting things out on the shelves and dresser so each item would be within easy reach, like baby wipes. He counted out the diapers and found that he had only five on hand. He'd need to pick up a supply tomorrow. He opened the suitcase, started organizing her clothes into neat stacks in each drawer. It didn't take him that long because there weren't that many outfits to put away.

He went out to the kitchen and found Nick's list tacked to the refrigerator and added the diapers and a nightlight to the bottom. He wiped down the high chair in preparation for breakfast. It wasn't until he started cleaning up the dishes that he realized he hadn't eaten anything since he'd been out on the water. Almost twelve hours had gone by since he'd had lunch and yet so much had changed.

He made himself a ham and cheese sandwich and got himself a beer. He took it over to the couch and plopped down. Merlin ambled up and put his head on the sofa.

"Yeah, buddy, things are changing in a big way. I'm not sure what to do about it. Are we really daddy material?" He ruffled the dog's fur. "I guess we'll find out."

He finished his food, drained his beer, and headed off to bed.

Merlin growled before Simon ever flipped on the light. Transfixed for several moments, Simon locked eyes with the man who sat in the corner in the Pottery Barn chair his mother had picked out a year earlier.

He thought of the M9 Beretta he kept in the nightstand drawer, but realized he'd never be able to get to it before the intruder made his move.

Scott Phillips held up both hands in surrender. "No need to freak out. It's only me."

"Who the hell is me?" Simon asked as he watched man's best friend trot over to sniff out the prowler. Instead of latching onto the man's arm with his teeth like he'd expected, Merlin simply wagged his tail.

"You don't recognize me? It has been a long time. Scott Phillips. You knew me as Captain."

Simon narrowed his eyes at the way the man was dressed---khaki shorts, a short-sleeved blue button-down shirt left open and worn over a pale-yellow T-shirt. He began inching his way toward the nightstand. "Scott Phillips is dead."

"You might want to lock up that Beretta now that there's a child in the house," Scott pointed out.

"How'd you get in here? I put in an alarm system when I moved in."

"Which in your haste to get to the hospital tonight you forgot to activate."

By this time Simon had opened the drawer and removed the weapon, aiming it across the room.

"That's not gonna do you much good as you've already pointed out that I'm no longer of this world." Scott got to his feet, stood spine straight. "But if you ask nicely, I'll think about leaving. I have several fancy exits that I've perfected over the years. There's the poof and I'm gone. I prefer that one. Then there's the exit through the wall. A little too over the top at times, but it gets them every time. Then there's the fade out, which usually freaks people out the most because I leave part of my body in the now."

Jokes aside, Simon found no humor in any of it. "You aren't real. I'm so exhausted I'm seeing things. Hallucinating. That's it. I'm just tired."

"You have had a rough day. It isn't every man who finds out he's a father from a snot-nosed, rude Boston lawyer."

"Word travels fast in a small town."

"It does. But I have an inside track. I'm usually found roaming the grounds somewhere around Promise Cove. Ask Jordan about me. Ask Nick. Hell, you can even ask Cord. They'll all tell you the same thing. I'm a permanent fixture around here."

"Then how come I've never seen you until tonight?"

"Until tonight, you haven't needed me. Put the gun down, Simon. Lock it away so Delaney won't get to it. You're not back in the war. You're not out on patrol. You don't need to light up the driver at seventy yards to protect a convoy. You're a changed man from the one who could so easily pull that trigger and not think twice about it."

"You don't know anything about me," Simon uttered quietly. "You of all people should know what I've done."

"In the name of war," Scott pointed out.

"Yeah, well, if I'd reacted quicker you'd still be alive."

"Absolute nonsense. Or maybe it's wishful thinking on your part. My Hummer hit an IED. No matter how many rounds you'd've gotten off, I'd still be dead. Land mines tend to work that way."

"You're awfully casual about it now."

"I've had years to deal with all the regret. You've tried so hard to put the war behind you. Don't let the demons take over now, now that you've connected with your daughter, don't let them win."

Simon loosened his grip on the M9. "She is mine, isn't she? I can see it in the eyes. They're the same blue as mine."

"Go with your gut. It's never failed you before. It won't now."

"Why are you here?"

"You saved my life once, before that day it all ended. You gave me an extra two months of living, breathing, of writing letters back home. I wish it could've been spent back here, but it was time I valued. I'm here to pay you back any way I can. You're here for a reason."

There was a second of understanding between man and ghost before the ghost simply wasn't there. Merlin woofed at the vanishing act, clearly confused as to what had just happened.

Simon was left holding the Beretta. "I guess that was the 'poof and I'm gone version,'" he muttered to the dog.

As he bent to put the weapon back in the drawer, he changed his mind. Instead, he reached up in the top of the closet and brought down a handgun case. After locking the pistol up, he fell into bed, exhausted.

Four

At three-thirty a.m., Gilly went through the shift change notes, updating Aubree Wright, the nurse who worked the next shift, with everything that had happened over the last twelve hours. "Ina Crawford's sister brought her in around six. Ina was having breathing problems, so I called Dr. Blackwood. He admitted her as a precaution. She's in Room 4. I sent Marabelle home, though, to get a good night's rest. She'll be back first thing to check on Ina. Around eight, Archer Gates brought his mother in complaining of stomach pains. Since this is her fifth bout, Dr. Blackwood had me call Dr. Nighthawk in to assess her situation."

"Does that mean she'll need surgery?" Aubree asked, knowing Gideon Nighthawk was the brand-new surgeon hired within the last month out of Chicago.

"Probably. Down the road," Gilly replied with a yawn. "Sorry. I'm running on my last bit of caffeine and I'm ready to drop into bed."

"Then go on home. I have it from here," Aubree assured her, brushing back a mop of raven-black hair. "What's this in the log about a fifteen-month-old?"

Gilly smiled, recalling Delaney and her pop. "Skittish new daddy. Don't be surprised if he comes back before dawn. I wrote down his name."

"Simon Bremmer," Aubree muttered, reading the details of the visit. "Are we talking about the same cute guy, a mop of brownish-blond hair, soulful blue eyes that look like they've seen the world but want to keep it all a secret, stands about six-one? That guy?"

"Six-two," Gilly confirmed.

"I've seen him at The Shipwreck a couple of times. He doesn't have a baby."

"He does now," Gilly underscored before another wide yawn took over. "I'm outta here. You have the bridge, Miss Aubree."

After clocking out, Gilly darted over the walkway to her ancient Subaru Outback, a 1998 dark blue station wagon with enough miles on it to have traveled around the world six times or more. But as long as Wally Pierce could keep it running, it would get her around town and that's all she needed.

She never went anywhere, never traveled very far from her base. Where was there to go with an active toddler anyway?

On automatic, as if the Outback had a mind of its own, she headed to her little one-story Craftsman at the corner of Crescent Street and Tradewinds Drive. It was more like a caretaker's cottage that she'd recently painted sea-moss green with white trim on the shutters. It had three tiny bedrooms and only one bath, but it had the original working fireplace in the living room and a decent-sized front porch.

When she'd bought it from Logan Donnelly, he'd insisted on redoing the inside before she moved in. That was fine by her. A first-time buyer didn't argue when someone wanted to knock out a few walls and open up the floor plan. The house might be small, but it had new flooring throughout and new appliances in the kitchen.

She turned into the longish driveway that led to a one-car detached garage. This was the only thing she really minded about getting off at four a.m.---the eerie darkness right before dawn that seemed more intimidating than any other time of night. She knew that made her sound like a Nervous Nellie. But a single mom had to be careful. She always dreaded getting out of the car and making that long walk to the back door. Or rather the dash *running* to the back door. She never walked at this time of night, she ran.

After getting inside and flipping on the lights, she looked around the kitchen at the tidy counters and spotless sink. One thing about having Mom for a babysitter, the former pediatric nurse hated the thought of dirt or clutter. And it showed. The stove gleamed and the cabinets were always neat with everything in its place.

Her mother, Connie Grant, now worked as Dr. Blackwood's receptionist and day nurse. She'd taken Sydney's place so that Sydney could go back to work at the hospital on the day shift and do what she did best---emergency medicine. Sydney went on duty at seven, handled any trauma cases or serious medical issues that cropped up during the day, assessing their situations, and stabilizing the patients until Quentin or Gideon could arrive.

Three nights a week, Connie babysat Jayden at her house, which was just down the street. Gilly would normally grab a few hours of shuteye until Connie dropped Jayden off around eight-thirty on her way to the doctor's office. That meant that three days a week Gilly survived on four hours of sleep or less. If she was lucky, she might catch an extra hour and a half when Jayden went down for a nap. Otherwise, it was hands-on the minute little Jayden walked in the door.

Some days if she just couldn't keep her eyes open, she'd cart him over to the Community Church and let their day care program do the job. Jayden went there anyway Monday through Wednesday during that void from three-thirty to five-thirty in the afternoon when Gilly left for work and Grandma still had two hours left at the doctor's office. Afterward, Connie would pick him up, feed him, and get him off to bed.

It was a tough schedule, a weird workaround that might drive others up the wall. But for Gilly and Connie, they made it work. That's why she considered herself fortunate to have her mother's help. She knew other moms who weren't as lucky.

For now, she carried that charmed feeling with her into the bedroom where she peeled off her scrubs, crawled beneath the covers, and yielded to bone-tired fatigue.

Five

Simon heard crying when it felt like he'd closed his eyes for no more than five minutes. But it was light outside, and Merlin was tugging on the covers. "Okay. Okay. I'm up."

He slipped on a pair of jeans but couldn't find his shirt. Meantime the crying continued, and Merlin became more agitated.

He followed the dog, padding across the wood-planked floor into the living room before crossing over to Delaney's room. The smell of poop hit him before he laid eyes on the crib or its occupant.

"Oh no. No. No. No. Not this. What kind of baby girl gets poop everywhere? Oh. No. It's in your hair? We need to get you into the shower. Now." He started peeling off her pajamas with the disgusting poop interspersed in the fabric. He weighed whether to toss the clothes in the garbage or try to wash the mess out, but he'd deal with that later.

For now, he broke the tabs on the disgusting diaper and wadded up the offending material, tossing it in the wastebasket, the one Nick had set out and placed in its most conspicuous spot. Simon now realized the value of location next to the crib.

Once he got Delaney down to bare skin he picked her up, then darted into the tiny bathroom and turned on the shower to let the water heat up. After testing the spray, he stepped under the stream, jeans and all, holding her away from his body until most of the stuff had dissolved.

With one hand, he soaped her from head to toe, a fragrant lavender smell taking over the poopy odor. After making sure her bottom was clean, he washed her hair. And when she giggled, it warmed his heart. "Look at us, we're all wet, but at least we smell like flowers."

Delaney mumbled something that sounded like "all wet" but he wasn't up on his baby jargon. Simon dried her off first and set her down on the floor. He was toweling his hair dry when she took off running down the hallway, naked.

Realizing the chase was on, Merlin took off after her. Simon was able to catch them both, and scooped her up, blowing raspberries on her belly as he toted her back into her room to get dressed. Five little outfits were all she had to choose from, something he'd remedy later. "What to wear on a Wednesday, Delaney? How about the pale blue overalls with a nice white top? Yes?"

The toddler clapped her hands. "Jes."

"Did you just say yes? That's affirmative."

"Ma-ma."

"Not here, baby. Diaper first."

She obliged by sitting down on the rug and falling backward, grabbing her toes.

Surprised that she knew the drill, he grinned. "Now we're cookin'." He got her diaper on and then pulled the Tee over her head. The overalls were next and then socks. Her pink tennis shoes slid over her feet.

"All done," Simon announced.

"Done," Delaney repeated.

"You're like a parrot," he gauged, stripping the bedding from the crib and gathering it all up in a ball, doing his best not to get any of the disgusting matter on him. He carried the soiled bundle out to the laundry room where he stuffed everything into the washer. Using the sanitize setting, he hoped it was enough to sterilize the smell out.

While Delaney ate her cereal, Simon dialed his mother's number. "Hey, Mom, hi."

On the other end of the line Gretchen Bremmer grinned into the phone. "Simon. What a wonderful surprise and it isn't even Sunday. To what do I owe this middle of the week call?" Like a mother's radar she went on alert. "Is everything okay?"

"I can call my mother on a Wednesday."

"Certainly, but your usual routine is check in on Sunday afternoons. So, what's wrong?"

"Depends on your definition of wrong. Remember that woman I told you about a couple of years ago. We met on Nauset Beach the summer I decided to leave the Army. We spent almost three months together."

"Amelia something, wasn't it? What about her?"

He walked her through the entire story or at least the last twenty-four hours. "Delaney's her name. And she's a spitfire. I have to say, she has my eyes."

"Goodness, I have a granddaughter. Oh, Simon, when can I see her? Are you bringing her out?"

"We could Skype, like we did when I was overseas. And I'll send you plenty of photos, starting this afternoon, maybe make a couple of videos of her running around. How's that for starters?"

"But I want to hold her. Can't you bring her here?"

"Mom, the truth is I'm barely beyond learning how to change a diaper. I'm not up for getting on a plane and flying across the country with a toddler who might cry the entire way. She just got here off a plane ride. Give me a few months to get it all down. Give me time to adjust. Maybe by Christmas I'll be better at this, enough to travel anyway. You could come out for a visit, though. That's what I'm hoping for. Get a home health nurse to take care of Lorraine for a week. That's all I'm asking."

"I could certainly use a break. I'll make the arrangements as soon as we hang up."

"That's flying into Santa Cruz. I'm pretty sure Delta and United offer a nonstop direct flight from Newport. I realize it'll be a long flight for you. But I'll pick you up. Well, we'll pick you up. No need to take a cab."

"Okay. I'm making notes. I haven't been out of Rhode Island in years, let alone on a plane. Simon, did you ever think this would happen?"

"Not in a million years. It wasn't even on my radar. Just come for a visit. Take the leap and leave the 401 behind for a week. You'll love it here. Look, I gotta go. There are a dozen things I have to get done today. The least of which is buying a vehicle that can haul around a kid."

His mother tittered with laughter. "Give up your motorcycle? Now I know you're serious. I also know you're dangling that child right in front of me as enticement."

"Is it working?"

"What do you think?"

"Good. Because I'm getting a kick out of your reaction. Are you worried about me taking care of a baby?"

Gretchen snickered again. "Oh, Simon. The one thing I'm absolutely certain of is that with you around that baby, she couldn't be in better hands."

"Thanks for that. But you're supposed to say stuff like that."

"Simon, you're the most capable man I know to protect anyone from anything. You always have been."

He blew out a breath and ran a hand through his hair. "I needed that. Thanks, Mom. Send me an email with your flight itinerary. Let me know if you have difficulty finding a nurse for Lorraine."

"And what will you do about it from three thousand miles away?"

"I'll pull some strings with the home health care place. I went to school with the guy who runs it. Remember?"

"I won't have a problem. Stop worrying. I'll make my flight arrangements and send you a copy."

They hung up and Simon began to tidy up the kitchen while Delaney slugged it out with one of the stuffed bears Jordan had sent over with Nick.

"How am I supposed to shower while you're awake?" Simon wondered aloud as he headed into the bedroom to get dressed.

The active toddler roamed each room with Merlin, inspecting her new surroundings before finally following Simon into the bedroom. She held up her hands to be picked up.

"Let's go, doodle-bug. We have to buy a car."

Their first stop of the day was Radcliff Motors.

"I need new wheels, something I can get a car seat into, something safe, something...you know, dads drive."

"I have a minivan that has only thirty-five thousand miles on it," Brad said, beginning his sales pitch. "New tires and a good used…"

"Anything but that. What about that SUV over there?"

Brad shook his head. "That SUV is on its way to the junk heap. Bad mistake on my part. Either Wally is going to take it for parts or out it goes. What about that sleek, black GMC Sierra pickup I have in the corner? It's a four-door model. Back seat has room enough for a car seat. Has less than thirty-five thousand miles on it. I can make you a good deal."

"I don't know. A pickup?"

"It is what dads drive," Brad pointed out. "And, if you get rear-ended the bed's gonna suffer the most damage buffering the back seat."

"Hmm. I'll take it for a test drive and see how it handles. But first I have to make sure the car seat fits in the back. If it doesn't that's a deal breaker."

"No problem. I'll put it in there myself."

Once Brad finished installing the car seat, Simon settled Delaney into the back and slid behind the wheel. The engine started right up. They were blasted by the sound of Abba and "Dancing Queen" coming from the speakers. Simon reached over and lowered the volume. Out of the corner of his eye, he saw Delaney bouncing to the music and clapping her hands to the song.

"Like that, do you?" He wasn't sure how or why anyone would've left behind an Abba CD loaded in the player of a pickup truck, but it might just be the key to calming her down when she was in fussy mode.

The two of them took the truck for a spin through town. "So what do you think, doodle-bug? Is this the vehicle for us? Yes? No? Should we keep looking?"

Delaney clapped her hands again.

"I'll take that as a yes."

After signing the papers, he put a call in to Nick. "Your beautiful wife can have her SUV back. I just bought a set of wheels."

"You didn't mess around."

"What would be the point of that? I left her SUV at Brad's. He promised to take good care of it."

"No problem. I'll drop Jordan off there at lunch. How'd it go last night with the baby?"

"Last night was okay. It was the morning after that started out a mess." Simon recapped the story of what happened before breakfast.

Nick burst out laughing. "I wish I could tell you it gets better, but the truth is, you could wake up tomorrow and have the same situation on your hands."

"Go through that every morning? You're just messing with me, right?"

"Some mornings are better than others," Nick assured him. "What's next on your agenda?"

"I've got a list of things she needs. She didn't come with a lot of clothes. I thought maybe Jordan could help me pick out some stuff online and get it delivered...fast."

"I'll mention that to her. Don't forget to childproof your cabinets. Now that I think about it, childproof your entire house."

"I wanted to talk to you about that. The house. I know you own Taggert Farms and everything on it, but is there any way you'd ever think about selling the house to me?"

"Aren't you making an awful lot of decisions since yesterday? It hasn't even been twenty-four hours yet. Give yourself a little time to adjust to daddyhood. Consider what you want for the long term before making that kind of leap. And if you're in the market for a house, why not buy one in town? Delaney would be closer to school. That's been an issue for us living so far out of town."

"Because I kind of like being away from people. Remember when you and I were doing all that work to the house after I got here, we decided the remodeling job was for the best. You paid to replace a lot of rotted wood and bad plumbing and I got to live on the farm. If I stick with the caretaker's cottage, at least I know what I'm getting. Any other house on the market might have issues."

"Just think about it before you make a permanent leap like that. I'm not trying to talk you out of it. If it's what you want, I could sell it to you. But I don't have to tell you that a house is a huge investment. I think you need to take some time and make sure it's what's best for you and Delaney. Talk to Troy or maybe even Logan. They could help you find exactly what you're looking for. They both know every house in town and all the problems that go with each one. These houses around here are all old and will need some tweaking to update wiring and plumbing, though."

"But I've already done all that to the caretaker's cottage."

"Simon, that house isn't perfect. There's no garage, no storage to speak of, and no place for a kid to play outside. I suppose you could fence in the backyard to some degree, but it wouldn't be an ideal location for a kid down the road. Not only that, it's a working farm. The noise from tractors and those huge harvesters might be an issue for a toddler. And what about the dust the machines kick up?"

Simon scratched the side of his jaw where he hadn't taken the time to shave. "I hadn't thought of that. I guess I'm so used to the noise and the dirt it didn't occur to me it might be a problem for Delaney. Okay, you're right. I'll see what other property is available out there. Thanks, Nick."

Kinsey had set up an appointment for him to talk to a woman named Ophelia Moore who headed up the child care program at the Community Church. Ophelia was a recent graduate of UC Santa Cruz with a degree in early childhood education. According to Kinsey, the woman loved working with preschoolers, jumpstarting their classroom experience, hoping they'd succeed early on and continue through elementary school.

Simon liked the young woman's enthusiasm, he just wasn't sure about her approach. "Do you have a spot for Delaney for short-term day care? Because my days off are sometimes in the middle of the week. I sometimes don't work a regular nine-to-five gig. The only time I'll need a full day of care is when I take a tour out for eight hours. Most of the trips, though, usually last for five. Kinsey Donnelly seemed to think I'd have to put her on a waiting list even for a drop-in situation."

"Since I've taken over the program, I've discovered there's been quite the baby boom in Pelican Pointe recently. Because of that, everyone needs us at different times. We're very flexible except for weekends. Our hours don't extend to Saturday and Sunday. We have so many use the program during the week that we're almost full up in every age group.

I'm sure that's what Kinsey meant. To prevent overcrowding, I've tried to maintain very small groups for better one on one, adding here and there, shifting when the kids move into a new group or when I think the classroom warrants a change. Right now, I can offer three very different programs. One for babies from newborn to one year. That's my smallest group. Then there are the toddlers from thirteen months through twenty-four months, and then preschoolers up to the age of four. Obviously, Delaney would fit into the middle group. That's Susan Hollenbeck's classroom."

"But a classroom? She's only fifteen months old. How much space could she take up? And like I said, she wouldn't be in here every day."

Ophelia smiled, patient as a nun. "Even toddlers that young learn at a rapid rate whenever they're in the right surroundings. Each age group uses one of the Sunday school classrooms. It's out of necessity and space. We don't make them sit at desks if that's what you're afraid of."

"Oh. Okay. That makes more sense. So I just drop her off when the situation warrants it and this Susan will make room for her?"

"It'd be nice if you could give us a heads up. But we realize situations change on a dime and we try to be flexible as much as possible." She handed him a business card. "You can also text us as soon as you know your plans so we can adjust accordingly."

Simon left trying to calculate how he could take Delaney to work with him without putting her in such a structured environment. He didn't object to school or learning new things. But he did think fifteen months was a little too early for even part of the day spent in a rigid setting.

From the church, he and Delaney stopped in to see Brent Cody, the chief of police. The lobby was empty, no one sitting behind the reception area, but Brent appeared in his office doorway right away.

"Hey, Simon. I already met the infamous munchkin yesterday. Delaney, right?"

"Yep. Then you also met Cruella de Vil, the Boston lawyer."

"Not the warm and fuzzy type, huh?"

"Hey, she dumped a kid on a total stranger and seemed just fine with it. In case you or anyone else wondered, Delaney survived the night just fine. I'm here to ask a favor. Can you do a background check on a deceased person?"

"Sure. Come on in and have a seat. Got a name in mind?"

Simon plopped down in one of the chairs and adjusted Delaney on his lap. "Amelia Langston. Boston." He reached in his jeans pocket and pulled out a piece of paper. "This was the last known address on the paperwork Cruella gave me. I want to know everything you can get on Amelia."

"Okay. You want to sit there while I pull up a snapshot summary or do you want a full-blown, in-depth…?"

He didn't let him finish. "I want to know where she worked, who her parents were, if she had siblings. I want to know what she ate for breakfast when she was ten."

Brent bobbed his head. "For that to happen, give me three days. What do you know about her…exactly?"

"When I met her, she claimed to be a photographer, claimed to have sold her pictures to *National Geographic*. But after she left, I checked on that, found out the magazine had no record of her. So I already know that was a lie. If she lied about that, what else was she hiding? Then last night, I remembered that every time I pressed her for more information, she was purposely vague. I recall asking about her family. Again, ambiguous answers, like she was making it up on the fly. You need to understand that until yesterday afternoon I hadn't given Amelia Langston another thought since that August she up and left. But when I think back to that summer, I realize now I knew very few facts or details about her that made any sense. I suspect she wasn't completely honest with me over the course of that summer. We're talking about a brief affair that didn't have much of a shelf life to it. She didn't make demands or anything like that. It was just the opposite. I woke up one morning the week before Labor Day and she'd packed up, left without so much as a goodbye. I thought it was odd then but shortly afterward Nick and Cord contacted me. And here I am. I never looked back."

"What is it you suspect exactly?"

Simon rubbed the stubble on his chin. "This is gonna sound a little paranoid. But I think she wanted a child and was on the hunt for a sperm donor. I was it. Don't get me wrong. The circumstances of how Delaney got here don't matter to me. She's here and I'm fine with that. But I need to know the truth. One day, she'll ask about her mother and I won't know what to say to her. I want something tangible."

"All right. I'll let you know as soon as I'm done with the criminal aspect of it. That's what'll take the longest, searching the different jurisdictions. Unless you just want the info that I find out from Massachusetts."

"Nope. I want the entire U.S. Approach this like you're hunting for a thief who just stole five million in diamonds."

"I figured as much."

"Something else. You were in the service, right?"

"An MP in Iraq."

"Is there a way to locate a soldier without the Army knowing about it?"

"Is he still on active duty?"

Simon shook his head. "No, but I heard through the grapevine that the Army doesn't much like civilians poking around in their databases. And I've lost track of him. From what I understand he's been having a rough time. He may even be homeless. I tried finding anyone remotely related to him but got nowhere."

"Give me a name. I still have a few contacts over there who can be trusted."

Simon took another piece of paper out of his pants pocket and slid it across the desk. "I wrote down the information I need. Could you let me know when you hear back?"

"You bet."

Simon made a few more stops, but Murphy's Market had to be the last one so that he could pick up groceries. They got a few stares from people who knew him when he plopped Delaney into the cart. He could see it in their eyes. Were they wondering if he'd kidnapped a baby overnight?

The idea made him chuckle as he pushed the cart toward the produce aisle. Murphy, who was also the town's mayor, stood in front of a large bin of honeycrisp apples, setting them in the display just so.

"Hey there, Simon. Who's the midget?"

"Delaney." He waited a beat before adding, "My daughter. We're out of food."

Unruffled, Murphy nodded. "You came to the right place. Toddler food is on aisle 6 along with Pampers. We carry the economy size in sensitive." When he saw Simon's blank stare, he added, "Most requested kind."

"Thanks for the heads-up. Might as well start there." He headed that way, stocking up on boxes of diapers and baby wipes. In the produce section, he tossed in bananas and apples, picking up jars of applesauce, just in case. After getting eggs, frozen waffles, yogurt, and of course, Cheerios, he was loading up on Graham crackers when the cute nurse approached from the opposite direction, a little boy sitting in the child seat.

"Fancy meeting you here," Gilly said, amused at the sight of father and daughter. "I see you survived the night. How's my patient doing?"

Simon grinned, the wheels turning in his head to come up with the nurse's name. "She's fine. I'm a little embarrassed at how I overreacted. This must be your boy."

"Jayden, say hi to Delaney and Simon."

Jayden stuck his finger in his mouth, turning bashful. Delaney reached over and patted the boy's face.

"Aren't you a friendly girl?" Gilly remarked. "Jayden can be shy on Wednesdays."

"You have a knack with kids," Simon commented, stalling until the woman's name popped into his head. "Gilly."

Even more amused at his demeanor, Gilly tipped up Delaney's chin. "You look a lot better than the last time I saw you. I have an idea. I have to be at work soon, but I'm off tomorrow. Why don't you guys come to my house for dinner tomorrow night?"

"I'd like that. What time?"

"Oh, sevenish or so is fine. If you get hung up with the doodle-bug, I'm flexible with the time."

Delaney yawned.

"Now see, Daddy. That's a sure signal right there it's nap time," Gilly pointed out with a wink. "I've gotta run anyway. I just came in here to pick up some milk and cereal, and maybe something for lunch."

"Before you go, would you happen to know where I could get a baby monitor?"

"Ferguson's Hardware stocks them."

"They do? I've been in there dozens of times before and never once noticed that."

Gilly snickered. "Now why would you go down the aisle with the baby stuff. If you're going, though, don't forget to pick up the childproof locks for cabinets and drawers."

"Good idea. One-stop shopping."

"I really do have to run. See you and Delaney Thursday night."

"What can we bring?" Simon asked as she darted down the aisle.

"Just bring yourselves."

She'd taken off like a spitfire, leaving him wondering where she got her energy. She had a marathon shift ahead of her. If she could endure twelve long hours on her feet, Simon could take care of one small bundle.

Nap time came and went for both of them. After catching up on sleep, he took Delaney out to his boat, getting her used to the sway of the water. He'd slathered layers of sunscreen on anything exposed to the sun or the wind and stuck a hat on her head that he'd picked up at Reclaimed Treasures, a little pink thing that tied under her chin to keep the sun out.

That's where Jordan found them, sitting together on the dock, looking out over the cove.

"This is a pretty spot for thinking," Jordan said as she plopped down beside them. "Nick said you might need help picking out a few outfits for Delaney."

The baby wanted down to run around with Merlin, but Simon held firm. "I'd really appreciate it. No idea what she needs as far as clothes. She didn't come with a lot."

Jordan nodded. "We'll wade through the choices together."

"I don't mean to bring this up, but before I went to bed last night I could've sworn I saw Scott. I know I was tired, but I even thought I had a conversation with him. I'm pretty sure it never happened. I'm certain it was all in my head."

"But it did," Jordan stated matter-of-factly as she took the squirming child out of his arms. "You weren't dreaming."

"How is that possible?"

"Honestly, I don't know. Scott…he just refuses to leave. He loves it here. He watches over Hutton every day of her life."

"Hutton is Scott's?"

"I thought you knew."

"No, I didn't. It never occurred to me."

"You and Nick never talk about what happened over there. You're both so much alike in that regard. While you may think you know everything about Nick, I bet there's one thing you don't know. When Nick first came here, when he first got out of the Guard, he was all messed up in his head for reasons I didn't understand. It took a few weeks before I realized he was suffering from guilt, PTSD, you name it. I think you have a lot of that inside you, too. Am I right? Nick mentioned to me once right after he got in touch with you that you'd been an Army sniper assigned to protect convoys. I can't even imagine what you've seen and the things you'll never be able to forget. I suppose those kinds of memories never quite go away."

Simon gave her the faintest of smiles. "Not when people keep bringing it up."

"Sorry. But you're so like Nick, unwilling to talk about what your life was like over there. Almost haunted. Is it really that surprising when any of you see Scott?"

"When you put it that way, I guess not. Wait. What do you mean? Has Nick seen him, too?" But he already knew the answer. "Cord. Ryder. Eastlyn."

"Notice a pattern?"

"It's eerie that we all ended up here."

"Not really. Not when you consider you all have super-bad memories from war. You all looked out for each other while you were over there. Why is it so out of the norm you'd still be doing it? You ended up here because Nick thought you might benefit from living in a town where people care about each other. Do you like living here, Simon?"

"I do."

"Why?"

"Like you said, people here seem to care. Just look at what happened yesterday. I was overwhelmed, knocked on my ass over the news. I was scared. But you guys rallied, stepped in, stepped up, and got me through the shock. I mean, I'm still in shock just looking at Delaney, but you guys were there for me. Nick and Cord putting up the crib. You sending over food for a toddler, knowing I had no clue what I needed to do for her. Where else would people do that?"

"Pelican Pointe hasn't always been like that, Simon. The day Nick drove up on that motorcycle of his, I was ready to give up, pack the house up that Scott had loved so much, and go back to the Bay Area to be with my family. I was that unhappy. I hated it here. I'd given up, so much so that I might've been on the verge of a mental breakdown. Living out here all alone, I suffered from a combination of depression and anger. I didn't know it at the time but some of the rage was aimed at Scott. I felt like he'd dumped me here, pregnant, and taken off to be with his Guard unit. I wasn't exactly the perfect military wife back home. I tried to be, but I was too miserable living out here in an unfriendly environment. The town was a huge disappointment for me. Scott had built this place up to be Paradise, which it definitely was not. But I couldn't afford to break down or give up because at the time Hutton was Delaney's age. What would've happened to her if I'd just buckled?"

"Then you know how I feel."

"I do. Nick's showing up when he did turned all that around, turned me around. He saved me, Simon. Do you understand what I'm saying? Nick came here because he was haunted by memories of Scott, by some stupid promise he made the day Scott died. That one decision saved my life. Because of him this Bed and Breakfast exists. And because it exists, you're here. We're all somehow an integral part of a dream Scott had for his hometown. And we're making it happen after his death, one person at a time. You're here for a reason. Don't ever forget that."

"I had no idea."

"Why would you know any of it? You've been here two years, had dinner with us at least a dozen times. And afterward, you play with the kids, build Lego sets, do puzzles, you laugh and carry on with them like you were their great-uncle, but you always hold something of yourself back. You're never totally, completely engaged. I see it in your eyes. You never say much about yourself, making sure to keep anything of a personal nature to yourself."

"I'm sorry. I didn't realize I was so distant. Maybe I have my reasons. Maybe I didn't want to bring my troubles into a house that's so…filled…with so much love. It seemed out of place. I seemed out of place being here, like I didn't belong."

Jordan reached over and laid her hand on top of his. "You're not out of place. Not here. Not ever. You're exactly where you're supposed to be." She took a shaky breath, thinking maybe she'd said too much, gone too far. "I'm not trying to interfere in your life, Simon. But something's bothering you deep inside. Don't let it get in the way of enjoying Delaney. That's all I'm saying. And if you want me to babysit tomorrow while you do your Treasure Island run, I will."

"I thought about taking her with me. I found her a lifejacket at the bait shop. They sell all kinds of boating supplies. And I picked up one of those backpack things for a kid. You know the ones that let you carry a toddler on your back."

She smiled. "You bought a carrier?"

"That's it, like a sling you put on your back." He shifted to face her. "Thanks for telling me all that stuff. I guess you never know what's truly going on in a person's life, even when things look so perfect from the outside."

"Things are rarely perfect, Simon. Why don't you think about forgiving yourself for whatever it is that's eating you up inside?" She handed off Delaney and stood up to go. "Think about it. And if you change your mind about me babysitting, give me a heads-up first, okay? Even though I only have four guests, they can be demanding."

"I know. You do a great job here. I couldn't do what you guys do."

"Sure you could." Jordan turned to Delaney and waved. "Bye-bye."

Simon picked up the girl's hand and waved. "Bye-bye, Jordan."

"Bye-bye," Delaney uttered and reached for the dog, trying to wrap her arms around his middle.

Simon sat there another half hour watching Delaney and Merlin bond with each other until the sun went down. "Come on, kids, time to head home for supper."

While he fixed dinner he put on music, beginning with the found Abba CD that Delaney seemed to like so much. "Dancing Queen" might've been her favorite, but he got a kick out of watching her move to the beat of "Super Trouper" with Merlin as her dance partner. And when Simon joined in, it became a party. "We're number one, Delaney! Number one." He showed her how to point, and all three rocked around the room in time to the music.

The menu tonight was macaroni and cheese and chicken. Surprisingly more went into her belly this time and less on the floor than the night before.

When it came time to get ready for bed, he put on a Donovan playlist and they listened to "Catch the Wind" during bath time. Afterward, he dressed her in a new pair of pajamas with pink and purple dinosaurs.

The tunes seemed to soothe her and settle her down enough to sit still for a bedtime story. He'd checked out some kid books from the new Ocean Street Library and decided on the one about a dragon. Delaney didn't make it to the end, falling asleep in his arms before the finale.

He watched her sleep until he realized he needed to play catch up and do all the things he couldn't do while she was awake. Like install all those childproof locks and take a shower.

He worked till almost midnight putting latches on every drawer and cabinet throughout the house. Thinking it would make too much noise, he didn't even use the drill, which is why it took him so long.

With the house quiet, and Merlin curled up in the corner snuggled in his dog bed, Simon took a quick shower before falling into bed. Within five minutes he was out like a light.

His day started out exactly like all the other days that came before it, days spent in this flea-infested sandbox with no way out, no escape.

Every sniper had a spotter and his was a guy known as Eagle Eye. The man had a warped sense of humor and would burst into his tent before dawn, shake him awake with the same tune that never changed. Eagle Eye loved Steppenwolf and somewhere in his civilian background someone had told him he could sing. God only knew why.

Eagle Eye sang at the top of his lungs the lyrics to "Born to be Wild." He heard that damn song so often it would eat into his brain all day long even as they trekked to the mess hall for some grub. It stayed with him as they headed to the motor pool where they'd pick up their ride, a Humvee so layered in dust that it was hard to tell what color it really was.

Eagle Eye would crawl behind the wheel, roaring out through the gates of the compound before the rest of the camp began to stir, still singing at the top of his lungs.

Sometimes they would drive to an abandoned house that had a clear view of the main supply route, the one used for transporting everything to all the advance units. Convoys came and went, but they all at one time or another passed this way, on this route, located near the only oasis within fifty miles of anything.

It was their job to ID any potential threat and eradicate it. Period. Anything out of the ordinary spotted approaching the encampment or the convoy transports was dealt with by eliminating it.

As far as Simon was concerned, every day was like a repeat of the day before. Every day seemed hotter than the last one. All he thought about was swimming in a cool ocean, sitting with a beer in his hand as the breeze hit his face instead of this blast furnace.

Some days nothing moved. They'd sit and bake until the sand fleas tried to eat at their faces. Other days, only a small herd of goats could be seen trotting toward the water, the herd driven back and forth by a twelve-year-old boy.

But it was the other days that were burned into his mind forever, the days when Eagle Eye would nudge him. That's when Simon would zero in on a target, a threat. Once he had the person in his crosshairs, he would assess the situation, and if need be, eliminate the threat.

Faces. There were a lot of faces that kept him up at night. Head shots. Young. Old. Male. Female. All had at one time or another tried to approach with some type of IED strapped to their bodies. When he closed his eyes and tried to sleep, he could still see their faces, sometimes blurred together, but always there. He tried to block the images by focusing on all the lives he'd saved with one flex of his index finger. His spotter always kept count. But Simon had instructed him to keep it to himself. He never wanted to know the actual number. He didn't need to know because he saw them in flashbacks almost every night.

When he got back stateside he never wanted to look at another human being through the crosshairs of a rifle scope.

He wanted a normal life, one where he could forget about every bad thing he'd ever done, one where death didn't visit quite so often.

Six

You're here for a reason.

In his dream those words blended together, merging from Scott's voice into Jordan's.

At the sound of baby babble, Simon cobwebbed out of his slumber and rolled out of bed. It was still dark outside, but he accepted the early morning hour just as he had for years in the military.

More together today than he had been yesterday, he started a pot of coffee before heading into Delaney's room. There was no mess like that first day and diaper changing went a great deal smoother. He let her wear pajamas during breakfast so there was only one change of clothes.

While he scrambled eggs, she ran around chasing Merlin. Every now and then, the pooch let her catch him, but mostly the dog dodged and darted like a game of tag.

She settled down long enough to eat but getting her dressed became a sing-song rhyming tune until the second shoe went on. Scooping her up, he plopped her on her feet and began to gather up dirty clothes. She trailed after him into the laundry room, beginning to explore more of her surroundings.

"I'm still not sure about taking you out on the water with me. Maybe you'd be better off staying with Jordan. I better text her," Simon said aloud as he started the washer, which now had become a daily routine.

Picking up his phone, he keyed in, *Jordan, are you still up for babysitting? I'm having second thoughts about taking Delaney on the boat all day. What if she doesn't like it? I won't be able to cut the trip short and leave the group to bring her back to the B&B. What's your take?*

Jordan's reply came back within a few minutes. *I think you're selling yourself short. Once the boat gets to the island, walk around with her. She'll be fine if she's with you no matter where it is.*

He smiled at that answer and texted back. *Then it's a go.*

For two years, spending time on the water had been Simon's refuge from all the wrong things he'd done in his life. Rain or shine, over the last few months he'd perfected his boating skills, even going out in bad weather to make sure he could handle the helm during rough seas. He never put others in jeopardy and never took out a tourist when it was stormy. But on his own, he pushed the limits, striving to become a better skipper just as he had always pushed himself to be the best each day he woke up in the Army.

Today, none of that was on his mind. Keeping Delaney safe and the others in his charge was his number one priority.

While Jordan fussed over the toddler, Nick helped him check off the guests, a professor who'd brought along five grad students from the plant biology department at UC Davis.

A youthful forty, professor Luca Waterman had a full crop of light brownish hair and a day's worth of beard. Turning to his entourage, three female students and two guys, Luca joked about his fondness for botany and flora. "This is my second trip out to the island. I came here two years ago with my girlfriend at the time and just happened to sign up for the tour on Treasure Island. I'm glad I did. You're in for a real treat today. There's so much to see. Prepare to experience native grasses in their natural habitat and California quail up close and personal."

"Bree took them out when they were here the last time," Jordan explained. "That was right before you came to town."

Simon could tell the professor and his group were anxious to get going and excited about gathering new samples. "I wasn't sure how Bree ever managed using such a compact boat to make all the trips she did in one day. I don't see how she carried so many back and forth. The woman had it down to a fine art to have hauled as many around as she did."

Luca snapped his fingers at the memory. "That's right. She had this small cabin cruiser. I remember it was overcrowded that day with all the gear everyone brought on board. I was glad to see that my girlfriend and I weren't the only ones who'd brought the kitchen sink with us. We'd lugged cameras, binoculars, and our field packs with us, along with the sample cases we didn't want to leave behind."

"Bree was good at what she did," Simon revealed. "The cabin cruiser was a nice outfit, but more in line for personal use rather than the tourist trade. Since then, business has doubled. That's why I like having the larger forty-six-footer. It cuts down on all the round trips Bree had to make."

Nick scratched his head. "Yeah. I remember her complaining about that. She'd make two and three expeditions out there a day, dropping off one bunch, usually family members, and then coming back to pick up the rest. I think the fun of it wore off after a while."

"Bree did a wonderful job for us," Luca pointed out. "No complaints. And she knew her stuff. Once we arrived on the island, she was an exceptional tour guide, able to point out all the interesting flora and fauna. She even helped us locate a rare white sage growing near a nest of quail and a patch of coastal grassland that I personally had never seen before. It was on that trip that I took a few samples back home with me. It's why I put in for a grant. When it finally came through this spring I had my funding, enough to bring my students back here for another round of visits. I'm hoping to take more samples and write a paper about the numerous plant species I've found growing there."

"It's a beautiful place that's stayed untouched and undisturbed by developers," Simon explained. "In this day and age that's a rarity. Which is why we'd best get going." He reached to take Delaney out of Jordan's arms. "We'll see you later this afternoon, that is unless…"

"If she fusses, bring her back," Jordan offered, gathering up the food baskets. "I have rooms to tidy and beds to change, but it'll take you that long to decide and bring her back if there's a problem."

Simon's brow creased into a frown. He glanced at Nick before turning back to Jordan. "I'll make it work. Delaney shouldn't be your problem."

Jordan grinned at his resolute attitude and patted his shoulder. "Nick will help you load up the boat while I get the kids ready for school. If you need help, don't hesitate to ask. Don't be so stubborn and think you can do it all by yourself. Who says I won't have time to babysit this little doll if you find out the hard way she doesn't like the water?"

"Hear that, Delaney? You gotta show us your sea legs, girl," Simon teased as he began smoothing sunblock over her arms and face and anything else exposed to the rays. When he was done, he rubbed his nose against her soft cheek before plopping her into the carryall. After adjusting the shoulder straps, he lifted the weight onto his back. "All set? We're counting on you to love the water as much as we do." He snapped his fingers to get the dog's attention. "Aren't we, Merlin? Come on. Let's show her how it's done."

Merlin woofed and took off out the back door, leading the way down to the water. The trek down the steep set of stairs had everyone holding onto the iron railing to get to the bottom.

After making sure everyone had safely boarded, Simon stood at the helm and throttled the engine, motoring his way out of the inlet. Under a solid blue sky, the breeze light from a westerly direction, he found the water smooth as silk.

"How do you know she won't barf in your hair?" the auburn-haired grad student asked, bobbing her head toward the toddler.

Simon could feel Delaney's weight on his back, but couldn't see her face. "I don't. Does she look like she's about to get sick?"

"No, she sorta looks like the dog does, leaning his head into the wind, taking in the breeze. How old is she?"

"Fifteen months."

"My son's a year and a half."

Simon's jaw dropped. The girl seemed too young to have a child.

She noticed his reaction and smiled. "I'm older than I look. Truth is I'm almost thirty, got a late start to getting my Ph.D. though, mostly due to an unplanned detour." She lifted a shoulder. "My name's Starla Miller. I went back to school two years ago when I decided I wanted to go into horticulture. Luca encouraged me to not let anything stop me."

Simon noticed Starla looked over adoringly at the professor. "How do you get it all done with a child?"

"My mother takes care of Danny for me during the week. Since I'm going to school year-round it helps to have a built-in babysitter. Am I wrong to wonder if this little cutie is your first?"

Simon chuckled. "Does my lack of experience show that much?"

"Hey, at least you're willing to bring her to work with you. I think that's great."

"I'm not that great, just trying to think outside the box for now. I'll eventually have to rely on daycare."

"Don't we all at one time or another. I heard the innkeeper back there. Be grateful you have backup. Single parents need all the help we can get."

Seven

At five-five, Gilly liked to think she was in shape, even though a portion of baby weight from three years back stubbornly wouldn't let go of her belly. She'd given up trying to make it to the treadmill three times a week and relied on getting her workout by keeping up with an active toddler. And when she dashed from patient to patient at the hospital wasn't that the same as a dozen hours of cardio and fat burning?

She'd once had a lean, athletic runner's build, was even on the girls' track team in high school. But now when she looked at herself in the mirror, she realized she could stand to lose a few pounds, especially around the hips. She'd let herself go because she never intended to date again. Not ever. And here she was waiting for a guy to show up for dinner.

"Well, you aren't going to lose ten pounds before he gets here," she mumbled to herself as she slid into her best summer dress, a black and white floral chiffon that made her feel more like Jennifer Lawrence walking the red carpet instead of a combat nurse stuck in scrubs every day of her life.

Jayden pushed the door open and scrambled on the bed to use it for a trampoline. She lifted him up and swung him around. "Not tonight, buddy. Let's go check on supper."

"Supper!"

"Yeah, well, I hope they like Italian," she muttered to Jayden, as she looped an apron around her neck so she wouldn't get marinara splatter on her best dress.

But standing at the stove in her little kitchen, dragging a spoon through her thick, homemade spaghetti sauce, it suddenly hit her. She'd overdressed for a simple dinner with a friend. "What was I thinking? Why didn't I just wear jeans?"

Jayden, who'd plopped down on the floor, was using his set of wooden building blocks to erect a fortress that cut off the only pathway in and out of the eating area.

Cutting her eyes to his project, she chewed her lip. "Oh, buddy, you're gonna have to move that at some point so people can get through."

Jayden shook his head. "No! Stays here. No!"

Gilly let out a mother's frustrated sigh. This is why she didn't have a lot of people over. She didn't really like the idea of standing her ground over a fort. Not tonight. She was already having second thoughts about extending the invitation. Why hadn't she invited them on a Friday night to allow herself at least one good night's sleep?

She dragged a hand through her hair. It would have been the smart thing to do. But no, her mouth had rolled over her strategic thinking right along with her common sense.

It had been so long since she'd been on a date, she was pretty sure this whole thing would end up in an awkward mess. She was fairly certain she couldn't remember how to act around a man in a social setting. Sure, she got a few looks and a couple of offers once or twice a year, but it was different entertaining in her own home.

"It's not a date. It's just dinner," she told herself as she glanced at the clock. Realizing there was no time to slip into a sensible pair of jeans, she decided to make the best of it.

Staring at the giant wall Jayden had built around himself, she heaved out a groan. "I'm sure the long-legged, lean Simon might be able to step over those blocks without any trouble, but I can't promise Delaney won't destroy all your hard work as soon as she sets eyes on it."

She started to sweat just thinking about a scene and knew she needed to calm down. "It's just one dinner between friends," she repeated. After fanning her face, she picked up a dish towel to wipe her sweaty palms when the doorbell rang.

Sucking in a deep breath to still her jitters, she took one giant step over the top of Jayden's head and cleared the wall he'd so carefully built.

As soon as she opened the door, her nerves slid away. There stood Simon holding the wiggly Delaney.

"Come on in. It's okay to put her down if you want. My house is pretty much childproof."

Simon looked around the tidy living room. It had an oversized, comfy sofa with a matching chair in durable tan canvas. "Your furniture looks in good shape for having a toddler around. Delaney got grape jelly on mine."

That made her laugh and let more anxiety slip away.

He plopped Delaney down on her feet and glanced over at Jayden. Noting the boy's creativity, he went over to where Jayden sat on the floor. "How's it going? What are you building there?"

"Big wall," the toddler exclaimed proudly, his arms outstretched to emphasize its width. "Big."

Simon saw trouble coming the minute Delaney got within reach.

She clapped her hands in delight and swooped in. "Bwocks."

"No!" Jayden shouted right before the first domino effect occurred.

Simon and Gilly stood back and watched as the wall toppled, the blocks crashing onto the floor.

In retaliation for destroying his work, Jayden shoved Delaney. The girl lost her balance and stumbled backward.

"Jayden, stop that," Gilly shouted. "There's no call for that. We can build back your wall."

By this time both toddlers were crimson-faced and in tears.

Simon lifted Delaney into his arms. "It's okay. You're okay. Shhh. Now tell Jayden you're sorry for knocking over his fort."

Delaney stuck out her lip in a pout. "Bwocks."

"I know. I know. You just wanted to play with the blocks. But how about this? How about we sit on the floor and help Jayden build it all back? How's that sound? Yes? No? Nod your head, doodle-bug."

The little girl hiccupped, stuck her finger in her mouth, and finally bobbed her head.

While Simon soothed over hurt feelings, so did Gilly, picking up Jayden and settling him on her hip. All at once, she sniffed the air. "Oh, my God. My sauce."

Scooting over to the stove, she took off the lid. "Oh, no. I forgot to turn the burner to simmer. I've ruined dinner."

Simon chuckled and went over to where she stood. "Don't worry about it. No harm done. Let's order a pizza instead. Longboard's delivers. We can also get some mac and cheese for the kids. Fischer makes it homestyle."

She leaned her head against Jayden's. "I can't believe I did that. I'm so sorry."

"It's okay, Mama," Jayden said, patting her cheeks in solace.

"Anyone for pizza?" Simon suggested again.

"Sure. I've got them on speed dial. I usually get half a plain cheese and pepperoni."

"Better order two then, one cheese and another pepperoni. I'm starving."

Jayden wanted down.

"Not until you say you're sorry to Delaney for pushing her."

"Sow-wy," Jayden whispered.

Patting him on the bottom, she set him down. "Good boy. Now go play with the blocks and this time share with Delaney," Gilly directed in her best Mom voice. "No sharing means no pizza."

Simon slid Delaney to the floor. "Go play with Jayden." After she'd toddled off to the corner of the kitchen, he leaned in and said, "You should know I'm taking notes. You handled that like a pro."

"I hope so," Gilly said with a smile as she dumped the ruined sauce down the sink and flipped on the garbage disposal. "I haven't burned dinner in years." She whirled around from the counter. "I was nervous about tonight. And I'm so very tired."

"I'm sure you are. You probably haven't had enough sleep. Should we do this another time?"

"No, of course not. I'm better now. I just don't do this kind of thing very often."

"Do what? Eat?"

That got a smile out of her. She scrubbed her hands over her face and rubbed the back of her neck.

He took her hand. "You look pretty tonight. I should've told you that as soon as you opened the door. You aren't the only one who's out of practice."

"Thanks. It's just that not many men want a kid."

"I'm sure the same applies in reverse to my situation. How long have you been a nurse?"

She blew out a breath. "Four years. Want a glass of wine or a beer?"

"Beer sounds great."

While getting the drinks from the refrigerator, her history seemed to pour out. "Before Dr. Blackwood built the hospital in town, my mom got me a job at San Sebastian General. She'd worked there for almost twenty years, so she had some pull with the personnel department. When I came back to town and announced I was pregnant, I needed to work. After all, I had a nursing degree. Nurses were in demand. Even though my mother was totally disappointed in me, she recommended me for a late-night shift, which are the hardest slots to fill. I didn't mind the hours because I eventually realized that working different shifts we'd be able to cover watching a newborn with less daycare expense. And once Jayden got here, I knew I'd need all the help I could get. Back at San Sebastian General we both had an even crazier schedule than we have now."

She paused to twist the cap off a local brew called Pelican Red. "Have you tried this stuff?"

Simon took a long pull. "I like it. Heavy on the barley, toss in plenty of smoke and tobacco with just a hint of cinnamon and allspice."

"Not bad. You nailed the flavors."

"I know beer. So, you've always worked the graveyard shift?"

"Gotta start somewhere. Besides, the pay is better. Although at the other hospital I worked five nights a week, eight-hour shifts. I prefer the way Dr. Blackwood and Sydney do the scheduling, even though nothing's perfect. I like the three days on part, four days off. It gives me more time to spend with Jayden. That's the upside."

Simon sipped his beer. "Lack of sleep is the downside. I like your house."

"Up until three months ago we were living with Mom. Sometime before last Christmas I got the distinct feeling that after three years sharing the same space, we were getting on each other's last nerve. Jayden and I needed our own place. The answer came when Dr. Blackwood announced he was building a new hospital here, small, but practically right around the corner. I approached Sydney and told her I'd be willing to do anything at the new clinic, work any job, any shift. She hired me on the spot, but I had to wait for all the construction to finish up. Once it opened last March, Mom and I gave up the commute we both hated and started working in town. We celebrated that night with champagne because, for the first time, we could work where we lived. After my first night on the job, I went to see Logan the next morning, was standing on his doorstep by seven-thirty asking about buying a house, how difficult it would be, that sort of thing. I knew he liked to flip houses. He talked me into taking the big plunge and I went to see Nick at the bank for my mortgage app."

"Is that why the sculptor doesn't do much sculpting these days?"

She lifted a shoulder. "With twins, who has the time? I understand the craziness of having small kids. And I know Kinsey has her hands full with all the legal work she does. I see Logan hauling the kids around town while she's busy with contracts and wills and stuff. I don't think he requires that artistic outlet like he once did. Or if he does, he's found a new venue for it. He mentioned that he prefers getting a crew together to restore a lot of these old houses around here. He's pretty good at it, too. He has a knack for knocking out walls and redesigning the interior. He did all the work in here and opened the place up. He even picked out the wood flooring for me."

"Nick says if I'm in the market for a house, I should go see him."

"Absolutely. He knows the properties inside and out, knows what the houses need and knows what they don't. He works with Troy a lot, who has his own business over on Ocean Street."

"Ah. That explains the call I got from Troy offering to show me some houses this weekend that have already been redone. Would you and Jayden like to join me and Delaney on the tour?"

"Why not? I probably know most of the properties already. I bet I know the one he's taking you to first. There's a classic Craftsman at the end of Tradewinds with a long front porch. In fact, we could walk down there after we eat. You could get an idea of what it's like. The walk might tire out the kids."

"I'm all for that."

The doorbell rang signaling dinner had arrived. Simon got up to pay.

Gilly balked. "You don't have to do that. I invited you."

"You get it next time."

Gilly had dragged out Jayden's old high chair for Delaney. And when they sat down at the table and dug in, it was a noisy, messy affair.

Needing to keep the adult conversation going, Gilly prompted, "You mentioned Delaney came from Boston. Is that where you grew up?"

"Me? No. Why'd you think that?"

"You mentioned you met Delaney's mother at Cape Cod. I just thought…"

"Amelia and I spent a summer together. That's it. I grew up in Newport, Rhode Island. My mother taught school. But my dad, he was a lawyer, one of those movers and shakers in mergers and acquisitions. He wanted his son to follow suit. But I was stubborn, determined to do things my way no matter what he said or the advice he tried to push on me. I wanted to move as far away from what he wanted me to do as I possibly could."

"Which isn't all that unusual. Relationships between fathers and sons are often tricky."

"True. But ours seemed worthy of a couple of lengthy novels about how rocky it was spending fifteen minutes together. My mother finally persuaded me to do what he wanted. Maybe bribed would be more accurate. And I went off to college with all the enthusiasm of a stupid kid determined to fail. I put up with it for a while."

"You went to college?"

"For two long years that seemed like twenty to an eighteen-year-old smartass."

"I thought all eighteen-year-olds were smartasses. Where?"

"Brown."

She tilted her head. "Brown University?"

"Oh, yeah. His alma mater. He picked the school and my major. Contract law just like him."

"But it wasn't for you?"

"Not only was it not for me, I hated the very idea of it. So one day after I made it through my sophomore year, I got a burr up my butt and joined the Army. It was spring. May. I went back home and shoved my decision in his face. He was livid, the maddest I'd ever seen him. 'How dare you defy me like that?'"

"Which was the point, I'm sure."

"Absolutely. At first, it was. But then we didn't speak for almost three years of my overseas stint, out of sight, out of mind, that sort of thing."

Delaney began to toss her food on the floor. Simon got to his feet, grabbing a paper towel to clean the sticky stuff off her face, and then went to work on the hardwood floor. He set her down to play.

By this time, it was Jayden's turn to announce he was done with his plate. He scurried over to make sure his blocks were protected from the interloper who'd knocked them down in the first place.

While the kids amused themselves, Gilly got the feeling Simon had something else to say. But the sun was also going down. "How about we take that walk to see the house before it gets dark? You have to see this place. We can clear the dishes when we get back."

"Sure. Let's go."

"You can use Jayden's stroller for Delaney." She bent down to her son. "You don't mind if Delaney sits in there while you take my hand like a big boy, do you, Jayden?"

Jayden stuck his finger in his mouth and nodded. "'kay."

They took off walking through the neighborhood to the tune of crickets singing and croaking frogs. Jayden tried to catch one of the slippery critters.

Simon decided to lend a hand, stopping their progress long enough to pick up a baby-sized tree frog with skin marbled the color of granite. "See his webbed feet and his bug eyes. It's okay to touch his head."

Jayden obliged, his little fingers exploring the frog's skin. "Can he jump?"

"He sure can. Let's put him down and watch him go back to his mom."

Jayden squatted down to check out the frog's movements. When it hopped away, he squealed in delight. "There he goes."

"Back to his mom."

Gilly watched the byplay and it warmed her heart. Her son rarely got the chance to interact with another male.

Simon must have sensed the connection because he met her eyes and sent her a mischievous grin, taking the boy's hand while she continued to push Delaney in the stroller. "Jayden has a curious nature."

"No kidding. That might explain why he thinks he's Bear Grylls."

"Boys and climbing go together."

"I suppose. I'll remind you of that when Delaney starts escaping from her crib."

Simon looked mortified. "When does that happen?"

"When you wake up one morning and they've spent the night on the floor."

"Oh wow. I thought the crib was a surefire way to keep her contained."

Gilly threw her head back and laughed. "Contained. Listen to you. Nothing is surefire with an infant. You learn that pretty quickly." She waited a beat before picking up their original topic. "So, despite your thinking you'd made a mistake by joining the Army, you still stuck it out for a long time, right? A dozen years is nothing to sneeze at. After all that time, why not just make it a career?"

The question took away his good mood. "Sure, I stuck it out, doesn't mean I liked every minute of it, though. And the idea of making it a career? No way. After that first tour, I couldn't very well quit after making such a point of shoving it in my father's face. It didn't take me long to realize the Army had…turned me into someone else. That was an eye-opener. And not in a good way. I'm not sure what I expected, but it wasn't what I thought it would be. What's the slogan they tout? 'Be all you can be.' I was more because I had to be. I had something to prove to myself and my dad. Because I knew almost immediately I'd made a huge error in judgment, I tried everything to make sure I wasn't a failure. I couldn't go back to Newport with my tail between my legs and admit how wrong I'd been. I was too stubborn. My pride was at stake."

He pivoted back to Gilly. "Unfortunately, my dad died before I could admit all that to him, admit how big of an ass I'd been, admit I'd been stupid. He died four months shy of my decision to finally quit the Army. By that time, I'd…done things, terrible things."

Gilly took his hand in hers. "Soldiers in war…"

Simon swallowed hard and shook his head. He lowered his voice. "No, you don't understand. I've done things, Gilly, things I'm not proud of, things I don't like thinking about, or talking about. Things I'll never be able to forget. Not ever."

"In Iraq and Afghanistan? Things you did in the Army?"

He tightened his jaw. His indigo eyes went hard. "Don't ever ask me about any of it. Don't ever ask me about what happened over there. I couldn't explain it to you if I had a dozen years to do so."

His eyes were so sad that she brought his head onto her shoulder. "Then we won't ever talk about it again. Not ever."

The silky softness in her voice drew him to her mouth. He brought his lips down to hers. She tasted like warm honey and sin, a sweet and spicy blend that pushed his hormones into overdrive.

He shifted into a slow melt toward tenderness, a give and take that hit him in the gut. With his hand still clutching Jayden's, he couldn't very well make the kiss anything more than a soft gesture, but it made him realize Gilly couldn't be a simple, brief affair.

When the single mother ran a hand down his cheek, it snapped him back to the situation. She had to point out the For Sale sign by clearing her throat. She threw out a breathless sigh. "Here we are."

Awkwardness hung in the air as he turned his head to stare at the cream and tan home that sat on a long, rectangular lot at the very end of the block.

She brought him further back to earth by pointing out the addition built over the double-car garage. "It's a huge playroom or maybe use it as a library."

Gilly lifted her eyes to the slanted, gabled roof and the row of front dormers and wide eaves at the top. "Classic Craftsman meets a touch of Cape Cod."

When she found him gawking at its size, she blurted out, "You should've seen this place before

Logan got hold of it. Rotted wood, broken windows, decades of neglect. Look at it now. It all but gleams. The front porch is an eye-catcher, huh?"

Simon gaped because he realized this was *the* house, the house he wanted for his own, the house he'd always wanted. "It reminds me of the house I grew up in."

"Really? Well, let's take a look then," she suggested, maneuvering the stroller up to the bottom of the steps and hauling Delaney onto her hip. She headed up to the front porch, cupping her face to peer through the window.

Simon followed with Jayden, taking his turn squinting into its interior. "Nice original hardwood floors."

"Buffed to a shine. That's not all. I got the impression from Logan he redid the entire house from top to bottom. It was out of my price range so I didn't even bother going to the open house after he finished the remodel. It's been on the market for a while. Who knows? Maybe he'd deal."

Feeling bold and daring, Gilly tried turning the door knob. Surprised when it opened, she giggled like a teenage girl. "It's a sign. I feel like it's meant to be that we get in here and find out if it's as nice as we think it is."

Since Simon felt drawn to explore the rooms, he followed her into the entryway. They opened closet doors and oohed and ahhed at all the space, including an office with French doors off the main living room. Still on the first floor, they bypassed the staircase to get to the huge dining room.

"I'd kill for this amount of storage," Gilly murmured after setting eyes on the kitchen, a wide room with an old fireplace Logan had left intact.

"Look at all these cabinets. Love the chestnut wood. This is *so* my dream kitchen." She lovingly ran a hand over the granite countertop. "With a kitchen like this, I hope you love to cook."

"I can manage scrambled eggs, maybe making a hot ham and cheese sandwich. I usually barbecue everything. So this room is probably overkill for a novice like me."

"Typical," Gilly uttered, staring out through the picture window into the massive backyard. "Lucky for you there's an outdoor grill as big as my stove."

"Really? Let me see that." It was a four-burner gas grill at the end of the patio. "Wow. You like burgers, Jayden? Just look at that. Great setup to throw on a couple of steaks."

"Hot dog," Jayden corrected.

Simon ruffled the boy's hair. "First chance we get, you got it."

They continued the tour, ending up in the mudroom / utility room off the kitchen. It was more than an afterthought. Here, Logan had provided a built-in box seat where one could sit down and take off their shoes. The bench had cabinets and storage for organizing shoes and outerwear, along with a stainless-steel washer and dryer that matched the appliances in the kitchen. An oversized, low-rise laundry sink seemed an ideal spot for giving the dog a bath.

"This is amazing," Simon admitted, taking out his cell phone.

"Let's go see the upstairs. I love the fact there's a back staircase right off the kitchen. Makes it so much easier when you need to check on the kids fast and get back to the kitchen in a hurry."

"I hadn't thought of that," Simon admitted, scratching his jawline. "It's as if Logan knew all the selling points that a large family requires. This might be more house than I know what to do with."

"You really are adorable," she said as she got to the upstairs landing and opened the door to a gigantic playroom.

Simon had seen enough. He pulled out his cell phone. "Do you have Logan's number? Never mind. I forgot it's the same as Kinsey's." He plugged in the numbers on the keypad.

"What are you doing?" Gilly asked.

"I need to know how much he wants for this place."

Eight

Logan Donnelly didn't resemble the same man who'd flown into Pelican Pointe several years earlier to find his sister's killer. The paparazzi left him alone these days because he no longer made headlines every time one of his sculptures sold. Nor was he partnered with crazy Brazilian models who like to throw things in public.

Nowadays, his life looked like a poster for domesticity. His wife, Kinsey, got the credit for that. She'd given him something he'd craved without knowing it was what he'd been missing in his life. He was an old married man now with kids. And he savored every minute of it.

Somehow his dabbling in real estate had turned into much more. It gave him an avenue for trying to give something back to the community, a town that had given him so much more than he felt he deserved.

By chance, he'd started fixing up old houses around town that had fallen into major disrepair. Needing an outlet just to stay busy, he couldn't stand seeing the homes become the eyesores everyone dreaded having next door. Giving them new life seemed like the right thing to do, and selling them off to young families seemed a natural progression.

Logan didn't do it for the money. It gave him pleasure to know that in some way he was providing a decent place for them to live. Those who desperately wanted their own home deserved a chance at making it happen.

So when his phone rang that night after dark, it wasn't the first time someone had reached out to him about a house he had for sale.

Simon rattled off the address and explained they were standing in the new addition over the garage. "I'm here with Gilly Grant. I mentioned I was in the market for a house. We went for a walk and the front door was unlocked."

"Troy said he'd agreed to take you house hunting this weekend. He'd planned to show it to you anyway. Sounds like you got an early start."

"I'm glad I did," Simon declared. "If the price is right, I want to buy it."

Logan reeled off the list price.

Simon did some quick calculations in his head. "Let me think about it. I'll have to talk to Nick to work out the paperwork."

"No problem. You need help with anything, let me know."

Simon disconnected the call and turned to look at a stunned Gilly.

"You weren't kidding around. Are you really serious about getting this house?"

"I'm really serious. The problem is my income is mostly seasonal. I don't know for sure what Nick's requirements are and what the bank's guidelines are for that kind of income."

She looped her arm through his. "I think you'll find Nick and the bank go hand in hand when it comes to making loans. That's the way it was with me. I'm a first-time home buyer, which means I'm certain Nick and Logan did some very creative financing to get me approved."

"Then maybe they'll do the same for me. Want to go get the kids some ice cream?"

"Ice cweam!" Jayden hollered, and the echo bounced off the bare walls.

"Way to go, new daddy. Mine really needed to get in bed. But how can I say no to a cone when it's such a beautiful evening."

"You shouldn't. The Hilltop Diner makes great chocolate shakes and it's right around the corner. We could get it to go. Besides, I promised to help you with the dishes."

Gilly warmed inside. "You order the ice cream. Delaney needs a diaper change. She's soaking wet. Did you bring the bag?"

Simon winced, knowing he'd left it by the front door at his house. "No. There's way too much stuff to keep track of. I'll run in the pharmacy and grab a box of Pampers."

"I'll do it," Gilly suggested. "You take Jayden with you. He adores Margie and the feeling is mutual. If I know Margie she'll probably give you the shakes on the house."

The drug store was next door to the Hilltop so Simon boosted Jayden onto his hip and went inside the oldest eatery in town.

Margie Rosterman started to greet Simon in her business-as-usual manner, until she spotted little Jayden. Her face broke into a wide grin and she began to gush. "How's my big boy today? Were you a good boy for your mama?"

Jayden bobbed his head up and down.

"What can I get you two tonight?"

"We're in the mood for chocolate shakes," Simon answered.

"Chocolate!" Jayden shouted. "Ice cweam!"

Margie laughed. "That boy doesn't have a middle notch, does he? He's either quiet as a mouse or at full volume. Am I right?"

"I've noticed that. Could we get these to go? Maybe two kid sizes and two mediums. We might want to take a walk along the water."

"No problem. You guys take a seat. I'll get 'em started for ya."

While Margie busied herself at the other end of the counter, Simon settled Jayden on his lap at one of the booths.

"Where's Mama?" Jayden wanted to know.

"She and Delaney went to pick up diapers because I forgot to bring supplies."

"Oh." He pointed to the door. "'Laney and Mama."

Simon looked up to see Gilly bouncing into the restaurant with his daughter. A missile of heat rocketed down his spine, shot straight to another part of his body. She made a picture carrying Delaney on her hip, looking as radiant as a burst of light.

Gilly slid into their booth. "Diaper change all taken care of. What'd you guys order?"

"Chocolate!" Jayden sang out.

Gilly chuckled. "That's my boy."

Margie brought over four milkshakes. When Simon tried to pay, the owner waved him off. "Connie and I go way back. This one, too. Gillian Rose has been coming into this place since she was no older than Jayden."

"Thanks, Margie," Gilly stated. "We love you, too."

"You guys enjoy that walk on the beach."

"Walk on the beach?" Gilly questioned.

"It's a nice night for it, Gillian Rose," Simon emphasized. "Pretty name."

She let out an embarrassed laugh. "Named after an aunt, my mother's sister."

The four of them headed off down Crescent Street toward the pier. Simon tried to help Delaney get the hang of the straw. "I guess I should've brought her sippy cup, too."

"Never go anywhere without the diaper bag and the sippy cup," Gilly cautioned. "You're asking for disaster if you do it again."

"I'm learning as I go. Where's your dad?"

"He died of a heart attack the year before I started nursing school. Saddest time of my life. I thought my mother might have a breakdown. It was that sudden. They'd planned to take a cruise to Alaska the next month, something they'd always wanted to do. Mom had already bought the tickets. I tried to talk her into going anyway, that we'd go together, thought it would be good for her to get away. She wouldn't hear of it."

"I'm sorry. What did he do for a living?"

"He was a surveyor for the county."

Simon leaned in and lowered his voice. "Is Jayden's father in the picture at all?"

"Lordy no. Vaughn's never even laid eyes on him. That's fine by me. After he kicked me out, I didn't expect anything else out of the loser. I've never looked back."

"But won't Jayden, I don't know, one day get curious? Who knows? Maybe the loser will have a change of heart."

"Too late. I've already dealt with it. He isn't listed on Jayden's birth certificate. And when Jayden ever gets to the point of asking me questions, I'll deal with that, too. Single moms do it all the time out of self-preservation."

They took a seat on one of the benches that lined the pier. Simon leaned over to her and asked, "Ever go fishing?"

Gilly wrinkled her nose. "You mean with worms? Ugh. No. I don't like the smell of fish that much."

"The bait isn't always worms. There are these little plastic things called lures. Besides, I didn't know nurses were squeamish."

"Let's just say I'm not a fan of...bait. And I know all about lures. The thing is, I have no desire to spend all day trying to catch a smelly fish. It's just so...not the way I want to spend my days off."

"How do you know if you've never tried?"

"I've tried. Wally Pierce tried his best to get me to like it."

"You and Wally at the gas station?"

"I've known Wally since we were old enough to fight over a bag of M&Ms. We were ten when he taught me how to surf. That I didn't mind. But fishing. Yuck. And tediously boring."

"Tired," Jayden announced, resting his head on his mother's lap to prove it.

"I'll carry him back," Simon offered.

"Thanks. We did say we wanted to wear them out. I guess we did."

On the walk back to Gilly's house, Delaney fell asleep in the stroller, and Jayden crumpled against Simon's chest. "I need to pick up one of these buggy things. Great way to get her to fall asleep."

"You're a fast learner, Mr. Bremmer."

He snaked his arm around her waist, pulling her closer. "I had fun tonight, more fun than I've had in years."

"So did I."

"Good. Have dinner with me Saturday night."

She looked up into his eyes as blue as the Pacific. "Do I need to get a sitter?"

"Nope. We make a good foursome."

After he left, Gilly carried Jayden to bed, all the while wondering if Simon Bremmer was too good to be true. She hadn't believed in men since that terrible experience with Vaughn Millar, a man she'd trusted enough to leave California. What a fool she'd been. She looked back at those days with embarrassment. But that time together had given her the most adorable little boy any mother would be proud to have. For that, she had to thank Loser Vaughn every day.

She made sure the little nightlight was plugged in, the one that bathed his room in sea creatures. Jayden was such a typical boy who adored all kinds of animals and little buggy critters---like the frog Simon had captured for him to hold.

Maybe Simon was for real. She couldn't deny her attraction. But she'd withhold judgment to protect her heart and to make sure she did the right thing for Jayden. As far as she was concerned, nobody was going to walk all over her again, or mess with her baby. So she'd proceed with caution. She could handle a casual fling. Nothing wrong with that. She could do it because maybe, after all this time, she deserved a sliver of happiness, just a small slice of not having to be alone every Friday and Saturday night. Was it so wrong to hope Simon could provide a little friendship, a little give and take, a little sex every now and again?

She didn't expect the moon. She was a single mom who did her best to stay grounded. But God, how great would it be to have someone to talk to.

On the drive back to the caretaker's cottage, Simon had similar thoughts and feelings. Vibrant and funny, Gilly had awakened something in him that he felt had been dead for years. But he didn't want to get too overly-optimistic about it. He could tell Gilly was leery of men, any men, which meant he had to take things slow. With two kids between them that shouldn't be a problem.

He pulled up to the farm and realized this was so different from the house on Tradewinds Drive. Was he ready to trade renting for a thirty-year mortgage? Going around to the back seat, he unbuckled his daughter out of her car seat. She muttered something in her sleep that sounded like mama.

Knowing she wasn't going to see her mother ever again, tugged at Simon's heartstrings. Just like Jayden would have questions about his dad, Simon believed Delaney would one day want to know about her mother.

Merlin waited inside the doorway and woofed a low bark at seeing them return.

"Hey, buddy. Shh, she's asleep. Let's not wake her up, okay?" He tiptoed to her room and slipped her into the crib.

Standing there, watching the baby sleep, brought a flood of emotions rushing back to that summer he'd spent with Amelia on the Cape. Delaney would never know her mother. But maybe he could keep her memory alive with bits and pieces of how her parents had spent their brief time together. No matter what Brent found out about Amelia's background, it wouldn't change things. She was still Delaney's mother. He'd need to remember that if he didn't want to disappoint a little girl down the road.

As he watched her breathe, he ran his fingers through her baby-fine hair. It hadn't taken but a few days for him to fall in love. So whatever Amelia's motives had been at the time, her decisions had brought him to this point.

And for that, he could be grateful.

Nine

Friday morning started out hectic. Delaney woke up cranky and pulling at her ear. Even a newbie like Simon knew that could spell trouble. But just to be sure, he put in a call to Cord.

Cord had been up all night with a sick stray pup that hadn't made it. Irritable from lack of sleep, he listened to Simon's concerns until he couldn't take it anymore. "Simon, you're right to be worried, but she probably has an ear infection. Didn't you tell me you were taking her for her well visit today anyway?"

"Yeah, but I just wanted to run it by you first."

"And now you have. The next step is showing up at Quentin's office. Can you handle that?"

His curt reply finally hit Simon the wrong way. "You're an ass. I'm just worried."

"That's because you're overreacting. Kids get ear infections. She got off a plane four days ago. What happens when you fly? The eardrum pushes outward. If she was already building up fluid, she might be feeling pressure in there. Look, man. I know this must be hard. You've got the doctor's appointment, get in there and see what he has to say before you come unglued."

"This is all new for me."

"I know and I'm trying to find my supportive gear."

Delaney wailed in the background.

"I gotta go. I don't like it when she cries. I feel helpless."

"I know that, too. According to Nick, this is all part of fatherhood, buddy. Get used to it before you buckle under the pressure. Take it day by day. Some days will be better than others."

Simon took that bit of advice and got Delaney ready for the trip into town. He showed up at the doctor's office, a Mission-style house two blocks off Main Street, two hours ahead of his scheduled appointment time and waited in the parking lot for someone to open up.

When a small, nondescript Chevy sedan pulled in beside him, he watched a lanky woman crawl out wearing a nurse's outfit in turquoise-colored scrubs. She had graying blond hair and looked like an older version of Gilly.

"You waiting for me?" she asked, a slight annoyance in her tone.

"I'm way early for my appointment but I think she's sick," he told the woman as he followed her to the front door and watched her stick a key into the lock. "I'm Simon Bremmer and this is Delaney."

"I remember the names of the patients on the docket for today," the woman snapped. "I'm Connie Grant, Gilly's mom. I'm the one who wrote you down in the appointment book."

"Nice to meet you. I had dinner with Gilly and Jayden last night."

Fifty-nine-year-old Connie Grant had a no-nonsense nature about her and a nurse's instinct that went back years. She'd worked in San Sebastian for so long and made the commute, she considered herself lucky now to be able to work in town less than three minutes from her house. In fact, Connie could've walked to work. She felt it was a miracle that Quentin Blackwood had given her a job. Which was probably why she'd bonded instantly with him. But at this stage of her life, Connie could be a tad overbearing with a sharp edge. She could also be overly protective, sometimes to a fault. She brought that attitude to work with her, fiercely guarding Dr. Blackwood's interests.

Now, her cautious nature flared up, raising her shields to protect Gilly and Jayden. Which probably was the reason she took such an instant dislike to Simon, a man she knew nothing about except that he mostly stayed to himself running his tourist business, a business she considered frivolous. From the moment her daughter had mentioned Simon Bremmer coming over for dinner, Connie's suspicious nature had kicked in. Now that she got a look at him for herself, she didn't trust those bluebonnet-colored eyes of his. They seemed too cocky, too over-confident.

Although his concern seemed genuine, especially with the toddler in his arms, she kept her reservations in place as the man followed her inside the office. "You told me when you made the appointment that this would be Delaney's well visit. Now you're saying she's ill?"

Simon had a hard time ignoring the cold attitude emanating off Connie Grant. It could've frozen Mother Teresa in her tracks. "Yeah. That's it. I think it might be an ear infection."

From years of dealing with a variety of panicky parents, Connie's skeptical nature kicked in again and she raised a brow. His rookie status was shining through loud and clear and she didn't like it. "We'll see if Dr. Blackwood shares your diagnosis, won't we?"

She went around to the front desk and picked up a clipboard and a pen, shoved both into his hands. "Fill this out. You can set her down to play with the toys we have set up over in the corner. It'll keep her occupied while you fill out the paperwork."

Simon did as he was told and was shocked when Delaney toddled over to the toy chest and plopped down to explore its contents, her mood changing from the cranky baby she'd been at home to almost normal. He quickly completed the insurance stuff and handed the clipboard back to Connie.

While she checked his information, Simon made small talk. Or tried to. "Gilly's the one who suggested I bring Delaney in and let the doc check her out, make sure she's okay. I thought it was a good idea."

"It's always a good idea to get established with a doctor when you have small children."

Simon couldn't get past the block of ice that was Connie. This woman was nothing like her daughter, that warm, caring individual he'd had dinner with the night before. When several more attempts at dialogue ended in frosty, clipped retorts, he finally gave up and took a seat in the reception area.

While other patients drifted in, the wait to see the doctor lasted another half hour.

Quentin came out wearing a white coat to greet him personally. The man had longish dark brown hair that turned up at his collar with cool gray eyes that seemed friendly and caring.

"Who do we have here?" Quentin asked, looking over at the toddler.

"That's Delaney."

From her desk, Connie piped up, "Dr. Blackwood, I'd intended to take them into an exam room later because they're an hour early for their appointment."

"That's okay," Quentin said. "They're here now." He looked around the waiting room and waved at the others. "I think we can squeeze you in."

"I hope everything you need is in the file because that's all they gave me on Monday," Simon explained, glancing over at a stern-faced Connie as he passed by her desk. Gilly's mother seemed either perturbed that her authority had been usurped or was disappointed that Dr. Blackwood hadn't kept him waiting longer. He thought he could actually see the nurse's ears perk up like radar. "I brought Delaney's medical records with me from Boston."

Quentin took the folder and led them into an exam room down the hallway. "Boston? That piques my interest. What's a Boston girl doing this far west?"

It wasn't until the doctor closed the door that Simon very quietly told him the story of how Delaney had come to be in Pelican Pointe.

Quentin took a seat on a rolling stool. "And for two years you'd had no contact with this woman?"

"Not a word or a postcard. She never even asked for child support. I hadn't heard the name until she died, and the lawyer showed up with all this paperwork that said Amelia had put me on the birth certificate as Delaney's father *and* made out a will that named me her legal guardian."

"Very strange indeed. These past few days you must've been overwhelmed with this coming out of left field the way it did."

"I was. I still am. I'm trying to figure out what's next."

"Is she eating okay since all this disruption in her life?"

"She eats okay, but sometimes likes to play at dinnertime. When I asked Jordan about it, she said that's normal. But then I've only had four nights to figure out normal. I did have a question about teething. She seems to chew on everything."

"Couple of things to try that might make teething more bearable. Take a banana and cut it into thirds, then push a popsicle stick in the middle of each piece and slide them into the freezer. When you notice she's fussy, hand her one of those and the ice-cold texture will help soothe the gums. Same is true with freezing any flavor of Kool-Aid in those pop-out trays with the stem. You can also try freezing apple rings. Just peel and core an apple, slice it so it looks like rings, then stick them into the freezer. They make great finger food. All three options give her something to chew that's cold."

Simon looked awestruck. "See? I didn't know any of that."

"If you don't know, use the Internet to look up a solution. I'm not suggesting you follow the medical advice you find there because there's a large amount that's downright crap. But there's nothing wrong with looking up a few shortcuts for things like teething."

"Good to know. There is something Kinsey thought you could help me with. I'd like you to do a paternity test."

Quentin nodded and continued to study the folder until he leaned closer. "The file says your girl is type O. By any chance do you know your blood type?"

"B positive."

"You're sure?"

"I was in the military, Doc. Believe me, I know my own blood type. Why?"

"If Delaney's type O, that would mean the mother must have been type A or O."

"Is that significant for paternity?"

"Not really. I'm looking at it purely from a medical perspective. If Delaney were to ever need a blood transfusion down the road, I'd have to rely on what's in here. It's good you're willing to do a quick test today to make sure. We'll have the results back by Monday."

"I think that's the way to go, check everything."

"Not a problem. Although you should know that a difference in blood type doesn't rule you out as Delaney's father. If that's what you're thinking, I could go into a detailed genealogy explanation or you could trust that I know what I'm talking about. With a type B father, Delaney could only be type O if the mother was A or O. Since we don't have the mother's medical records it makes sense to find out for certain, even if you weren't going for paternity."

"Does that mean drawing blood?"

"Nope, just a little stick to the finger just to be sure. And since we're sticking both of you, truth won't come without a little pain. But I see here she's due for her DTP immunizations anyway, so..."

"Even if I think she might have an ear infection?"

"Ah. Let's take a look at that." Quentin picked up his otoscope to check the ear canal. "There is some redness and fluid in both ears." He used a digital thermometer to take her temperature. "Ninety-nine, which means she might be on the cusp of an infection."

"She had ninety-nine Monday night, too. That's the reason I took her to the hospital. She wouldn't stop crying. That's where I met Gilly."

"Gilly knows her stuff. I'd say, it looks like all this stress in Delaney's little life is finally catching up with her. Tell you what…" From a drawer, he pulled out a prescription pad. "Let's put her on Amoxycillin for ten days and get her completely healthy before we do the immunizations. I think that's best with all the stress she's gone through lately. Her medical records indicate she isn't allergic to penicillin, which we're counting on to be right. I'm delaying the booster because when you bring her back in healthy, we'll no doubt want to add her measles and chicken pox shots in there to get her up to speed." He stood up as if finished. "I'll send Connie in to prick your fingers and get that started."

"Does it have to be Connie? Couldn't you just do it?"

Quentin's gray eyes warmed. "So you and Connie didn't hit it off, is that it? Well, you aren't the first one to hint at that kind of friction. Between you and me, I miss my wife here in the office. But she's a superb ER nurse and it's best for the hospital if she's there during the day rather than being stuck here, helping me with the everyday routine stuff."

"What happens when there's an emergency?"

"We have that covered. Sydney assesses the situation and then calls either me or Gideon. At night, if there's an accident or someone goes into labor, I rely on the duty nurse to make the call. That's either Gilly, Aubree Wright, or Sheena Howser."

"Everyone working different shifts is confusing."

"It may sound that way, but we have it worked out, team-wise. We all know our role in an emergency situation. Sydney and I are very proud of how we lured Sheena down from the Bay Area. We stole her away from a top-notch facility and gave her the hours she wanted. Our staff might be new, but we're motivated to be the best for our patients. In fact, we're having a fundraiser for the hospital toward the end of October, right before Halloween. You should plan to participate."

"What's involved?"

Quentin rubbed his fingers together in a money gesture. "Bread. Moolah. We need to build up our cash reserve to continue to operate down the road. Don't get me wrong. We still get our grant from the feds but having cash on hand always makes it easier to buy everything we need. Drugs and supplies don't come cheap."

"How much are you looking to raise?"

Quentin tossed out a low six figure. "We're not asking for the moon."

"That sounds doable."

"Sydney's been planning this bash since July. An auction with food, music, dancing, the whole bit."

"And you're getting dragged into all of it."

"Not really. Sydney's drafted a handful of recruits to help her. And I'm gladly letting her take the lead."

"I'm about to buy a house, but hey, count on me to help out. I'm good for a contribution."

"Then why are you squirming?"

Simon scratched his jaw. "Is Connie any good at that blood-drawing thing?"

Quentin's lips curved. "I'd think a tough Army guy like yourself wouldn't have a problem with needles."

"Usually I don't. But that woman doesn't like me and it's obvious."

The smile left Quentin's face. "At one time, I thought Connie was one of the best hires I'd made. Her skills and instincts are what you'd expect from a nurse who's been doing this for decades. But I learned early on that if she doesn't like you, it tends to show. She wears her feelings on her sleeve and doesn't bother to hide them at all."

"Oh, it shows," Simon admitted. "I'm not sure what I did except have dinner with her daughter and grandson."

"There you go," Quentin muttered. "She tends to make snap judgments."

"I thought Gilly and I had hit it off because I asked her to come out to the farm for dinner Saturday night. I didn't realize I might have to clear it with the mother first."

"Connie's been a tough read for me. I thought I had her all figured out until an incident with another patient last week. She seemed to get upset over nothing and it went from a little thing to a big blowup. Drama is something I don't put up with around here."

"Who wants to put up with a confrontational nurse? All I want to know is, can she prick my finger without making it black and blue? I've had blood drawn before, Doc. And it's all in the technique."

Quentin chuckled. "All right. I'll do the slide for both you and Delaney. I should have the results back on Monday. We'll talk in greater detail then."

After getting Delaney's prescription filled, Simon stopped at the bank to talk to Nick. He waited longer to see him than he had waited to see Quentin.

Nick had a string of people, six total, waiting in his outer office. When it was Simon's turn, he watched a young married couple emerge he didn't recognize. But since they came out of Nick's office all smiles, Simon figured they must've received good news.

"I found a house," Simon announced before going into a litany of its features. He stopped when he noticed Nick wasn't as enthusiastic.

Nick simply leaned back in his chair. "Simon, should I worry about these impulsive decisions you're making?"

"No. Why?"

"Because…I'm not sure how to say this."

Simon frowned, his good mood going south. "Just say it. I've found that's the best way."

"All right. You're making all these life changing decisions. What if—and I'm just playing devil's advocate here—what if you discover Delaney isn't yours? What if you find out this Amelia person has family somewhere that wants to fight you for legal custody? What happens then? Have you even heard from Brent about the background check? What if all this comes tumbling down around you and you somehow discover it's all been…some kind of trick?"

Simon dropped into a chair. "You don't think I haven't considered all that? Because I have. I just left the doctor's office. Quentin is essentially doing a paternity test. You think my stomach isn't in a knot knowing Amelia may have lied about this whole thing? That Delaney might not even be mine? But tell me this, Nick. What am I supposed to do? Let someone else take care of her? Put her in foster care?

Try to find a bunch of strangers on her mother's side and then dump her on them? That isn't me."

Nick blew out a heavy breath. "I know it's not. And I think that's why you're in the spot you're in. Without knowing anything about Amelia other than what you've said, I think she knew you were a stand-up kind of guy."

"So you don't think Delaney's mine?"

"I didn't say that. She certainly looks like you, especially around the eyes. But as your friend, I have to consider the most basic question of all. Why didn't she want child support from you? Have you asked yourself that? It's highly irregular."

"I don't know. I have a lot of questions. I'm afraid of the answers. I already told my mom and she's flying out here next week, full of excitement. Amelia isn't just playing with my feelings from the grave, she's at the root of my getting my mother all jazzed about being a grandmother. It's all...so very confusing and scary. Amelia and I do have history. I keep thinking it isn't just possible, it's probable."

"Okay, but do me a favor. Step back from the house angle until Monday. Give yourself a weekend to digest everything. If by then, you want to buy that house on Tradewinds, fine. I'll make it happen. But try not to make any more of these big decisions until a couple of things happen. One, you get the results back from the paternity test. And two, you get Brent's findings from the background check. That's all I'm suggesting. If it turns out that Delaney isn't yours, then you can still be her father. No one's gonna make her go away. I see you've fallen in love with her just like I did with Hutton. And Hutton isn't mine by blood. But that child is as much mine as she is Scott's. So I know the bond you're feeling. All I'm saying is just slow down, take a breath, maybe get out of hyperdrive for two minutes. You already have a shitload of paperwork that says at the very least, you're Delaney's legal guardian. No one can change that, not even Amelia's family, if there is any. That's huge."

"Unless it's all phony documentation," Simon stated flatly. "I've thought of that angle, too. I'm not stupid."

"No, you're one of the sharpest men I know. And one more reason to proceed with caution. At the very least, you'll know the truth, and from there be able to know what's real and what isn't."

Simon decided it was good strategy. As he got to his feet and turned to go, he stopped and stared at Nick. "But I really want that house. Could you at least call Logan and make sure no one else buys it?"

Nick cracked a grin. "I don't think you have anything to worry about. That house has been sitting empty for quite some time. But I'll make the call just in case."

Simon cocked his head and stared at his friend. "Now it's my turn to give you some advice. Did you ever think about spending more time at home away from this rat race you've built up? Hutton's right. I know you help people but…you look tired all the time."

Nick took a deep, soul-cleansing breath. "I'm exhausted by the time I get home in the evening. There's never time for the kids anymore. So about a month ago I decided to start interviewing for a VP, who can take care of a lot of this paperwork. I've got a few lined up, good candidates. Hopefully I can make a decision soon and get them in here as quickly as possible."

"I'll hold you to that."

"Simon, has Jordan said anything to you about this?"

Simon was no fool to stir up trouble between couples. "Not a word. But anyone can see you're struggling to breathe under all this bureaucracy. It's not you."

That evening, Simon and Delaney settled in at home because the toddler was still running a fever. After supper, he took her outside on the porch where they could sit in the rocking chair and take in the sights and sounds on the farm.

With Merlin at his feet, he rocked back and forth, talking softly about things around them, things she didn't understand. But he'd read on the Internet that it didn't matter. Just talking to her was an important part of bonding. Her hearing his voice was important, the subject matter immaterial.

Silas had harvested the corn that day, along with a batch of arugula and spinach, squash and zucchini. Nearby, in another field, Sammy sat atop one of the huge tractors, busy plowing a patch of ground where he'd replant kale and broccoli.

They'd finished picking the cherries that day and a few workers were still carting them into the packing house.

Simon waved to the seasonal farmhands, hard at work under the setting sun, their bodies bent, picking strawberries and blueberries destined for markets north and south.

"The same crew comes every June," Simon told Delaney. "They travel from the central valley to the coast and bring their families, live in trailers or RVs, camping out near the farm. I never understood until now just how hard that has to be, traveling from one farm to the next with kids in tow to find work."

Delaney answered with baby babble.

"That's what I'm thinking," Simon returned. "Maybe we should do something about that. I can't imagine doing all that moving around with you."

His perspectives were morphing into a man's outlook that he didn't quite recognize. But that was okay. Since mustering out of the Army, he knew well that change could often bring on a badly needed attitude adjustment. It could be a good thing.

"Now you're beginning to get the picture," Scott said from the other side of the porch. "You're here for a reason."

Simon slowly turned his head to see Scott sitting in the other rocking chair, swaying back and forth as if in sync with the harvester's engine sounds. He tried to keep his voice level when he leaned past Delaney to answer. "I'm here to make sure farm workers have a better lot in life?"

"Stop worrying. You're not the next Cesar Chavez," Scott cautioned. "Although you could speak to Nick about building better housing for the farmhands; a bunkhouse for the single guys would work. And maybe a few two-bedroom units for any head of household who wants to stay on for longer than a season. If you went out there right now and took a poll, most of those workers would tell you they'd love to settle down in one spot, but the opportunity just isn't there. This farm is a tremendous cash cow. Finding the money for housing shouldn't be a problem. Look at this place. It isn't working for you and Delaney, but it could work for another family. You talking to Nick about hiring more permanent workers would eliminate the hassle each year of trying to find enough quality people to get the job done, folks who'll stick around and send their kids to school in town and contribute to the community."

"Jordan's right. You love this town."

"Everything about it deserves to be better."

"Why don't you talk to Nick yourself? From what I hear, you don't have a problem bugging anyone for any reason."

"I don't need to bug Nick when I have you. Besides, Nick has other important things to take care of before going home to all the other necessary stuff he does for family. He's spreading himself too thin. Maybe you should bring that up to him the next time he starts preaching to you about what's wrong with your life."

"Thanks for the tip."

"You like Gilly?"

"Oh, God. Don't tell me you've zeroed in on my love life."

"You don't have a love life."

"Neither do you," Simon shot back.

"But you aren't dead," Scott countered. "You forget that I know what Amelia did to you. I know the real reason you haven't bothered with women since you've been here."

Simon bristled, the hilarity gone. "Some things should be kept private. You don't get to stick your nose into everything just because no one can stop you."

"Fair enough. But remember this. Gilly has her own secrets."

By the time he opened his mouth to respond, Scott was gone. He propped his chin on the top of

Delaney's head. "Remind me to tell you a bedtime story. No ghosts allowed."

Delaney pointed toward the strawberry field.

Simon followed the track of her eyes and realized she was pointing at Scott, who was now standing in the middle of the farmland surrounded by the pickers. "Do you see that man?"

"Man," Delaney repeated.

"Weird," Simon muttered. "Very weird."

Ten

Back in town, Gilly was dealing with her own weird scene. This one with her mother.

Connie Grant had become agitated over seemingly nothing.

"What has gotten into you?" Gilly said, her voice rising in anger. "I'm not asking you to babysit."

"You never listen to me, that's what I'm saying. I'm telling you I don't think it's a good idea to start up with this Simon Bremmer fellow. He's no good."

"Why? What did he ever do to you?"

"Well, for one thing, he's not that different from Jayden's father. This guy got a woman pregnant and left her on her own to deal with a baby just like Vaughn did to you. I'd think you'd want to avoid men like that."

"So you're telling me you know the details of what happened between Simon and Delaney's mother? Really? Is that it, Mom? Did Simon confide in you while he was at the doctor's office today and tell you the intimate details of his breakup?"

Connie looked like she'd been slapped. "No. I didn't even get into the exam room to have a conversation with him. All I did was read their charts...afterward. Although I did mention his situation to Margie."

Gilly narrowed her eyes, afraid of the quagmire in front of her. "Was there a need-to-know basis for you to go over his file? Were you looking for any details that had to do with a follow-up? Were you adding pertinent facts to their visit for next time? Were you jotting down notes for the follow-up appointment at the instructions of Dr. Blackwood? Or was your curiosity the only reason you read his file? Because otherwise every detail in that chart is confidential."

"I certainly wasn't snooping, if that's what you're getting at."

"Sounds like it to me. Why is it you didn't interact with them in the exam room? Isn't that what you do? Take vitals and ask pertinent questions pre-exam?"

Connie lifted her chin. "Yes. But Dr. Blackwood took care of it. Without me. I didn't even get to draw their blood, something I've been doing since Dr. Blackwood was in grade school. He didn't even come get me. It's insulting."

"Mom…"

"I've been working for him since March, ever since Sydney joined the hospital staff. I've done everything Dr. Blackwood has asked me to do, and more. And yet, he treats me like I'm not even needed or wanted."

Gilly tried again. "Mom…"

Connie bowled right over her and went on, "I have a right to be angry when I've been nothing but loyal and fiercely supportive of him. I can't help it if I've tried to streamline his patient load by making it easier for him. It's time someone said no to people without the proper insurance."

Gilly was mortified. "What? You know good and well Doc Prescott never turned anyone away. Not a soul. I hadn't planned on telling you this, but there's growing rumors around town about your abrasive treatment of certain patients. Shelby Jennings said you swore at her last week. I overheard Dr. Nighthawk talking to Sydney about your surly behavior. Apparently, you had some negative interaction with him before he dropped the bomb that he was the new surgeon."

"He should have introduced himself to me the proper way," Connie stated, still in defensive mode.

"What's the proper way?" Gilly fired back. "What's going on with you lately? I never noticed this bitter outlook until just recently. You've always been so...so normal before you made the switch from San Sebastian to working here. It was supposed to be less stressful. Less of a commute. It was the perfect job. And you're screwing it up by snooping in files, repeating what you read, and behaving like a jerk."

Connie dropped into a kitchen chair and put her head in her hands. "Honestly, I don't know. I seem to be rude to everyone who gets within two feet of me."

"Maybe it's hormonal."

"I don't think so. I'm still on hormone replacement."

Gilly took a seat next to her mother. "Then what is it?"

"I didn't want to say anything, but I think some days I feel like I'm losing my mind. I can't remember stuff. I get so angry whenever it happens that I just want to explode."

"Maybe you should see a specialist. Better still, talk to Dr. Blackwood."

"I'm pretty sure he's unhappy with me, with my work performance. I don't know how to fix it. I've never been in that situation before."

"What makes you think he's upset?"

"Because he's quieter than when I first started. Instead of us forming a workable bond and cementing our relationship, it seems we spend all day at odds with one another."

"Over the way you treat people," Gilly concluded. "I'm beginning to see a pattern."

"What should I do?"

"Start by talking with Sydney. She'll know the best way to approach Dr. Blackwood."

"What if he wants to fire me?"

"It couldn't be any worse than waiting for the axe to fall." Gilly put her hands over Connie's. "I think it's best to find out what's causing you to feel the way you do. I'm sure the first thing Sydney will suggest is a head-to-toe exam."

"Maybe I should just go back to San Sebastian and see the doctor I had there."

"That's nonsense, Mom. We have a perfectly good team in place here. Is there something you specifically don't like about Dr. Nighthawk?"

"No. He has good credentials. I looked him up myself."

"Then what is it?"

Fat tears formed in Connie's eyes. "If it's something serious, I'm afraid everyone in town will know."

"That's ridiculous and maybe a bit of an insult. We're all professionals. We don't go around gossiping about our patients. Privacy has always been paramount."

"Don't you want to know what I found out in Simon's file today?"

Gilly looked horror-stricken. "No! Of course not. What did I just say? That's an abuse of doctor-patient privilege and I don't want any part of it. My God, Mom, you know better."

"See? I don't seem to be able to help myself."

"This is worse than I imagined. It goes beyond being rude to patients. I want you to promise me you won't…" Gilly stopped in mid-sentence. "Have you told anyone else what you've read in other people's charts?"

But before Connie could reply, Gilly could see the answer in her mother's eyes. "Who did you tell?"

"I might've mentioned to Ina Crawford that Abby Bonner was pregnant again."

"Before she told anyone else?"

"And I might've told Emma Colter that Prissie Gates will probably need stomach surgery."

Gilly had heard enough and pushed back from the table. "You know what? I can't believe I'm saying this. Maybe you do need to look for another line of work."

"What?"

"Mom, what you did is so highly unethical I won't even begin to defend you. I don't even want to try."

"Gilly Grant, how dare you talk to me that way."

"How long have you been passing along privileged information? When did this start exactly? Were you doing this the entire time you worked in San Sebastian?"

"Of course not."

"Then why did it start here? I thought this was your ideal job. When did you start becoming such a blabbermouth when it comes to patient files?"

Connie hid her face in her hands. "A few months ago."

"That might explain why you're so worried about going to see a doctor here and the fact you think the staff might blab about you, too. Unbelievable."

Gilly ran a hand through her hair and stood up to pace. "You do realize this will get out. Ina will say something to Abby or Emma, and in turn, someone will tell Prissie how they found out...about a personal medical condition that should stay private. This isn't something we can hide anymore. The minute Dr. Blackwood finds out, he'll can you so fast it'll ruin your career."

"Then what do I do?"

"I don't know," Gilly snapped. "Maybe keep your mouth shut and stop spilling what you know about patients until we can figure things out."

"I refuse to sit here and be spoken to like that," Connie wailed. "I'm leaving."

Even though Connie had come for supper, Gilly didn't try to stop her. "That's probably a good idea. Unless you intend to tell half the town that we think Jayden might have an ADHD problem."

"What difference does it make? Julianne Dickinson will find out in two years anyway when he goes to kindergarten. I'm sure Neenah told her before I did."

Gilly looked betrayed. "Why did you do that? You know very well Dr. Blackwood said he might outgrow his impulsivity by that time."

Connie lifted a shoulder. "Neenah and I go way back. I was just trying to help her with Jayden's problem when he acts out so much. Plus, she had some issues with his inability to sit still."

"He likes to blurt out the answers. So what? He's three!" Gilly shouted, almost irrational in her anger. "I've talked to the other moms and their kids do exactly the same thing sometimes. They can't all be hyper. Jayden shouldn't be singled out that way."

"Why are you yelling at me? It's not my fault something might be wrong with Jayden."

Gilly held her hands up to her face. "Oh, Mom. Just go. I'll talk to you later."

After Connie went home, Gilly booted up her computer to specifically hunt down any reasons she could find for her mother's weird behavior. She made notes about Alzheimer's and Parkinson's and compared symptoms.

When it was time to put Jayden to bed, she read him a story and was grateful to get him down without a fuss.

Back in the kitchen, she reached for the bottle of wine she had left over from the night before. Before draining the contents into a glass, she decided she needed someone to talk to instead. Out of desperation, she dialed Simon's number.

"Hi, have you put Delaney down for the night?"

"Yeah. What's up?"

"I need a sounding board and you're the first person I thought of. Jayden's asleep so I can't have this conversation in person. Is this a good time? It's about my mother."

That last part had Simon reluctant to gab. "Uh, I met her today."

"I know. And I understand she was on the rude side."

"You could say that. For some reason she took an instant dislike to me. Ordinarily I wouldn't mind that so much, but it also seemed to lap over to Delaney. I'm not sure what we did to make her act so…surly toward us, except that I showed up really early for my appointment, like two hours."

"Trust me, it was nothing you did. I'm beginning to suspect there might be something medically wrong with her."

"Like what? How does that work? She suddenly starts treating strangers like dirt? I'm the one who showed up early. She didn't have to take whatever she was feeling out on Delaney."

"I agree. But I just had a huge argument with her and it was very revealing. She's just not acting like herself."

"Sounds like an old sci-fi movie where the town is slowly replaced by alien lookalikes."

"If only that would explain it," Gilly moaned. "I think she might be experiencing the early stages of Alzheimer's."

"For real? Wow. That's like my Aunt Lorraine. Although she's not as testy. But now that I think about it, I wasn't around when she started experiencing her symptoms. If you want, I could ask my mother what Lorraine's behavior was like back then."

"That would be great. The thing is I have this bad feeling she's sick or something." And with that one statement, Gilly let all of her pent-up frustrations out in the open, violating the mother and daughter pact that had been sacrosanct for years. She confided in someone other than her mom.

Eleven

Gilly still felt guilty about it the next morning, but not enough to ignore her mother's strange behavior. She called Sydney, who set up a meeting with Dr. Blackwood for noon at the clinic. She hoped by meeting on a Saturday her mother wouldn't suspect anything.

Simon had agreed to watch Jayden at his place so that if Connie dropped by the house it looked like she'd gone out to run weekend errands and nothing more.

She went through her closet, throwing on a plain white, short-sleeve ribbed top, pairing it with a dark green skirt that had big white and red flowers in the pattern.

She fussed with her hair, eventually twisting it into a tight knot, unfurling a few loose strands to fall around her face.

After loading Jayden's gear and a few of his favorite toys into the station wagon, the pair headed for Taggert Farms.

Winding through the countryside, Gilly pointed out the coastline to her son. "Look at that, Jayden. Waves! Whitecaps! See the boat way out there in the distance?"

"Waves! Boat! Read the story!" Jayden shouted.

The story he referred to was one Gilly knew by heart. "I'm driving, bud. But I can recite it from memory." Dutiful mom that she was, she proceeded to deliver the tale about a tugboat captain and his loyal dog.

It kept him entertained until she pulled up in front of Simon's place. A huge hairy block of energy was the first thing to bound out of the house.

"What is that?" Gilly screeched.

From the porch steps, Simon called to the dog. "That's Merlin. He's big but harmless."

Gilly eased out of the car and went around to let Jayden free of his car seat. But when she set the toddler down, Merlin almost knocked him over.

"Be careful, Merlin," Simon cautioned, leaping off the steps to take the pooch by his collar.

"Bear!" Jayden hollered and hid behind his mother's legs. "Big bear."

"No, sweetie. It's a doggie. You like doggies," Gilly reminded her son.

Simon bent down to Jayden's level. "I know Merlin looks huge and his face might look like a bear, but he won't hurt you. I promise."

"Scared."

"It's okay to be scared. But watch." Simon brought the dog closer to let Merlin lick his own hand. "He's friendly. He's not gonna eat you up. I wouldn't lie to you."

Jayden let go of his mother's legs and stepped toward the dog. Merlin stuck out his big tongue and slurped the boy's face.

Jayden scrunched up his nose and giggled. "It tickles."

"It does, I know."

"Thanks for this," Gilly said to Simon as she watched her son relax enough to latch onto Merlin's fur. "Oh, he'll love being around your dog. He loves animals, just not big bears. You sure you're okay to handle two toddlers? By yourself."

He glanced over at Delaney who was backing down the porch steps on all fours to get to the grass on her own. "I guess we'll see. I'm counting on them getting along well enough to entertain each other."

"I brought some of Jayden's Matchbox cars and his favorite stuffed elephant. If you have any problems, text me and I'll come right back."

Simon chuckled and stared at her bare legs. They seemed to go on and on. "You look good, even though I can see you're not too convinced of my parenting skills."

"New parent," she pointed out with a grin. "Which I have to admit gave me pause. On the drive here, I had my reservations. But watching you with Jayden and the dog just now, I think he's in good hands. At least for a couple of hours. Just remember, Jayden can be a handful at times because he's a tad hyper." She quickly added, "But he's not destructive or anything like that. Need me to pick up anything at the store for dinner tonight?"

"I have it handled. I hope you like grilled steak."

"Love it. Okay, I'm out of here then. Just let me know if you need anything."

But she didn't budge.

Her nervousness made her so damn cute, he wanted to plant a kiss on those lips to make her stop fidgeting. He leaned in and so did she. He took her by the arms, bringing her closer. Their lips met in a smoldering blast of heat. It felt like they'd slammed into the sun.

She blew out a breath and licked her lips. "That was... I really need to go."

He grinned and let go of her arms. "We'll finish that later. Now get out of here before you're late for your meeting."

Gilly stumbled around the car and fumbled with the door handle.

Simon trailed, then reached around her and opened the door. "Drive safe."

"Okay."

She barely remembered backing out and heading down the driveway. This wasn't like her. She was usually level-headed and in total control. When she reached the highway, she muttered to herself, "This is your fault, Mom. You've gotten me all out of sorts."

But she knew it wasn't true. Simon Bremmer had a way of making a body feel like they were floating on air. Or maybe gliding right before they fell into bed.

Fanning herself at the thought of the two of them in bed, she rolled the window down for some fresh air and tried to take several deep breaths to bring her feet back down to earth.

She had to have her wits about her when she talked to Dr. Blackwood, not feeling all moony-eyed over the new boy in town.

She arrived at the clinic a few minutes past noon. Sydney greeted her at the door holding a can of Coke in her hand. "Quentin will be with us in a few. He had a compound fracture to deal with at the hospital."

"Oh, no. Who got hurt?"

"Tandy Gilliam. He fell from the pier onto his boat and cracked a bone in his leg, multiple breaks. Quentin says he'll be fine, but he'll probably need a home health care nurse to look in on him now and again until he completely heals."

"That's something in short supply around here. San Sebastian has an agency that provides that service, otherwise you'll have to find one out of Santa Cruz."

"You and I both know how hard it is to get an RN to travel to Pelican Pointe. If I hadn't gone to work for Doc Prescott, I would've been making the commute somewhere else. Help yourself to a soda," Sydney offered as she led the way into the breakroom. "There's plenty in the fridge."

Beginning to relax, Gilly popped the top on a Cherry Coke and took a seat at the kitchen table. "I'm still pinching myself that I got hired on at the hospital."

"Same here. I can't believe I'm back in the ER again."

"Didn't you like working for Dr. Blackwood?"

"Honestly? I loved it. But it was nothing like emergency medicine. Don't tell Quentin but I miss working with him."

"You still get to…sort of…whenever he's called to the hospital or there making rounds."

"It's not the same thing. But someone has to be in the office to see patients, day in and day out, and that's Quentin. He's very good with people, better than any doctor I've been around. He just can't…you know…perform surgery."

"Which is why we have Dr. Nighthawk here. What happened to Quentin?"

"He took a bullet. One night this crazy guy shot him. It's the world we live in. Violence is so much a part of society these days. I remember thinking right after he came here what a pompous ass he was." Her lips curved. "There was a time I didn't completely trust him. Of course, I was wrong about everything."

"You didn't like him at first? Get out."

"I'm not kidding. I thought his bedside manner was…atrocious."

"Are you talking about me again?" Quentin asked from the doorway. "I turn my back for five seconds and…"

Sydney lifted her cheek for a kiss. "I'm explaining to Gilly how we got off on the wrong foot."

Quentin leaned down, obliged with a sweet peck on his wife's mouth. "This one wanted to run me out of town on a rail. All she needed was the pitchfork, the tar, and the feathers. After I arrived here, I hated this place."

"But without you we wouldn't have the hospital. So what changed?" Gilly wanted to know.

"It took time to settle in and find my groove. And then I met Beckham and his terminally ill grandmother. That whole experience taught me that my problems weren't so huge after all."

Quentin got out a bottle of water and sat down across from Gilly. "So what's up with your mom?"

"First off, she can't know I'm going behind her back like this," Gilly began. "And I wouldn't be if I didn't feel that her behavior is getting so bizarre that it shouldn't be ignored. She's been so critical of everything and everybody lately. She's acting like someone I don't even know."

"I'll be honest. Her sharp tongue is a problem, even more so than when I hired her," Quentin admitted. "Which might mean that whatever is happening, it's getting worse."

Gilly squirmed in her chair. "Is there any way her abrupt change in personality could be triggered by a medical condition? I spent last night searching online for a reasonable explanation but couldn't find anything other than Alzheimer's. It doesn't run in our family, but...who knows."

Sydney nodded. "Sometimes, in addition to the memory lapses, patients become irritable for no apparent reason. They're unable to work well with others because they simply can't get along with anyone around them. Not just coworkers either, but family members seem to get them all riled up even worse. It comes out of the blue, kind of like when they pull inappropriate things out of thin air."

"Exactly. Her attitude reminds me of the way she behaved after my dad died," Gilly stated. "I honestly thought there for a while she was headed for a breakdown. But that's been close to ten years ago. That's why I thought this heads-up meeting might be a good idea."

Sydney finished her Coke and got up to throw the can in the recycle bin. "I once had a woman come into the ER right after having a stroke. Miraculously, it hadn't affected her speech. But because she couldn't move her right arm, she got so frustrated she started cursing. These horrible things came rolling out of her mouth. Her kids were horrified at her language."

Quentin sipped his drink. "What Sydney's trying to say is that sometimes when the brain is getting mixed signals, it reacts with difficulties in hand-eye coordination, odd gaits, and even strange behavior. I didn't want to mention this but last week, Connie had trouble getting up out of a chair. And she almost tipped over while taking a patient's blood pressure. Is it possible to coax her into having a full physical?"

"That's what I'm hoping for. I'm also hoping you'll give me some time to talk her into it before you fire her."

"You think I'd do that? Her job is safe…for now."

"Well, she isn't exactly racking up brownie points for good behavior, now is she? You need to know that up to now she's always had a stellar run as one of the best nurses at San Sebastian General," Gilly declared. "She excelled on the pediatric ward. I know because I heard heartwarming stories from the staff. They were always coming up to me with things she'd done above and beyond her job that were nothing like this. I just want a chance to understand why this is happening. If it's medical, that is."

"Then persuade her to go in for a complete physical."

"I will. There's something else you need to know, though." Gilly cleared her throat. "She's turned away a few patients because they didn't have insurance."

Quentin traded looks with Sydney, but it was Quentin's face that tightened with disappointment and pure anger. "That's not good. Do you know which ones?"

"I'm sorry, I don't. My mother has lived here a long time, so she'd know the names of the people she sent away. I could ask."

"Please do that. Doc Prescott and I didn't have a whole lot in common, but one thing we agreed on was that treating people took precedence over their ability to pay. The hospital's named for a woman who didn't have a lot of money. There's a reason we decided to go with that."

"I understand. But you need to know this simply isn't like my mom to do something so cruel."

"I'll take your word for it. As long as she agrees to go in for a checkup, I'll maintain a positive outlook on her continued employment. You have to understand where I'm coming from, rudeness is one thing; turning away patients is something I won't abide."

"Nor would I," Gilly said with relief. "I'll make the appointment myself."

"How will you get her in without telling her about this conversation?" Sydney asked.

"I don't know. But I have a couple of days to figure it out."

Gilly stewed on it after she left until her head spun with different ways to approach her mom. She'd always been good at meeting a problem head on. But could she really talk her stubborn mother into going in to see the doctor without having a big fight about it?

To hell with it, she thought as she walked down the street to the house where she'd grown up. Connie's mid-century ranch sat in the middle of the block. Its tidy lawn, still green and wet from the sprinkler, showed off a thick St. Augustine carpet that badly needed mowing. The well-tended flower beds, laden with purple hydrangeas, blue foxglove, and deep violet pansies guarded each side of the porch like a troop of soldiers. A tall, enormous valley oak that had stood for decades extended over the entrance, its branches providing a canopy of summer green.

Her dad had always taken pride in his lawn, ripping out the tiniest weeds lest it take root and infect his yard. She remembered following him around with the mower or raking and picking up leaves right up through Christmas when he would string lights around the eaves. Those fond memories of happier times morphed back into the reason she was here.

Ordinarily she'd just open the front door and walk in, but since she was on the outs with the woman on the other side of the door, she politely rang the bell.

Connie inched the door back. "Are you here to apologize?"

"Sure," Gilly said if it would get her inside where she could reason with her mother.

The house still had the original parquet oak flooring in the living room and the gold and white laminate in the kitchen. There were bookshelves lining one wall with trinkets and photographs from decades back.

"Well?" Connie prompted, arms crossed. "Where's my apology?"

"Mom, do you realize that you're sitting on a keg of dynamite if Dr. Blackwood finds out you've turned away patients?"

"I'm looking out for his best interests."

"I doubt he'd agree with that. Do you remember when Doc Prescott helped people even if they didn't have insurance?"

"Doc Prescott was a fool."

"You're kidding? Jack Prescott was a former chief resident of emergency medicine in one of San Francisco's busiest ERs. He might've been a lot of things, but he was no fool. He cared about people. Same goes for Quentin Blackwood."

"What are you saying, Gilly? Because you're beginning to get on my last nerve."

Gilly noticed her mother's hand start to shake. "Mom, have you noticed other changes lately? Not just the blowups and the anger, but differences in how you're able to do things?"

"Right now, I'm upset with you and you're giving me a major headache."

"Then go see a doctor. When's the last time you had a physical?"

"I had my mammogram last October."

"No, I mean a thorough checkup."

"Oh, two years back or so. Why?"

"Because I want you to go in and see Dr. Nighthawk."

"What? Why? He's a surgeon."

"Because everyone your age needs a once-a-year physical."

"I don't have time for that."

"You either make time this Wednesday or I tell Dr. Blackwood that you've turned away patients."

"You wouldn't."

"I would." To prove it, she went to the seventy-ish olive-green phone hanging on the kitchen wall and picked up the receiver. She used the ancient rotary to dial the first three digits. "Do I continue, or will you agree to go in for a checkup this Wednesday?"

"Oh, for Pete's sake," Connie moaned, letting out a huge sigh. "I suppose. What have you done with Jayden?"

Gilly dropped the receiver into place and coolly thought up a lie. "He's on a playdate with Nate Cody."

"That's nice. I suppose he needs to make more little friends. Want a cup of coffee? I made a fresh pot before you got here."

And just like that, thought Gilly, her mother seemed to have morphed into her normal self again. "Sure. I could use the caffeine."

"Are you still going out with that Simon person?"

Gilly gritted her teeth. Normal hadn't lasted for long. "Yes, Mom, I'm still having dinner tonight with Simon at his place. I'm looking forward to it."

"Figures. Losers are the only men you seem to attract."

Her jaw unclenched enough to spout off what was really on her mind. "Forget the coffee. I'm sorry you have such a low opinion of your own daughter. I'm done with trying to convince you something's wrong. Just listen to yourself."

Connie slid into a kitchen chair. "I'm a bundle of nerves these days. I can't seem to focus on anything but my anger. I'm always on edge."

"What it is about Simon that gets you so peeved?"

"He has such an arrogant look about him. I don't like it. And he should never be allowed to raise that kid by himself. He's ill-equipped."

Gilly had heard enough and got to her feet. "You know, Mom, some people might say the same thing about me, a single mother, never been married with a little boy who just wants some attention. I've never known you to be so judgmental. But I'm beginning to see you're slowly becoming such a bitter person I don't even recognize." With that, she marched out the front door and down the street.

She was still fuming when she texted Simon. *On my way to pick up Jayden. How is he?*

He's fine. Why not just plan to stay and I'll fix us an early dinner?

Sounds great. See you both soon.

Once she got back to her own car, she tried to calm down enough to drive. She needed a better mood, an attitude adjustment.

As she backed out of the driveway, she wondered when her mother had turned into such an angry person willing to judge so easily? When had it happened? Since March, things had been going along so well for both of them. When exactly had her mother started exhibiting this back-biting, bitter personality?

As she took a shortcut toward Taggert Farms, she thought back over the past few months. She was able to pinpoint a day not too long ago when her mother had taken a tumble right outside the drug store and hit her elbow on the concrete, even scratched up a knee. Had she taken a hit to the head as well and no one noticed?

Gilly had a bad feeling she already knew the answer and would have to remember to tell Dr. Nighthawk about the fall. Which meant maybe she'd been too rough on her mother. She decided to turn around and try to make amends.

But when she reached Connie's house, there stood her mother standing in the front yard with a broom, swatting the branches of the big oak tree.

"Mom, what are you doing?"

"I can't get these bats to leave me alone."

"What?" Gilly took a step closer. "What bats?" She stood beneath the tree and searched for anything that looked like a bat. She didn't see so much as a crow or blackbird. But the next thing out of her mother's mouth told her there was cause for alarm.

"Those black things up in the tree. See? They keep flying around and scaring Blossom."

"Our orange tabby that died two years ago? Mom, stop." Gilly caught the broom handle and stopped Connie's whacking motion. "It's okay, Mom. There are no bats bothering Blossom. Let's get you back inside."

Twelve

When Gilly relayed the story to Simon, he took on such a sweet, understanding role that she was certain he was too good to be true. After all, Vaughn had been that way in the beginning.

"Maybe you're right about your mother's abrasiveness being medical. Because that sounds a lot like how my Aunt Lorraine started. According to my mom, instead of swiping at bats, Lorraine would freak out at sunset, clawing to get out the door if she couldn't get the knob to work. She claimed she needed to find her mother, who was always in some type of distress."

"Did you see it for yourself?"

"Once when I was home on leave. It broke my heart to see Lorraine act more like a petulant twelve-year-old than the aunt I remembered. She'd always been active, always taking up causes for the underdog. She always loved the water and used to row out in her own skiff with no help from anyone, fearless."

Simon shook his head. "Not anymore. Alzheimer's is a strange disease. While dementia totally engulfs Lorraine, my mother, her sister, shows no signs of the disease. My mother's been tested for the gene. She doesn't have it. And yet, poor Lorraine gets worse by the month."

Gilly put her head in her hands. "But the onset has been so sudden. I'm a nurse. I'm supposed to recognize these things. Instead, I went behind her back and talked to her boss. Probably putting her job in further jeopardy."

"Look, if your mother is suffering from this illness, she can't perform her duties, even as a receptionist. You already said she's angry all the time. I saw it firsthand. Maybe the stress of her job is making the symptoms come to light sooner than they normally would and making her worse."

"I suppose that's true."

"You need to find out what's going on. The best way is to have her checked out. The sooner, the better."

"Wednesday. I scheduled it for this coming Wednesday when I'll be able to go with her to the hospital."

"On very little sleep," Simon pointed out.

"It can't be helped. It's either get her into the ER or a regular appointment. But after watching her chase down imaginary bats, believe me the ER is tempting."

"I have a bottle of chardonnay I picked up at Murphy's. Want to try it?"

"You read my mind." Gilly realized he had no idea how much spending the afternoon with him meant to her, how much it helped her cope with the worry. The bat thing hadn't just unnerved her, the crazy look in her mother's eyes had sent a chilling fear up her spine. She was afraid things were about to change, felt it in the air. And now, watching Simon open the wine calmed her down.

Simon filled their glasses and went over to the stone hearth, plopped down in front of the fireplace to pick up the guitar leaning against the wall.

Tilting her head to study him, she leaned back on the sofa to get comfortable. "You're a man of surprises."

"I taught myself how to play a couple of years ago because I like music and I needed…an outlet at the time."

"Who doesn't like music? But I can't play a tune to save my life…on anything."

"I like creating different songs using different notes. Delaney seems to like this one." He showed her what he meant, strumming a few bars of "Catch the Wind."

"I like it. What did you decide to do about the house in town?"

"Nick suggested I use the weekend to think about it."

Gilly's brow wrinkled. "What's really going on? You were so excited about it Thursday night. Now you're not."

He told her about the paternity test.

"That's normal. Any guy would want to know for certain. No reason to be shy about wanting to get at the truth."

When Delaney toddled over, he put down his guitar and brought her onto his lap, bouncing her up and down until she giggled.

Watching the affection and the way he interacted with his daughter made Gilly's heart melt into mush. How many guys out there could morph into an instant dad like he'd done? Not many.

"What?" he asked.

He'd caught her staring. "Um, do you need help starting dinner?"

"Not unless you want to fire up the grill. Are you guys hungry?"

"I wanna hot dog," Jayden announced, rubbing his eyes like he was sleepy.

Delaney spit out her pacifier, trying to imitate Jayden's words. Merlin retrieved it by scooping it up in his mouth, chomping down, and then dropping it at Simon's feet.

"Now that's what I call service," Gilly commented, rubbing the dog's ears.

Simon picked the thing up covered in dog slobber. "Happens a lot around here. I'll wash it off and then fire up the grill."

But as soon as he stepped outside on the little patio, Gavin Kendall pointed to the sky and hollered, "Better hurry up. Looks like storms are moving in."

For the first time all day, Simon realized the sky had turned a bluish black. "Maybe no time for steaks."

"Not unless you like them rare," Gavin returned. "Looks like it could open up and pour any minute."

"We do need the shower, but I wish it would've held off a little longer. The one time I use the grill…"

Thunder rumbled, bringing Gilly outside. "Just toss on the package of hot dogs. I'll go make some mac and cheese. Dinner."

"You sure?"

"It's fine. I don't need steak."

She had a down-to-earth way about her. It was a rallying point for him. The opposite of Amelia in every way and the realization hit him that her genuineness is what he liked most about her. It caused him to get his head out of the clouds and get busy with dinner.

The first plump splats of rain started falling just as he took the hot dogs off the fire. "This isn't exactly the meal I'd planned."

"It's okay. Betty White swears eating a hot dog every day is what got her to a ripe old age. And she's nearing a hundred," Gilly declared with a grin.

"The only reason I bought the package is because Jayden said he liked hot dogs. And I promised him one. Didn't I, Jayden?"

With his mouth full, the boy merely bobbed his head up and down.

Gilly reached over and cut Delaney's hot dog into smaller bites that became finger food.

The gesture made Simon smile.

"What are you grinning at?" Gilly wanted to know.

As the rain picked up and pounded the new roof he'd re-shingled last year, he met her eyes. "I don't know. I guess I'm happy. For the first time in a long time, I'm just…content."

"You're still haunted by all the things you saw in the Army though. I can tell."

He heard himself describing his greatest fears that he'd admitted to no one else. Maybe because she was so easy to talk to, he let down his guard. "It's faces mostly. That's what I see sometimes when I try to close my eyes to sleep. All ages. Young. Old. And everything in between."

His voice was barely above a whisper. But it made her want to hold him like she did Jayden when her boy had a bad dream. But she doubted Simon would appreciate it at the moment. Instead, in her unflappable style, she pushed Delaney's hair off her face, tossed Merlin part of a hot dog, and adjusted Jayden in his chair so he wouldn't tumble off the seat. "How is it you don't have one of those weird accents from back east?"

To Simon, all those gestures she did in one fluid motion garnered her another point in the win column. "My mother claims I lost it in the Army. I don't know that I ever had it, though. If I did you can bet the guys probably razzed me out of talking that way. I do miss the old homestead at times. Places like Del's. Best lemonade stand evah. They serve a wicked good slush."

Merlin sidled up to her for another handout. Ruffling the dog's fur, she let him gobble out of her hand. "Now see, that time I heard a definite eastern twang, somewhere between heavy New Yorker and Boston."

"Nah. But I know a guy," imitating a definite Rhode Island monotone.

She laughed. "There it is again."

"Wait until you hear my mom. Boston born and raised. Now there's a twang."

"If you don't mind my asking, how is it you hooked up with Delaney's mother on Cape Cod?"

He went into the explanation, not minding the walk down memory lane so much. He felt relaxed and loose around her.

She sat back, listening to the story. He wasn't aware of it, but that accent slipped in every so often. "How long has the beach house been in your family?"

"Grandparents bought the place around 1940, right before the war broke out."

"So you've always lived around the water, the beach, like here?"

"I guess I have."

"How in the world did you cope being out in desert conditions for such long deployments? I remember how much I missed the ocean when I lived in landlocked Lubbock with Vaughn for six months. I can't imagine being away from the water for so long."

"It was tough. But remember I didn't want to admit my mistake. That stubborn streak kept me putting one foot in front of the other for twelve years."

"And your family has owned that piece of beach since before the war? No conflict among relatives about the land?"

Before Simon could answer, Jayden started another kind of conflict by tossing bits of mac and cheese toward Delaney.

Without raising her voice, Gilly took hold of the three-year-old's chin. "Young man, you know better than that. Tell her you're sorry for throwing food. Right now."

"Sow-wy."

She got up to wet a paper towel to wipe off the toddler's mouth. "If you're done, go play with your cars." She watched as he hopped down and flew into the living room. "Want me to clean Delaney up too while I'm at it?"

It blew his mind that she'd offer. "Sure. I'll get the tray and wash it off."

After Delaney waddled off to play, Gilly picked up her wine glass and drained the contents.

"You're just now beginning to relax," Simon noted.

"I guess I am. That scene with my mom has me worried and wore me out."

Simon tipped up the bottle to fill her glass before topping off his. "Then it's time we both kicked back and chilled out tonight."

She flashed him a brilliant smile. "On a rainy night, too. Want to pop in a movie? I'll pop the corn."

"Now you're talking."

"Um, probably not a good idea to sound so thrilled. We're talking about the animated variety to entertain the kids."

Simon laughed, realizing she was right. He scratched his chin. "I don't think I have anything like that on hand."

She went to the huge bag she'd brought and dug into its depths. "No problem. I came prepared." She held up three DVDs. "You get *Toy Story*, *Madagascar*, or *Cars*."

"How many times has Jayden seen *Cars*?"

"How many fingers do you have?"

"That many, huh? I don't know. You pick. I'm no expert on any of those."

"All right. No way we could go wrong with *Madagascar*. Talking animals. An adventure into the wild. A funny ring-tailed lemur."

The kids fell asleep long before the credits rolled. It was barely eight-thirty.

"I'm tucking Delaney into bed."

"Should Jayden and I hit the road?"

"No way. Want to put Jayden in the guest room? I put clean sheets on the bed two days ago because my mother's coming at the end of the week."

"Sure."

Scooping Jayden into his arms, he headed down the hallway again. "There's a queen size bed. He can spread out."

With the kids asleep, the house grew so quiet you could hear a pin drop. They settled back on the sofa.

"When they're in bed it's like this calm overtakes everything," Gilly commented, picking up her wine glass.

"Is Jayden a good sleeper?"

"Mostly. Is Delaney?"

"Seems to be. It's still coming down out there," Simon noted. "I'm about to say something that might upset you. Don't take it the wrong way."

"It's a little early in the relationship to sleep together."

His lips curved. "As great as that sounds, that wasn't it. You could stay here tonight. Hear me out. Instead of driving home in this downpour…Jayden's already conked out…spending the night here isn't that farfetched."

"I have had a little too much wine."

"Then it's settled." Simon went over to his collection of CDs and began flipping through the selections. "What kind of music do you like?"

"My tastes vary. I didn't know anyone kept CDs anymore."

"They're from my misspent youth. Outdated tunes. But I'd rather listen to them than anything on the radio these days."

"Then you pick. I'm sure I'll like it."

Simon slid in a disc and took a seat next to her. Eddie Vedder's lilting voice flowed from the speakers.

"Nailed it," she said with a smile.

She leaned her head on his shoulder. She was so close he could smell her shampoo. It reminded him of that perfect aroma right after a spring shower, when everything is lush and radiant.

He nuzzled her hair. She lifted her chin. Their lips met. He changed the angle, sending the kiss into a searing demand for more. He felt her hand grip his shirt, felt her shoulders relax, felt her drop into the kiss. When he bothered to open his eyes and stare into hers, he recognized arousal and skimmed a finger along her cheek.

"You look sleepy," he said. "Why don't you go on to bed?"

"No, I need to help you with the dishes."

"Gilly, you look exhausted. Go on. Go to bed. I'll clean up."

"If you're sure; I am tired. It's the wine. Was that my goodnight kiss?"

"Not yet."

She took that for rejection and let out a sigh.

Her disappointed look amused him. "I haven't walked you to your door yet."

"Ah." She brightened, bumping his shoulder. "A girl deserves a goodnight kiss."

"Mmm, and you're not just any girl." Locking his fingers with hers, he dragged her up, snaked an arm around her waist.

Her arms circled his neck.

With each step they got closer to the guest room with its closed door and little Jayden on the other side asleep.

"I had a nice time tonight," she began. "Maybe we could do it again sometime."

His lips pressed hers. "A real date, just you and me. Sitters for the kids."

"That sounds wonderful."

"You talk too much."

"Then why are you letting me…?"

His mouth covered hers. The sizzle heated his blood. If the kiss made her tremble in his arms, he wondered what making love to her would be like. There was something so heady about her body responding to his like that, he had to force himself to let her go.

"We're going to need to finish this...and soon."

"Yes. Soon."

Thirteen

Thunder rattled the little cottage around six, booming so loudly that it woke up the kids. First Jayden's boisterous welcome to the day to make sure everyone knew he was awake. And then Delaney, who wanted out of her crib to run after Jayden.

Simon stumbled into the kitchen---stepping over Jayden zooming around the floor with his little cars and Delaney crawling after them---only to find Gilly had already put on coffee and was cracking eggs into a bowl. "I wondered how she got out of her crib."

"I heard her shortly after Jayden stormed right past her door."

He eyed the coffee pot again. "Great idea. How'd you sleep?"

"Like a rock. My head hit the pillow and that's all I remember."

"You needed it."

"My head was so full of worry about my mom that I drank way too much wine. Sorry. I don't usually do that."

"Don't apologize to me. I've done the same thing. Lots of times."

"But I have a toddler to look after."

He poured himself a cup of coffee. "Stop beating yourself up for letting your hair down for one evening."

She blew out a breath. "My shift starts this afternoon at four."

"You have to head to work in…" he glanced at his watch, "nine hours?"

"Less than. But yeah. I don't even know if my mom should continue to watch Jayden. And the church doesn't provide daycare on a Sunday for my benefit, so I can't drop him off."

"How does this thing work with your mom and babysitting? Because I'll be honest, the way you explained it to me, it's confusing."

"I work four p.m. to four a.m., three nights a week beginning Sundays. On those nights, I'll drop him off at her house around three, get him settled in, and then head to work. When four a.m. comes around, I go home to catch some sleep, usually three to four hours. It varies. Down the street, my mom gets Jayden dressed, fixes his breakfast, and then runs him back over to my house around eight-thirty before going to the office." Her shoulders drooped. "I guess it is confusing."

"No, no, I get it now. You're off four days, but those three when you work are hectic as hell."

"Yep. But now…I don't know if Mom can handle it. What if she forgets the routine, forgets about Jayden? What if she forgets just one of those necessary steps?"

"Maybe I could do it."

"What?"

"I'm serious. You could drop him off this afternoon. He could sleep here. I have to fix breakfast anyway for Delaney. What's another mouth to feed?

And tomorrow Jordan's booked a hiking tour. She texted me late last night. I can't take Delaney on an all-day hike, so I'll have to drop her off at daycare before I head over to the B&B. Early. That means I'm headed to town anyway. Jayden might as well tag along for the ride until you feel like picking him up."

"I couldn't ask you to do that."

"You didn't ask. I offered."

"I…I don't know what to say. That's incredibly generous of you. I could pay you."

"Please. Don't insult me like that. I'm happy to help out a friend, especially one parent to another, especially one who's so beautiful." Simon swallowed hard. "Maybe that came out wrong. Or it's inappropriate. These days, I'm never sure. Bottom line is, Jayden's welcome to stay here. Delaney seems to like him. Only thing is, I don't have a car seat for him, but I could ask Jordan if she has a…"

"I'll get one," Gilly said quickly. "You think I'm beautiful, really?"

Simon smiled. "Incredibly."

Because she couldn't remember the last time anyone had called her beautiful, her blush spread to her neck. "We'll get out of your hair after breakfast."

"No need to rush."

"There kinda is. I should probably go check on my mom," Gilly stated. "And if Jayden's coming over here, I have to figure out a way to explain why. Something else we need to think about, if we're picking up and dropping off at the daycare for each other, we probably want to sign permission slips, authorizing each other to have access."

"Good thinking." He saw the troubled look on her face. "What's wrong? Having second thoughts already?"

"Only about telling my mom."

"It's been my experience that honesty is the best way to go. Explain to her that until you know what's going on with her medical situation, maybe taking away the little guy will ease some of her stress issues."

"That's actually not a bad approach. You're a genius."

"I wish. A genius would've held on to his Amazon stock."

She roared out a belly laugh. "You've really picked my spirits up since I got here yesterday. Thank you for that."

"Same here. It's lonely being the only single father who doesn't know what he's doing half the time."

"You know who else is a single father? Malachi Rafferty. And he likes to play guitar. You two should meet."

"Malachi Rafferty? Surely you aren't referring to *the* Malachi Rafferty?"

"I don't even know what that means."

"By any chance is this guy from L.A.?"

"I think he used to live there. Yeah. Why? Who's Malachi Rafferty?"

"You remember a band called Moss Radley, a grunge band in the 90s?"

"Um, sure. Everybody I knew was inconsolable when they broke up."

"Over a woman," Simon supplied. "Or so the story goes. The lead singer and guitarist was a guy named Malachi Rafferty."

"Wow. No way. It can't be the same guy. This Malachi's wife died right after they moved here and ever since he sticks pretty close to his T-shirt shop. He has two teenage daughters."

"Then it probably isn't him. Just in case, though, I'm gonna make a point to find out."

After a simple breakfast of scrambled eggs and frozen waffles, Gilly got up to clear the table.

He stood up with a couple of plates. "You cooked, I can handle clean up."

"You sure?"

"Go. Check on your mom before you crack a bone. I can tell you want to."

She threw her arms around him and kissed the corner of his mouth.

But he didn't let her get off that easy. He glided his lips down to meet hers. Together, they slid into a quiet and desperate euphoria, building up to a lust neither could act on. When Jayden made a booming noise with his car hitting the baseboard, they broke apart like they'd been shot out of a cannon.

But the kids were oblivious, playing and laughing.

Simon noticed Gilly was still clinging to him as if unwilling to let go.

"What time do you want Jayden back here tonight?" she whispered, her words still breathless from the kiss.

Simon took hold of her chin. "Whatever time works best for you."

"Three o'clock okay?"

"That'll work."

"Thanks for doing this. It won't be for long, just until I find out what's going on with her. Three nights tops."

Ten minutes later, when Delaney figured out Jayden was leaving, she started bawling.

Simon scooped her up. "Don't worry, doodle-bug, he's coming back this afternoon. He has to go home and get his stuff to spend the night."

Gilly took hold of Delaney's hand. "It's okay. I think someone's ready for her nap already."

Between the crying, Simon helped Gilly load up the car as the steady rain continued to beat down. "Maybe one day we can spend a rainy day together."

"We just spent a rainy night together. Will you still go on the hike tomorrow if it's raining?"

"I checked the forecast. This storm will be gone by tonight."

She leaned in to kiss him again, but just as she was ready to tilt her head for better access, Brent Cody pulled up in his police cruiser. Instead of a smoldering goodbye, she lowered her voice, "I'll see you at three."

Simon waved goodbye and turned to Brent, who seemed to be bursting with news.

"You want the long version of what I discovered or the short?" Brent asked.

"What do you think? Come on in and I'll make a pot of fresh coffee."

"Make it strong. You're gonna need it. You were right about some of what you suspected. But in order for you to get the full gist of it all, I need to start at the very beginning." Brent followed him inside and took a seat at the kitchen table. He stared at Delaney who was crawling around on the tile floor. "She seems to be settling in just fine."

"She is. So far. Tomorrow's her first time at day care. I'm a little nervous."

"No need to be. My kids go there all the time. Ophelia has taken a good program and made it better."

"I keep hearing good things about it," Simon remarked. "I'm hoping it lives up to the glowing reviews." He turned from the counter as the Cuisinart coffeemaker began to gurgle to life. "What have you got for me?"

Brent cleared his throat. "The woman you knew on Cape Cod didn't start out in life as Amelia Langston."

"You're kidding?"

"I wish I was. She was born Muriel Bondurant in Gallentine, Louisiana."

Simon dropped into one of the chairs across from Brent. "Louisiana? That explains the hint of a southern drawl I detected when she'd drop her guard every now and again. It wasn't obvious, but it certainly came through at times when she wasn't trying so hard. What else?"

"Her family practically owns the little town where she grew up. They're deep into politics, father was mayor twenty years ago, now the brothers take turns running the place. The Bondurants own real estate, businesses, have a hefty portfolio. It seems Muriel was the black sheep. Got into trouble early on, at the age of fifteen when she was picked up for shoplifting. After that, she bypassed anything petty and went straight to the high dollar stuff, stealing a convertible on her sixteenth birthday and driving it off the showroom floor before wrecking the thing on the highway."

Simon frowned. "Are you sure you have the right person?"

"I'm sure. Photo verified. Amelia Langston was just one of the many aliases Muriel Bondurant used over the years. The car theft happened to be the first time the family covered up her misdeeds and paid her way out of trouble for the rest. Her rap sheet includes fifteen other arrests for various thefts between Louisiana and Massachusetts. And I'm not talking about the incidental taking gum at the convenience store. Not this woman."

Simon mulled that over. "Then I take it her family got the dealership to drop the charges."

"Yep. That happened dozens of times. By the time she reached eighteen, they even shipped her off to some fancy rehabilitation school in Canada, hoping they could break her of the habit of stealing. It didn't take. She spent a little more than a month there before taking off. When she tried to contact her family, they told her they were done with her and that she was on her own."

"Ouch. When did she become Amelia Langston?"

"I'll get to that."

"Was she ever a travel photographer?"

"Sorry, she did work at a studio once, picked up a camera fetish, took lots of pictures, but never sold anything other than a few online photos. She worked a lot of low-paying jobs because with her record she couldn't get anything above minimum wage. She did settle down once, after meeting a man willing to put up with her shoplifting. That happened when she was around twenty-five. Hearing the rest may hurt. According to her friends in the Boston area, she wanted a child. Badly. This particular man did not share her feelings about kids. At all. I tracked him down and he admitted they broke up sometime between Thanksgiving and Christmas four years ago because he was adamant that having kids for him was off the table. After that, she made several inquiries into adoption but got turned down every time because of her arrest record."

"This must be where I come in, some stupid, horny ex-soldier spending the summer on Cape Cod."

"Not so fast. I'm getting there. I'm told she went in search of a wealthy benefactor using all kinds of social media apps to find the kind of guy she wanted. She signed up on all the dating sites and finally hooked a fish, a guy named Houghton Wellington, who was a Wall Street banker in his prime. Wellington routinely summered on Cape Cod."

"Oh jeez. I wonder. She did disappear for more than a few afternoons and didn't come back until the evenings."

"Interesting. Since Wellington was almost forty-six years older than she was, maybe she had to put him to bed before she came back to you."

"She swore she was mailing photos to the magazine. She'd come back with dinner, so you're probably right."

"From what I understand from the Wellington family, he would have given her the moon."

"But not a baby," Simon stated, beginning to catch on.

"Nope. Turns out, Houghton's second wife insisted that he get a vasectomy back in the 80s, so Wellington couldn't have given her a child."

"I feel like I'm waiting for the other shoe to drop. So she spent the summer with me, trying to get pregnant, all the while she was with this rich old guy?"

"That about sums it up."

"Did this Wellington fella dump her or what?"

"Not that. By this time, she had officially changed her name to Amelia Langston, living life as Wellington's mistress. During her pregnancy, the old guy had a heart attack, leaving her a sizeable chunk of his estate, not all of it, according to his kids, but enough that Amelia would be comfortable. She probably thought she was fixed for life. But I guess karma has a way of coming around and making things right again, dues to pay and all that. There's a price to pay for deception. The day of the accident, Muriel..."

"Amelia," Simon corrected.

"Yeah, okay, whatever. Amelia was coming back from her yoga class when a delivery truck ran a stop sign in the heart of Boston and T-boned the driver's side door. She was dead on arrival at the hospital. She'd taken a blow to the left temple and it apparently caused an immediate cerebral hemorrhage. She never made it to the ER, died en route."

Simon looked over at Delaney, playing with her blocks. "She could've been in that car."

"She could have been, but she wasn't. The strange thing is Amelia was only a few blocks away from the townhouse Wellington had given her."

"What a fraud, nothing she told me was true."

"Well, I doubt you'd have dabbled in an affair if she'd admitted up front that all she wanted was your man juice."

Simon couldn't hold back the laughter. "I suppose you're right. Well, like an idiot I got played."

"You aren't the first guy who was duped and used for a sperm donor."

"If that's supposed to make me feel less stupid..."

"No, but it might explain how desperate she was. You crossed paths with her at a time in her life when she very much wanted a kid, wanted it enough to do anything to get one. That's how I see it. It's less about tricking you and more about getting what she wanted. Anything else or are you satisfied with the outcome?"

"Part of me wanted to verify I'd been played. And then I suppose I wanted to make sure no one else was out there who might lay claim to Delaney down the road."

"You might get some interest from the Bondurant family *if* they knew about the baby. But I don't think they have a clue. I didn't tip them off. I'm almost certain they didn't even have an idea where Muriel ended up. Boston authorities saw you listed as next of kin and that was it. For Muriel that had to be like thumbing her nose at the Bondurants. Pretty sure they don't care. That's my impression."

"I hope you're right."

"The day I talked to them, my questions were strictly on a law enforcement basis. I just wanted to know what they knew. And they were reluctant to talk. Period. In fact, one brother pretty much told me to never call him again."

"I can handle never. Thanks, Brent. Want that coffee now?"

"Nah. I'll pass. You drink it. What's with you and Gilly Grant?"

"We're friends. A single dad. A single mom. We need someone to talk to."

Brent's mouth quirked up. "Friends. Yeah. Right."

"I met her the same day I met Delaney. It's all new."

"Want my opinion?"

"Sure."

"You couldn't ask for a better person than Gilly Grant. Having said that, have you noticed anything strange about Connie, her mother, lately?"

Simon lifted a shoulder. "Something's off there. That seems to be the consensus. How do you know about it?"

"Because last night Eastlyn got a call from the neighbors. Connie was out walking around in her nightgown at ten-thirty. Eastlyn had to go over, corral her, and coax her back into the house."

"Wow. Gilly was here last night. Why didn't Eastlyn call Gilly?"

"Don't know. But I can make a notation in her file to call Gilly if it happens again. Is Connie looking at an Alzheimer's diagnosis?"

"Sure sounds like it to me. But she doesn't know anything yet. She's trying to get her mother in on Wednesday for a checkup."

"I'll note that in the file, too." Brent stood up. "I gotta go. River has some proposal she's working on, due tomorrow, and I have to watch the kids."

Simon stuck out his hand. "Thanks for doing all the background."

"No problem. I didn't much like the lawyer from Boston either."

"That makes two of us."

After Brent left, Simon fed Delaney lunch and put her down for a nap, then texted Gilly.

How's your mom?

Seems fine today. She's spent the last hour not bashing anyone so that has to count for something, right?

Did she tell you Eastlyn found her wandering around the neighborhood in her nightgown?

OMG. No! Why didn't Eastlyn call me?

Brent put it in his notes to do that next time. Have you told her Jayden's staying here tonight?

Not yet. I know, I know. I'm chicken.

Tell her.

I will. I'll use that wandering around in her nightgown thing as the reason.

Gilly fixed her mother a grilled cheese sandwich and sat down on the back porch with a glass of tea.

She decided it was better if she simply ripped off the Band-Aid quickly. "Mom, I'm not bringing Jayden over here tonight."

"Really? Did you get the night off?"

"No. He's staying overnight with someone else."

"Why? You mean like a sleepover?"

"No. Mom, I found out about your late-night foray into the neighborhood wearing your nightgown. And it worries me. I have second thoughts about leaving a three-year-old in your care when I'm not convinced you can take care of yourself. You do have to admit your weird behavior is getting worse. Fast."

"I don't remember unlocking the door and going outside."

Gilly laid a hand over hers. "Wednesday can't come soon enough for me so that I can find out why you're acting like this. It's scaring me, Mom."

"It's scaring me, too."

"Okay, then we agree that until we know what's happening Jayden will stay with someone else?"

"I suppose it's for the best. It won't be the same around here without him."

"It's not like I'm hitting the road and you'll never see him again. He's still right down the street whenever you get to feeling better. Are you still having headaches? Does anything else hurt?"

"A little pain in the top of my head now and then. It's the shaking I don't like. I tried to crack an egg this morning and couldn't."

Gilly let out a long groan. "I have to be at work in three hours, is there any way I could talk you into coming into the ER before then?"

"I'm fine. I'm sure it's just a bug I picked up from all the patients that come into the clinic. After all, I work around sick people, you know. Sometimes you catch what they have. How was your date last night? Did that Simon behave himself?"

"*That Simon* has a funny sense of humor. And I think you'd be surprised just how good a dad he is. I hope, at some point, you'll give him a chance to show you."

But Gilly realized Connie wasn't listening. Her mother had found something to stare at in the corner of the kitchen. Eyes fixated on whatever it was, Connie couldn't seem to focus on anything else. Not even the sound of her daughter's voice.

Gilly put her head in her hands and felt like crying. Wednesday couldn't get here fast enough.

Fourteen

Simon might be a newbie, but he'd learned fast that if you found a place to let kids run around, they'd exert enough energy to eventually collapse in exhaustion.

Even though the rain had stopped, puddles were everywhere, overflowing along the deep, pock-marked wet patches of ground. Simon decided that taking them to the beach would be a mistake in such muddy conditions. Instead, he got the brilliant idea to cart them around the farm to look at all the chickens and ducks.

Everything was fine until Simon started up a conversation with Gavin. He turned his back for maybe two minutes and then spotted the kids splashing in a shallow, muddy hole with Merlin right there egging them on.

He ran over to put a stop to it, but they were already filthy dirty.

Gavin stood there watching. "You'll have to hose them off. Otherwise, you'll never get the muck out of their hair. You can use my kids' wagon to haul them back to the house."

Which is how Simon ended up pulling an all-terrain red wagon all the way down the road until it dead-ended and back to his house.

"Don't stand up," he cautioned Delaney when she tried to get to her feet. "You sit right there until I get you cleaned up."

By the time he reached the back porch, they'd smeared the mud onto each side so that he had a bigger mess than before.

"Who wants to go first?"

Jayden roared with laughter and hollered, "Me!"

"Me," Delaney repeated.

"Together then," Simon decided as he plopped them down one after the other on the concrete patio and went to unfurl the hose.

He set the nozzle to a gentle soak, but that didn't do the job. He increased the pressure until their clothing was drenched and both kids were slightly mud-free. That's when he realized he needed towels. Opening the back door, he herded them inside into the utility room where they both dripped water on the floor. He got them out of their wet clothes, dumping their outfits into the washer.

Jayden took off running into the kitchen and beyond, naked as the day he was born, while Simon scooped up Delaney. After putting her in a clean diaper and tugging on one of her new romper things, he had to dig in the massive bag Gilly had brought to find Jayden's change of clothes. Then he had to chase down Jayden who refused to be caught and thought it was all a funny game.

Eventually Simon corralled the boy and persuaded him to stand still long enough to put on a clean pair of underwear with dinosaurs as a theme, a dry T-shirt, and shorts. "Thank goodness your mom brought you extra clothes."

"Done," Jayden pronounced and made a dive for his cars. When he saw Delaney picking one up, he yelled, "Mine," and jerked it out of her hands.

Delaney started to pucker up and cry.

"They do belong to Jayden," Simon pointed out, holding out the bear she'd become fond of dragging everywhere. "How about this? We'll get you some cars of your own tomorrow. How does that sound?"

She hugged the blue bear to her chest. "Mine."

"Yep. You learn fast. Bear is all yours."

Simon turned his attention to fixing supper and decided he couldn't look at macaroni again. He'd picked up dinosaur-shaped chicken nuggets that were quick and easy to heat in the oven. And Gilly had mentioned that Jayden liked apricots served over rice. She swore that throwing everything into a bowl, the toddlers would gobble it up.

Simon was less than convinced. He used instant rice because the stuff cooked in five minutes. Once he took the chicken out of the oven, he cut it up into chunks and poured the apricots, juice and all, over the hot meat and served the concoction over the rice.

He stood back and waited for the kids to balk, but when they began to stuff their faces, he looked on in wonder. "You guys eat the weirdest things."

"Weird but good," Jayden stated.

Simon ruffled the boy's hair. "That's all that counts."

When his cell phone rang, Simon looked at the display. "This is your mom."

Gilly was almost breathless with worry on the other end. "Hey, how is everything going? Any problems?"

"We're surviving. You were right about that chicken dish."

"I know. It may sound disgusting to us, but I got the idea off the Internet."

He told her about the tour of the farm and the consequences that followed.

"No problem, I've hosed Jayden off lots of times."

"I never would've thought of it if Gavin hadn't tossed out the idea. How's your shift going?"

"Quiet so far. I have three patients who were admitted over the weekend so I'm not alone."

"Do you ever get scared working there by yourself?"

"No. Thanks for putting that in my head, though."

"Sorry, it's just that I've been in isolated places and it's a bit unnerving."

"You were actually scared?"

"Sure. I've been afraid a bunch of times. Nothing wrong with admitting it."

"I gotta go. Looks like Dr. Blackwood is here to do rounds. Remember, try to get Jayden in bed by eight-thirty, no later than nine. That is if you can. If not, don't sweat it. He'll run out of energy long before midnight."

"Midnight?"

"Just kidding? Gotta go. Call if there's a problem. Talk to you later."

After making himself a ham sandwich and cleaning up the supper dishes, he loaded one of the music CDs that Gilly had packed in Jayden's bag into the player. Jayden started dancing to tunes from They Might Be Giants, and then later hauled a bouncing Delaney around the room to the rhythm from another band called The Twigs.

Both kids were bobbing up and down and hopping until bedtime. Since they'd already been cleaned up, all Simon had to do was get them into pajamas.

He fixed Delaney a bottle and plopped down on the sofa to read them a bedtime story from a book Gilly had thought to bring. It made him realize that he needed to do some major shopping for Delaney. She had very few clothes and needed toys and books.

Getting both kids off to bed proved less of a challenge than he thought. Jayden nodded off halfway through the story and Delaney's eyes kept fluttering before she finished her bottle. Simon simply carried both to their bedrooms.

Exhausted, he rewarded himself with a beer and sat down in his favorite chair to enjoy the silence.

Gilly stayed busy that evening. Murphy sliced open his hand on a box cutter and needed stitches. Abby Bonner brought her little girl in after she complained of a stomach ache. Joey Pierce had fallen into a patch of poison ivy and scratched himself until he'd made the rash bleed.

Lucky for the patients, Gilly had the skillset to handle each of these non-life-threatening emergencies without having to contact the doctors.

She stitched up Murphy's hand and put a warm compress on the five-year-old's belly until it stopped hurting.

She applied anti-itch cream to Joey's ugly red lesions, sending him home with his dad along with instructions on how to keep them from getting infected.

"Thanks, Gilly," Wally said as he signed paperwork.

"That's what I'm here for."

"And we're mighty glad to have our own hospital. How's Jayden?"

"Energetic as ever."

"And your mom?"

Gilly had known Wally too long not to recognize concern. She brought him up to speed on the situation.

"I knew something was wrong. She brought her car in the other day and asked me to change the oil."

"What's wrong with that?"

"She wrote down the make of the car as a Buick. Remember the Park Avenue. She thought that's what she was driving. Connie hasn't driven that thing since we had to worry about Y2K."

Gilly's heart dropped. "I don't know what else to do except wait until she gets checked out. But it seems her condition is escalating."

Wally wrapped an arm around her shoulder. "You need anything at all, you don't hesitate to call. You shouldn't go through something like this on your own."

"Thanks, Wally. But I'll be okay. You take good care of Joey."

Around midnight, she had just sat down to take a break when she heard the double automatic doors open. Letting out a sigh, she got to her feet and went out to the registration desk. It took her a couple of seconds to realize that it was Ophelia Moore, face battered with black and blue marks on both cheeks, hand prints around her throat, a cut on her forehead, and a busted lip that just kept oozing blood.

"Who on earth did this to you?" Gilly asked as she ushered the woman into an exam room.

"Please don't tell anybody," Ophelia moaned, holding her ribs.

"Who did this?" Gilly demanded, more emphatic this time.

"I think I hurt my side," Ophelia stated, ignoring Gilly's requests for information.

Gilly examined the cut over her eye and got out antiseptic from the cabinet. "It won't need stitches but it's still a deep slash on a very noticeable place on your face. Made from a ring I'm guessing."

"How did you know?"

"I can still see the imprint."

"He wears this stupid twenty-four-karat-gold ring with flashy diamonds in an onyx setting."

"Drug dealer?"

"No, just rich. He comes from a family that has more money than they know what to do with."

"And his name, Ophelia, is…?"

She started to cry. "My ex-boyfriend, Robby Ogilvie. Robert. He seems to think he can bully me into getting back together with him. I thought moving here he'd get the message."

"Bullies never just get the message. And I say that from experience. Where is he now?"

"Let's hope he's headed back to Santa Cruz."

"How long ago did this happen?"

"About an hour. My side started hurting or I would've taken care of it myself."

"Let's get you into X-ray. You do realize I'll have to report this to Brent."

"No. No. Please don't. It's embarrassing enough that I'll have to call in sick tomorrow."

Gilly took her chin. "Makeup might cover the purple, but it won't do anything about the gash on your forehead. Let's make sure your head's okay before we talk about work tomorrow."

After studying the film, Gilly put in a call to Dr. Blackwood. With the late hour, it took several rings before Quentin picked up the phone.

"Sorry to bother you this time of night, but I have a female patient who's been badly beaten about the face and head. Domestic violence situation. Her head X-ray looks okay to me, but I think you should make a determination for the record because she also has a cracked rib. And she doesn't want me calling Brent even though I told her it was required by law."

"Make the call to Brent. I think it's Eastlyn who's on duty tonight. Give me ten minutes."

After making the call to Eastlyn, Gilly turned to prep the young teacher and let her know that the police would be here soon to take her report. "He's done this before, I take it?"

"A few times, that's why I tried moving away."

"Then you know he won't stop beating on you until you report it and press charges."

"No. Don't make me do that because it won't do any good. His family has money. They'll get him off."

"You have to take a stand, Ophelia. And I have to follow the law. Eastlyn Richmond will be walking in that door any minute to take your statement. You've been attacked and beaten so badly you may not be able to go to work tomorrow. That's serious…and it's wrong for you not to be able to feel safe in your own home."

"But he'll kill me if I report this. He said so."

"And he'll kill you eventually if you don't put a stop to it. If you need somewhere safe to go, there are plenty of people who'll help you."

"Gilly's right," Eastlyn said from the doorway of the exam room. She wore her blond hair short and was dressed in a crisp blue uniform with a Glock 22 strapped to her waist. "All bullies threaten their victims to keep them silent. It's how they maintain control and keep the manipulation going. 'If you don't do what I say,'" she mimicked. "They use threats as a control thing, a 'fill in the blank' situation. 'I'll kill you, kill the kids, kill your parents,' that sort of thing. Obviously, he made a serious threat against you and we don't take that lightly."

"But I don't have children. Just the ones in my charge at the daycare center. And my mom and dad live in Lake Tahoe."

"Then it sounds like you're his main target," Eastlyn supplied. "Tell me what triggered the incident."

Ophelia took a shaky breath. "He showed up at my house around nine, begging me to come with him. He'd been drinking. When I refused, he turned mean. He always turns mean when he doesn't get his way."

Dr. Blackwood listened from the hallway and cleared his throat before making his way to the side of Ophelia's exam table. He'd seen her around town but hadn't yet met her. He held out his hand. "Quentin Blackwood. How are you feeling?"

"Stupid. I always feel stupid after he beats me up. This time he threw me against a wall."

Quentin studied the X-rays Gilly had attached to the screen. "Is that how he damaged the ribs?"

"No, that happened when he punched me."

"Do you think he's still in town?" Eastlyn said, raising her voice at that kind of brutal attack taking place on her watch. "What does he drive?"

"I'm pretty sure he took off…probably in his brand-new Porsche, one of those 911s. I have the license plate number at home if it'll help."

"That's good, but how about taking me through the details of what happened?"

Quentin held up a hand and turned to Ophelia. "Are we talking about rape here?"

Ophelia shook her head and wiped her nose. "No. But it wasn't for lack of trying. I fought him."

"Okay," he grunted and shifted back to Eastlyn. "Maybe you could question her after the examination. She suffered one broken rib, but also two others have hairline fractures, all three are around the lung."

Gilly stepped closer to the monitor. "Oh, wow. I'm glad I called you. I missed those other two."

"It's easy enough to do. See the two very thin lines, very faint. They're worrisome because they may cause her some breathing difficulty since they're in the same vicinity. It's as though this guy smashed her hard with his fist. See the circular pattern?"

"I do now," Gilly admitted.

He pivoted toward Eastlyn. "It might be easier for her to talk once I get the area wrapped. The longer I wait, the more pain she'll experience."

"Sure, Doc," Eastlyn said. "You do what you have to do and let me know when I can finish up."

Quentin swung back to the patient, got out his little flashlight, and looked into her eyes. "Pupils are fine. Any headache?"

"Maybe in the back."

"Do you remember whether or not you hit your head on the wall or the floor?"

"Both, I think. To tell you the truth I was too busy fighting him off. I know I ended up on the floor and he was on top of me, that's when he went for my face."

"We'll do a CT scan as a precaution. I'm going to admit you, Ophelia. Mainly because we'll need to watch you for any signs of concussion. Plus, you're in for several days of extreme pain. We want to make sure you're able to get that under control. After that, you'll have to deal with considerable soreness every time you move. I won't lie, rib fractures are bad, especially this close to the lung. The damage is mostly to your left side. Let us know if you have any problems breathing. And you'll need to limit your physical activity until you heal completely. Six weeks."

"Really? That long? But do I have to stay in the hospital tonight?"

"Do you have anyone at home who'll take care of you? Look after you?"

She shook her head. "No. But I'm friends with Abby Anderson. She works at the Marine Rescue Center. I could ask her if I could stay at her place."

"Tomorrow," Quentin insisted. "Abby might need to pick you up."

"I drove myself here. My car's parked outside."

"We'll see if you can drive tomorrow. For now, I see Gilly has already treated your cuts and bruises. The nasty gash on the head might not need stitches but it will require changing the bandage often." He patted her hand. "We'll get the CT scan out of the way and then you can rest. Afterward, Gilly will give you a shot for pain so you're able to get a good night's sleep."

He angled toward Eastlyn. "She's all yours after that. We appreciate you waiting."

"No problem. I've already taken a few face and throat pics for evidence, but I'll take more of the ribs. Then I'll take it to a judge to get a warrant. I'll drive over to Santa Cruz myself if I have to and pick up the rich SOB."

"Let me know when you have him in custody. I'd like to see what kind of man does this to a woman."

Before Quentin headed home, he took Gilly aside in the hallway. "Great job with the diagnosis."

"Really? But I missed those hairlines."

"Easy to do. I'm glad you called me in to evaluate."

"I hesitated since it was so late, but I decided in the end you should see the whole picture for yourself."

"Don't ever hesitate calling me. Same is true for Gideon. It comes with the territory and we know that going in. We're lucky to have you."

"Thanks for that. I feel so bad for Ophelia. He could've killed her. I wanted to quiz her more, find out why he stopped the attack? Find out why he left so abruptly? But I thought maybe Eastlyn would find that out...later."

"I'm betting on Eastlyn."

After things quieted down, Gilly asked Eastlyn those very questions.

The cop twisted up her mouth. "Ophelia says he stopped choking her because someone banged on the front door. He ran off like the big chicken he is."

"Who was at the door?"

"I'm guessing Emma Colter, Ophelia's next-door neighbor. But because Ophelia didn't answer the door, Emma went back home."

"It's a shame Emma didn't call the police. Ophelia could've used a ride to the hospital."

"Be glad she got herself here and started the ball rolling to end this," Eastlyn stated. "Now the system just has to show her it works and not let her down."

"Go get him, girl," Gilly rooted. "If you need anything from me, I could be a witness, I'm here for her."

The calm settled in, and nearing four a.m., she handed off the reins to Aubree who came on duty, yawning. After giving her the rundown on each patient, Gilly grabbed her purse. But Aubree was in the mood to talk.

"Any chance we might possibly get these hours readjusted, rethink this whole twelve-hour shift thing? I'm having trouble with getting here at four a.m. and staying until four in the afternoon. Makes for a very long day."

"Tell me about it. Maybe we should bring it up to Dr. Blackwood," Gilly said in agreement. "I'm not exactly in a position to complain, though."

"Me either. I need this job," Aubree admitted. "Maybe ten-hour shifts, four days a week would work better, though."

"I don't know. I love having those four days off."

"Not exactly like it's advertised, though, is it? Or maybe it just goes by way too fast."

"We could approach Sydney about it. Look, Aub, I'm sorry, but I gotta get some sleep. My mother's having…issues. I had to leave Jayden with Simon Bremmer last night."

Aubree's jaw dropped, her interest piqued. "Oh. My. God. Do I detect Gilly Grant inching toward an actual relationship with a man? Alert the media."

"Too early to tell," Gilly said, her mouth falling open in a huge yawn. "I'm dragging myself home and sleeping for…" she glanced at the clock on the wall. "…five glorious hours."

Fifteen

The phone rang at six a.m., bringing Simon out of a deep sleep. He picked up his phone plugged in on the nightstand to check the readout. Through brain fog, he didn't recognize the 617 area code. Newport was 401, so it wasn't his mother. Groggy, it took him a few minutes to recognize it as Boston.

"Bremmer," he grunted into the receiver.

"Mr. Bremmer, this is Margaret Tyler. I just wanted to let you know that as of last Friday the judge signed off on all Ms. Langston's estate. Probate's completed. I have the balance of the monies in her accounts---minus my fees of course---ready to hand off to you. If you'll just let me know how you want to handle the transfer, we're done until her townhouse sells."

"Um, transfer? You mean the money Delaney inherited from her mother?"

"The trust is set up, yes, with you as the executor."

"Then I guess just put the check in the mail. Will it be made out to Delaney?"

Simon could hear her impatience on the other end of the line.

"No, it's made out to you as Delaney's legal guardian and Amelia's request that you oversee the trust. How many times must I explain it to you?"

"I know what a trust is," Simon snapped.

"Well then you should know how this works. Are you sure you want me to mail the check and not send it by wire transfer?"

"No, just put it in an envelope," Simon retorted, ready to get rid of the ornery attorney and be done with her.

"Okay, if that's what you want. You should also know that I secured a mover to pack up Delaney's things and transport them to California. The truck left last Thursday so it should arrive in seven to ten days. It's been my experience that movers always give themselves a long, protracted, estimated time of arrival, so it could be sooner."

"Wait. You mean her stuff from Boston is being delivered here?"

"Well, of course. The child had furniture and toys so her entire nursery is headed your way. I'm still in the process of liquidating the rest, like the contents of Amelia's townhouse, and then after that, the townhouse itself. That'll come in separate checks. No need to bug me about it. I did leave money in the account for my expenses. I did mention that earlier. You do understand that much, right? I don't do this for free."

"Believe me, I got that part the first day I met you. Just keep me posted on all of it. I'll expect a detailed accounting of your fees, too."

After Mrs. Tyler verified his address, he disconnected the call. Disgusted because the lawyer hadn't once asked about Delaney's welfare or how she was doing in her new surroundings, he crawled out of bed in a foul mood and decided to take a shower before the kids woke up.

As soon as he cut the water off, Merlin alerted him that the troops were on the march. He quickly got dressed, forgoing a razor, and went in to check on his charges.

Jayden was already on the living room floor banging his cars into each other.

Simon ruffled the kid's hair.

"Laney's crying," the boy advised.

"Which means her lungs work really well, right? She wants out of her cage." Simon walked into the room, holding his breath and hoping he didn't have to deal with poop everywhere again.

As soon as the baby spotted him, the crying ceased and she started babbling.

"First time at daycare today. Let's dry those tears and get you looking pretty. Daddy has a group of tourists staying at the B&B from Ireland and they want to see the California coast on foot."

"Da-da," Delaney crooned.

On the way to her closet, Simon stopped in his tracks. "What did you say?"

"Da-da."

He snatched her out of the crib and hugged her to his chest, emotions of all kinds running through him. "First time you've called me that. Lots of firsts today. Let's get you into a clean diaper. Jayden, what are you into out there? You're awfully quiet."

Jayden's head popped around the doorframe. "I wanna listen to music."

"I'll be right there. What do you want for breakfast?"

"Cocoa Puffs!"

"No argument there," Simon muttered. "Who doesn't like Cocoa Puffs?" After the clean diaper went on, he set Delaney down to toddle.

As he moved through the living room, he hit the button on the CD player. Kid music blared out of the speakers.

When he reached the kitchen, he poured food in the dog's dish before going over to the cabinet to get down bowls.

The minute Jayden heard cereal dropping into his bowl, he responded by scrambling up to the table, waiting for Simon to deliver on the milk.

"I see somebody's hungry," Simon remarked, ruffling the boy's hair.

Simon got Delaney settled into her high chair, filling her bowl up with Cheerios. While the kids ate, he started a pot of much-needed coffee.

The kids were noisy. The music loud. But they ate without a fuss, which Simon celebrated as he enjoyed his first hit of caffeine.

But afterward, coaxing Jayden to put his clothes on took patience and creativity. He all but had to tackle the boy just to get him to settle down enough to dress. After finally getting the second shoe tied, it was Delaney's turn.

"Just as much of a hassle," Simon grumbled as he tried to capture her constantly moving legs and stick them down into a pair of overalls.

By the time he loaded up the truck with kids and dog and made sure each was secured in their car seats, his patience was frazzled and all he wanted to do was get on the road.

Running late, he pulled up to the Community Church and had to unbuckle and unload. As he went up the steps, River Cody hurried out the door. "Hey, Simon. How's the tourist business treating you? Oh, my God, who's this little cherub?"

"This is Delaney. You probably know Jayden."

"Oh, hey there, kiddo."

"You dropping off your brood?" Simon asked.

"Yep. I've got a meeting at the Museum with the docents from the Chumash tribe at ten and I haven't even finished my PowerPoint presentation. Brent's running down some guy who skipped out on his court date, so he couldn't help. Typical manic Monday. Where are you headed?"

"Got a bunch of tourists from Donegal County who want to compare notes on Irish cliffs versus ours."

"Lucky you. At least you aren't stuck inside on a beautiful day like today. I'm sorry, Simon, but I have to get going. That proposal has to be finished by the time the docents arrive and if I miss this window, I'll have to wait another month to get the elders to agree on a date. We'll catch up later."

"No problem. I need to get Delaney settled. I'm a little nervous. It's our first time here."

River waved him off, hot-footing it to her car in a jog. "She'll be fine. Since Ophelia took over, this place has a better teacher-to-student ratio than it did. She's hired several full-time staff members who dote on the preschoolers, giving them a lot more attention than before."

Simon took that nugget and hoped it was true because he felt like he was abandoning his daughter to the mercy of strangers. But it couldn't be helped. He looked around for Ophelia but didn't see her. Instead an older lady met him at the door.

"Hello, Jayden. Good to see you this morning."

"Miss Neenah!" Jayden yelled. The older woman laughed and turned to Simon. "I'm Neenah Brewer. Jayden's in my class. I was expecting to see Connie. She usually drops him off."

With his hands full and in a hurry, Simon merely nodded. "Then you must be used to Jayden's volume. I'm Simon Bremmer, dropping him off while Gilly gets in a few extra winks. I'm hoping Susan has room for Delaney this morning."

"Susan's classroom is down the hall, third on the left. It's Monday so I'm sure she'll have room. We're always less crowded the first two days of the week."

Simon moved on down the corridor, but as he looked back he saw that Jayden marched into Neenah's classroom like an old pro, not even taking the time to wave goodbye.

In contrast, Delaney acted timid toward Susan, a woman in her twenties with big brown eyes behind a trendy pair of glasses.

Simon surrendered his daughter to the stranger. It broke his heart when the baby began to cry and reach out for him.

"This often happens the first time," Susan said. "She'll calm down."

"I'm sorry," Simon uttered, watching his daughter turn red in the face and squirm in the woman's arms trying to get down. "I've got to go to work, honey. Daddy will be back for you this afternoon. I promise."

"She'll be fine," Susan assured him as she struggled to hold onto the writhing child who didn't want to be there and didn't want her daddy to go.

"I'll call and check on her throughout the day." Simon promised again.

"That's fine."

But those weak words didn't make him feel any better. In fact, as he walked out of the building and back to his truck, he felt like the worst dad on the planet, who'd just relinquished his daughter to a total stranger and abandoned her without a backward glance.

With Merlin riding shotgun, he fretted over it all the way to the B&B where, he found eight eager college students waiting for him to show them what California had to offer, a hike he no longer felt that enthusiastic about completing.

Gilly was pulled out of a deep sleep by a ringing phone. She reached over to the nightstand, felt around on the tabletop until she located her Smartphone. "Hello."

"Gilly, this is Quentin Blackwood. Your mother collapsed at work this morning and is in the hospital."

"Oh, no. What time is it?"

"Nine-thirty."

"How is she?"

"She's unconscious. We're about to do an MRI."

"Give me time to get dressed and I'll be there." But after she hung up, she realized she still had to run by and get Jayden. Disoriented and trying to wake up, she tried to think what to do next. Knowing Ophelia wasn't at the church, she dialed the number for Neenah Brewer.

"Neenah, it's Gilly. Mom's been taken to the hospital. Is it okay if I leave Jayden there until I find out what's going on?"

"Don't worry about Jayden, he's having the time of his life. Let me know about Connie. She's been…not herself for days."

"You noticed that too, huh? I'll text you when I know something."

Gilly slipped on jeans and a pullover top and grabbed her keys. She was out the door within seconds.

She drove fast, too fast, to get to the parking lot. While she made the walk over the bridge to get to the automatic front doors, it occurred to her that she'd just left this place hours earlier.

Aubree came running up and ushered her into Connie's empty exam room. "She's not here. Quentin took her to get the scan done."

"How was she? Did she say anything?"

Aubree shook her head and clasped Gilly's hand in hers. "She'll be okay. Her vitals were within normal range."

"Then I don't understand what's wrong with her?"

"She'll be okay. Dr. Nighthawk and Dr. Blackwood are both in with her."

During the wait for answers, Gilly called Simon, but it went directly to voicemail. "When you get this message, call me. My mom's in the hospital. I'm here now. Jayden's still at daycare with Delaney. Call me."

Gilly ended the call to pace. Even though she knew Nighthawk's credentials were stellar and her mother was in good hands, it didn't keep her from biting her nails.

Gideon Nighthawk had completed his residency at Northwestern Memorial Hospital, a Level I trauma center in the downtown section of Chicago, staying on as one of their staff neurosurgeons until one of his best friends made him an offer he couldn't refuse.

Quentin's call came at a time when Gideon wanted out of the traffic and the bitter cold of the Midwest. His colleagues had warned him that leaving for a small-time post in California was a major step down in his career. But Gideon didn't see it like that. Small town folks deserved quality medical care just like those living in the urban sprawl.

He was determined to provide that care and shared Quentin's dedication to do so. It's what made them a great team.

On the other end of worry, Gilly stood outside the X-ray wing until she saw Gideon emerge through the steel doors.

He held up his hands. "I just looked over your mother's CT scan. It's not a tumor and it isn't Alzheimer's."

"Thank God. So what's wrong with her?"

"She has what's known as normal pressure hydrocephalus or NPH."

"I've never heard of it and I'm a nurse."

"Most people haven't. That's because its symptoms mimic Alzheimer's, Parkinson's, or Creutzfeldt-Jakob disease. The treatment is completely different for NPH so it gets misdiagnosed. Some doctors think they're treating one of the big three when what they're dealing with is NPH, which continues to impair the brain's motor function until it manifests as dementia and then slowly robs the body of mobility."

Gilly ran a hand through her hair. "I see why it's misdiagnosed. What is it exactly?"

"It causes a gradual buildup of cerebrospinal fluid in the brain, which messes with the normal flow of fluid and ends up blocking the receptors. Over time, it causes memory loss, a change in personality, the inability to control muscles, and therefore eventually leads to incontinence. It can also affect hand-eye coordination to the point that holding a pen or using the fingers becomes increasingly difficult."

"Memory loss and a couple of those other things sound exactly like Alzheimer's and the symptoms Mom's been having—not being able to remember things, walking around in the yard in her gown, erratic behavior. What causes it?"

"Stroke, meningitis, a blow to the head, bleeding around the brain or brain tumor."

"Wait. She did recently fall outside the drug store. She tripped and fell off the curb. I'm thinking she might've hit her head. Could that have been the cause?"

"Possibly. But if she fell, she might've been having problems that made her fall. She didn't see a doctor?"

"No. She had a few scrapes and bruises but refused to get checked out. Look, bottom line is, what do we do about this?"

"The good news is NPH is treatable."

"And that is...?"

"I make an incision and put in a permanent shunt that should take care of the excess fluid."

Gilly made a face. "That leaves the fluid to drain..."

"Into the abdomen," Gideon said with a nod, "Where it's absorbed in the..."

"Routine circulatory process," Gilly finished for him. "I get it. What else?"

"In due time, she can resume her normal physical activities. But I doubt she'll ever be able to go back to nursing full-time unless it's a situation where she doesn't have to have pinpoint accuracy."

"In other words, giving shots and drawing blood are likely behind her."

"I'm afraid so."

"So basically, it's good news, bad news."

"I'm sorry. I thought you'd be glad it was treatable."

"Oh, I am. It's just that...what kind of nursing doesn't require the whole package? I'll have to break it to her that...her nursing career is over." Gilly cut her eyes to Quentin, who'd been standing to the side, listening. "At least you know she wasn't being rude on purpose and the reason was something medical that she couldn't help." She blinked back tears. "In my gut, I knew something had to be wrong, enough that it had her acting so...weird."

Quentin put his hand on her shoulder. "I'm truly sorry, Gilly. I'll stop in to see Connie after her surgery."

Gideon exchanged looks with Quentin. "Cancel the rest of your appointments and suit up. You're assisting."

Even though Quentin couldn't handle a scalpel with the precision he'd once had, he'd been trained in anesthesia. It was the one area where he could contribute during surgery.

Gilly turned back to Gideon. "Did she wake up during the MRI? Can I talk to her before she goes in?"

"Absolutely," Gideon said, watching her walk off toward Connie's exam room.

After she'd gone, Gideon scratched his chin. "I don't understand why she had such a long face. I thought she'd be glad to know the shunt will make her mother better."

Quentin slapped his colleague on the back. "You have a lot to learn about the human psyche. Connie Grant spent most of her adult life doing what she loved to do. Nursing was her passion. As someone who used to be a highly-touted trauma surgeon and had to morph into becoming a country doctor, I understand how Connie will take the news. Now she has to accept another stage in her life, one completely different than the one she's used to. Just like I did. At any age, that's a hard pill to swallow."

Around noon, while Gilly waited for her mother to come out of surgery, she saw Quentin and Aubree discharge Ophelia Moore. The teacher, dealing with a black and blue face and a busted mouth, checked out surrounded by her friends, Abby Anderson and Jessica St. John.

"If you need anything," Gilly began, squeezing Ophelia's hand. "Don't hesitate to call."

"She's with us now," Jessica said, arm around Ophelia's waist. "I called Wally to change the locks and Troy to rebuild the door where that asshole broke it down. Eastlyn already finished her investigation and let us know it was okay to go back inside."

"But we aren't," Abby added, "going back inside, that is. Not until the new locks are installed. Ophelia's staying with me until she feels better."

"She can barely walk as it is," Jessica pointed out.

"She's lucky to have friends like you two," Gilly said.

"She's lucky that asshole didn't kill her," Abby muttered.

"Next time he just might," Jessica uttered.

"There won't be a next time," Ophelia assured them through swollen lips. "Eastlyn talked me into taking out a restraining order."

Abby rolled her eyes. "Yeah, well, I've heard protection orders just make them madder and more dangerous. He tries coming around my place and he's in for a big surprise. An old boyfriend left me his baseball bat when he moved out. I'd just love to take a swing at Robby Ogilvie."

"Be careful what you wish for," Jessica cautioned. "The guy is seriously whacked."

Sixteen

Simon's Irish companions were in awe of the cliffs and the coastline. He knew because they'd taken tons of pictures to document their outing and couldn't stop talking his ear off about the scenery. The group had tried, to no avail, to use their cell phones to update their social media accounts with the glowing comments about their experience but couldn't understand why they lacked service. "I thought America had cell phone towers everywhere."

"We lost the nearest one a few miles back," Simon explained to the twenty-something young woman with flame-red hair and a penchant for asking dozens of questions. "Surely, you don't want us to stick a cell tower on a scenic overlook and mar the beauty. Don't worry. Now that we're on our way back, we should pick up service in less than thirty minutes."

"You've done this before?" the woman named Fiona replied in a brogue so thick Simon sometimes had trouble understanding her.

"I trekked over this same ground a hundred times since moving here. The thing is I always find some angle that's different than before and see something special on each trip that I didn't see on the last one."

"I love the California coast better than I thought I would," the girl they called Christy admitted.

"What brought all of you here?"

"My boyfriend booked us on a summer tour, bumming around the countryside, seeing America for the first time. Pelican Pointe is the best place we've seen so far."

Simon could relate. But as enjoyable as the hike had been, he was anxious to get within range of the tower to check his texts and messages. He'd been expecting a call from Gilly, or maybe an update from the daycare on Delaney, and certainly news from Quentin about the results of the paternity test. He'd also left Merlin behind with Quake.

But when they got closer to the B&B, there was nothing on his phone except several voicemails from Gilly about her mother.

He picked up his pace through the hilly scrub. But behind him, some of his charges were beginning to tire and drag. "Come on, guys. Just a few more miles and you'll be back soaking your feet in your posh rooms. I promise you Mrs. Harris will have a nice supper waiting. If it's Monday, the menu is pot roast and mashed potatoes."

"Like shepherd's pie back home?" one of them wanted to know.

"Yeah. But better," Simon said with a wink.

When he finally reached the courtyard, Merlin ran up to greet him like he'd been away for a dozen years. Simon grabbed the dog around the collar and plopped down in one of the chairs to return Gilly's calls while the others headed inside. With the privacy he'd been craving, he punched in her number. "Hey, how's your mom?"

"Out of surgery and resting. No need to go by the church because Neenah Brewer took the kids home with her."

"Then I'll head there and pick them up."

"Are you sure, Simon? You don't have to take Jayden."

"Well, it's up to you, but I don't mind taking him home with me. Delaney seems to like having him around."

"But isn't he too hyper for you?"

"Nah. He's just an inquisitive kid with a ton of energy."

That answer made her flush with pleasure. "As long as you're sure. I don't want you to think I'm pushing him off on you."

"I don't think that at all."

"Then Neenah lives on Cape May." She gave him the address. "You can always stop by and pick up my house key from the hospital and gather up more clothes for him."

"Will your mom be okay?"

"Her vitals are good, but she'll have to stay here for at least another three days to see how the shunt does."

"Are you okay? Need me to bring you anything?"

Again, her heart felt like it flipped in her chest. "Food. I could use a burger from the Diner and some fries."

Simon could hear her stomach rumble through the phone. "You got it. Anything for your mom?"

"She's not able to eat that kind of greasy food yet."

"Okay, then I'll pick up the kids, grab the burgers, and we'll all eat together. Plan to take your break in about an hour." He thought about stopping by Blackwood's office and altered his arrival time. "On second thought, add half an hour to that. I need to talk to Quentin."

"He's here at the hospital. Want me to mention that you need to talk?"

"That would be great. See you in an hour."

It took Simon the entire hour to run all the errands and reach the hospital around suppertime. Gilly ran out to the parking lot to greet them. "How's my gang doing?" she said, scooping Jayden up in a hug.

"Mama!"

"How's my big boy? Are you being good for Simon?"

Jayden bobbed his head.

They made their way inside to the breakroom where Simon unpacked the food.

"Eat first or see Quentin?" Gilly asked. "I can see you're anxious."

"How long will he be here? I don't want to miss him and have to go to his house for my answer. I thought he'd call."

"Probably until eight. He's been wrapped up in a patient dealing with stomach issues."

"Then let's eat first and hope I catch him before he leaves."

Simon had learned by now that meals with kids were never dull---an overturned sippy cup, a messy face that needed swiping, all the contagious giggles and laughter that seemed to accompany eating with toddlers. For a solitary guy, the disordered hubbub should've been annoying. But Simon found a kind of comfort in the racket.

Tonight, Gilly seemed the same. She ran her fingers through Jayden's hair as he nibbled a fry. "I have to work tonight and Grandma is here with me."

"Is Grandma sick?"

"She's feeling better, but she won't be able to look after you tonight, maybe not for several more days.

Do you want to stay with Simon and Delaney again? Would that be okay?"

Jayden bobbed his head.

"Is he sleeping okay?"

Simon scratched his chin. "I think so. I put him to bed and he stayed there until morning. Merlin found him playing in the living room."

"He gets up early."

"So does Delaney. You'd think they were both in the Army. Look, I need to corner Quentin before he leaves. Where's his office?"

"Go around behind the reception area, first door on the left."

After settling Delaney on his hip, he started out of the room. "I'll be right back. It'll give you some alone time with Jayden."

Quentin was standing outside his office talking to his wife when he spotted Simon. "I was expecting you to call. You didn't have to hunt me down, I would've phoned you tonight."

"It's already tonight. I couldn't wait any longer," Simon declared. "I've waited for a week as it is."

Sydney sent him a smile and ran a hand across Delaney's mop of golden hair. "I'll leave you guys alone then. Want me to entertain your little monkey?"

"Do you have that kind of time?"

"I'll make time," Sydney declared, taking the toddler out of Simon's arms. "If you need us, we'll be playing nurse."

Quentin rounded his desk and opened a file folder. "I'm not gonna build up to the results. You're Delaney's father, plain and simple. DNA markers line up perfect as a match."

"I figured as much. Even though my blood type is B positive?"

Quentin nodded. "Even though. As I said on Friday, the mother was probably either A or O. What's important is that now we're certain about Delaney's blood type. Yours too. And prepared for anything medical down the road. Aside from that, there's no mistake about the DNA. You did father that child."

Simon blew out a breath. "Whew!"

Quentin smiled. "Good to know it's a relief. How's her ear?"

"She's better. The antibiotics have helped. I feel like I should...do something...celebrate. But Gilly is here at work and I'm helping her out babysitting Jayden. With all that going on, I don't think Gilly will feel much like partying during her free time, at least not until the weekend gets here."

"Let me guess, Connie doesn't approve."

"You got it. Still not sure why."

"Don't take it personal. Now that we have a diagnosis, Connie may go back to her old self again," Quentin explained. "It could happen."

"Is there a possibility she won't?"

"Since you aren't family, I'm not allowed to discuss Connie's specifics, other than her procedure went well. It's wait and see now."

"For Gilly's sake, I hope she has a complete recovery."

"We all do," Quentin said. Getting to his feet, he changed the topic back to parenthood. "I'm glad to know you're happy about the paternity results. Since Sydney and I adopted Beckham we're experiencing a whole new area of our lives. Nothing about it is easy, though."

Simon got a brief glimpse of horror...Delaney growing up and hitting puberty. "Oh, my God, she'll be a teenager one day. I'll have to fight off boys."

Quentin slapped him on the back. "Circle of life, my friend. Learn to deal. Having kids is a whole other experience."

"So I'm learning on the job." Simon shook Quentin's hand and left to go find his daughter. *His daughter.* Instead of dwelling on why Amelia had chosen to cut him out of the picture, he focused on the present and the future.

He couldn't wait to share the test results with Gilly.

She took the news in total Gilly fashion. "We should throw you a party. As soon as Mom is back home and able to function, I'll get Jordan to help me with the food. No one caters a shower better than Jordan."

"A shower? You mean for a baby? But I'm a guy."

"But you're still in need of baby things."

"Not sure I could sit through that. Besides, that lawyer is supposed to be sending her stuff here." He gave her a chaste smack on the lips. "We'll talk about it later. I've gotta get the kids to bed. When my mother gets to town, maybe you'll let me take you out to dinner."

"You mean like a real date without the kids?" She tilted her head with newfound interest at the prospect. "When is your mom getting here exactly?"

"I'm picking her up from the airport on Thursday."

"Are you working tomorrow?"

"Nope. Not unless something last minute pops to the top. I'll have all day to spend with the kids."

"I'll walk you to the car. Come on, Jayden. Mama has to get back to work. You be good for Simon tonight. Okay? Go right to sleep after your story. Promise me. No getting up playing with your action figures."

Jayden's face puckered up before he stuck out his lower lip in disappointment. "Aww."

Simon traded a glance with Gilly and then bursted out laughing. "Your kid is a riot. He gets these looks on his face like he's practicing his actor poses."

"I know. He's like a miniature Leo DiCaprio."

Later, after the kids were asleep, Simon put in a call to Logan. "I want the house on Tradewinds."

"Nick said you needed time to think it over."

"I've thought it over and I need a house. The farm's noisy for a kid and because it's commercial, there are a lot of trucks going in and out of the gate. It isn't safe for a toddler."

"I have other houses for sale. I could email you the list. Look over the descriptions and the locations and see which one fits the bill."

"Nah. I want this one. I've never bought a house before, how does this work?"

Logan went through the steps, but added, "Nick says you were preapproved and that makes the paperwork so much easier. You've already done the hard part, now you basically sign away your life to a thirty-year mortgage at closing. It takes a few weeks because the loan department at the bank is so backed up. Nick's looking for help, but so far he hasn't found anyone willing to move here."

"Is that the hold up? No one wants to live here? Their loss. Will you let me know when it's time to sign the offer letter? In this case, there's no real estate agent to ask."

"I have a standard letter I've used in the past. I'd say get a lawyer, but that would be my wife, so whether it comes from me or Kinsey, it's the same letter."

"Let's get the ball rolling because I'm ready to move on this."

Simon went to bed happy about his decision but beat. It had been a long day and he was ready to crawl between the sheets.

Needing shuteye, he unwillingly slid into nightmares that were forever dragging him back to where he didn't want to go.

The wind whipped through the arid desert blowing dust so thick the eyes had a hard time getting a fix on the target.

But focus he did.

Protecting convoys came with a deadly aim and Simon had one. Sitting atop a hill, overlooking the village, Eagle Eye scanned the horizon for any movement. They knew the 1st Battalion would be rolling in with supplies at any moment. It was their job to make sure there was no ambush, no surprises from the enemy.

Eagle Eye went on alert and pointed toward two men crawling belly-first on the ground at a thousand yards.

Simon couldn't get the image out of his head. It seemed too much for a twenty-year-old to handle, even if that young man had been a swaggering, tough guy with a big mouth. He'd been too naïve to think it wouldn't affect him. But it had been his first kills, two Taliban shooters creeping in from an odd angle. They wouldn't be his last. Nor would it be the last time he'd experience flesh and bone disintegrating right before his eyes. A .50 caliber tended to damage anything beyond repair, least of all a human being.

If he wasn't reliving those images, there were the firefights, up close, personal. Sangin. Helmand. Ganjgul. Gunfire erupting from all sides. Facing off with the enemy, often armed with AK-47s. And all the ambushes they'd walked into, leaving them surrounded, outgunned, outnumbered.

Simon woke in a sweat, trembling. He felt fur and realized Merlin's head rested on the side of the bed. It was like the dog knew his distress and had come over to comfort him.

"You're a good boy, aren't you?"

The dog woofed.

Simon patted the side of the bed and the Newfie hopped up, curling into his side. Simon wrapped the dog up, resting his head on Merlin's, glad for the company, and hoping to drift back to sleep.

Working the graveyard shift didn't come without its eerie spookiness that often occurred somewhere around the witching hour. Having grown up in town, Gilly had long been aware that the hospital had once been a working cannery, abandoned for decades after the business fell on hard times. It had remained in that rundown condition until Quentin had moved to town and acted on the brilliant idea to turn the place into a state of the art treatment center.

Even now, she could hear the water lapping at the pilings where Logan and his crew had structurally reinforced the beams. But that hardly compared to the noises she sometimes heard coming from the lower level, an old, dark, and dank storage area that could still make her conjure up ghosts and goblins---and that was during daylight hours. She never went down there while she was on duty. It was just too creepy.

Even the fog that rolled in and engulfed the building could often get the imagination spinning into overdrive on those quiet nights when the place was devoid of sick people. She could usually look out over the water and enjoy the serene setting. But on those nights when the mist was especially thick and heavy, its color could change from green to blue depending on the whip of the wind.

Having had his own brush with death in a hospital parking lot, Quentin made sure there were surveillance cameras inside and out. He often stressed that security was of the utmost importance. And since the police chief lived right across the street, Brent Cody had assured him that patrols would be a routine practice. That's mainly why Gilly could do her job without spending long hours alone and afraid.

But tonight, something had her feeling uneasy, like she was being watched. She was alone in the half-circle reception area, but not alone in the building. Her mother was still down the corridor in room number 3, and Prissie Gates, who'd been admitted earlier, slept soundly in room number 4.

She checked the cameras outside but saw no movement on the bridge or in the parking lot. She rechecked all the hallways but saw nothing out of the ordinary. After going over the entire building via surveillance, she headed to the breakroom to get a bottle of water, assuring herself that she was simply edgy from lack of sleep.

Afraid he was back in the fight, Simon shot straight up again, wide awake, sweat beading off his face and trickling down to his neck.

When he kicked off the covers, he heard Merlin whine.

"Sorry, boy. It's just a dream," Simon reminded himself. He was here, not back in a war zone. He swung his legs around and started to get to his feet when he spotted Scott sitting in that same chair in the corner.

"Do you ever knock?" Simon groaned, holding his head in his hands.

"What would be the point?"

"Invading a person's privacy like this is so…wrong."

"You needed to talk."

"How do you know? Never mind. I don't want to know. On second thought, how long do these nightmares last?"

"Over time, they fade, but you'll never completely be rid of them."

"Gee, thanks. You really know how to give a pep talk. Not."

"You've had your share of them through the years. Gung ho. Military-style. You don't need another one from me. If you're worried that Gilly won't understand, she will."

"How do you know? Are you having conversations with her now, too?"

"There's no safe way to approach a single mom. But suffice to say, I watch out for her, especially when she's alone at night at the hospital."

Simon's hard edge, softened. "Damn. You're a regular invisible sentry. Thanks for that."

"It's what I do."

"What else do you do besides watch over Hutton?"

"She'll always come first. But there are so many here that need a little guidance. It never hurts to offer a helping hand."

"I should text Gilly."

"That'd be nice. But then you'd have to explain why you're up at this hour."

"You said she'd understand, right?"

Scott smiled. "Don't text. Call her. You're here for a reason."

"Why do you keep saying that?" But there was only silence. Simon glanced over at the empty chair. "Damn, that's annoying."

He picked up his phone and punched in Gilly's mobile. "Hey, what are you up to?"

She smiled at the sound of his voice. "I'm rethinking working these hours in such a small hospital. I'm hearing things."

Simon's spine straightened. "Like what? Is someone bothering you?"

She laughed. "No, that's just it, there's no one here. This is an old building and I think it might be haunted."

If only he could tell her that ghosts were not unfamiliar to him. He knew all about seeing the faces of the dead. "Want me to come over and sit with you?"

She went into a little happy dance, knowing he couldn't while watching the kids, but loving the idea of him showing up to protect her. "Sure," she said, playing along. "Be sure to wear your armor. I couldn't bear the thought of you getting hurt."

"Me? It's you I'm afraid will get hurt acting all Florence Nightingale."

"But you're the one risking life and limb going into battle. It's probably a good thing that I didn't know you when you were a soldier. I'd worry constantly. How did your mother handle that?"

He leaned back into his pillow, beginning to relax. "You can ask her when she comes to town. By the way, what are you wearing? Scrubs I hope. You look so sexy in them."

That had her giggling. "I'm not sure anyone's ever thought scrubs were sexy."

"Then I'm the first. I love your hazel eyes with just the right amount of brown around the fringes. They get darker whenever you get flustered."

"You noticed my eyes?"

"The first time I saw you."

"The first time you were pretty wound up dealing with Delaney."

"Doesn't mean I didn't notice the cute way you moved."

Heating up, she said the first thing that popped into her head. "I could stand to lose a few pounds."

"Why? You're perfect the way you are."

"Wait a minute, is this conversation for real? Maybe I fell asleep hours ago, and I'm really dreaming."

"Gilly, you're beautiful. How is it you don't know that?"

"History."

"Forget history. I thought I was the one plagued by demons."

"Nope. Just a different kind."

Seventeen

On Wednesday, Gilly brought Connie home from the hospital and dealt with all the friends who stopped by to wish her mother well. Margie brought one of Max's pies and offered to sit with her friend or help her get around if need be. Neenah Brewer offered to clean the house anytime she needed it. And Emma Colter had knitted her a pink and blue cap to cover up her shaved head.

"There now, you look pretty in pink and blue," Emma drawled, trying not to stare at the huge bare spot on the right side of Connie's head behind her ear.

"I'd planned on getting a haircut anyway," Connie shot back. "I just wish Abby could've prettied me up before I came home."

"You have to let the incision heal," Gilly said, swatting her mom's hand away from the bandage. "Stop acting like you're Jayden's age. Leave the thing alone."

"It itches," Connie complained for the umpteenth time.

Margie noticed Gilly's frustration and steered her out of the bedroom. "Look, take Jayden and get out of here for a little while. You need a breather. I'll sit with your mom."

Gilly looked at the older woman, her hair no longer as red as it used to be. "What about the Diner?"

"Max has things covered. I wouldn't be here otherwise. Connie is my oldest friend. She once sat up all night with me when I had the flu. That was fifteen years ago, and this is the first time the woman's been in a position where I can pay her back. Now go home and relax. I'll stay with her tonight."

"The entire night?"

"That's what I said."

Gilly was so thrilled she grabbed Margie in a hug. "You have no idea how much this means to me. I needed some downtime."

"I know you do. You've been at the hospital almost round the clock. Get out of here and get some rest."

"Thank you."

Downtime meant she could soak in a tub once she got Jayden to bed. But as she started for her mother's front door, she bumped smack dab into Simon standing on the stoop, carrying a sack of groceries.

"Hey, I thought I'd cook supper for everybody. I have spaghetti fixins in here."

Margie came up behind Gilly. "Great idea. Gilly's headed home. You can fix dinner for her and Jayden. I have things covered here."

The expression on Simon's face said if he could, he would've kissed Margie and spun her into a jig. "No problem. I can cook there as well as here."

Margie all but pushed Gilly and her boy out the door. "Y'all have a good time."

After they left, Margie headed back into Connie's bedroom. "I know you don't like Simon, but that man has the hots for your daughter."

Connie leaned her head back on the pillow and sighed. "That was him, wasn't it? He just keeps trying to worm his way in."

"A man that good-looking can worm his way into my bed any time."

"Margie! What would Max do if he heard you talking like that?"

"Probably get me one of them nice romantic dinners and a movie and then an early night to bed."

Connie shook her head. "I should've known you'd make this all about sex. I'm just trying to talk some sense into Gilly," she pointed out in her own defense. "I don't want her getting hurt again. That's all."

"Have you seen the way he looks at her? If you have, you wouldn't worry about it. Do I have to remind you that he showed up to make dinner for all of you? What kind of a guy does that these days? Not many. You ought to give him a chance, Connie. Gilly adores the man. I can tell. I've known her since she was Jayden's age and she's smitten."

Connie groaned. "That's what I'm afraid of."

Down the block, Simon stood at the stove pushing a spoon through his thick marinara sauce, a recipe he'd begged out of his mother before she'd packed for her trip and headed west.

Gilly stood next to him, dropping thin spaghetti into a big pot of boiling water. "It's so sweet of you to do this."

"Cook dinner? I feel responsible for ruining your last batch of Bolognese. That night Delaney barreled in like a tornado and destroyed Jayden's fort, I thought we might go to war. And I feel like I owe you for pointing me to the house down the street."

"Does that mean you've decided to buy it?"

He nodded, pulling the spoon out dripping with sauce and holding it up for her to taste. "I put in my offer letter, so the paperwork is crunching. Here, try this." He slid the spoon past her lips.

"Very good. Wow. That might be better than mine."

As she licked her lips, he moved closer, savoring the moment. "The least I can do is cook dinner. Besides, you've been stressed out with everything going on. And we all have to eat, might as well do it together."

She leaned in and nibbled on the side of his jaw. "You're making it more difficult by the minute for me to resist you."

"Why would you want to?"

"Why indeed? I'd better set the table." After rattling plates down from the cabinet, she grabbed silverware out of the drawer. "We're having a fundraiser for the hospital the last week of October."

"I heard."

"Sydney put me in charge of planning the theme. I had this idea. Tell me if you think it's corny."

Simon dished up the sauce and waited. "Well? I have to hear it first before I can make the call."

"Everyone will be wearing costumes anyway because it's near Halloween. So instead of tuxedos and formal wear, I thought it would be really cool to throw a masquerade ball, you know, like they did back in the 17th century."

Simon winced at the notion of wearing a silly get-up with feathers and a mask. But he saw the excitement on her face and didn't have the heart to shoot down the idea. "Could I dress in all-black and just put a mask over my face?"

"Sure. I guess." She went back over to the stove and ran her hands around his shoulders and down his arms. "But a really supportive guy would go all in and at least wear a ruffled shirt, maybe a wig."

"I'm not wearing a wig. That's non-negotiable. And I'm pretty sure I speak for most of the men in town."

She batted her eyes. "How about one of those Venetian hats?"

"No. Dressing up like Dread Pirate Roberts is the best I can do. All black. A bandana on my head."

"Westley from *Princess Bride*? Deal." She stuck out her hand to shake.

"You totally maneuvered me into that, didn't you?" he said, nibbling on her fingers.

"Me? Let's eat. I'm suddenly starving."

After wrangling the kids to the table, when they finally sat down, he noticed Gilly picking at her food. "Don't like it?"

"It isn't that. It's probably better than mine."

"Then what's wrong?"

"I'm just trying to lose a few pounds. I've been eating like a horse lately and I want to be able to fit into the ball gown I have in mind." The last thing she wanted to admit was that she wanted to look her very best when they finally slept together.

"Gilly, you're not overweight."

"How would you know? You haven't seen me…you know…without clothes."

His eyes locked on hers because he suddenly was ignoring the kids. "As fantastic as that would be, I'm looking at you right now. You're beautiful.

Gorgeous." He held up his hands. "But you should do what you want to do."

"Maybe I'll start jogging or exercising more. I've been a slug lately."

"When have you had the time?" Realizing there was no point to arguing, he changed the subject. "My mom will want to meet you while she's here."

"She'll be here for a week, right?"

"Something like that. And since I want to take you out Saturday night, if you need her to look after Jayden, I think there's no reason to get a sitter."

"She can handle two?"

"She used to teach school. She can handle kids."

Afterward, there were messy faces to scrub, sticky fingers to clean, and runny noses to wipe. With dinner over and cleanup done, they headed outside to the backyard where the kids could run around the sycamore trees and tire themselves out.

Gilly and Simon supervised from the old picnic table, the one she'd dragged down the street from her mother's house. "My dad built this thing. It has great sentimental value. I carved my name into the wood on the other end the day he finished it. See?"

Simon spotted the name written in block letters. "How old were you?"

"Six."

There was also a plus sign with another name next to hers. "Who's Rudy?"

"My first boyfriend. We were eight. He added his name without me knowing it. I came outside one day to swing and there he was, whittling away on the family picnic table. I thought it was cute. My dad wasn't so understanding."

"What was it like growing up here?"

"Nothing much happened. Or so we thought. Turns out, we had a scandalous mayor no one knew about. That would be Quentin's uncle. And a serial killer who used to bury some of his victims up near the old lighthouse. Logan's sister was one of his victims."

"Wow. And I thought you were going to say it was like Mayberry. That puts a whole new spin on what happens behind closed doors."

"There was also a double homicide that happened under the pier. Cooper Richmond's father was shot and killed by his own mother. She also killed his teacher."

"This just keeps getting creepier."

"Every town has its secrets." Gilly thought of poor Ophelia and decided she needed to stop by and check on her.

When Jayden got stuck trying to go down the slide, Simon got to his feet and went over to help him out, leaving Gilly to stare at the man's backside all the way across the yard.

Lordy, she thought, he did fill out a tight pair of jeans. She counted the years since she'd had sex and audibly groaned at the number. She started mentally preparing for the day or night when she and Simon could hit the sheets. It couldn't be Saturday night. What would his mother think of her if she stayed out all night on their very first official date only to do the walk of shame the next morning to pick up Jayden? No way could they sleep together Saturday night. Or could they? Maybe she could bring Simon back here to the house after dinner.

After all, he didn't have to spend the night. And if she got someone else to babysit Jayden for the entire night, she wouldn't have to face his mother. It might work.

She sighed as she watched him swing Jayden around in a dizzying circle, then tickle his belly when her boy plopped to the ground in uncontrollable laughter. She couldn't help it. Her belly slid further into lust. Her heart filled with emotions she couldn't stop, feelings she'd tried to quash, but couldn't.

If she had decided to sleep with him, then she'd have to go shopping for new underwear and maybe a new dress for Saturday night. Her mind started spinning with a to-do list. She might not be able to drop a single pound in three days, but if she planned it right, she'd keep him so busy he wouldn't notice.

Simon caught her zoning out. "You look deep in thought. What were you thinking about just now?"

Your ass, she wanted to say. Instead, she smiled and met his eyes. "We have two sweaty kids to get ready for bed. Just how long have you known that you're good with kids?"

Simon nipped her around the waist. "About as long as I've known you." He pressed his lips to hers and lingered there until he made her breathless. "If my mother weren't coming to town... I'm ready for Saturday night to get here."

She patted his chest. "You aren't the only one."

Eighteen

Just shy of her sixtieth birthday, Gretchen Bremmer walked down the jetway and followed the signs to the lower level. Fit and trim, with a crop of short, sandy blond hair, a few strands turning gray, she looked like she played tennis every other day and hosted bridge club to take up the slack.

Neither was accurate.

She'd once had an active social life, mostly heading committees doing her part for charity. But since becoming a widow, all that had changed. She spent her days taking care of a sister she adored who was locked in a world of dementia and would never find her way out. With all her heart, Gretchen believed her sister deserved private care so she refused to pack her off to a home that specialized in long-term situations.

Her life had taken that turn, but Gretchen Bremmer was not a complainer.

She'd spent the last two years trying to stay in shape on the faint hope that one day she'd be able to run around after grandkids. With an only child and one who didn't even date all that much, her prospects were looking mighty slim. That is, until Simon's phone call. And now, here she was on California soil about to meet her granddaughter.

The skycap helped her roll her luggage through baggage claim and out the double doors to the curb. She tipped the porter with a ten-spot and texted Simon to let him know where she stood waiting. He texted back the make and model of the truck he'd bought since their last phone call. In subsequent efforts to get her here for a visit, she'd balked at riding on the back of a motorcycle. If she made the effort to visit, he promised he'd rent a car to haul her around for the duration. Still she'd stayed put in Newport.

But now she was here. And when she finally spotted the pickup, she got his attention in typical Gretchen fashion. She put her fingers between her teeth and let out a whistle.

Simon pulled to the curb, hopped out, wrapped her up in a quick bear hug, the only kind that TSA walking the beat allowed, before snatching up the oversized bag, and tossing it into the bed of the pickup. "What've you got in this thing? It weighs a ton."

"I brought presents so be careful how you throw it around."

"Stuff in here breaks? What did you bring, Mom?"

"You'll just have to wait and see and be surprised." She settled into the front seat as Merlin woofed in greeting. "How's my big handsome boy doing?" she asked, scratching under his chin.

"I take it you don't mean me. Hear that, Merlin? You get the handsome boy before I do."

"Why on earth didn't you buy one of those minivans instead of a truck?"

"Because I'm not driving around town in a minivan."

She pivoted in her seat, angled where she could try and get a good look at the baby. "My God, Simon, she's absolutely gorgeous. But you already knew that, didn't you, baby girl?" She tugged on a little tennis shoe, grabbing hold of a toe. "Why is she facing backward like that? I'm not allowed to look at my grandchild?"

"State law," Simon announced and turned in his seat to get Delaney's attention. "What shall we call Grandma-ma, Delaney? Any ideas?"

"Ma-ma," Delaney piped up, clapping her hands.

"She says that a lot, and Ma-ma's not around," Simon explained.

"That's just so heartbreaking. My only grandchild is motherless."

"I know. But if Amelia hadn't had the accident, both of us would still be in the dark about Delaney's existence. Think about that."

"I have, all the way from Rhode Island. What a cruel thing to do to the father of her child."

"You don't know the half of it. But we'll talk about it later. I know all Amelia's secrets now because I had her investigated."

From the back seat, Delaney sang out in a string of baby babble.

"She's very vocal," Gretchen said proudly. "That's a good sign."

"Yeah, if only I knew what she was trying to say. By my count she knows a handful of words. Bye, Ma-ma, yes, no, and I think something that sounds like 'more.' Oh, and the other day, she said Da-Da."

"How thrilling. Maybe she'll say it for me."

"She understands other words and phrases, like 'go get your shoes' and it's apparent she likes books."

"Good, because her Nana brought her a few."

"Nana?"

"That's right, what's wrong with Nana? I think it suits me. It's better than Grandma-ma. What do you think, Delaney? You like Nana?"

But Delaney kept babbling in sing-song fashion.

"That's okay, honey. You talk Daddy's ear off. Payback. That's what he did to your Nana when he was a little boy."

"How about some lunch?"

"I'm famished. I still can't get used to the airlines not feeding you anymore on a cross-country flight."

Simon squeezed his mother's hand. "We'll get you fed and then get you settled in at home. We have lots to talk about."

He took her to a sidewalk café along the boardwalk that Brent Cody had recommended where they could sit and look out with a view of the ocean and bring Merlin along.

"I can see why you like it here. It reminds me of early Newport," she commented as she fed Delaney part of a peanut butter and jelly sandwich off the kids' menu.

"It does, doesn't it? I want to introduce you around to the people I've met. I think you'll like them."

"And what about this Gilly? I want to meet her, too."

"Don't worry, you will. First things first. I want you to enjoy yourself while you're here. You need a break from taking care of Lorraine."

"It felt so weird leaving her behind this morning when the taxi drove away from the house. I got to the airport and almost had second thoughts about coming."

"I knew you would. I wasn't even sure you'd follow through until I got your text from the plane that you'd boarded."

"It's been such a tough two years, Simon. Everything I knew has changed. Your father's not around to lean on so I've had to go my own way on a lot of things. It's been rough without you there, too."

"I'm sorry, Mom, but I just couldn't stay back east. I couldn't. After the Army I needed a completely different change of scenery. Nick and Cord persuaded me that to get a brand-new start, I'd be better off here. Starting my business from the B&B has been a leg up that I couldn't have gotten back in Newport."

"I know that. A good mother doesn't hold her child back for selfish reasons." She laughed and picked up her glass of tea. "At least, that's what I tell myself."

"Lorraine won't always be around…"

She put a hand over his. "Let's not go down that road just yet."

"Then I'll pay the bill and we can head home, home for now anyway. It'll soon be time for Delaney's nap."

"I'd love to be the one to put her down and read her a story."

"Then what are we waiting for?"

On the drive back to the farm, mother and son caught up on family business and people they knew in common.

"You remember Elena Faris? She graduated the same year you did from Rogers."

"I remember. Go Vikings."

"Elena's on her sixth marriage."

"You're kidding?"

"Nope. Her mother and I are still good friends. Elena's gone to rehab so many times her mother can't keep up."

"Look, I know you said you didn't want to talk about it, but...do you ever think about what's going to happen when Lorraine...when it's Lorraine's time?"

"I think about it every day. Why?"

"Whenever it...happens, you're welcome to move here."

"Oh, Simon, as wonderful as that sounds, my life has always been back east. You know that. I'm living in the same house your father and I bought six months after you came along." She let out a loud sigh. "But let me think about it. Because getting to be around this precious baby would be enough of a lure for me to start over. But at my age? And three thousand miles away in such a strange setting? That's a scary proposition for me, sweetheart."

"It's not the other side of the moon, Mom."

"I know that. The thing is, I have thought long and hard about selling the house on Cape Cod. No one in the family's used it since you were there last, and that was two years ago. We rent it out during the summers, but that can be a headache. Tim Simonds, the caretaker, died last spring and I haven't had anyone there who wants to take care of the place, do repairs, and collect the rent like he did."

"A management company would do all that. I'd really hate to see you sell it."

"Then for now I won't. But sometimes I think Lorraine might be, I don't know, more cognizant about her surroundings if she were on Nauset instead of Newport. We did practically grow up there. But then she fades away again without acknowledging me and I think there's no point in moving her to the beach when she doesn't even know who I am."

"Mom, Lorraine will never get any better."

"I know that, honey."

"As long as you're aware that the prognosis will never improve." He paused, looking back at Delaney. "I've decided to buy a house."

Gretchen smiled. "Why, Simon Graham Bremmer, I do believe you're settling down for real. Do you need money for a down payment?"

"I make my own way, Mom. You know that. I've been putting money aside for twelve years now, saving every dollar. And these last two years with the business booming, I've managed to save quite a bit."

Simon pulled down the long driveway to the caretaker's cottage. "This place has been great for me. Nick wouldn't even take much in rent. Delaney and I could live here like this for years, but it isn't kid-friendly."

She reached across the bench seat and cupped his face in her hands. "You are so like your father. Responsible but stubborn to the core. I've known it ever since you quit Brown and left for the Army. You've always been independent, fiercely so. But don't forget you have family who care about your welfare and that baby back there."

"I've never doubted for a minute I was loved."

"That's because you always have been, from the day we brought you home from the hospital."

"Let's get this little munchkin in for a nap."

Gretchen watched her big, strong son reach into the back seat and pick up the tiny girl. Her heart soared with a mother's pride.

After getting Delaney down, Gretchen stood at the baby's door and lowered her voice. "I can't believe I'm standing here watching my grandchild sleep."

Simon kissed her cheek. "I had the same feeling the first night."

As he turned to go, she grabbed his arm. "If you need money for that house don't be foolish enough to pass up my help."

"Mom…"

She led him into the living room, dropping onto the sofa, tucking her legs under her to get comfortable. "Just listen for a minute. When your father died he left me without a financial worry in the world. Again, his trademark. No philandering or gambling away the life savings for Lowell Bremmer. These past two years, I've tried to keep the investments going, the ones he favored. But our family attorney is getting old, Simon. Jacob Pittman is pushing eighty. He recently stopped by and told me he's decided to finally close his practice at the end of the year. He says he'll continue being the estate attorney until then. But Simon, the day of his visit, Jacob couldn't even remember how to get back outside to his car. It makes me worry."

"That's not good. Want me to research who can take his place?"

"I was hoping you'd do it. I hate to ask now that you're so busy with Delaney, but someone has to make sure the investments don't shrink."

"Me?"

"Why are you so surprised?"

"It's a big responsibility."

"Like you'd shirk that. Look, I deal with Lorraine practically twenty-four-seven. This is the first time I've been out of Rhode Island in four years. That should tell you something. And at my age I'd rather make sure both of us have the money for our futures. Now there's Delaney to think about. I can't think of another person I trust more."

"Okay. I'd be happy to take a look at the portfolio Dad put together."

"Super. So if you want to get a house, I'd say let me help you."

"I love you, Mom."

"I love you, too. What's the place look like? Is there any way I can get to see it today?"

"See it? I insist you help me decorate it."

"What about asking Gilly Grant to do that?"

"I suppose I could. But she has her hands full right now with her mother. I told you about Connie's…weird behavior."

Gretchen nodded. "Dealing with Lorraine, I'm used to weird behavior. Maybe her mother will improve after the shunt."

"Let's hope so. I could get Gilly's input. You should see what she's done with her little house. So yeah, why wouldn't I ask a friend to give me some pointers?"

Gretchen stared at her son. "Is that all she is? A friend?"

Simon squinted into the afternoon sun streaming in a wide path through the kitchen patio door. "I don't know what she is yet. She has her own set of problems." He tried to think how to phrase it. "Why is it women think they're overweight when they're not?"

"Because the media and fashion magazines have been telling us for years how awful we are if we don't wear a size two. My hairdresser, whom I've known for going on thirty-five years, still tries to talk me into keeping the gray out of my hair, thinks it makes me look old. I say, it makes me look wiser than everyone else."

"You look great to me. You know I have to help Silas with the planting tomorrow. It'll probably get very dusty around here, there'll be a cloud surrounding this place."

"Do you want me to take Delaney and go into town while you do that?"

"Would you mind?"

"Simon, stop trying to be so polite. I'm here to help you out. Just point me in the direction of how to do that and stop tiptoeing around."

"Well then, I need to ask a favor. And it's a big one. What do you say to babysitting Saturday night?"

"Now you're talking. That's why I traveled three thousand miles to try out my Nana skills. Please tell me you're taking Gilly out for the evening."

"That's the plan. I'm not sure who she has watching Jayden, but when I offered you, she said she had it covered."

Gilly not only had it covered, she'd shopped until her credit cards felt the burn. She'd left her mother and Jayden in the care of Emma Colter long enough to make a quick trip over to San Sebastian for new lingerie. She'd splurged on a cream-colored chemise that looked gorgeous, but it was the lace bustier and thong in silky black she thought might get Simon's juices flowing the quickest. And for dinner and a movie, she'd bought a slinky, V-neck cocktail dress in black that should keep him interested before they got to the main event.

As she made the turn onto Ocean Street, Gilly braked and did a U-turn toward Ophelia's place, wondering if the teacher was back home yet. She sent Ophelia a text to ask, pulling to the side of the road to wait for a reply. It came a few minutes later.

Yes, I'm back home.
Feel like company?
Sure.

The home where Ophelia lived was a tiny Arts and Crafts cottage about the size of a doll house that she rented from Logan. Built with cedar shingles and nestled under an umbrella of magnolias, it looked like it belonged in a storybook setting.

Gilly knocked on the bright yellow door and heard Ophelia twisting several locks on the other side before she finally opened it a crack with a chain still visible. "Hey, you okay?"

"I'm fine," Ophelia said, sliding the chain back so she could let Gilly inside. As soon as Gilly got far enough in, Ophelia snapped the door shut and flipped all the locks again. "Logan installed extra ones. I don't know how he found out, but he called Abby yesterday and said it was a done deal. And Isabella came by to bring me groceries, so I wouldn't have to go to the store."

Gilly dug in her purse. "I brought you something, too." She handed off an envelope.

"Oh, my God. There must be five hundred dollars here."

"We knew you missed work all week, so the staff took up a collection to help you offset your time off."

Ophelia put her arms out for a hug. "Thank you. I'll write them a note right now."

The woman turned and ran into the kitchen, but Gilly recognized distress when she saw it and trailed after her. "If you're afraid of staying here, I have a guest room."

"No. You've done enough. I'll be fine. Eastlyn went with the Santa Cruz police to pick him up. He's been charged with assault. Of course, he didn't stay in jail two minutes before his parents bailed him out. But Eastlyn also served the protection order. He's not supposed to come near me."

Gilly had seen the results from restraining orders. She considered them mostly useless, depending on the aggressor's willingness to follow the law. Rob Ogilvie didn't seem like the type to follow orders written on a piece of paper. But she didn't share that view with Ophelia.

"I got an email from Dottie Whitcomb. She wanted to let everyone know that the deacon has hired a new pastor. He'll be here first of next week."

"That's great."

"Maybe I should leave."

"Why on earth would you do that?"

"Look at me. I'll be lucky if I'm ready to attend church on Sunday, let alone meet the new reverend. My face is still a mess. How can I go and look the parents in the eye, the same ones who trust me with their kids? I can't even handle my own personal life."

"Stop it. Your face is looking a lot better. And in two days it'll look even less yellowish." Gilly tried to think of anything to talk about except her bruised face. "Who is this guy they hired?"

"His name's Seth Larrabee from South Dakota, or maybe it's North. I just don't want the new reverend to see me looking like this when he gets here."

"Let's try some makeup."

"Did that already. Abby spent almost an hour applying that thick goop, only to watch me wash it all off because it made me look worse. It's a myth that foundation covers purple. It doesn't. Maybe I should just quit my job, pack up and try somewhere else, somewhere Rob can't find me."

"You shouldn't have to run."

"That's just it. We both know a restraining order is a weak way to counter a guy like Rob."

"You could stay with Abby."

"Abby and Keegan both want me to move into the Rescue Center, where there's a gate that's locked at night to keep the animals inside if one should accidentally get out."

"That sounds like a plan. So why don't you?"

"Because this is my home and I shouldn't have to leave it to stay safe."

"No argument there. How about asking Eastlyn to sit out in front of your house?"

"She does that anyway."

"But you still don't feel safe. I get it. What do you want me to do?"

Ophelia pulled out a piece of paper from a drawer. "Here's the information to get in touch with my parents. If anything should happen to me, just make sure you tell them that I tried to get away from Rob. Make sure they know. I've told Abby the same thing. And Keegan. I just want everyone to know that I did the best I could to get him out of my life."

Ophelia's fear and pain broke Gilly's heart, maybe because she'd lived it once. After she arrived back home she brought it up to her mother.

As she peeled potatoes for dinner, she turned to Connie. "Did you ever feel that way when I was with Vaughn?"

"All the time. Are you finally admitting that he was abusive?"

"I guess I am."

"I never could understand why you put up with it. You weren't raised that way."

Gilly wondered that, too. "I suppose I wanted a man in my life and was willing to compromise on certain things."

"Compromise on him hitting you? I don't understand that."

"Well, if it's any consolation, I'll never do it again."

Connie went over to the counter where Gilly stood. "Want me to help?" It was her way of mending fences and putting the conversation to an end.

"Do you feel like it?"

"I'd like to see if I can peel a potato."

Gilly handed her the paring knife. "Would the peeler work better?"

"Maybe."

Gilly watched her mother painstakingly use the knife to work her way around the spud. "Looks like you have it handled. Did Quentin talk to you yet?"

"If you're asking if he let me go, the answer is yes. Well, sort of. Oh, it's okay. He let me down easy enough, said I could work part-time there in the office, which I gladly accepted. But he'll have to hire a nurse for the shots and other day to day routine stuff. But I know I might as well get ready for him to phase me out altogether, probably by the end of the year."

"I'm sorry, Mom."

"At least I'm beginning to feel like my old self again," Connie admitted as she began to slice and dice with pauses in between.

"Did you two discuss hours?"

"Mid-day. That way you and I aren't in such a rush like before. I agreed to five hours a day from ten to three. That way you no longer have to drop Jayden at daycare."

"Sounds great. Is that enough money for you to live on, though?"

"Your pop left me in good shape. And I've put a little money aside in savings. I think I'll be fine."

Relieved to hear that, Gilly huffed out a breath and broached another slippery topic. "Would you like to meet Simon's mother while she's here in town?"

"If you plan on dating him, I suppose I should."

Gilly figured that was the closest thing she'd get to a détente and took it, smiling as she turned on the burner to boil the potatoes.

While Delaney played with a new set of blocks Gretchen had brought, Simon made dinner, a simple stir-fry with beef tips and veggies. While he stood at the stove, his phone dinged with a text from Gilly.

Sneaking this in but I think my mom has finally turned a corner. I think we should set something up for her to meet yours.

Really? How'd you manage that?

Nothing I did. She's slowly getting back to normal. Fingers crossed. Maybe get the moms together tomorrow night?

Sure. But I'm nervous about being around your mom.

Come on. Big tough guy like you afraid of my mother? I don't think so.

She scares me.

Buck up. We'll do dinner at my house.

Fine. But make sure she's not armed.

Very funny. Not. Gotta go.

See, you're scared of her too.

Hahaha. On second thought…

When his mother caught him texting and beaming into his phone, she peered over his shoulder. "You're grinning like a teenager again. Brings back memories of when you dated Paige Brookings all through high school."

"Jeez, I haven't thought of Paige in years. She dumped me right before senior prom. I still have no idea why. Maybe don't bring that up tomorrow night at dinner, though."

Gretchen did a mock salute. "Yes, sir."

"I'm not kidding. Connie dislikes me."

Gretchen waved him off. "Leave it to me. By the time we get out of there, she'll be your biggest fan."

"If only. Personally, I think that's overly optimistic. You don't know this woman."

"That's the point." She scanned the food simmering in the pan. "You've become quite the cook. I don't remember you doing this sort of thing when you were home on leave."

"You get hungry, you learn to cook. Pelican Pointe doesn't have any fast food joints. You come in late off the water, starving, and you're forced to fend for yourself."

Gretchen watched him plate the food and went to herd Delaney into the kitchen. The toddler didn't want to leave her blocks. "Time to eat."

"No!" Delaney screamed when Nana tried to pick her up and turned red with temper. She tried pushing out of Gretchen's arms. "No!"

Simon and his mother exchanged looks. "There's that little girl who's been hiding from grandma, uh Nana, since she got here. You're showing Nana your dark side."

Simon finally got her to calm down and settled into her high chair. "I hope she doesn't act this way in front of Connie tomorrow night."

Gretchen's brow crinkled with concern. "You really want this woman to like you. Normally you wouldn't give a hang one way or the other."

"It just bugs me that she was so hostile to me, us, Delaney and me, after only meeting us one time. I'm not sure a medical procedure will correct that. It's like she didn't approve of us or something."

"Hmm, that old saying like mother, like daughter?"

"Well, it's there in the back of my head…somewhere…that Gilly could one day be like that."

"You're kidding?"

"Hey, you weren't there the day I took Delaney to see the doctor and met Connie in the parking lot. It was like instant loathing. Here I've got a kid in my arms who clearly doesn't feel well, and this nurse is annoyed I showed up at all. I have to admit, Gilly was the opposite. The night I sought out help at the hospital, Gilly was like, 'what can I do to help?' She listened. She immediately went into action. Not her mother. I honestly think if it had been up to her, Connie would've kicked me and Delaney to the curb that day."

"Simon, are you sure you aren't overreacting? That sounds awfully harsh for the staff of a local clinic."

"I don't think I am. And Gilly admitted her mother's been...unpredictable. And don't forget Quentin is having reservations about his decision to hire her. So no, I don't think I'm exaggerating."

That night after supper and the dishes were done, Delaney fell asleep on the floor using Merlin for a pillow.

"Look at that," Gretchen said. "We need a picture."

Simon obliged using his camera phone and then scooped the baby up to carry her to bed. "Want to lay her down?"

"You know I do. Look at you, being a daddy. I'm so proud of you, honey."

"I'm kind of proud of me, too. Never in a million years did I think I'd ever be left with a baby."

"Just goes to show how life takes twists and turns you never expect."

Nineteen

After spending most of the day sitting at the wheel of a tractor, Simon needed a shower before heading out to Gilly's. As he strode toward the office to update Silas on where he'd stopped for the day, he spotted Gavin Kendall waving him over.

While Nick had given Silas and Sammy free rein to run all the planting stages on the farm, he'd promoted Gavin from caretaker to a hands-on position in the smaller specialty field growing hard-to-raise herbs.

When Gavin had been brought on board years earlier by Ryder McLachlan, no one realized that the man possessed such a green thumb. Gavin could grow anything and proved it by cultivating massive quantities of edible lavender used in ice cream. Although the garden next to the lighthouse grew plenty for the locals, it had been his idea to produce a variety commercially to sell to restaurants, creating another revenue stream. It went with the line of gourmet garlic he produced favored by fancy eateries like The Pointe. He also experimented in growing ginseng from seedlings even though the zone was reportedly too hot to grow it with any success. Gavin did.

Simon knew all this, but he also recognized that the affable gardener and husband was quite the hands-on father. He'd seen Gavin in one of the vacant fields playing with his kids and thought the guy made fatherhood look almost effortless. And that was before Delaney had arrived.

"I got some of your mail here," Gavin said. "It was stuck inside a bunch of circulars."

Simon saw the return address read Boston and stuffed it in his pocket. "I wanted to ask you something."

"If it's about my decision to go ahead and pack up the lavender for shipment, I thought it was the best way to stay on schedule. And the customer approved it ahead of time, said he needed the batch sooner rather than waiting for the entire shipment to go out."

"Who am I to squabble about when you ship a purple flower that people like to eat?"

Gavin chortled with laughter. "Well, it's certainly more popular than the endive."

"That bitter stuff? Smells better than endive anyway. But that isn't what I was wondering about. I noticed you and your wife manage two kids. How do you work and still get to spend time with them? With all the different areas, this place stays hopping."

Gavin gave him an odd look and took off his cap to scratch his head. "I never had anyone ask me that before. It's just what we do. My wife and me. We share the load. My wife, Maggie, is the glue that holds us all together. She's terrific at helping the kids with their homework during the week and doing all the extra activities after school, like Scouts and music lessons, while I focus on bringing home a paycheck. I get my job done and what's left over is my time. Usually weekends I try to take up the slack. But even then, I have work to get done. Gardening doesn't take a day off. But I usually try to take the kids out to the greenhouse with me and let them participate in the growing, get them involved that way so we can spend some time together."

"It must be nice to be on the same page like that."

"Oh yeah. On weekends, I sometimes make breakfast and cook dinner, and then I set aside some time to play dolls or Legos, whatever they want to do at the time. And during the summer months, I like taking the kids camping just to spend a little alone time with each of them. I even put up the tent under that big maple tree in the back just to show them we don't have to head to Yellowstone to get away. They have great fun now, but Maggie tells me they'll soon outgrow wanting to spend time with Dad."

"But what's your secret to being a good father?"

"Is this about the baby I've seen you hauling back and forth? I bet you were shocked when she showed up."

"Shocked is putting it mildly. So what can you tell me?"

"Well, having an understanding partner helps. That says it all. Because Maggie's a rock. She doesn't come unglued at every little thing and go nuts like some women do. She keeps me grounded. And she's supportive when she knows I have a lot on my plate. This farm doesn't run itself. When we first got here, I had zero experience at commercial growing. All I knew was how to put a seed in the ground and get it to sprout. Maggie knew I was feeling a little insecure and nervous about the whole thing. Did she give me a hard time? Nope. She made me feel like I could do anything. That's the key to how we make it work. We're a team. Never underestimate a partner who makes you feel on top of the world. I think that's what it takes, two people on the same page to make things work. At least it does for us."

That didn't help much, Simon decided as he walked back toward his house. Stepping inside, Merlin woofed in greeting as Simon stared at his mother, sitting cross-legged on the floor with Delaney and a Cabbage Patch doll in her lap. "What did I do to deserve such beautiful women waiting for me at the end of a long day?"

"Look, Daddy's home!" Nana said.

Delaney clapped her hands and got up to go to Simon. "Da-da."

He scooped her up, noticing she was decked out in a new pink and purple outfit with a mermaid on the top. "Did you and Nana go shopping?"

"We did. We wanted to look extra pretty for our big dinner tonight," Gretchen said, sniffing the air. "You smell like compost."

"That's why I need to grab a shower. I'm gonna make it quick before we leave for Gilly's." He plopped Delaney down and headed off into the bedroom, unbuttoning his shirt as he went. He removed the envelope from Boston and ripped it open. Flipping the estate check around, he did a double take when he saw the seven-figure dollar amount. "Holy crap! Would you look at this?"

Gretchen stood in the doorway. "Look at what?"

"Mom, Amelia's estate is over a million dollars."

"What? I thought you said the attorney told you it'd be no more than twenty-five thousand at best and that was before expenses."

"That's what she said. Which means this is a mistake. That stupid law firm has obviously made a whopping accounting error. Where's my phone? I need to call that Tyler woman. Now."

"Not on a Friday evening you won't. On the east coast, they're already closed this time of day. You'll have to wait until Monday to get it straightened out."

He plopped down on the bed to take off his shoes. "Damn. What a mess this is. This just proves Margaret Tyler can't do anything right."

Gilly had ditched her barbecue idea in lieu of a picnic in the backyard, complete with fried chicken and potato salad. And when she opened the door she was glad she'd changed her mind about having Simon stand at the grill. He looked tired and edgy. That's why she was surprised when he snatched her around the waist in front of everyone and planted a big kiss on her lips.

"I'm glad to see you, too," Gilly said with a grin.

"This is my mom, Gretchen. Mom, meet Gilly and her mother, Connie. And that little guy hiding behind his mom's legs is Jayden. Hey there, Jayden."

In greeting, Jayden popped out from behind his mother and latched onto Simon's legs. "I got cars."

"I know, buddy. And Delaney brought some of her own this time so she won't be swiping yours."

"It's such a nice night I thought we'd eat outside," Gilly announced as she shepherded her little flock through the kitchen and out the back door. "What can I get you to drink, Mrs. Bremmer?"

"Call me Gretchen. And I'd love a glass of white wine if you have it."

"White wine it is. Mom?"

"I'll take the same."

"Simon, would you like a beer?"

"Sure. I'll help you get the drinks."

They moved into the kitchen away from prying eyes and Simon used the moment to grab her around the waist again, pulling her in for a heated kiss that showed why he'd acted so edgy. There was need and greed that slammed them both into a tailspin. He rested his forehead on hers and muttered, "I don't know about you, but I've been looking forward to that."

The emotion whipped through her like a fierce wind. "I should've had my head examined for this idea. Why didn't you stop me? I'd much rather have spent the evening alone, just the two of us."

"Too late for that. We can't very well run out the door like teenagers and abandon it all. Although that's not a bad idea. Tomorrow night is ours. We'll make the best of it for now. And I spotted your fried chicken on the counter. That's worth a Friday night of torture right there."

Gilly handed him a bottle of wine. "Let's just get through the evening and hope my mother keeps the snide remarks to a minimum."

She made up a tray with the drinks and carried them out to the mothers. She almost stumbled over her own feet when she saw her mother laughing, in deep conversation sitting next to Gretchen.

"Ladies," Gilly said, offering up the wine.

"I was just telling your mother about the time Simon tried to put a Band-Aid on his dog. When he couldn't get the strip to adhere to all that fur, he tried using glue. I couldn't believe Toby, that was the golden retriever we had, sat still long enough for Simon to slather Elmer's glue on him that air-dried onto his nose. It was Simon's first attempt at playing nurse."

Gilly grinned, knowing full well Gretchen's intent was to bring Connie into Simon's corner. "How old was he at the time?"

"Five. Rambunctious as Jayden is now."

Gilly beamed at the comparison. "You mean Simon was that energetic?"

"That's a polite way of saying he'd climb to the rafters. And he was loud," Gretchen added.

"I should've mentioned that it's okay if you guys wanted to bring Merlin tonight. Jayden adores that dog. Talks about him all the time."

Simon had been listening to the byplay. "I think Merlin was ready to get rid of all of us, get the house to himself. He's been looking forward to some peace and quiet. Now's his chance."

"Does he mind being left alone?" Gilly asked. "Does he chew things up?"

"No. Never has. But then the place has a doggie door, so Merlin pretty much comes and goes as he pleases. I often find him sitting on the porch waiting for me to drive up. It's like he has my routine down five days a week. On weekends, he changes things up to mesh with mine."

"He must love living on the farm," Gilly said. "Will he adjust to moving to town?"

"Cord says it won't be a problem. Merlin just wants to be where I am."

"Is this house nearby?" Gretchen wanted to know.

Gilly looked surprised. "It's down the street. You haven't seen it yet? Let's go do a walkthrough after we eat."

"I'd love that." Gretchen turned in her seat toward Connie. "Are you up for it?"

"Sure. I'm supposed to resume my normal activities."

Gretchen nodded. "When do you go back to work?"

"Not for another two weeks. I'll start taking care of Jayden on Sunday night, though, when Gilly heads to work. That way, Simon won't have to mess with him."

Simon glanced over at the hyper three-year-old. "It was no problem. In fact, Delaney and I will miss his high-energy mornings, music blaring, and little cars shooting across the floor."

"Really?" Connie said, her brow furrowing. "You didn't mind his little mouth running all the time?"

"I look at it this way. Jayden's running his mouth seems to make Delaney want to talk more. That's a good thing in my book."

Jayden came running up with a soccer ball. "Kick it hard!"

Simon obliged by sending it to the back fence and watched the tyke scamper after it.

Gilly looped her arm through Simon's. "Help me bring the food out."

"If it means we're closer to eating, you bet. I'm starving."

Alone together in the kitchen, Gilly put her arms around his waist and tiptoed to press a kiss on his lips. "Did you mean that?"

"I don't normally say stuff I don't mean."

"I like that about you. I also adore your mother."

Simon's lips curved. "Never underestimate Gretchen Bremmer. She's a spitfire when she needs to be. Now let me at that chicken before I keel over from hunger."

They carted plates out to the picnic table already covered with a bright blue-green tablecloth that fluttered in the breeze. Simon carried the platter full of chicken while Gilly brought out two different kinds of salads and a casserole.

Simon scooped up the kids in a bundle together as they squealed in delight and plopped them down onto the bench. "You guys ready for some chow?"

"Chow!" Jayden hollered.

"Chow!" mimicked Delaney.

"See. It's like an echo," Simon pointed out, ruffling the boy's hair. He snapped a bib on Delaney to protect her brand-new outfit and kissed the top of her head. "I'm trying the potato salad first and then digging into the pasta. I think the cheesy rice casserole has my name on it."

"There's so much food here," Gretchen said, checking out all the different choices. "And you obviously know something about making stuff toddlers will eat. You must've worked on this all day. Thanks so much for going to all this trouble."

The flutters long gone, Gilly had calmed down quite a bit and relished in the compliment. "My pleasure. I love having people over, it's just not something I've done lately."

The meal brought out booms of laughter and conversation. Knock-knock jokes were bantered back and forth that made Jayden laugh. Connie even relaxed enough to compare notes with Gretchen about gardening and argue about the best way to grow orchids.

The little group seemed to bond as the stars twinkled out and glittered over them like a protective canopy.

Simon stood up and started gathering up paper plates and tossing them into a huge plastic trash bag. "We'll clean this mess up and head out to tour the house before it gets too late."

"You're really buying that house?" Connie asked.

"Yep. Really. The farm's no place for Delaney."

"That seems very considerate," Connie grudgingly admitted. "This tour business of yours, does it make any money? Can you afford that big house?"

"Mom!" Gilly bellowed. "That's none of your business."

"It's okay," Simon assured her. "I do fine, Mrs. Grant. Bree Dayton built up a steady customer base that I've expanded. I have a rapport with repeat tourists. Nick and Jordan have so many guests who keep coming back year after year, sometimes three times in one twelve-month period, that I have a steady flow of traffic. And I'm starting to branch out, fill the void with my own fishing tours. I advertise online and have a website that allows people to book reservations right from their laptops. It might even grow one day to where I have to add on another boat."

"You don't miss the Army?" Connie wondered.

"No."

Since Gretchen knew that was all he intended to say on the subject, she put her hand over her son's. "Let's go see this house. Come on, Delaney. Let's go check out your new room."

Twenty

"So you really like it?"

It was the fifth time he'd asked her opinion about the house since the night before. Gretchen merely smiled and poured Delaney her bowl of Cheerios. "Yes, Simon, I think it's been very nicely renovated and has a ton of charm. I don't think you could find a better house anywhere in town. And I love the back staircase. I know exactly why you love it, too. The house reminds you where you grew up."

"Is it that obvious?"

"It's obvious you're looking for a home, a permanent one where you can finally settle down after all those years spent on foreign soil. I think it's perfect."

Simon kissed her cheek. "That's what I wanted to hear."

"Aren't you gonna ask me what I thought about Gilly?"

"I was working up to it."

"Not only is she gorgeous, but I watched her with her boy. Gilly's a good mother, a strong single mom who's working ungodly hours. That kind of spirit and determination keeps her going. Kind of like someone else I know."

"And what did you think of Connie?"

"Well-intentioned, but a little too judgmental for my taste. She mentioned four times while we went through the house that she didn't think you could afford the place. Four times."

Simon shook his head. "I'm not sure I care what she thinks anymore. She seems to think Jayden has problems. I don't like it."

"I noticed that. What I saw was a sweet little boy who's loud and active and loves an audience. But it's something else Connie seems to be fixated on and it annoys Gilly."

"Exactly. She's brought it up several times. She hoped her mother's attitude had something to do with her medical condition. I'm not so sure."

"There's tension there. So where are you taking this spirited, beautiful woman tonight for dinner?"

"I made reservations at The Pointe, got a table looking out over the water. Romantic, right?"

"That's my boy, knows how to treat a woman right."

He grinned and held up his car keys. "You and Delaney gonna be okay? I've gotta get going. Silas wants that northwest corner cleared today. All of it. You've got the truck if you want to explore."

Gretchen waved him away. "We'll be fine. I'm taking my granddaughter to the park where she can take in some sunshine without getting dust all over her. When do you close on that house?"

Simon lifted a shoulder. "Two weeks. But I haven't heard from Nick yet as to when I sign the papers. Why?"

"I wish it could happen while I'm here. I'd like to be able to see you two settled before I head back east."

"We'll be fine, Mom. In case you haven't noticed, there are a lot of people to help." He kissed his daughter's head and headed out the door.

Gretchen looked at Delaney. "He just doesn't get it, does he? A mother likes to be around to see her child…" She stopped short. "Oh, baby, your mother will never be able to check up on you, will she? You'll never know her. You'll grow up without having that bond. Which means it's that much more important for your daddy to find that very special person to share his life with. Is Gilly the one? I don't know, sweetie. Let's go test the waters a bit and find out."

Gretchen was definitely sticking her nose where it didn't belong. But if she wanted to have peace of mind back in Rhode Island, it was the only way.

Phillips Park was in the middle of downtown, between Main Street and Tradewinds Drive. She already knew Connie lived down the street.

She unloaded Delaney's borrowed stroller from the pickup and set out to meander through the neighborhood. It was good exercise on a beautiful day with soft breezes coming off the ocean. Her goal was to walk back and forth until she either caught a glimpse of Connie in her yard or Gilly in hers. She gave it forty-five minutes. And when that didn't work, she simply marched up to Connie's door and rang the bell.

"Hi there," Gretchen began. "How about having lunch with me today? We could invite Gilly and Jayden."

"Oh, lord, no. Gilly's getting ready for her big date tonight and Jayden's such a handful when you take him out to eat I don't bother with that."

"Are you babysitting him tonight?"

"No, thank goodness. Emma Colter volunteered to keep him overnight."

"I would've done it."

"Why don't you come on in and we can have lunch here. I was just sitting down to a tuna fish sandwich. There's plenty."

"Okay. I'll leave the stroller out here on the porch. Are you sure having Delaney here won't upset your peace and quiet?"

"She seems to be well-behaved enough."

Gretchen wasn't sure how to respond to that and wondered if she should keep Delaney sitting on her lap. But the child wanted down. "All kids are a handful sometimes, aren't they?"

"I suppose. But Jayden throws things and runs around like a little heathen at times. He won't sit still long enough to watch a cartoon. I keep telling Gillian she should put the boy on medication to calm him down, but she refuses."

Good for Gilly, Gretchen thought, but kept her mouth firmly shut and her teeth clenched in a jaw-tightened lockdown.

"Want some lemonade with your sandwich? Or maybe some tea?"

"Lemonade's fine," Gretchen replied, trying to make sure Delaney didn't break anything as she toddled around the living room, a room filled with knickknacks on every table. Gretchen wanted to point out that those little figurines sitting around, and well within a child's reach, were mighty tempting to a toddler. To them, the collectibles could easily be mistaken for toys.

Gretchen realized then and there she didn't have a chance in hell of changing Connie Grant's mind about Simon, nor her habits or her long-held beliefs. It didn't even seem to Gretchen as if Connie liked her own grandson very much. Gretchen couldn't fathom the notion of that.

After an awkward beginning, the meal could only be described as tense and unrewarding. She sat through it on pins and needles, mostly because she was afraid Delaney might knock over one of those precious mementos that Connie seemed so fond of displaying. Which was her right to do so, Gretchen realized. But since she favored having a clutter-free zone when it came to letting toddlers move around without worry, there didn't seem to be any point to bringing it up.

At the first opportunity after she swallowed the last bite, she and Delaney got out of there, practically scooting down the street and back to where she'd parked Simon's truck.

Just as she started to lift Delaney out of the stroller, she heard a voice ask, "Need some help there?"

She turned to see a lanky man her age with a crop of dark-colored hair graying at the temples, standing a few feet away. He was dressed in jogging attire with earbuds hanging around his neck like he'd been listening to music. He had the most endearing brown eyes she'd ever seen. "I think I've got it, but thanks for the offer."

"No problem. I'm John Dickinson. You're new in town?"

"I'm just visiting my new grandbaby and my son. Simon Bremmer. You might know him."

"The guy who owns the *Sea Dragon*? Sure. You're his mother? You don't look old enough to have a boy that age."

Gretchen laughed and introduced herself. "And

this is Delaney."

He bent down to shake her little hand. "My daughter is principal at the elementary school. I bet she'll be meeting you one day soon." John straightened up and turned to Gretchen again. "Her name's Julianne, last name's McLachlan now. I moved here last June after retiring and selling off my contractor business in Santa Cruz. Love it here. And I get to be closer to my only daughter."

"That's what matters, isn't it? Family. My son lives so far away now. This is my first visit here since he moved. But now that he has Delaney…"

"My guess is, that grandbaby will get you out here a lot more often."

"You're probably right."

"How long are you in town?"

"I leave next Thursday. Six more days." She told him about her sister with Alzheimer's. "It's tough getting away and leaving her in the care of strangers."

"If you'd like to have coffee before you go back, maybe someone to talk to about it, we could meet at the Diner," John said. "Max makes a mean cinnamon roll."

Gretchen scooped up Delaney and almost stumbled over her own feet at the offer. "You're asking me to have coffee with you? How do you know I'm not married?"

John grinned and held up his hands. "I'm not psychic. I went out with Simon on the *Sea Dragon* last summer to go fishing. He mentioned his dad died two years back. And it's just a cup of coffee. It's not like we're sneaking out to meet at midnight."

That brought a chuckle out of Gretchen. "I haven't been out at midnight in a long time. I might turn into a pumpkin."

"We wouldn't want that. So how about it? I'll buy Simon's mom a cup of coffee as a thank you for having such a great guy for a son. I caught twelve striped bass the day we went out on the boat."

"It's a nice, friendly gesture by one of the locals. Okay, let's do it. Let's meet up for coffee. How about Monday morning? I'll have to bring Delaney because Simon has a tour leaving at seven."

"That's fine. Bring her along. Is nine okay?"

"It's fine."

"Got your phone with you?"

"Sure," she said and couldn't believe she was setting up a date. It felt weird handing off the device to someone else, especially a man.

John keyed in his phone number and handed it back. "There. You call me if you chicken out."

"I won't."

"You sure?"

"I'm sure."

And on the drive back to the farm, she wasn't just sure, she was intrigued. Imagine, a man asking her out for the first time in…decades, and she'd said yes. Coffee or not, it was a first for her since Lowell died. She looked in the rearview mirror and muttered to Delaney, "Has Nana still got it or what?"

Delaney answered with a series of baby babble that summed up Gretchen's mood. She didn't want to turn out like Connie Grant. Having coffee with John Dickinson was a first step in doing something about it.

It had been a long time since Simon had gone out on a date, let alone dressed up for one. He put on a charcoal gray suit that made him feel like he was headed to the prom or a wedding or maybe a funeral. The tie began to feel like it was choking him before he ever left the house.

"Stop fidgeting," Gretchen scolded, as she straightened his tie. "You're like a schoolboy who won't stand still. Oh jeez, I sound like Connie complaining about poor Jayden."

"She's rough on that kid, isn't she?"

Gretchen wasn't about to cop to her earlier meddling. "Connie's an odd duck, that's for sure. She mentioned Jayden is staying with someone else tonight."

"That's almost a relief," Simon noted, looking over at his own daughter who was straddling Merlin like a horse. "Come on, honey. Let's get you into your pajamas."

"I'll do that. You go on. My time's short here and I want to be the one who gets her ready for bed. If I didn't know better, I'd say you're stalling."

"I'm not. I'm just…I feel stupid in this suit."

"You look handsome. Now go. Get out of here and enjoy yourself."

His nervousness lasted right up to Gilly's house. But once she opened the door, that all fell away. "Wow! You look…fantastic."

She wore an off-the-shoulder skater dress in burgundy and heels in the same color that showed off her legs.

"I do?"

He whistled. "You do."

"You don't look so bad yourself. Although I can tell you're not comfortable wearing that tie. Why not ditch it?"

"Really? You wouldn't mind?"

"Silly. Of course not. Come on in." She dragged him inside. "I just have to get my purse."

He loosened the knot on the tie and pulled it from around his neck. "It's certainly quiet around here without Jayden."

"I wondered which one of us would mention the kids first. I should've known it'd be you."

"Why's that?"

"Because you're just that kind of guy."

"I made reservations at The Pointe."

"Nice. I've never eaten there before."

"I've gotten take out, a steak to-go." He couldn't take his eyes off her and twirled her around for a kiss.

"You start that, and we won't make it out the door," she assured him.

"That's not a bad idea."

"Thirty minutes ago, I would've agreed with you. But since I look too gorgeous to stay at home, I want the full treatment. Wine and dine me, Bremmer." Her eyes glinted with mischief.

"Tease."

"Yep, that's me."

"You're almost dressed too fancy to ride in a truck," he stated as they finally headed out the door.

"See? You say the sweetest things."

He pulled up to the red-brick building with its faint white lettering on the side and waited for the valet to open Gilly's door.

Perry Altman had taken a rundown old fish hatchery near the wharf and turned it into a five-star restaurant complete with upscale atmosphere that included all the elegance one would expect for the prices. Anniversaries were celebrated here the same as special moments like birthdays or first dates. With live classical piano music playing in the background, candles flickering on the tabletops that were draped in fine white linen, and some of the best seafood within fifty miles served on stylish china, The Pointe offered its clientele first-rate service. Waiters dressed in formal black and white buzzed around the tables, flitting back and forth, filling water glasses or tipping fine wine into a glass.

Perky hostess Jolene Sanders greeted them with all the flair she'd mustered over the years. Though she didn't work for tips, she knew her boss expected her to receive everyone like they were old friends. "That's a reservation for Bremmer, right?"

"That's us," Simon said cheerily. "By the window."

Jolene gathered two menus and showed them to their table.

They settled in with a bayside view and began to peruse the choices.

"I'm having steak," Simon announced. "With a baked potato and everything on it."

"I lost two pounds this week and I'm not about to ruin it by splurging on carbs. I'm sticking with the spinach salad and the baked halibut."

Simon frowned. "I thought you didn't like fish?"

"I don't but I like being able to fit into this dress."

"What are you, a size 4?"

"Good guess, but I'd like to be..." She held up a hand. "Let's not ruin this moment arguing about it. I know you think I'm making a big deal out of this, but...women know their ideal weight and constantly fight to be five pounds lighter."

"Why?" He linked her fingers with his. "You're beautiful just the way you are."

She let out a flustered breath. "Look, maybe I'm going through a phase that reeks lack of self-confidence."

"Have you...?" His question was interrupted by the waiter who asked for their drink order. "How about a bottle of your best chardonnay?"

The young waiter nodded. "We have a very nice 2013 from the Sonoma Valley that integrates rich oak with honeysuckle and melon."

Simon looked at Gilly. "You're more the wine expert. How does that sound? Because I'm not even sure what it means."

Gilly's lips curved. "That sounds great." After the waiter left, she leaned in, "I bet it tastes better than the cheap stuff I usually buy. Why didn't you order a beer?"

"Because tonight's special. It warrants more than a pint." He glanced around at the other diners. "They all look like they know their wine on a personal level."

She giggled. "That's probably true. What was it you wanted to say before the waiter came?"

"Have you ever experienced a lack of self-confidence before now?"

"Not really."

"Then why now, with me?"

Gilly bit her lip. "Good question. Maybe because you're this put-together military guy who clearly succeeded..."

Simon shifted in his chair. "Former military guy," he corrected. "And succeeding meant...I don't want to talk about this. I'm not sure what that has to do with your obsession about losing weight."

"I just wanted to look…perfect for you," she finally admitted.

"You couldn't be any more perfect if I'd conjured you up in a dream. You're beautiful, a great mother, a caring daughter. You knocked me off my feet that night I walked into the hospital with a bawling baby and I haven't been the same since."

Her cheeks blushed at the praise, so he added, "Not to mention your fried chicken is out of this world."

That brought out another belly laugh. "You like my cooking?"

"All except the spaghetti sauce you torched that first night."

"That was your fault."

"Hey, I was trying to play referee and keep your son from pummeling my daughter."

"They act a lot like siblings, don't they? Maybe they'll be best friends one of these days."

"Like you used to be with Wally Pierce?"

"Maybe. Wally was my first major crush."

The waiter brought over their bottle of wine, uncorked it, and filled their glasses. "What can I get you this evening for dinner?"

"Gilly?"

She traded looks with Simon and changed her order. "I'll have the filet, cooked medium, with a plain baked potato. No sense going overboard, right?"

"I'll take the same. But I want the works on the potato. And could you bring the lady a salad?"

"Absolutely. What type of dressing?"

Gilly leaned back in her chair and sipped her wine. "Any type of vinaigrette is fine."

The waiter marched off and Gilly tilted her head in Simon's direction. "You don't like salad?"

"Not with vinaigrette. I like watching your eyes change color when you shift topics, though. Sometimes they look amber, sometimes they glisten green, and sometimes they're somewhere in between. Like now, in the candlelight they're golden. And you're blushing."

"I am not. I don't blush."

"You are. I love it." He cracked a mischievous grin. "In fact, you have golden fire in your eyes right now."

"Stop it. I do not."

"You don't take compliments very well, do you? I hadn't noticed that before tonight."

She shifted in her seat. "You know very well why I'm nervous. Don't pretend otherwise."

He did, but he wanted her to spell it out. "Do tell."

She took the bait. "I'm hoping tonight…after dropping me back home…you won't leave right away." Just getting that statement out there felt like she'd run a marathon. "Whew! Now you think I'm forward, but you should know, I bought new lingerie." She couldn't seem to stop her mouth from moving. "Too much information, huh?"

"Are you serious? Watch me scarf down my dinner in record time. I want to see what you bought."

"The wait for food here is notoriously long," she pointed out.

"Maybe I'm not hungry anymore."

Gilly cut her eyes to the waiter, who picked that moment to plop down a huge tray with their plates on it.

They dug in just to get the meal out of the way, anticipation humming between them with each bite. They even guzzled down Sonoma County's finest without bothering to enjoy the aroma or the flavor.

Before the waiter could hand out the bill, Simon handed his credit card off to Jolene. "Will you take this to our waiter. We're in kind of a hurry."

"Sure. I'll take care of it for you."

"They are obliging here," Simon uttered. "We'll have to try it again sometime when we're not..."

"So eager?" she finished.

"Exactly."

After signing the receipt on the way out the door, he watched her stride in those heels to the truck. For the first time he wished he drove something sleeker, something spiffy that was worthy of her outfit.

"Oh, by the way, do you know what's playing tonight at the Driftwood?"

"Hmm. That would be no."

She looped an arm through his. "*Princess Bride*."

"How did you manage that?"

"Me? Whatever do you mean? It's a coincidence." She leaned in and whispered, "I actually thought we'd be heading to the movies tonight instead of heading back to my place."

"Do you have Jayden covered for the night or do we need to go pick him up?"

If she'd had any reservations about sleeping with him this soon into their relationship, his concern for her baby erased all doubt. And he'd used the word "we." Her heart swooned a little bit like it had in ninth grade with Wally Pierce. She poked him in the ribs. "Emma Colter is more than happy to keep him until morning."

He brought her into his chest. "Then let's make the most of our time without the kids."

Twenty-One

Simon made sure the short trip to her house took less time than usual. As soon as she opened the front door, she turned in his arms. Without words, he backed her against the wall. Mouth pressed against mouth. They tasted and devoured. He deepened the kiss, let it spin out until it dizzied them both.

"I need to see all of you." He slid the zipper all the way down on the back of that slinky fabric. Her skin felt like silk, warm and soft beneath his touch. He pressed a kiss to her shoulders and felt her skin tingle. He watched as the dress pooled in a heap on the top of her heels.

Her breath hitched as his fingers found the swell of her breast through the lace of her bra. Deftly, he unsnapped the front closure. His blood went thick, his breath backed up in his lungs. The look of her in the dim light brought out needs, long denied.

It was the purr in her throat at his touch that reminded him to slow things down. She deserved a rhythm, a pace where he could linger and savor every trace of bare skin. Measured kisses that went on and on caused the pulse to race.

"I want to take you on a bed, not here against the wall."

She tugged him down her little hallway to her bedroom, a room she'd already prepped with the gentle glow of a nightlight. She'd left the window open and moonlight drifted in, bathing them in the perfect prelude to lust.

He rid himself of the suit jacket and she took care of unbuttoning his shirt. She skimmed his torso with her nails getting to the belt and trousers. Her hands explored his broad shoulders, his hard body, muscles lean and firm from the toil of his labor.

With one simple, gentle caress, arousal hung between them, they fell to the bed, bunched together in a ball of heat and lust.

He ran his fingers along her cheek, bringing her mouth to meet his. Lips brought out the pleasure, sinking into a playful seduction. His tongue slid down to her breast, gliding over the swell and curve, sampling, savoring each pull and tug.

He took his time trailing wet kisses down her body, relishing soft skin. He lingered at a curve, flicked along her belly before moving to taste other delectable flesh. Teasing out a moan, he thrilled to that moment of silk and satin until her breath became shallow, her focus on him.

She witnessed moonlight turn golden as he took her up and over, climbing to that hot, gilded peak where release came fast and hard.

He covered her mouth again, capturing each little sigh she eked out. They blended into one, movement and rhythm, syncing and sliding toward that same ribbon of wonder. It swirled and floated around them, lingering long and lovely, until neither could hold back. Together they fell, weightless, into the chasm that glowed and glimmered with everything they needed, they gave to each other.

"I'm not sure I can move," Simon admitted, out of breath, placing a kiss on the corner of her mouth.

"Maybe I don't want you to."

"I'm crushing you," he said, as he slid to the side and cracked out a laugh. "I saw more than your underwear."

"I let you."

"I'm forever grateful you did."

"I haven't done that in so long…"

"Same here."

"You're kidding?"

"Nope. I'd adopted a forced abstinence since moving here. Too busy with getting the business to grow and not enough hours in the day to go in pursuit of…companionship. You?"

She rolled to her side, nuzzling into his chest. "Just taking care of my boy, working hard to buy a house. I'd given up on men."

He kissed her hair. "I hope you don't feel that way about me."

"You're the reason I bought new undies. You're the reason I'm right here in this spot." Her eyes fluttered closed. "Let's take a little nap before you have to go, just for a few minutes to recharge."

"Mmm," he replied, already nodding off.

In the dream he aimed his .300 Win Mag at a man's head and squeezed the trigger. The action resulted in an explosion of deadly aim and power. Where the enemy had once stood was now nothing more than a mass of blood and bone.

The scene made him shiver. He tried to block out the image, but it wouldn't go away. He tried to leave the area, to go somewhere else. But his feet refused to move from his perch.

Eagle Eye sat next to him, pointing at another target. It seemed never-ending.

Simon dutifully zeroed in, repeating the process from before. Another target exterminated, another target down.

He felt like he wanted to throw up, like his food might return at any minute. It wouldn't be the first time. But he needed to get out of the prying eyes of his spotter. He began to move, to shake, to feel himself floating away.

Gilly woke to the man beside her thrashing in his sleep. Simon was so fitful, she touched his arm. It caused him to bolt upright, knocking her back. "Hey. Hey. It's just me. It's okay," she said, rubbing his back.

She noticed his torso gleaming wet.

"I drifted off."

"How often do you do that?"

"Do what?"

"Toss and turn and wake up drenched in sweat."

"I don't know." When he saw the look she gave him, he closed his eyes. "Okay. It always happens. Every night."

"Is this like PTSD?"

"It's like guilt," he snapped. "Look, I don't wanna talk about it."

He started to crawl out of bed, but she yanked him back. "It's okay, Simon. I get it. Just remember, this is the second part of your life. As you pointed out to me earlier, you're no longer in the Army. You no longer need to suffer like this because you did your job. Think about what might've happened if you'd failed. How many lives would've been lost then? You need to start working on forgiving yourself. Now. Tonight."

He'd heard it all before and twisted to peer over her shoulder at the time on the clock. "It's already five-thirty. I need to get home."

She noticed the strong man she'd come to know almost crumble in panic. "Simon, don't go like this."

"I have to, Gilly. I promised my mom I'd take her out on the boat today. There are things I have to get done. I'd like it if you and Jayden could join us."

"What time?"

"As soon as I can get the boat ready. Nine-ish maybe?"

"I'd love to, but I can't. Sydney's forcing a group of us to attend a mandatory meeting for the fundraiser. It's a brainstorming session slash brunch at her house at eleven. And then I have to be at work by four."

"Damn. I was hoping we could spend some more time together. My mother's going back at the end of the week. I promised to show her the area. I want her to like it here."

She watched him get dressed and let out a sigh, starting to feel a little panic creep in herself. "When do we get to do this again?"

"Whenever we can." He ran a finger down her cheek and tilted her chin up. Pressing his lips to hers, the kiss felt electric. A new wave of lust hit. "I hate to go like this. You should go back to sleep. What time are you picking up Jayden?"

"Around eight. I'm taking him with me to Sydney's. She said it was okay. Other kids will be there, too."

"Then he's covered for tonight?"

She nodded. "My mother wants to give it a try."

"Is that wise?"

"We'll see, I guess."

"Call me if you need anything."

"Okay."

He kissed her again with a deep soul-rendering emotion that left her head spinning. And then he was out the door, gone, leaving her alone with a void, a feeling that something important was missing.

Twenty-Two

Gilly found out that Sydney's notion of hosting the planning party was to keep the pitchers of margaritas coming. The suggestions tended to flow better when alcohol was involved.

"The best idea so far is Gilly's masquerade ball," Sydney announced. "And if we act on that we need to get moving on making it happen, settling on a venue."

"Nick's not exactly thrilled about wearing a costume," Jordan admitted.

"Same with Ethan," Hayden confessed. "I'll have to make it worth his while if we decide on that direction."

"Brent feels the same way," River piped up. "But he'll do it for a good cause. Raising money for the hospital is the best cause I know. I mean, no one wants to lose our brand-new facility."

"Exactly," Jordan said. "All of us need to step up and do what it takes to make sure it's always there. Besides, it isn't like we're asking the men to put on some stupid getup."

"What is it about guys not wanting to dress up?" Gilly noted. "All they have to do is wear a suit and tie and put a mask over their face for one evening. A mask equals a costume ball right there." She couldn't very well partake of the booze because in four hours she'd be on duty, but it didn't mean she couldn't enjoy the get-together and all it had to offer. She stuck a single chip down in a green sea of guacamole. "Who made this? It's delicious."

"Logan did," Kinsey answered. "He's quite the cook these days. He made a lasagna last night to die for."

"Isn't it great when men cook?" Isabella added, scooping up her own portion of the dip. "Thane doesn't just bring home pizza from Longboard's anymore, he actually makes breakfast at least four mornings a week."

Gilly glanced over at baby Jace, now almost six months old. "He's growing like a weed."

Isabella chuckled. "He is, but then he started out huge. Jace weighed almost nine pounds at birth."

"Try pushing out two," Kinsey bemoaned, peering over at the baby and latching on to one of his chubby little fingers. "Logan's talking about having another one. I might have to give in since Jace is so adorable." She shifted gears and leaned into Gilly. "What's this I hear about you and Simon joining forces?"

"I know small town living is like a grapevine, but we haven't put out a press release yet."

Kinsey bumped her shoulder. "Your mother has."

Gilly rolled her eyes. "And did she elaborate on how she felt about him?"

"What do you think? Yeah, she made it known she's not a fan. Don't know why exactly. The guy has served so many tours of duty overseas that I've lost count. He's a bona fide hero who doesn't even talk about his service."

It made her blood boil that her mother couldn't seem to keep her opinions to herself. But she maintained an even keel, refusing to let the annoyance show. "I don't get it either."

But as she stood there, her mind drifted to the way he'd been tossing and turning. She'd seen firsthand what all those tours had done to him. She was pretty sure that trouble sleeping was only part of it. People didn't realize the man suffered from a bad case of PTSD. Those thoughts were interrupted when she heard Jayden let out a squeal from the backyard. "I'd better go check on him."

Kinsey trailed after her. "I better go check on mine. They tend to act up when I take them out in public."

Gilly snorted out a laugh. "I'm almost afraid to look." But what she saw through the open doorway was Beckham Blackwood and Faye DeMarco entertaining all the preschoolers with a lively, interactive puppet show about magical dragons. Naturally, Jayden enjoyed it so much he had to shout out his enthusiasm full throttle.

"We should persuade those two that we need them for babysitting duty the night of the ball. Look how enthralled the kids are with the show."

"That's not a bad idea," Kinsey said. "We should make an offer. Teenagers always need a few extra bucks. And with half the town showing up we'll need extra hands to take care of so many kids."

"I'll approach Ophelia with that idea. Where is this event taking place?"

Kinsey pulled her back inside. "We need to talk about that. The elementary school cafeteria would work. What about it, Sydney?"

"It's probably our only option."

"Not really," Gilly began. "What about the grand foyer in the new library? It isn't fully stocked yet, which leaves room for a few hundred people. And it's more elegant than the school gym." She looked around at the faces. "Sorry, but the school gym just sounds so drab for a masquerade ball."

"No. No, you're right." Sydney began to pace and consider the possibilities. "There's room for a band in that raised space near the big window. It would work as a stage. And if we moved the furniture completely out of the lobby we could shove in another fifty people."

"We should check the fire codes," Kinsey prompted. "Make sure we don't violate any regulations. I'll call the county and set up an appointment for them to come out, maybe sit in on our final plans."

As that idea took shape, Gilly thought about Simon out on the water with his mother and daughter, enjoying the beautiful fall day.

Heat rose in her cheeks recalling their short, brief union, so fleeting she wondered if it had actually taken place. She knew it had. Her body felt different, felt like she'd been thoroughly made love to, and made to feel special, albeit briefly. But that wasn't his fault. As single parents, their circumstances were such that family had to take priority. She didn't feel cheated, she felt elated to finally have those first-night-together jitters out of the way, put to rest for good.

She glanced out the window at her boy, still giggling and laughing at the puppet show. That was her main goal, to keep Jayden happy and well-loved. If she could toss in a few stolen hours of happiness herself with a man like Simon, she'd take those precious times together and build on them for down the road. She hadn't expected to ever feel this way about a man; certainly it was different from the way she'd felt about Vaughn. But the man had given her Jayden and for that she could appreciate the role he'd played in changing her life.

Simon wasn't Vaughn. The two had zero traits in common. Something else to be grateful for, she muttered to herself as she looked at her watch and realized her Sunday had already been gobbled up. It was time to get ready for work.

On what was a somewhat boring start to her shift, Gilly was two hours in when she got a frantic phone call from her mother.

"You have to come and do something about Jayden. He's all wound up and I can't get him to settle down to go to bed."

"Bed? Mom, it's barely six o'clock. Have you given him supper?" Her worry shot up when she heard Jayden crying in the background.

"I made him peanut butter and jelly. Just come pick him up. He won't stop crying."

Gilly didn't know what had turned her happy toddler into a bawling mess, but she tried to figure it out. "Maybe he's worn out. He spent a long afternoon running around in the yard with the other kids."

"That's no excuse for knocking over one of my oldest figurines, the one with the birds on it."

"You're upset because he broke one of your porcelain pieces?"

"Your father bought that for me for my fortieth birthday."

"Okay. I understand you're upset. Let me call Sydney and see if I can get someone to cover for me. I'll take my lunch break early and be right there." After she hung up, she sent Sydney several text messages, hoping for a quick reply. But when the texts weren't returned right away, she realized the planning session must still be going strong. Which meant the other nurses like Aubree Wright would certainly have been drinking. With few options left, she decided to call Simon.

"What's wrong?"

"How did you know something was wrong?"

"I figure you're at work, right? You're not calling to shoot the bull."

She went into a detailed account that covered her mother's agitation at Jayden. "She's having a meltdown over a broken figurine. I know it's asking a lot but…could you go get him?"

"Stop it. I'll leave right now. What about a car seat?"

"You could borrow mine."

"Okay. Do you want me to stop off at the hospital after I pick him up and let you take a look at him, make sure for yourself that he's all right?"

At that moment, love, deep and solid, hit her squarely in the chest. In three years, she'd had no one who'd showed her this kind of affection, caring, or concern. She'd had no one to lean on, to call in times of crisis.

"That would be great. You don't mind?"

"If it were me, I'd want to see for myself that he's okay."

After hanging up, she waited, doing a dozen little chores for the patients under her care. She checked on Hattie Bledsoe, who'd been admitted the night before with a blood clot in her leg. She changed a bandage for Wade Hawkins, who'd driven a nail through his foot a week ago and was now dealing with sepsis from the wound. By the time she brought juice to Alice Mayfield, who suffered from a staph infection that had spread to her sinus cavity, she heard the double doors open out front.

Darting past the reception area, she watched Simon carry Jayden into the lobby. "How's my big guy doing?" Gilly asked, trying to remain upbeat and calm.

"Mama! Simon gonna take me for ice cream."

Simon relinquished him to his mom.

She settled him on her hip. "Ice cream, huh? And I don't get any?"

Jayden bobbed his head. "You can have mine."

"That's generous of you, buddy. Wanna tell me what happened at grandma's house?"

The toddler laid his head on her shoulder. "I...uh...I...bwoke her thing...and she got mad."

Simon put a hand on the boy's head. "I break things all the time. Accidents happen."

"Okay, baby, are you okay to go with Simon?"

Jayden nodded his head. "Ice cweam."

"Oh, yeah, mustn't forget the ice cream. Tell Margie I said hi, okay?"

"'K. Bye, Mama."

"Bye, baby."

Simon took Jayden out of her arms and leaned over to give her a chaste peck on the cheek. "Don't worry, he'll be fine."

"I won't worry, not now. Did Mom give you a change of clothes, his pajamas, his toothbrush?"

"She had a bag sitting by the door when I got there. We'll be fine."

"I know." Gilly bit her lip. "Thanks, Simon."

He took her chin because the woman looked like she might cry. "No problem. Text us when you get a break. We'll be playing with our cars."

That made her laugh. "Okay. Simon?"

"What?"

"Drive carefully."

He waved his free hand in the air as he exited through the automatic doors.

Gretchen had taken up a position on the front porch with Delaney on her lap to wait for them to get back. As soon as she spotted the pickup, she whispered in Delaney's ear. "Daddy's back. See? And he brought Jayden."

Delaney wanted down and started trying to maneuver the steps on her own. Gretchen helped her toddle out to the truck where Simon unbuckled Jayden from the back seat. "Jayden, tell them we brought ice cream."

"Ice cweam!" Jayden yelled.

"What kind?" Gretchen asked.

Simon waited for Jayden to come up with the answer. When he didn't, he leaned down and whispered in the boy's ear.

"Chocolate and stwabewwy."

"Yum. We like those, don't we, Delaney."

Simon handed off the bag to his mother so he could scoop up Delaney. "Did she eat her supper?"

"She wanted to wait for Daddy."

"Then let's get you something to eat before the ice cream melts. Jayden, let's get you unpacked and set up before bedtime."

"Jayden can have my room. I don't mind sleeping on the sofa."

Simon shook his head. "Nonsense. I'll bunk on the couch, you take my room."

"Are you sure?"

"I'm sure. The couch is fine compared to some of the places I've slept."

During her break, Gilly called to say goodnight to Jayden. But a three-year-old was much more interested in playing with the buttons than talking to his mother. After several minutes he got bored and handed the phone back to Simon, dashing off to continue smashing cars.

"I forgot to mention that since your mom is in the guest room, you can use a sleeping bag for Jayden and tell him he's camping out like big boys."

"It's not necessary." He went over the sleeping arrangements again. "Stop worrying. I have everything under control."

"I'm sure you can handle anything that comes your way. But wrangling two kids under the age of three is not for the faint of heart."

"Didn't you know? I'm fearless. Want me to bring you something to eat?"

"You'd do that?"

To get to see her, he would've driven to Fresno and back. "My mom's here for the kids. I could make you a homemade roast beef sandwich, two hours out of the oven."

As great as that sounded, should she cop to bringing leftovers from Friday night's spread? "You don't have to do that. You have to get two kids to bed."

Simon looked over at a drowsy Delaney and an animated Jayden, who was bumping his cars into the furniture and making loud roaring sounds. "One's already nodding off. The other is…having fun."

"You are so politically correct. I can hear him in the background zooming around the room. That's what he does."

"He'll wind down soon enough."

"Are you always this patient?"

"What's to get upset about? He's a kid. Maybe he's rowdy, but he's a typical, normal little guy, even my mom thinks so."

"She does? Did she say that?"

"She did."

For the first time in days, Gilly felt like the universe had lined up. "I gotta get back to work. Will you text me later?"

"Count on it."

With help from his mother, Simon let her put Delaney to bed while he corralled Jayden. "Maybe giving you sugar so close to bedtime wasn't the smartest move I've ever made. Want to hear a story about a seriously whacked monkey in the zoo?"

"Uh huh."

"Then let's get you a bath and put your PJs on."

Bath time was quick and messy. But he could tell Jayden was winding down. By the time he cracked open the book, Jayden had already drifted off to sleep.

Gretchen tiptoed out of Delaney's room and plopped down on the sofa. "I hate to say this, but after my visit to Connie's the other day, I'm not surprised she came unglued around Jayden."

"Really? You went to see Connie? When?"

She'd walked right into that. "Okay, I went there Saturday morning to see if I could get a better handle on why she disliked you so much. I was ready to take up for my boy. But she seemed even more fragile than she had on Friday night, obsessing about Jayden and his hyperactivity."

"Well, she proved that tonight. I felt bad for Gilly. I thought she might burst into tears before I got Jayden out of there. Gilly, not Connie."

"Poor thing. I get the impression that Connie's erratic behavior is beginning to take a toll. Stop and think about it. Connie's been her only support system since Jayden's been here. A person relies on family to get them through the tough times. Now she's realizing Connie is either unwilling or unable to continue in that capacity. She has to be worried at this point."

"That about sums up what I saw this afternoon. What did you intend to do to try and persuade Connie that I'm a nice enough guy? More cute stories about me as an adorable kid? Something tells me Connie's immune."

Gretchen leaned over and slapped him on the knee. "You could be right. I did try some of my best stuff. It seemed to go right over her head." She noticed Simon's glum look. "What else is bothering you?"

"I think I'm falling for Gilly."

"Why so down about it?"

"Not down, maybe…scared."

Gretchen let out a laugh. "Oh, Simon. How long has it been since you've been in love? High school?

"Not like this. Besides, I don't want to scare her off by telling her too quickly. Thoughts? Advice?"

"Gauge the way she acts around you and go from there. It's the best I can do. Look, I'm exhausted. I think I'll head to bed."

"Just let me get some blankets out of the closet."

He made up the couch, but laid there, wide awake. After a while, he sent a text to Gilly.

What are you wearing?

That teddy you didn't get to see.

Unfair.

What are you wearing?

Not a thing. See how that unfair thing works?

I'm picturing you right now. Hot. Bothered.

I'm picturing the teddy and taking it off you.

Now you're talking. Oops. Gotta go, one of my patients just buzzed.

Get your mind out of the gutter first.

He got a smiley face in return.

A little wired from the suggestive byplay, it took him a while, but he eventually dozed off. That is, until he heard a noise coming from outside on the porch. With his gun locked away in a closet in the other room, he picked up the only thing handy---the poker in front of the fireplace.

Looking out the window, he didn't see anyone until a shadow crossed in front of him. He threw back the door, only to see Scott sitting in one of the chairs like he owned the place.

"You scared the bejesus out of me. There are kids inside. What the hell are you doing out here?"

"Look at your watch. What time is it?"

"What? I didn't think time existed in your world. It's three-fifteen. That's a.m. in case you were wondering."

"Go put some clothes on and be there when Gilly gets off work."

"That's a great idea. Is she in trouble?"

"Not if you show up and surprise her."

"That's what you came here to tell me? My God, Scott Phillips is a romantic."

"I know. I didn't realize it was wasted on the living until I died."

"Okay. You can go now. Message received. But I'll have to wake my mother up to let her know to listen for the kids."

Scott stood up. "She's already awake."

Simon stepped back inside but when he looked back, Scott had disappeared. "That is just plain weird," he muttered under his breath. "*Twilight Zone* weird,"

"Who are you talking to?" Gretchen whispered. "What's wrong?"

"Nothing. An old friend stopped by," Simon muttered, pulling on his jeans. "I need for you to make sure you can hear the kids in case they wake up."

"Sure. But where will you be?"

He pulled a T-shirt over his head and started to put on his Nikes. "After I go to the hospital, I'm hoping to end up at Gilly's. I'll be back first thing in the morning. Do you mind very much?"

Gretchen smiled. "Go. Enjoy yourself the same way you did Saturday night."

He gave her a wink. "That's the plan. Thanks, Mom."

Simon had spent many pre-dawn hours on high alert. But the road into town was downright spooky. It made him appreciate the hours Gilly worked and how she did it with total composure and spunk. Third shift wasn't for sissies.

He pulled into the hospital parking lot, which had only two cars there, parked next to her Subaru. And waited.

Fifteen minutes later she came out through a side door. He knew the minute she spotted him because she broke out into a wide smile and darted toward him, jumping into his arms.

His mouth covered hers. There was a moment of sheer need and utter lust. "I'll follow you home."

"Are you staying?"

"Do you want me to?"

"Absolutely. The kids?"

"Mom has them covered for at least four hours."

"Then why are we standing around here?"

Lovers who found a way to carve out precious moments to be together made the most of their time.

They barely made it into Gilly's house before ripping at each other's clothes. They toed off shoes, peeled off scrubs and shirts and shorts, tossing them on the living room floor as they bumped into the walls, latching onto each other, making their way into the bedroom.

They couldn't get to the bed fast enough. It was all heat and need. Hurrying to get down to flesh, to feel skin. Tongues explored, devoured. Wet and slick, teeth nipped. He'd known he could take her to the gilded edge of all reason and proved it, as they both tumbled onto the bed.

Her senses were on overload as he slicked his tongue again over curves, taking his time to savor her taste.

"I want you inside me," she said, breathless with need.

"Not yet." There were peaks to climb, valleys yet to conquer.

She arched her back, shuddering at the pleasure spooling around her. She fisted the sheet in her hand and held on while his mouth did the rest.

This was finally the love she'd needed without knowing it existed. She soared toward that ribbon of light, seeking the ultimate assent. When it hit, she floated, drunk and dizzy into the circle of his embrace.

"Now, Simon! Now!"

He pressed his lips to hers. Joined, mated, he began to move, taking her higher. Desire as smooth as silk danced along the fringes. Like velvet, they glided up and up, sailing through the bluest blue. Swirling, swirling they flew. Gilly moaned as she raced toward that jagged rim, inching closer, faster. It was her sexy little whimper that let Simon claw his way toward the edge. He buried his face in her hair and let himself fall into the same glow.

Sprawled over her sleek body, he had to drum up the energy to move.

"Wow," Gilly managed. "Just. Wow."

Simon finally rolled to his back. "I'll take that as a compliment."

Snuggled next to each other, entwined, they tried to sleep. But it eluded them. They napped but it wasn't the same as that gateway to deep slumber. So when sunlight began to filter through the drapes despite their best efforts to ignore it, Simon cracked open one eye to snatch a look at the time.

"Where did the last few hours go?" Gilly whispered hoarsely, yawning widely.

He twined a blond strand of her hair around his finger, toyed with a bare breast. "Time flies when you're having fun."

"Mmm." She rolled over him, straddled him. "Want to enjoy yourself again?"

She didn't wait for an answer. Instead, she ravaged his mouth, his throat, moving down his chest, hungry to feed a primal greed that seemed to have come alive over the last two days.

Their eyes locked. His hands reached out and laced his fingers with hers. They began a rhythm, a faster pace than the last as if they knew the sand drifted through the hourglass at a rapid rate and they didn't have a whole lot of time.

Gilly capitalized on that, made it her own. She wanted to give back to him before they had to wait until the next available opportunity presented itself.

From her vantage point, she rode, taking the lead, intense and focused. Her mouth came down on his in fierce need. He lifted her, urging her on. Her blood pumped, pulsing toward that one goal, release. When pleasure flooded her senses, she let go, tumbling, spinning, into the brilliant bliss.

He ran his hands down her hips. "You're incredible."

She threw her arms in the air. "You've made me feel alive again. Even though I'm running on fumes, that was…exhilarating. Thanks for waiting for me outside the hospital. Whatever made you think of that?"

He wasn't about to cop to a ghost for inspiration. "I wanted to be with you."

She wriggled off him to plop back on her side of the bed. "How will we deal with no sleep today?"

"You have to be fresh for your shift at four. That means, you're gonna to stay here and get some shuteye."

"Simon, I can't let you do that. Jayden's a handful."

"Look, I got the planting all done until Silas gives me another task. No tours today from the B&B. I can catch a few winks when Delaney goes down for her nap."

"But Jayden rarely naps."

"That's okay. Maybe my mom will entertain him. Don't worry about it." He stood up to get dressed. "But I probably need to hit the road while I'm able to walk."

She burst out laughing. "I'll wear you out anytime you want, just say the word."

He planted a smoldering kiss on her mouth. "That's a plan I can live with."

Twenty-Three

Simon was shocked to hear the house so quiet when he walked into the living room. His mother had fallen asleep on the sofa and was slumped into the pillows, softly snoring. He tiptoed past her and into the bathroom to grab a hot shower. It only lasted a quick five minutes or so, but in that short amount of time, as he was drying off, he heard voices, one louder than the rest, ginning up for the day.

He grabbed a clean pair of jeans and a shirt and opened the door to his bedroom, prepared to face the chaos. Pandemonium loomed. Jayden, ever the lover of anything with wheels, careened his cars into Delaney's feet, causing her to lose her balance and hit the floor.

"I'm sowwy," Jayden hollered.

Simon picked up the now screaming child and held her close. "It's okay. It's okay. You're okay."

"I'm sowwy," Jayden said again.

Simon traded looks with his mother who stood back waiting for him to handle the situation. He took a seat in one of the living room chairs. "I know you are, Jayden. It was an accident. But you gotta be more careful around her. She's younger than you are and doesn't walk as steady as you do yet. She'll get there, but right now she's wobbly on her feet."

As Delaney sniffed and hiccupped in his arms, Jayden put his face close to hers. "I'm sowwy."

Her hand jabbed out fast with a quick right, aiming to hit him in the face in retaliation.

"Delaney, none of that," Simon calmly said. "You two should be friends. Jayden, I want you to give her a hug. Delaney, hug Jayden back. Now."

He watched as they made an awkward attempt to put their arms around each other. Forced as it was, it did the trick. "There. All better? Are we ready to eat breakfast now or do we still want to fuss at each other?"

"Eat!" Jayden yelled.

"Eat," Delaney repeated.

"Good because it's too early for sniping. No more fighting or fussing. Delaney, do you want to get down now and play before breakfast?"

She crawled out of Simon's lap and made a beeline for Jayden's cars. Simon waited for the blow up, but Jayden seemed to accept that he needed to share.

Gretchen shook her head and marveled at the sight. "You're actually pretty good at this."

"Who knew, right? I need caffeine."

"And sleep. You didn't get a wink of sleep, I bet."

At the sink, Simon filled a decanter with water and poured the contents into the reservoir before measuring out coffee beans to grind. "What do you think? But then I didn't go over there to sleep. My morning's free and hers isn't, so I'm keeping Jayden while she gets some rest since she has to be fresh for her shift this afternoon."

He removed a carton of eggs from the fridge and began to crack them into a bowl and then whipped them with a fork for scrambling.

Gretchen remembered her coffee date with John. She could cancel. It wasn't like it was set in stone. But then maybe there was a workaround. "Want me to look after the kids while you take a nap? I could take them to the park and let them run around there. Who knows? Maybe Jayden would take a nap."

"It's not necessary unless you just want to spend time with Delaney. You still have a few days left. Your flight leaves Thursday, right?"

"At eleven." Why didn't she simply tell him about the coffee date? It might make things easier. "I met someone in the park Saturday morning."

"Yeah? Who?"

"A man by the name of John Dickinson. He asked me to have coffee with him this morning and I said yes."

Simon's mouth fell open. He'd never thought about his mother's social life including a man. But she was young enough, sixty was hardly having one foot in the grave. And he of all people knew how short life could be and ever-changing in an instant. Once the idea sunk in, the implication became clear. "And you want to keep this date, right?"

"For coffee," Gretchen emphasized. "Just to talk. I so seldom get to do that with people my own age anymore. Back home, if they don't drop in to see me, I don't go out of my way to see them. I slowly gave up doing my charity work after your father died, and without meaning to, I gave friends I'd known for years the impression I wanted to be left alone. Those contacts have slowly dried up for me. That includes most of my old bridge partners, who've chosen to avoid stopping by to visit. I'm not sure if it's their circumstances keeping them away, or maybe they're super busy, or maybe they really do want to avoid being around Lorraine. People are like that sometimes. They don't know what to say, so they avoid saying anything at all."

He'd known all along what a challenge his mother faced every day taking care of his aunt. But he didn't realize it had put a ding in her once active social life. He could see it now on her face. Maybe she was dreading going back home to that strained situation, one that had no good ending on the horizon. "Then do it. Don't cancel this thing with John. But you don't have to take the kids. I have to call that Margaret person in Boston and get the check thing straightened out anyway."

"But that's just it. I could meet John in the park and bring the kids with me. Watch them while they play. And still have coffee with John."

Simon saw the eagerness in his mother's eyes. "Sure." As he scrambled the eggs, he prompted, "So tell me about this John guy. Who is he exactly?"

"Small town and you don't know? His daughter is the principal of the elementary school."

"Julianne McLachlan is his daughter?"

"You know her?"

"I've seen her around town. I know Ryder better. Good guy. He has a boatbuilding business over on Ocean Street. His wife also opened her own shop called Reclaimed Treasures, that store on Main that carries fashionable and trendy upcycled stuff. Julianne is the one who found my sofa. She'll do that sort of thing if you ask her to look out for a certain hard-to-find item."

"John didn't mention the store. But he seems like any proud daddy when he talks about his daughter."

Simon began to feel better about the man.

After calling the kids to the table and getting them situated, he and his mother continued their conversation over coffee. "I should've realized how hard it was taking care of Lorraine all these years."

"She's my sister. We used to do everything together. We're barely a year apart. I wasn't about to turn her over to strangers and let them take care of her. But...it's been five years since she started behaving in odd ways, couldn't remember where she'd left her car keys. And odd things would come out of her mouth. She's gone steadily downhill in the last year. She doesn't even know where she is most of the time, let alone recognizing me. Makes me wonder...about Connie. She's acting a lot like Lorraine did before her diagnosis."

"But the doctors say Connie doesn't have Alzheimer's."

"Which is good. But I wonder if the shunt hasn't had time to get rid of all the excess fluid yet and it's still doing weird things to her brain."

"According to Gilly, her mother wasn't like this until recently. It's gotta be the right diagnosis."

"You'd think. What if this Boston lawyer didn't make a mistake? You said the man Amelia was with was wealthy. What if that check is Delaney's inheritance?"

"A million-dollar inheritance?" He thought back to that summer on Cape Cod. There were indications Amelia Langston favored expensive things. She carried trendy handbags, the upscale kind made of Italian calfskin leather. But he hadn't bothered checking the price tags. Why would he? He knew the camera she used to capture all those photos wasn't cheap, somewhere in the neighborhood of three grand, maybe more. And her outfits never failed to get his attention. But again, he hadn't bothered checking labels. He could admit now that he hadn't paid enough attention to details that summer. He was too caught up in the escape, the newness of being out of the Army, the freedom to do whatever he wanted, not to mention all the sex an arm's reach away.

"It's possible it isn't a mistake," Gretchen insisted.

"It has to be. Things like that don't happen to people like us," Simon stated. He glanced at his watch, noted the time. "But we'll know in a few minutes because Boston is open for business."

He shut himself off in the bedroom to make the call so there'd be less noise from the kids. After Tyler's secretary put him through to her majesty, Simon went into all the questions he'd built up over the last three days.

"Remember when you dropped Delaney off that day, you said something about Amelia's estate totaling no more than twenty-five grand. That's what I expected the check to read when I opened the envelope. How could you make this kind of error?"

On the other end of the line, Simon thought the ice-cold Margaret Tyler seemed to squirm in her chair. "If you'll recall, that day I had a lot on my plate. I might've misspoken. I didn't realize at the time the true extent of her estate. Up until then I had been focused on getting your daughter situated. I would think you'd appreciate that fact first."

"So what are you saying?"

"The amount of the check isn't a mistake."

"You're kidding?"

"Would I kid about this? That's why I asked before sending that amount through the mail. But you werc so insistent."

"How was I supposed to know you were talking about that kind of money?"

He heard Margaret sigh into the phone. "I'm sorry there's been this kind of miscommunication, but I assure you the only thing left is to sell the townhouse her...benefactor left to her. As it turns out, his grown children were attempting to file a lawsuit for their share of what he left Ms. Langston. I thought I was doing you a favor by going ahead and distributing the funds. I feel that little girl deserves what her mother left her. The only mistake she made was not putting the money in a trust so it wouldn't have to go through probate."

"All right. Where do we go from here? Because that's exactly my intent, putting the money into a trust for her is the only option. She won't even know about it until she reaches twenty-one. Or maybe twenty-five."

"That's good. At least she'll know her mother cared enough to leave her everything she had. I would suggest you get a good trust attorney immediately to set up an ironclad fund that only she benefits from, no matter whom she marries, they won't be able to squander away her inheritance. After you've done all the paperwork, send me a copy for my files."

He wondered if that last part was a dig at him. It didn't sound like Ms. Tyler had any faith that he'd follow through on the plan, which is why he set up an appointment with Kinsey for eleven that morning.

Having the kids with her made Gretchen feel more at ease. Not that she thought John was a perv or a weirdo or anything like that. But meeting up in the park with the children seemed to be the best way to gauge his interest and possibly his intent.

She sat on the park bench under a beautiful clear sky, a soft ocean breeze on her face. Birds flitted back and forth like springtime. The difference in weather here was startling. Back in Rhode Island it would soon be cold and dreary, snow on the ground until March or April. How nice it would be to live here year-round. How great it would be to get up in the morning just to see Delaney's little face more often than once a year.

She was deep in those kinds of thoughts when John ambled up and took a seat next to her, holding two containers of coffee and a bag between his fingers. He handed one to-go cup off to her.

"Thanks for meeting me here instead of the Diner."

"No problem. Better than your canceling on me altogether. Besides, I like the outdoors. Busy morning?"

She let out a laugh and looked over at the energetic kids playing in the sandbox. "Those two make sure mornings aren't boring. You didn't say anything about grandkids."

"That's because I think my daughter and son-in-law have been trying but…they've been unsuccessful so far, if you know what I mean. I find it best to avoid bringing up the subject at all. I refuse to play the role of nosy in-law."

"Good for you. Isn't life strange, though? My son had Delaney and for almost sixteen months didn't even know she existed. Now, it seems she's his whole reason for getting up in the morning. Life can bring change in the oddest ways."

He nodded and held out the bag to her. "Max's famous cinnamon rolls guaranteed to melt in your mouth. Try one."

Gretchen obliged, taking a bite out of the gooey pastry, then licking the icing off her fingertips.

"Is your coffee okay?"

"It's fine. Good. Strong the way I like it."

"Margie makes the best coffee in town. Swears she cleans the pot every four hours to keep it from going stale. When you texted me with a change in plans I wasn't sure if you were trying to ditch me or not."

"If I'd wanted to do that I wouldn't be sitting here now."

"I'm glad. You didn't ditch me, that is. Would you consider letting me buy you dinner before you go back east?"

Flattered, she tilted her head to study him, more forward than what she was used to in her neck of the woods. A long-forgotten pull in the belly hit her. She barely recognized the tug, but it made her realize she was attracted to him. "Are we talking about a date?"

"I am. Not sure what you consider it to be. We could be friends, but that's not what I'm hoping for."

"Really? And what about the fact that we live on opposite ends of the country?"

"I thought about that some. Is there any way we could keep in touch once you get back to Newport? Get to know each other better."

"You want to?"

"We could email back and forth. Julianne taught me how to use Skype not too long ago. I could show you how to set it up and when we get the urge we could talk. It's cheaper than long distance and you don't have to eat into your minutes on the cell. Is that too forward?"

She lifted a shoulder. "Don't ask me. I'm no expert. I haven't…" She'd started to use the word "dated" and stopped, realizing that might be presumptuous, even premature. "Whatever this is?"

"I'll be honest, I haven't done much dating lately. I spent years raising my daughter alone. My wife took off not long after Julianne came along and left me to raise her by myself. I was way too busy back then to seek out company on a regular basis. Had a girlfriend a time or two, but they got tired of waiting for me to marry them. And I just…got cold feet every time I tried to think like that. You should know I'm a little gun shy when that subject comes up."

"That's understandable, given your first wife. Now for me, as long as you know up front that I've only been a widow for two years, which means I have no idea what to expect from any kind of dating scenario. It sounds like you're more the expert. Plus, I'm taking care of my older sister who's getting worse every day. I seem to have no one to talk to about it because my friends have slowly distanced themselves from the situation over the years, especially since Lowell died. And now my son has given me this ultimate gift, a grandchild, who happens to be three thousand miles away from where I live. How unfair is that?"

John smiled. "You're right. Life is truly strange. It hands us all kinds of twists and turns we don't expect. I don't see what the harm is to having dinner before you go."

Gretchen took a deep breath and remembered Connie's situation, then Lorraine's. Things could get a lot worse and life was just too short to pass up the possibilities. "I say don't waste a minute on regrets. How about tomorrow night? It can't be Wednesday because I have to set aside time to see Simon and Delaney my last night in town."

"Tuesday night's fine. You can come to my house. I fix a mean grilled snapper."

The Tudor-style home on Landings Bay that Kinsey used for her law office had grown larger over the years to accommodate a growing family. Logan had made sure that the space expanded into two wings. One for hearth and home, another for tending to clients, complete with Aaron Hartley's law library.

Simon sat in a study surrounded by books. After explaining to Kinsey what was going on, and producing the large check, he watched her reaction.

"Wow! This is from the woman on Cape Cod? The one who wanted a baby so badly…?"

"That she slept with me? Yeah."

"I didn't mean it like that."

"I know what you meant, but it's the reality of the situation. Tyler seems to think the adult children of this guy will come after the money."

Kinsey shook her head. "Nope. Not happening. That should've been done before probate. Although I can check the laws of Massachusetts for you if you'd like, even go so far as to make a call to this Tyler woman myself. But I'm ninety-nine percent certain the window of opportunity has passed. My guess, without having all the facts on hand, is that your Amelia put most of the money he left her in an offshore account, hid it away from these grown children for that very purpose. She had access whenever she needed to draw from the account.

These kids likely didn't know anything about it so they couldn't very well contest her assets until it was too late. At some point, Amelia must've made a lawyer aware of the account so that it showed up in her estate, otherwise you wouldn't be holding that check. Probably at the same time she made out a will stating Delaney belonged to you and was to go to you if anything happened to her."

"Smart woman, but let's not lessen the fact she was also cunning. Figuring all the angles is what she did best."

"She figured this one pretty well, Simon. For her only daughter. She did what she thought was best for her daughter's future."

"I guess. Though it seems…too weird to suit me. I don't want to cut Delaney out of anything, but the money…it isn't that important to me and I personally won't be touching it."

"But it might be important to Delaney one day, something from her mother that validates Amelia existed. She'll never remember her, Simon, not even a slight memory. She's too young. Do you have any photos from that summer, from your time together?"

"That's the first I've thought of it. A ton. Amelia didn't go anywhere or do anything without a camera in her hand. Those pictures have to be somewhere. Although Tyler did tell me I should expect a moving pod to arrive any day now."

"Great. Then maybe there are personal effects in there that you can hang onto and show her from that brief time you and her mother had together." She waved the check in the air. "I'll get the paperwork started after we take this puppy to the bank. Once the money's safely there, you pick the name you want for the trust, and I'll take it from there."

"Does that mean you'll administer the money?"

"Nope. Not me. That's you unless you want to change the specifics. Do you have a current will? Because you should probably name someone to care for Delaney if anything should happen to you."

Simon twisted in his chair. "Not a bad idea. I do have a will, but I haven't added anything about Delaney. I should do that."

Kinsey leveled a finger at him. "Parents can't afford to put off that kind of stuff. Amelia is proof of that. You walk out the door in the morning and you never know what's around that bend in the road."

After all his errands were done, Simon caught up with his mother for a late lunch at Longboard's Pizza. "How'd it go with John?"

"I'm having dinner with him tomorrow night."

"Wow, this guy sounds like a mover and a shaker who doesn't waste any time. Maybe he could give me some pointers."

She playfully punched his arm. "Since when do you need pointers?"

"Since I got played by a beautiful woman who wanted a baby and didn't care how she got it?"

"You have to stop saying things like that, Simon, especially in front of Delaney."

He scrubbed his hands over his face. "You're right. I'm sorry. I'm tired and not used to watching what I say."

Just as Fischer brought out their order, Gilly sailed into the eatery with a big smile on her face. "Hey guys. Perfect timing. Feed me."

"Mama!" Jayden burst out.

"Hi, baby," Gilly said, wrapping her arms around the boy before sliding into the booth beside Simon. "Are you being a good boy for Simon and Mrs. Bremmer?"

"Jes."

"Shouldn't you be sleeping?" Simon asked.

"Thanks to you, I got in six hours. I'm good."

"You hungry?" Gretchen asked, cutting a piece of the pie so that Delaney could use it as finger food. "There's plenty. We ordered two large so there'd be leftovers."

"Yeah. No one wants to cook tonight."

After taking a slice off the tray and handing it to Jayden, Gilly took Simon's chin. "You didn't get any sleep."

"I had errands to get done. But I'm not complaining."

"Neither am I," she whispered. "So what else have you guys been up to?"

"Mom had a date in the park," Simon said with a grin. "She took the kids along for protection."

Gilly let out a laugh. "Do tell. Who's this mystery man?"

"I haven't kept it a mystery." Eyeing Simon, she added, "Although I'm beginning to think I should have. His name's John Dickinson."

Gilly took a slice for herself and stared at Gretchen. "I know John. He built the cover over my patio. Logan recommended him, said he was reliable and wouldn't charge an arm and a leg. Turns out, John did it for peanuts and had the work done within a week."

"See? He's good with his hands," Simon cracked.

Gretchen blushed, but sent him a reluctant grin. "You aren't as upset about this as I thought you'd be."

"You want I should go beat him up?"

"Of course not. I'm not dead, you know. I should have a life."

"Not saying otherwise. I think you should get out there and live. I'd like you to do it here around your granddaughter, but I know you won't budge as long as Lorraine needs you." He patted his mother's hand. "I'm not trying to guilt you. Just the opposite. After you leave, I'll miss having you here."

Water formed in Gretchen's eyes causing her to snatch up a few paper napkins from the dispenser to dab them dry. "I've enjoyed getting to know Delaney and spending this time with you."

Gilly couldn't believe what she was hearing. "Hey, you still have two days. Don't be so down. There's still time to have fun. You two. Fun."

"Well, I did agree to have dinner with John Tuesday night."

Simon choked on the bite of pizza he'd just chewed. "I thought you were kidding. You're going on a date when the clock's ticking on our time together?"

Now Gretchen heard annoyance in his voice. "I'll cancel if you want me to, but the plan is to put Delaney to bed and then he'll pick me up. We're going back to his place. He said he'd cook."

Simon had to grab his soda to wash down the wad of pie that stuck in his throat. Just as he was about to lose it, he looked at his mother's face, saw real pain there that he hadn't noticed before. Hadn't he just told her she needed to get out there, to live her life? He swallowed his objections and, like Gilly, thought it best to focus on enjoying the rest of his mother's time here in town. "I talked to Nick today and got a firm date for closing. Two weeks from today."

"I wish I could be here for it," Gretchen said, still teary eyed.

Gilly frowned. "On a Monday? I was hoping to help you out."

"Don't worry about it. I'll round up the guys and we'll knock it out in a few hours. I don't have that much stuff. But I should probably start packing things up."

"No, I think I'll ask Sydney for the day off, give her plenty of time to switch around schedules. We do it all the time. That way, I can at least watch Delaney for you. And it isn't easy packing with a toddler. Now you're dealing with Jayden. I'll help you pack this weekend." She wiped Jayden's messy mouth and then turned to do the same with Delaney.

It was all so normal to sit around like a family, Simon thought, as if it was the most natural thing in the world, as if they'd been doing it forever. He listened to Gilly go over decorating ideas with his Mom. For *his* house. They were already like a team. This was so surreal. Instead of panicking, his shoulders relaxed. There were no egos at play here.

With the kind of life he'd lived, nothing he'd ever imagined would have brought him to this point, to this woman. And yet, here he was, listening to the woman he loved…

Whoa. Where had that come from? Loved? He glanced over and stared at Gilly, watching her interact with the kids. She was so good at everything she did and so down to earth. When exactly had he fallen off that cliff?

He knew she was like a burst of bright sunlight, someone he enjoyed being around. He'd even fallen for her kid. He glanced over at Jayden's face, messy again from tomato sauce. How had he gotten a ready-made family so fast? And why didn't it scare the bejesus out of him?

Twenty-Four

There wasn't a lot of time for Simon to sort out fears like that.

Early Tuesday morning, a truck rumbled up the lane and dropped off the pod from Boston containing all Delaney's stuff. It took Simon and his mother three hours to make sense of what was inside.

Gretchen stood, hands on hips, surveying all the various items that hadn't been packed away in cartons but rather loaded into the storage container and left to tumble around on the cross-country trip here. "Everything's a mess. It's like whoever packed up her townhouse crammed it all in here without tying anything down."

"I wonder if Margaret Tyler was even there to supervise the removal of this stuff. I blame her for this."

Gretchen huffed out a breath. "At least you can give Gilly back her stroller. There are two in the back there. Did you notice that?"

"I like Jayden's stroller better than these, although one is pink and white, girly, but it looks like a luggage cart."

"Honey, those must've cost at least a thousand dollars apiece."

"You're kidding? Why would anyone pay that for a stroller?"

"Beats me. But apparently money was no object for your…"

Simon cut her off. "I wish people would stop using that word. *Your*. It irritates me."

"Would you prefer *that woman*?"

Simon ran a hand through his hair. "Not really. But Amelia wasn't mine. We had no future together. Not ever. If she and her lover had lived, I wouldn't even know I'd ever had a daughter, until a stranger, a grown female at that, showed up at my door thirty, forty years down the road."

"You're still bitter about that."

"Angry," he corrected. "You try learning you've fathered a child, standing in the living room at the B&B. It was…"

"Humiliating?"

"Yeah. And then some. But I need to let it go and stop bringing it up, don't I?"

She rubbed his arm. "Too many other more productive things that need doing right now. Are you okay to sort this mess out after you move in?"

"After I get this thing over to the new place, I'll unload it bit by bit into the garage and go through it then. The toys she had have to be in here somewhere."

"She's doing fine with what she has. *This*, a truckload of stuff, isn't what she needs right now."

He knew it was true. Delaney seemed like a happy little girl, a fact that meant he was doing something right.

He couldn't explain the thrill he felt at the sight of her holding out her arms to him when she wanted to be picked up. Any parent could relate to that deep emotional connection running through their veins when their child needed them.

Gilly knew. She understood. But it wasn't their only bond. The sex had been incredible. And wasn't that the best boon to it all. Without much effort, his mind drifted into that memory of mating, slipping into her body and sharing that link.

He forced himself to shake out of the fogbank of sex and focus on the task at hand. Getting movers lined up was a helluva drop from thinking about Gilly's curvy body and how he wanted to explore every inch of it the next time they were together.

Gilly didn't have time to think about sex. She'd arrived for her shift to find it busy and hopping. She'd just given Zach Dennison, who'd almost lost a finger using a table saw at his workplace, a shot of lidocaine before Dr. Nighthawk sutured the wound.

"When's the last time you had a tetanus shot?" she asked.

"Don't know. Don't remember. Don't like blood. Don't like shots either."

Gilly patted his arm. "Then don't look. But you're getting a tetanus shot before you go home."

She'd just cruised out of his exam room when she spotted her mother teetering this side of the automatic front doors. She darted toward her and watched as her mother collapsed in the waiting area.

"Dr. Nighthawk!"

Gideon, who'd been about to tend to Zach, rushed over to where Connie had crumpled. "Get Sydney. We'll need help getting her onto a stretcher."

But Sydney had already heard the commotion and come running. All three managed to lift an unconscious Connie and transferred her to a gurney.

Sydney wheeled her into another exam room. "You stay out here and take care of Zach," Sydney told Gilly. "You know the rules."

"I do." But Gilly had to calm down enough to do her job and stitch up Zach's sliced finger, all the while her mother was on the other side of a blue curtain.

She slapped on latex gloves, brought over the suture tray and got busy.

She estimated Zach's ring finger would take seven stitches. Normally, a piece of cake. She took her time with each suture, not wanting to rush. Before she was finished, Bree and Troy pushed back the curtain to check on his progress.

Gilly was used to dealing with worried family members who wanted to hover, but at this juncture, she was having none of it. "Visitors wait outside until we're done. Your brother's doing fine, Bree. Aren't you, Zach?"

Zach nodded.

The couple backed out without an argument, either because they didn't want to see the procedure or didn't want to upset the person holding the tapered needle.

Thirty minutes later, she finished up with Zach, complete with tetanus shot and extra bandages, and discharged him to his waiting family.

She took care of half a dozen other chores, seeing to patients down the hall, until finally Dr. Nighthawk emerged with news.

"She's fine," Gideon assured her. "She's developed an infection which is quite common in shunt recipients. I'm admitting her, so we can pump enough antibiotics into her and deal with it."

"I'd just checked on her before I came to work. You're sure she'll be okay?"

"I think so, yes. You know as well as I do that infections related to shunts can develop rapidly, cause the body to go into shock. That's what happened to Connie."

Gilly dropped into one of the chairs near the reception area. "Thank goodness she was able to get herself here. I looked up and...there she was. I watched her collapse right in front of me."

Gideon put a hand on her shoulder. "And like the professional you are, you went on to do your job. We're trained to keep our heads in a crisis. I think you exemplified that just now."

"Thanks. When I can see her?"

"Sydney's wheeled her into room 2. Take your break now and tend to your mom."

Her mother looked pale and fragile, but at least she was awake. "Hey, Mom. How're you feeling?"

"Like I've walked ten miles uphill."

"Why didn't you call me?"

"I didn't have my phone with me. I started out on a walk, got halfway down Crescent Street and began to feel sick, you know, dizzy like I could pass out. I didn't have much choice but to try and make it here."

Gilly squeezed her fingers. "You did a great job." She had to be grateful her mother hadn't fainted anywhere along the route.

"Am I going to be okay, Gilly? Tell me the truth. I'm not used to this, not used to feeling sick."

"You'll be fine, Mom. From now on we'll monitor your white cell count for infection on a more regular basis. Stay on top of anything that doesn't feel quite right."

"I'm sorry I upset you with Jayden the other day."

"It's okay, Mom. You haven't been yourself. But we'll make you better. I promise. Now get some sleep."

After leaving her alone, Gilly leaned up against the wall in the hallway. She reached out to the one person she could, not through text, but she needed to hear Simon's voice.

Simon was in the middle of the floor, wrestling with Jayden when his phone buzzed. "That's your mom," he told the toddler. "Time out."

He answered the phone in a mocking voice. "Hello, this is Jayden's latest victim. I need help. The boy is strong and keeps knocking me down. Help. Come save me."

In the background, Gilly could hear Jayden giggle and make zooming noises. And she laughed, grateful for this part of her world. "I'm Nurse Grant coming to the rescue."

"How's everything going? Work okay?"

She told him about her mother.

Instantly, he was up off the floor. "Do you need anything?"

"I'm fine. Talking to you is what I needed. Hearing your voice. Knowing Jayden's okay. That's what I need right now."

He wanted to reach through the phone and wrap her up. "When's your break?"

"I'm on it now. I needed some time to get it together."

"I'd be there, even with the kids. Mom has that date tonight. Just say the word."

"Simon, you've been blowing and going for days now. Take a night off. I'll be fine. Knowing you have everything under control means the world to me. And tell Gretchen to go out and kick up her heels tonight."

There was a sadness in her voice he hadn't heard before. He thought he understood. "Close calls like that take a lot out of us, but we rebound."

She took a deep breath. "What would I do without you?"

"I don't want you finding out."

"I've got to get back. I'll text you if I can."

Simon went from being in a good mood to taking on some of Gilly's burden. He needed to think and suggested they all go for a walk.

"Why don't I start dinner?" Gretchen offered. "You take the kids out for a little bit. You look like you could use the fresh air."

The three of them headed toward the pumpkin patch, where the big and bright orange balls caught Delaney's eye.

Their pace wasn't fast, but rather a slow methodical amble down rows and rows of green vines, holding onto fruit that would surely end up as someone's jack o'lantern soon. It was almost the end of September, time for the fruit stand at the end of the driveway to bustle with busloads of school children coming from as far away as San Sebastian to pick out pumpkins. It was one of the farm's oldest fall traditions.

He looked over in time to see Delaney try to pick up one of the orange balls. "Not budging, huh, munchkin?"

"I'll get it," Jayden offered. He tried to push and pull to no avail.

"Gotta find one that's ripe first," Simon noted, scanning the bigger plants until he found a likely prospect. "To tell if it's ripe, you gotta thump it, like this." Simon used his finger to tap the skin. "If it sounds hollow, it's time to pick." He took out his pocket knife and bent down to cut the stem. "Uh-oh. Now we've done it. What do we do with our pumpkin?"

Jayden put his finger in his mouth to think. "Porch."

"Good thinking."

Sammy came over, all smiles. "What did you bring me this afternoon, Simon? New workers?"

"Looks like. They're eager to get started. What should we have them do first?"

"Harvest these pumpkins. But I see problems. Two kids, one pumpkin. Seems to me like someone's gonna be shortchanged."

"You're right. Who wants to go pick out another one?"

"Me!" Jayden hollered. "'Laney can have this one."

"Don't forget to thump it," Simon directed, watching Delaney circle her newly acquired, oversized squash and try to sit on it.

"You shoulda brought a wagon," Sammy suggested, scrubbing his chin. "Want me to go get that old cart next to the barn? That way they can ride back."

"Great idea. Wish I'd thought of it." He trailed after Jayden, waiting for the boy to find one he wanted.

"This one!"

Simon started laughing, noting how large it was, probably eighteen inches in circumference. "That has to be the first prize winner, Jayden. That thing must weigh almost as much as you."

When Sammy came back he had the steel metal cart attached to the back of the tractor. Simon had to hold Jayden in place to keep him from running up to it while in motion.

The kid was fascinated with the huge wheels, which he had to inspect from all angles.

Simon moved them along by loading up their haul and setting the kids inside to head back. "Hold on," he cautioned. "It gets bumpy through here."

He noted his step was just a little lighter. His attitude better. His somber mood had lifted. The power of kids, he thought. Never in a million years would he have considered they held such influence on how differently he looked at things.

The kids chattered away like two magpies.

Simon was certain Delaney's vocabulary had increased since being around Jayden. It was understandable, the boy talked nonstop. That was okay with Simon. It showed the three-year-old's development was on track. He knew because he'd looked it up online.

Once they reached the house, Simon plucked the two out of the cart and let them run around on the grass until his mother stepped out onto the porch. "Dinner's ready."

"Hear that," Simon called. "Time to eat!"

Hands had to be washed and bibs in place to eat the ravioli his mother had made from scratch.

"I didn't know I had the ingredients in the pantry for all this," Simon stated, spooning out her homemade sauce and drizzling it over his pasta. "Good stuff."

"Good stuff," Jayden repeated, his mouth rimmed with red sauce.

"Good 'tuff," Delaney echoed.

"I have rolls," Gretchen offered.

"Hot buttered rolls, too? What did we do to deserve this feast? Can you tell Nana thank you for making this great supper?"

"Thank you!" Jayden said.

Again, Delaney tried to utter the same words.

"I think it's unanimous, Nana. Your supper's a hit."

Gretchen took a seat between Simon and Delaney. "I'm going to miss this."

"Same here," Simon acknowledged. "We're just glad you got to make the trip."

Immediately after supper was done, Simon noticed his mother getting anxious. "Forget the dishes. Forget bathing the kids. Go get dressed for your date."

"You sure?"

"Go. I'll get the kids ready for bed."

She didn't need to be told twice. She darted off to the bedroom to fuss with her short hair, experimenting with several ways to wear her bangs. She hadn't brought a lot of clothes with her, just a few essentials she wore on a regular basis. But she'd recently purchased a dressy floral skirt online in mint green that was just the right thing for a dinner and a movie. Not that he had mentioned a movie, she thought, beginning to panic a little.

Drawing in a deep breath, she reached for a plain, short-sleeved white button-down blouse she'd ironed that very morning. Turning to the mirror, she decided to add a gold belt at the waist that would accentuate her figure.

She slid a pair of matching hoops into her pierced ears and wrapped a string of favored, oversized beads in the same color green around her neck. By the time she slipped into a pair of sandals, she felt almost pretty, almost like a girl again getting ready for a big date.

New at this, she spritzed on perfume and then realized maybe she'd sprayed too much. She opened the bedroom door to ask for Simon's opinion and found John already waiting for her in the living room.

"I didn't hear the doorbell," she announced.

Simon smiled. "We don't have a doorbell, Mom. John knocked. We've been sitting out here waiting for you to make your entrance."

"And what an entrance," John noted. "You look beautiful."

Simon hated to admit it, but she did indeed look radiant. Pride swelled in his chest. At sixty, Gretchen Bremmer still had what it took to turn a man's head. And the look on John's face told Simon the man was already smitten.

"Are the kids in bed?"

"Delaney was tuckered out and Jayden wasn't far behind. All that running around in the garden did the trick. You two get out of here now and have fun." He held out his hand to John. "You take care of my mother tonight. I'd hate to have to hunt you down and hurt you."

John grinned. "I won't even speed."

Simon slapped the man on the back. "Now that's the right answer."

After they left, Simon made himself comfortable in front of his big-screen TV to watch a late-starting playoff game between the Seattle Mariners and Red Sox. But instead of watching a pitching duel, his head fell back on the cushions and he was asleep within minutes.

Gretchen, however, was totally psyched to be out and about, at what for her was eleven o'clock on the east coast. The three-hour time difference meant she'd normally be crawling into bed right about now. She looked out the passenger side window at the clear night sky. "It's beautiful here. Look at that moon shining on the water."

"If I weren't so hungry, I'd take you for a walk along the beach. But we can do that after we eat."

"Promise? Because that sounds wonderful."

"You bet."

It was a short drive to Athena Circle, a cul de sac with beach bungalows of different styles. John turned into the driveway of one on the corner of Ocean Street, painted white with blue shutters and a bright red door to set it apart from the rest.

Gretchen decided it could only be described as a doll house, nestled among other similar cottages built during the 1930s. "What a lovely beach house."

"Thanks. I put a lot of work into it. You wouldn't believe what it looked like when I moved in. Rotten shingles, termites. I guess it's best if I keep that to myself. A lady like you might not want to eat in there."

"A lady like me?"

"Refined lady."

"Am I?"

John unlocked the front door and let her go inside first. "You are. It shows in the way you carry yourself."

"I'm not sure what to say to that." She sniffed the air. "Did you already start dinner?"

He grinned. "Not the fish. But I did make a potato casserole as a side that I left warming in the oven. It should be nice and crispy by now."

"You weren't kidding when you boasted you could cook."

He puttered around the stove and brought out a pan. "Hey, with a kid, I had to learn and learn quick. Over the years I've come up with all sorts of tasty dishes. You stick around, I'll give you the chance to sample the full buffet." He paused. "That was meant to be a joke."

She hooted with laughter. "Simon was right about you."

"How's that?"

"You don't waste time."

"I figure at my age, why waste a minute." He removed the fish from the refrigerator, freshly caught snapper, and added it to the pan to sear.

"Did you catch that yourself?"

"You bet. I have a little boat I take out into the bay, motor out to this spot and sit there looking back on our little village."

"Anything I can do to help?"

"You can toss the salad. I made a nice dressing I like with fish."

Impressed, Gretchen watched him out of the corner of her eye. He handled the cooking like a pro, like a chef on one of those foodie shows. "You said you were a contractor, but I think you've taken some classes."

He gave her the sexiest smile. Her heart did a little flutter.

"When I lived in Santa Cruz I lived next door to a lady who could flat out cook. Lindeen Cody's her name. Just happens to be our chief of police's mother. She's the one who sat me down one day and read me the riot act for feeding Julianne a frozen TV dinner. Lectured me about nutrition and all that. She pushed me into doing what little cooking I did with more fresh fruits and veggies. Apparently, I wasn't a fast enough learner to suit her, so she started schooling me in what she meant. Turns out, it wasn't that hard once I got the hang of it. I've been cooking ever since."

He had a cadence in his voice she liked, a soft tone that had an almost lyrical quality to it. "Are you a California native?"

"Born and raised. You a Rhode Island native?"

"Boston. I didn't move to Newport until after I married Lowell. Went down to Cape Cod every summer as a girl. As I get older I realize how magical those days were."

"Living by the beach can still be magical. Your accent isn't that heavy like some others I've heard."

"Maybe because in junior high my grandfather had a stroke. Part of his recovery process was taking speech lessons three times a week. My mother said that after I sat in on so many of his therapy sessions, spanning almost two years, my speech became clearer. I'd had a bit of a lisp before that. Anyway, the lisp got better and maybe the lessons improved my accent."

John plated the snapper and dished out the casserole. "I hope you like fish."

She chuckled. "You're talking to a Cape Codder. I grew up living off the sea, catching my supper as a girl, trailing after my dad with a fishing pole in my hand." She hadn't thought of that in years.

"I think I'm in heaven. A woman who fishes is a woman after my own heart. I'd love to take you fishing for Pacific snapper sometime. It's also known as rockfish out here and it's a bit different than what you're used to on the Cape. Listen to me going on about fish with the expert."

"Me? An expert on fish? I doubt that. I'm not the one who spends so much time on the water." But she had to admit it sounded like something she'd love to do.

He uncorked a bottle of Riesling. "I'm no wine connoisseur, but I prefer this with the snapper, brings out the nutty flavor and matches sweet for sweet."

She held up her glass. "Here's to new friendships."

"And a man hoping for a lot more."

Her lips curved. "I do expect that walk on the beach."

"You got it. But you should know that I'm hoping to steal a kiss in the moonlight."

Simon waited up. He couldn't help it. His mother was out there at…last time he checked…one-thirty in the morning with a man she really didn't know very well. When he heard John's truck pull up outside, he pretended to be asleep on the sofa. It seemed to take forever for his mother to get out of the car.

But when she did, he saw her entrance; she glided into the house like a schoolgirl.

"You look like you had fun."

Gretchen came to a sudden stop. "Oh, Simon, I had the best time. We've spent all this evening after dinner walking on the beach, talking like we've known each other for ages."

"I guess when you connect, you connect for real."

"I know, it's crazy. We'll have to get to know each other more from a distance, though."

For some reason, knowing that, the wad of worry in his gut unknotted a bit. Whatever this was between them seemed to be moving at lightning speed. He needed breathing room. But he could tell his mother was already infatuated. As sorry as he was to see his mother head back east, maybe it was for the best, to give this thing with John some time to…run its course. Army life had taught him long distance relationships were hard to maintain.

"You're not saying anything," Gretchen accused.

"It's late, Mom. I'm sleepy. But I had to wait up because that's what a good son does in case you two kids decided to run off to Las Vegas and tie the knot."

Gretchen let out a laugh and slapped his knee. "Okay, then. Just checking. I'm off to bed now. You should get some sleep."

Simon could only shake his head as he watched his level-headed mother float out of the room like she'd just been on her very first date. It was like a scene out of *Back to the Future* minus the part about kissing his mother. He just needed Doc Brown's DeLorean, the time machine, so he could go back in time and make all this with John Dickinson go away.

Twenty-Five

Gilly made a point to go with Simon when he dropped Gretchen off at the airport. It was a tearful goodbye as they watched her pull her suitcase past the double doors and disappear into the terminal.

Afterward, Gilly noticed he didn't speak as he drove through the winding stretch of roadway toward the exit ramp. He turned the music up for the kids, letting the tunes absorb part of the sadness, the void that seemed to hang in the truck with Gretchen gone.

She waited, drumming her fingers on her thigh, letting him deal with his emotions, which seemed to be visibly raw and tattered at the edges. Wondering if something deeper could be going on, she thought back to the night before.

They'd had a perfectly delightful evening, the five of them sitting around the dinner table gorging on the burgers Simon had cooked on the grill and the skinny fries his mother had made from scratch. The mood had been relaxed, the atmosphere cheery.

Maybe that was the problem, she decided. Simon realized his mother had nothing like that back home waiting for her. No babies running around, only a dreary routine she'd grown tired of facing each day.

It was only when the kids began to get restless that Simon reached out to her and clasped her hand in his.

"Thanks for coming with me."

"Your mom is so cool."

Simon chuckled. "Yeah. She is. My sixty-year-old mother is dating."

"At least she didn't meet him online."

"You ever try that online stuff?"

"Me? God no. Too many of my friends at work have been burned that way. You?"

"Uh-uh. It's been my experience that you can't even find a decent plumber online, never mind a suitable date."

She hooted with laughter. "At least John's well known around town. I asked a few people and they all said the same thing. He's a rock, a good guy, a good neighbor. And he would do anything for Julianne. That has to count for something."

"It does. But this is my mom we're talking about. I never even considered the possibility that she might, you know, have those kinds of feelings in her. Your mom doesn't, and she's been a widow for a lot longer than mine."

"Yes, but your mom acts like she's years younger. It's her approach to life, maybe. I don't know. But I'm sure you couldn't even get my mother to consider going out with a man. She's just not willing to reach out there and grab life by the balls the way your mom does."

Simon cracked up. "I hope you meant that as a pun."

"I did. Kinda."

"Because that is *not* anything I want to conjure up in my head, especially while I'm going sixty-five down the highway."

"Since I know John, neither do I."

Simon skirted the 101 and hit the Pelican Pointe city limits using the Pacific Coast Highway. As he connected with Main Street, he realized this sleepy little village had grown on him. In the two years he'd been here, he'd often avoided coming into town. But now, he was anxious to make it his forever home.

He made a right at Beach Street and a left at Tradewinds. "Want to go by the house? Logan went ahead and dropped off the key last night."

"That's so like Logan. He did the same thing with me, gave me the key ahead of closing. Let's go inside and measure everything, make plans where your furniture should go."

Recognizing that the excitement in her voice equaled his, he brought her hand up to his lips, pressed a kiss to the palm. "You realize we'll be neighbors. Maybe you'll get tired of having me around."

"Maybe you'll get tired of me first."

Keeping it light, he fired back, "Possibly, since you're so annoying."

She jabbed his arm.

"Hey, kids in the car. Never attack the driver," Simon pointed out as he pulled into the driveway of his house. *His house.* He sat there for a minute, taking it all in. But since the vehicle had stopped moving, the kids either wanted to keep going or get out of the confined back seat.

After getting inside, Delaney toddled around like she had the first time, slow and methodical. While Jayden was a blur, going room to room, unable to settle on where he should send his cars flying toward the baseboards.

They measured everything twice. Gilly took notes. "To remind you later about what you don't have now, but will need after moving in."

Didn't the house have everything he needed already? Stainless-steel appliances, a huge walk-in pantry, an island, gorgeous cabinets. What could he possibly need? "Like what?"

"Window coverings for one thing. Some of the rooms already have blinds up, but the ones that don't…you'll need to decide if you want to go with drapes or more blinds."

"Maybe I'll just leave them uncovered, let the light in."

She gave him a pathetic look. "That's okay for now, but down the road you'll want to be able to have something for privacy. Or is that just because I'm a single mom and have read way too many books about serial killers who started out as peepers?"

Simon made a face. "There's a lot to this house thing."

"You don't have to do it all at once. Gradually is more fun anyway, shopping for things, adding a piece here and there after spending weeks looking for just the right rug or artwork."

That didn't sound like great fun to Simon. But Gilly was going on and on about color schemes and something called Feng Shui she'd read in a magazine.

"This is why I let my mother order me a Pottery Barn chair two years ago. I didn't have to do anything to get it. One day, a truck pulled up, dumped it off, and I watched two guys rip off the plastic wrap. Boom, it was there for me to enjoy."

Gilly put her hands on her hips. "This is starting to get a little too real for you, isn't it?"

"I just wanted a house, a decent place for Delaney to grow up. Now, I suddenly have to worry about décor, worry if what I have in the cottage will work here. It's discouraging, intimidating."

She hid a laugh because his face said it all. He was so serious. She could've sworn his usual clear-blue eyes showed such real alarm they'd turned the color of frosty ice. "Look, don't mind me. I get like this sometimes. I should've known better than to bring this all up now because right before I signed on the dotted line, signed my life away really, I remember feeling this overwhelming sense of panic. Could I make this work? What happens when I miss a payment? What if work dries up around here and I'm back commuting to San Sebastian?"

"So you're saying this tightness in my chest is normal?"

"I think so." She ran a hand up his arm. "I'm sorry I got you worked up."

His hand reached out to cup the back of her neck. "I'm hoping you get me worked up more often, just not about buying this house."

She poked him in the ribs. "No second-guessing allowed. You're doing the right thing, even though the farm is fine for a visit. By the way, Jayden and I love our pumpkin. We put it right on the porch. I told him you'd turn it into a jack o'lantern."

"Me?"

She went over to the French doors and swung them open. Jayden came running through the kitchen, followed by Delaney. Both kids scooted out into the yard where the lawn was lush and green. "See? Backyards, grass, all this room to run around, magnets for kids."

Watching Delaney flap her arms and fall into the grass lifted him up out of the sheer fear he'd felt. He ran his hand across the island counter. "I'll be able to stand here and fix her lunch for school, maybe a Fluffernutter or two."

"A what?"

"You know, a sandwich."

"Never heard of it. Is that a Rhode Island thing?"

"Surely not. No kid heads off to school without a Fluffernutter in their lunch box. You take two pieces of white bread, spread on peanut butter, nice and thick, and smear marshmallow Fluff over the top."

Gilly made a face. "Eww. That sounds disgusting."

"Not as disgusting as peanut butter and bananas."

"I don't eat that either. Let's finish the walkthrough and go get lunch."

They enticed the kids back inside, so they could tour the upstairs, Simon carrying Delaney and Gilly toting Jayden on her hip.

"What have you decided to do with this big playroom?"

"No idea yet. But I think I'll put Delaney in this corner bedroom farthest away from the stairs."

"Probably a good idea." Roaming the end of the hallway to the landing, Gilly stopped at the middle bedroom doorway. It had the cutest little nook built into one of the corner walls that she'd missed on earlier visits. "This would make a great place for a teenager to sit and read. Her bed would look great over there. I'd go with this room for Delaney instead of the other one."

Simon shook his head. "I just got a punch to the gut thinking of her as a teenager."

"Get used to it, pal. That girl is growing like a spring weed. Before you know it, she'll be fighting off the boys."

He knew it was true. Life seemed to be racing along at a fast clip, which was why he tabled his angst about the house. "Let's get out of here and get some chow."

"Chow!" Jayden yelled into his mother's ear.

Delaney took hold of his face with both hands. "Da-da."

"I love it when she says that."

"It is pretty cool," Gilly said in agreement. "Where to from here?"

"Let's go grab sandwiches and eat at the beach. We could even eat on the boat. It's moored in Smuggler's Bay."

"As long as you're not offering to whip up those nutter things."

"Fluffernutters."

"Whatever. You know I have to go to another one of Sydney's fundraiser meetings on Friday night."

"How's that coming?"

"We agreed the masquerade ball was a go."

"I don't get it. Where's the fundraiser part come in?"

"There'll be an auction. Nick and Logan are working on that. Apparently, they have some fantastic prizes lined up to bid on. Although I haven't seen the list yet, rumors say they're auctioning off stuff around town."

"Like what?"

"Like that empty storefront next to the church. They want someone to open up another business and this is a good way for them to get it dirt cheap."

"Interesting. What kind of business?"

"That's up to the person who wins the auction."

They ended up at Gilly's house, making tuna fish sandwiches for themselves and peanut butter and jelly for the kids. After bagging the food, they headed off toward the Bay, each pushing a stroller.

Simon had dug out Delaney's from the cargo container, loaded it up in the back of his truck, and returned Jayden's to Gilly. "I'm beginning to think I might've made a mistake buying the pickup."

"Oh, no, Simon. Really?"

"It doesn't have the space in the interior I need. It's hard to cram in the diaper bag and all the other crap and still have room for other passengers. Just look at this morning and how jampacked we were on the way to the airport. You had to sit sandwiched in between two car seats."

"What are you gonna do about it?"

"I'm thinking about asking Brad to find…God help me…a minivan."

"Was there a thirty-day return clause?"

"I doubt it."

"How much money would you lose?"

"You know what they say about driving a car off the lot. It loses ten percent of its value before you get to the first stop sign."

Simon pointed to the *Sea Dragon* in a slip next to the pier. "It doesn't have wheels, Jayden, but she can really move when I want her to."

Jayden sat up in his stroller to get a better view. "Boats!"

Simon helped Gilly aboard first carrying Delaney and then came back for Jayden. "Welcome aboard."

The deck rolled under Gilly's feet. Her free hand latched onto the railing to steady herself with Delaney.

"Got a get your sea legs," Simon called out. "Maybe you should sit down."

She took his advice and plopped her fanny down next to her son.

Simon pointed to a pelican perched on top of a nearby pylon. "Look at that, she's waiting to catch her lunch."

"Dat's a big bird," Jayden noted. Unlike his mother, the toddler was right at home with the sway and give.

Overhead, seagulls sailed gracefully through the air, calling to each other, their squawking booming out over the sapphire water.

Once Gilly got her balance back, she passed around the sandwiches.

As the gentle waves lapped and rocked the sides, they ate in silence. But Gilly couldn't take her eyes off Simon. She got it now. It was as if the man had been born for the water. The breeze lifted all that golden-touched brown hair, reminding her he could've been Jack Sparrow, and this was his personal armada.

"Why didn't you join the Navy?" she heard herself ask. "You obviously adore the water, grew up around it."

"No logical answer to that. But the Army recruiter was a little more heavy-handed than the Navy guy. And I was sure the Army would piss off my father more. Turns out, I was right." He squinted into the afternoon sun. "How do you go about righting so many wrongs over the years?"

"That's easy. Forgive yourself."

"How do I do that?"

She bounced Delaney on her knee. "Pick one and start with that. I've thought about what you said earlier, about being neighbors. I won't get tired of having you around."

Their eyes met. "Whether you believe it or not, I'll be someone you can count on. Always."

"Always is a long time, Simon."

"So, what are we talking about here? If I'm off base…"

"No, it's not that. It's more like I'm in shock hearing you use the word 'always.'"

So much for telling her how he really felt. No way was he going to bring up the L word now. "Maybe we should both take a page from Gretchen Bremmer's playbook. She's trying to get on with her life, trying to reach for something she hasn't had in two years."

"Try never. That's me. I've never had real love in a relationship. Not ever. I know that now, so I relate to how your mother must feel when it comes to meeting John. At least she had your dad all those years." Gilly looked out over the shimmering sun-kissed water and bit her lip. "I want that kind of commitment."

"Then we are on the same page."

"I think we're getting there, at least I hope we are."

Twenty-Six

Maybe it was that positive mindset about the future that carried them through those first few days after Gretchen left.

As September slid without fanfare into October, signs of autumn began popping up around town. Nowhere was that more evident than in Drea's Flower Shop. The florist had filled her front window with locally grown colorful blooms from The Plant Habitat. Golden chrysanthemums, vibrant orange and scarlet celosia, and spiky, lemon-cream asters, adorned the shop, enticing the passerby to order early for homecoming, the first such event at Ocean Street Academy.

Hayden had decorated the stoop outside her bookstore with pots of various sizes containing black-eyed Susan, simple marigolds, and bright yellow pansies.

Doorsteps and porches throughout the neighborhood displayed their pumpkins and scarecrows perched on bales of hay along with leafy golden wreaths on the front doors.

Time for a change of seasons. Fall was officially in the air.

The autumn days had an Indian summer feel to them. Warm sunshiny days and beautiful clear nights kept people outdoors, especially guests booked into the B&B who wanted to take advantage of special end-of-season rates and all that the coast had to offer. The good weather meant Simon was busier than ever.

But Gilly still had her three-day-on shifts to contend with, and those were the most hectic times of all. While Connie's health was still in question and she recuperated from the nasty infection, Simon continued to look after Jayden.

Crazy work schedules meant being even twenty minutes late could blow the best laid plans out of the water. The church's daycare program acted as their stop-gap measure; getting from one hour to the next in the afternoon sometimes meant lining it up at the last minute. The staff got used to the couple's requirements in short order. Everyone agreed the most important thing was getting the kids covered.

With the big move coming tomorrow, they'd discovered that packing up the cottage with toddlers around was impossible, so they'd foisted the kids and the dog off on a willing Neenah Brewer. She'd promised to keep them the entire day if Simon would mow her grass. He eagerly took the offer.

So far, it had paid off. They'd finished up in the kitchen, wrapping dishes and glassware securely for the bumpy ride into town.

"It's time for a break," Simon announced, after taping up the last box and looking around at the bare cabinets. "It's almost two. Why don't we grab some lunch? And don't suggest we eat in this dustbowl." He fanned the air where little bits of dust particles tried to cling to his face. "I need to get out and experience fresh air."

"Where would that be? I'm sick of pizza."

"Me too. What about The Shipwreck?"

"Bar food?" She wrinkled her nose. "As long as I don't have to cook, I'm in for…whatever."

"I heard that Durke hired an actual cook. No more microwaving junk food and charging six bucks for jar salsa and chips out of a bag."

"I haven't been in there since the initial opening when I went with Aubree and Kinsey for a night out. Sure. I'm willing to support local fare even if it probably tastes like crap."

They hopped in his truck—Brad Radcliff was still trying to find him a good price on a minivan—and headed for town.

"I'll be so glad when this move is over."

Gilly twisted in the passenger seat. "Have you heard from your mom?"

"I talked to her mid-week. She mentions John every other sentence."

"And that bothers you."

"I wouldn't say bothers, more like…it's different, my mother bringing up this guy in odd ways. He's actually planning to pay her a visit, fly to Newport in two weeks. According to her, they spend every night Skyping."

Gilly let out a laugh. "You gotta love their enthusiasm."

"I guess." Simon found a place to park near the wharf and went around to open the door for Gilly. He draped an arm over her shoulder as they walked into the newly revamped bar. Usually hopping with chatter and music so loud it could perforate an eardrum, on this Saturday afternoon the place was dead.

Waitress Geniece Darrow met them at the door with a one-page menu done on glossy cardstock. "Hey, there. Late lunch? Sit anywhere. Your choice."

They beelined for a table in the back. Geniece came over to take their drink orders.

Gilly went with a glass of red.

"Beer for me," Simon stated, skimming the simple menu. "I've only had the wings here, but I see Durke added three sandwiches, lobster rolls, roast beef, and turkey club."

Geniece nodded. "He started serving them last summer for the tourists. They were so popular with the beachgoers, he decided to keep them permanently. Or as permanently as we are around here. Roast beef is the real deal, piled high on a French roll with au jus. Lobster is fresh, the club is served on thick slices of bread. All of them come with fries."

Gilly had given up trying to lose a few pounds. "I'll have the club."

"I'll go with the lobster roll."

After Geniece hurried off to the kitchen, Gilly crossed her arms on the table. She loved studying him. Today he wore a green T-shirt with White Horse Tavern emblazoned on it and a pair of stonewashed jeans so ancient they'd lost their denim color. His hair was ruffled and always seemed to be needing a comb. His arms were tanned, his body lean and loose. Her heart did a slow roll into lust.

She met his eyes. Leaning closer, and barely above a whisper, her voice went raspy from wicked thoughts. "It occurs to me we have free time to ourselves. Very rare lately. We can either spend it between the sheets…"

Simon's eyes went wide and didn't let her finish. "I vote for that."

She reached across the table and locked her fingers with his. "I need a shower. And my place is less than five minutes from here."

He frowned. "Why didn't you mention this before we ordered?"

"I thought you were hungry."

"Not that hungry." He signaled for Geniece. "Any way we could get those sandwiches to go?"

"Sure thing. I'll go bag them up."

He sent Gilly a confident look. "There. Problem solved."

They couldn't get to Gilly's house or the shower fast enough. They were hungry, but not for food. They yanked off shoes and tugged off clothes as they spun their way down the hallway and into the bathroom. Simon reached over and turned the knob for the water. As it heated up, so did he. Their need snapped and spun, untangling knots and tensions. When they stepped under the spray together, it was all slick bodies and slippery hands, feeling, exploring, stroking.

He gripped her butt, lifted her up against the tile. She wrapped her legs around him, threw her head back. His vision went ragged as she shuddered, the tremble making his heart hammer in his chest.

Her nails scraped down his back, her teeth nipped his shoulder. He thought he heard a muffled moan as she went lax in his arms. He'd held out, but now took that pulsing rhythm to a higher arc. Letting himself go, he drove deeper, sending them both toward that energy field of ecstasy, that higher rapture, where raw need meets heaven.

Afterward, they ate sitting cross-legged on the bed, devouring cold fries and soggy sandwiches.

Sampling each other's menu choices, Gilly broke off a corner of the lobster roll. "I should've ordered that."

"I was just thinking the same thing about the club."

They traded.

"What time do we pick up the kids?"

"Less than an hour. What shall we do tonight?"

"I was thinking a walk on the beach."

"Really? That's so funny. I live this close to the water, and yet, I don't do that often enough. I'm always in a hurry to get home or get somewhere else."

"It's the perfect night for it. We should take the kids through the Marine Rescue Center sometime. They'd love all the animals."

"Once you get settled, we'll make a point of doing that."

Simon was about to agree when his cell phone buzzed, the sound coming from down the hallway. Naked, he got out of bed to retrieve the device he'd stuffed down in his jeans and left on the floor near the bathroom. He looked at the readout but didn't recognize the area code. "Hello?"

He heard static on the other end of the line. "Hello?" he repeated.

"Bro, is that you?"

Simon recognized the familiar voice right away, especially hearing it break out in a rendition of "Born to be Wild." Eagle Eye sounded stoned or drunk.

"Where are you?"

Instead of getting an answer, Simon heard more singing. Then the line went dead. He hit redial, but no one picked up.

Puzzled and annoyed, he gathered up their scattered clothes and walked back to the bedroom to Gilly.

Almost immediately, she could tell something was bothering him. "Who was that?"

"Nobody."

His mood had changed, a definite somber demeanor had replaced the carefree, after-sex glow. She let it go because they needed to head to Neenah's house to get the kids.

But even then, he was subdued to the point of distracted. All during their meal at the Diner, and then on their leisurely stroll at the beach, he kept looking at his phone, redialing a number over and over again.

Her first instinct was, of course, dark. Was he cheating on her? She dismissed that notion almost right away. Where on earth had he carved out the time to see someone else? They could barely keep up with their own space and time, let alone bringing in a third party.

From the pier, they watched the sun go down over the glistening water. They sat there, neither one talking, until dusk, watching the lights wink on up and down the strand.

It wasn't until a drowsy Delaney turned in her arms that she realized the baby had fallen asleep. She tugged on Simon's sleeve. "I think we should go."

"Oh. Sure. Absolutely." He bundled Jayden up in his arms, called to Merlin, and set off toward Crescent Street with the boy clutched to his chest.

Once they reached the house, Gilly wanted to know, "Are you staying tonight?"

He set Jayden on his feet and watched as the tyke ran off to get his cars. "How does this work exactly if Delaney doesn't have her crib?"

"I dug out Jayden's and put it together yesterday afternoon. I set it up in the guest room for Delaney."

"Oh. Well, I'm not an expert at this. In fact, maybe I have no right to even have a kid."

"Where's this coming from? Tell me what's wrong. You've been acting weird since that phone call."

He shook his head. "I can't talk about it."

"Can't or won't?"

Noticing the rise in her tone, he quietly pointed out, "If you plan on yelling at me, maybe you should take Delaney in the other room."

She growled low in her throat. "Simon, I don't want to yell. But you said you wanted to be there for me. Always. That's what you said. Your words, not mine. Then when I try to poke a secret out of that brain of yours, to find out why you're so down, I hit the silent wall. Always is a long time to keep secrets."

"Maybe you have a few I don't know about," he muttered.

"What would that be? Oh. Wait. I'm not supposed to tell anyone that Logan's auctioning off a trip to Greece, where he still owns a house there. Maybe you should just…leave…get out of here."

"Fine. Come on, Merlin. Let's go back to our place."

The dog wasn't sure if he wanted to go. But when she transferred the baby to Simon's arms and watched him walk out the door, Merlin trotted after him, albeit reluctantly.

She'd thrown his words back at him and he couldn't blame her. He'd been an idiot, but he didn't admit that until he sat alone with Merlin in the dark, sulking.

Delaney had gone down without any effort at all. He'd searched his CDs for some soul-wrenching strings and piano and listened as Bach drifted out of the speakers. It fit his mood perfectly.

Merlin let out a low whine. But it was the eyes Simon saw first. Scott's eyes.

"I'm not in the mood," Simon said in a faint, raspy voice.

"Maybe you should get in the mood."

"Back off." He held up his middle finger to go with the warning.

"Del Rio couldn't possibly have made you this upset."

"What do you know about it?"

"Just that your kill count could've sparked a movie." Even in the dim shadows, Scott saw Simon pale.

"Gilly keeps bugging me about it."

"That's actually not true," Scott said.

"Take her side then."

"There are no sides to this, Simon. You've killed for your country, you've done things that followed you back home. No one can prevent you from feeling guilty about it. But we can help you heal. You aren't the first soldier to do it and you won't be the last. They'll be other wars, other snipers with more kills to their credit than you. Del Rio needs help. He reached out to *you*. No one else."

"What do you want me to do? Go get him? I don't even know for sure where he is. And even if I did I don't know that I can be around him without dredging up bad memories. Don't you get it? Really bad memories. Are ghosts that dumb? I want to help the guy out, I do, but I might not be able to handle having him around. It might not be the best thing for me. Get it now?"

"It'll take weeks to track him down. Del Rio. He won't get here in time."

"In time for what? What are you talking about?"

"You're here for a reason."

"And what would that be? To screw up Gilly's life more than it already is?"

"Maybe you should start by telling her that one of your own, one of your friends needs your help, that you're worried about a buddy. Then take it from there. Tell her everything. Truth, Simon, is better than any pride or stowing secrets in here." Scott tapped his chest. "Be the man Gilly thinks you are. Be the friend Del Rio needs."

Simon's eyes watered. He put his head in his hands. When he started to speak, he looked back up, but he was alone again in the room.

He picked up his phone and texted Gilly.

I'm sorry. Is the offer still open to talk?

Of course. I'll be there in ten minutes.

True to her word, she showed up on his porch with Jayden in her arms, sound asleep. After putting the toddler to bed in the guest room, she took a seat on the sofa. And waited. She watched him pace, back and forth, back and forth, until she couldn't take it any longer.

"Why tell me now, Simon? What's changed?"

"Because you deserve to know what kind of person I am." Once he started talking, everything poured out, the faces, young and old, male and female, and those he couldn't save. Buddies he'd known for years. He told her about the tortured dreams, his guilt, and now someone was calling him who needed help, someone worse off than him, someone who dredged up all the lousy memories, someone who brought them back into focus as if it all had happened yesterday.

"I don't know if I can do it. Don't you see? It'll be too painful seeing him every day. I don't have that kind of courage inside me anymore."

She patted the seat next to her and watched as he dropped, exhausted, into the cushions. She wrapped him up in her arms, just like she had Jayden an hour earlier. "Simon, you're the strongest man I've ever known. Stop selling yourself short. You need to do this for yourself and your friend. It'll be okay. It'll all be okay."

He sank deeper into her arms, wondering what he'd done to deserve a woman like this, who could see past his faults, and could forgive him for the unforgivable.

Twenty-Seven

On Monday morning, while Gilly looked after Delaney, Simon waited outside the First Bank of Pelican Pointe, for it to open.

An attractive brunette he didn't recognize came around the corner, dressed in a gray business suit, her hair held back in a bun. He didn't know women wore buns anymore, not even his mother. He wasn't sure whether she was trying to look older than her years, or just very conservative in her dress.

"You're either a very eager customer here to make a deposit or cash a check or you're here to rob me on my very first day on the job."

"What? No. I'm Simon Bremmer. I have an appointment. I'm here to sign my life away or at least thirty years of it. I bought a house. Today is closing. Please tell me you know what I'm talking about."

She waved a hand through the air. "Sorry. I'm nervous. I'm Naomi Townsend. I'll walk you through all the paperwork."

"Where's Nick?"

"He's taking the week off," Naomi explained, showing Simon to her office, a smaller one right next to Nick's.

"Good for him. He needs a month off."

"That's why he hired me. I'm more than willing to take up the slack while he recharges. When I asked him where he planned to go, I thought he'd say somewhere exotic, but all he plans to do is hang out with his kids at home."

"You'll find around here, family is high on the old totem pole. So you're Nick's new hire?"

She made a slight nod and slid into business mode. "Second in command, the new bank vice president. I'm a transplant from a small town, much like this one, but in the heart of the Midwest, Grand Island, Nebraska, to be exact."

"Ah, that's a long way from here. I thought I detected a cornhusker twang."

"Yes, well, you're not from here either," she stated. "Back east somewhere I'd guess, from the definite accent."

"Rhode Island. Can you really take care of closing, or do I have to wait another week for Nick to get back? I have movers all lined up and everything for today."

"No, no. I'm happy to help you. It's a simple process for the bank. I'd normally offer you a cup of coffee right about now, but I'd have to make it first and you seem like you're in a hurry to get this done."

"Had a gallon of the stuff already. And yeah, I'd appreciate getting this show on the road."

"No problem. Give me a minute to locate your file and we'll be in business."

She disappeared into Nick's office and while Simon waited, one of the tellers showed up for work. Heidi Radford swung by Naomi's office. "Everything okay in here? Want coffee?"

"No thanks, I'm fine."

When Naomi returned she had an armload of file folders.

Simon swallowed hard. "Is that all mine?"

"No," Naomi said with a laugh. "You're just one of many today and the first to get here." She took him through the paperwork, line by line, explaining each notation, spelling out the terms. She went over homeowners' insurance and details that scared him just a little bit.

"I put the down payment in escrow when I made the offer on the house."

"Again, not what I'm used to, but it'll make today's closing that much easier." She showed him the places to sign and initial.

His fear slid away as he scrawled his name on the documents, signing where she indicated. He watched her fold the fat papers and stuff them all into a large white envelope with his name on it. She then handed it off with a set of keys.

He stood up, ready to get out of there. "That must be an extra set. Logan gave me the keys two weeks ago."

Naomi smiled widely. "That's certainly different than what I'm used to doing, too, but I get it. Pelican Pointe is a much smaller community."

Simon was in a hurry, but he cocked his head to study her. "Which causes me to wonder why you'd pick here."

"We all have our secrets, Mr. Bremmer. I'm happy to be the first one to congratulate you on purchasing your new home. You're now a homeowner."

He drove by the house and took a picture to text to Gilly on his way back to the farm.

It's official. This sucker is all mine.
Woohoo!!!! Congratulations!

From there, the move went smoothly. It tended to do that when help came from anyone who owned a truck. Logan had put out the word and men showed up to haul boxes, headboards, couches, and chairs into their pickups.

Cord, Troy, and Ryder McLachlan cleared out each room, one by one. The men were able to get every stick of furniture out of the cottage in one trip.

Like a caravan they drove out of the farm and into town, pulling up in front of the cream and tan Craftsman with the long front porch.

"This is a nice place," Cord said, slapping Simon on the back. "You're practically right across the street from the clinic. I can come over now anytime and bum lunch off you."

"Yeah? Well, don't make it a habit," Simon fired back. "Although the beer and pizza are on me after we finish."

"I guess we better get started then," Troy stated.

The guys organized the boxes by room and cleared out those first. Then they turned their attention to the heavy stuff, muscling tables, sofas, and chairs into the appropriate places downstairs. They saved what went upstairs for last, heaving beds and dressers up the steps and past the landing.

Because Simon and Gilly had pre-determined where the stuff went, it cut down on any confusion.

All in all, the operation went smoothly with only one smashed finger, no boxes rattling with obvious broken dishes, and everything out of the trucks.

While everyone caught their breath, Simon went into his kitchen and pulled out cold beer from the fridge. "Start on this while I call in the pizza. I'm ordering three large meat-lovers all around so stop me if you want veggies."

Troy shook his head. "Bree's been on a health kick lately. This is my chance to avoid anything green or yellow that's supposed to be good for me."

"My sentiments exactly," Simon stated in agreement. But after placing the order, he pulled Cord aside in the living room. "I got a call from Del Rio Saturday night. At least, I think it was him. He sounded drunk or high."

Cord took the end of his shirt and wiped the sweat off his face. "Last time I heard, Eagle Eye was living in a New Mexico mobile home park out in the middle of the desert. The nearest town five miles away. We could ask Brent to see what he can dig up on him. One or both of us will have to go check it out."

"He sounded in a bad way. Who knows where I would've ended up if you and Nick hadn't persuaded me to try here."

"Come on, Bremmer. You wouldn't have spiraled downward like Del Rio. He's got no one. Never has. Different circumstances altogether."

"You want to get the search started, or should I?"

"I'll take care of it. You have a lot on your plate right now getting settled."

Simon noticed Ryder holding back from the rest. "You sure you don't want that beer?"

"I've gotta get back to work. I just wanted to talk to you about John, Julianne's dad. He told us he's booked on the next flight to Newport."

"That soon, huh?"

"Looks like. Are you as stunned as we are?"

Simon chuckled. "You could say that."

"Look, I'll be honest. John's dated before, but he's never been this serious about a woman to fly clear across the country like this."

"Are you saying he's a player?"

Ryder balked at that. "John? No way."

"Just checking. It's only been two years since my dad died. Well, maybe two and a half. She really likes this guy. But if he hurts her…"

Ryder grinned. "I get it. He told us about that."

Simon held out his hand. "Thanks for the help moving. You didn't have to do it, but you showed up. Thanks."

"Hey, that's what neighbors do. Besides, Gilly took real good care of Zach when he sliced his finger open. It's a great comfort to us all having the hospital there when accidents like Zach's happen."

"Does that mean you're gonna show up in a costume for this fundraiser?"

Ryder used the back of his hand to wipe sweat off his brow. "Julianne is still working that angle. I'm not sure if I like the idea or not. What about you?"

"I'm not wearing a frilly outfit. Gilly already knows that. I'll wear black and put on a mask and that's it."

"Yeah. I think that's a plan I can live with. We should probably stick together on that score. Enjoy your house. Have fun unpacking, because that's the hard part."

"Don't I know it."

As Ryder went out the door, a new face appeared on the porch, a man in his mid-twenties with wire-rim glasses and a studious expression in his eyes. Dressed casually in jeans and a white Oxford shirt, he stood looking, peering into the doorway.

"Need something?" Simon asked.

"Hey there, I'm Seth Larrabee, the new pastor at the Community Church. Today's my first day on the job. I was out taking a walk and spotted all the moving activity and wanted to introduce myself."

Simon shook his hand. "I hope you know, you're inheriting a first-rate daycare program."

"I'm aware of that. Ophelia has done an outstanding job. But the church also needs new parishioners. That's why I'm here. If you're new to the area, like me, I was wondering if you'd think about attending services."

Simon rubbed the back of his neck, trying to loosen a tight muscle there. "I'll be honest. I'm not much of a churchgoer, although I was raised Catholic, I haven't taken communion in…" He laughed, trying to think of the last time he'd gone to Mass. "Let's just say twelve years or so and leave it at that."

"We're a non-denominational bunch. We accept all faiths and hold no judgments."

"That might be a first," Simon mumbled. He did feel a nagging obligation to promise the man something, make some type of pledge, because Delaney had been spending a lot of time there lately. "Okay. When things settle down, I'll give it a whirl."

"Awesome. Sunday school is at nine. Services start at ten-thirty. Are you all moved in?"

"I think so. I want to do something special for my first night here, like get my girl some flowers."

Seth smiled. "Would you like me to say a blessing?"

"Sure. Why not?"

The young pastor stepped inside and stood in the foyer, bowed his head. "Your home is your safe harbor; may it shelter you from the outside world during tough times and happy ones. May you find peace and harmony here for as long as you call this place home. For all who enter, may God bless. Amen."

"Thank you. That was nice." And short, thought Simon. "What do I call you? Reverend Larrabee?"

The man chuckled. "Seth. You can call me Seth. Your accent sounds like a mix of New York and Boston."

It was Simon's turn to smile. "And you don't sound one bit like a surfer dude who's seen the light."

"Minnesota, North Star State, born and raised. Go Wild."

"Hockey fan, huh? Rhode Island, Ocean State, born and raised. Bruins fan. We kicked your butts in the playoffs last year."

"You just got lucky is all. Just wait until this season. We're primed. We've improved our offense."

"Won't matter," Simon boasted, slapping the new preacher on the back. "Sorry. But my money says you're in for a quick exit again."

That night, thunder cracked overhead as rain beat down on the roof. His roof. It was a night made for staying home curled up by the fire. So Simon built one in the living room and one in the kitchen for good measure.

Just to be on the safe side, even though the house had passed inspection by a pro, he went around checking all the rooms upstairs for leaks in the roofline and was ecstatic when he found the ceilings bone dry.

Merlin made himself at home right away by gravitating to the fireplace in the kitchen, choosing this spot as his favorite place to curl up. The dog had adjusted to having kids around him, tots who made lots of noise and sometimes treated him like a stuffed animal or a pillow or a riding toy. Merlin didn't seem to mind the extra attention or the hectic pace that surrounded him.

Gilly had arrived with take-out from the Diner, Max Bingham's Monday night special, a feast that included fried chicken, mashed potatoes, homemade rolls, and chocolate cake for dessert. She'd stopped by Murphy's and bought a bottle of champagne for later.

They ate on paper plates and drank out of plastic cups until the dishes could be unpacked.

"You actually met the new pastor?"

"I'm telling you the guy came right in and said a prayer in the living room. Not exactly what I expected in a preacher, though. He couldn't be more than twenty-five with a dab of peach fuzz on his chin."

"He's twenty-seven," Gilly corrected, eager to share new details. "Ophelia thought he was from one of the Dakotas."

"Nope. Minnesota."

"Cottage Grove. I looked it up. Ten miles south of St. Paul on the Mississippi River. According to his own words, he got into some trouble there as a teenager, but somewhere along the way, he must've turned his life around."

"Really? He looks like a clean-cut kid who's never done anything more serious than TPing someone's house."

"Looks can be deceiving."

"Ain't that the truth. Look, I know you're not that fond of getting out on the water, but your next day off, I wish you'd let me take you out on the boat. Just you and me. We'll make a day of it. Leave the kids at daycare and enjoy a lazy day on the water."

"I don't dislike it. And you seemed to know what you're doing well enough. But wouldn't it be like spending your day off working?"

"No. You're not a tourist. We wouldn't even have to go that far out, maybe just to the end of the Bay. Have you checked out that little island due west of Promise Cove? That's another great spot."

"My dad took me over there when I was a kid." She could see he had no intention of letting this go. "All right. We could have a picnic there, which is on land."

He couldn't fathom being landlocked again after spending so much time in the desert overseas. "I don't get it. Your aversion to water. You said you surfed when you were a kid."

Shrugging it off, she chalked it up to disinterest. "I just got out of the habit is all. Wally went on to someone else and I went to the beach to ride my bike instead."

"Breakups can be tough," he teased.

She whacked him on the arm. "We were probably eleven at the time. I'm pretty sure he took a shine to Keegan Fanning after that."

"No hard feelings?"

Gilly laughed. "No. I fancied Frank Martin back then. That lasted a year or so. Frank used to be a vice president at the bank until Nick booted him out. He moved off somewhere to Arizona, I think. Look, if we intend to drink that champagne we need to put the kids to bed. The bedding is in one of those boxes upstairs we haven't gone through yet. So one of us gets to dig through the cartons and get the beds ready while the other deals with bath time. Which is it?"

He shoved back from the table, started gathering up the leftovers and discarding the trash. "I'll take care of the bedding while you get the troops clean."

Finding the right box took some time, but he eventually got sheets on all the beds. Rain still poured down outside. With a cold front coming in, the temperature was expected to dip into the forties, which was the reason he went in search of the right comforters and blankets. It would be a chilly fall night that suited him perfectly.

After getting the munchkins settled for the night, Gilly decided to rearrange the living room, just as Simon brought out the champagne from the kitchen. He held a silver tray he'd found that he didn't even know he owned and watched her from the doorway.

"What happened to the furniture?" he asked when he saw her pushing the sofa in front of the roaring fire.

"I thought it'd be cozier this way. What do you think?"

Simon wasn't stupid enough to offer an opinion one way or another. "If it looks better this way...."

He ran a finger down her cheekbone. "I'm just happy you're here."

She eyed the two glasses he'd already poured, picking one up off the platter. "What shall we drink to?"

"The future."

"Simon?"

He picked up on the different tone. "What?"

"Jayden is beginning to get attached to you."

"And you don't like that?"

"What if...?"

"I could say the same thing about Delaney. She holds onto you like I assume she would her mother."

"Then we have to be very careful here. For the kids."

"I know that. Have I done something that makes you think I'm about to bolt? Is our conversation from last night…giving you reason to have second thoughts?"

"No. The future…scares me just a little, though."

He snatched her around the waist. "Baby, we signed our life away to own homes. You down the street and me here. Now that's what's freaking scary. This, what we have together right now, this is the icing on the cake. Not a problem for two people like us who work hard and try to build something together."

"But we've never, you know, used the L word."

"Is that what's bothering you? I love you, Gilly. I've known it for weeks now."

"You do? Then why didn't you say something before now?"

"I tried to tell you that day, but you didn't want to talk about it."

She drew a calming breath in and out. "I love you, too."

He crushed his mouth to hers and slid a hand under her shirt. "Why don't we bring the champagne upstairs? The bed's ready and waiting for us."

"There's just one thing I need to do first."

"What's that? Find that sexy teddy I didn't get to see before? Now you're talking."

She patted his chest. "Great thought, but no. I bought a child safety gate at Ferguson's hardware for the landing at the top of the stairs. Could we put it up before going to bed? I don't want Jayden getting up early and tumbling down the stairs or wandering around down here by himself before we get up."

"There are two staircases," he reminded her.

"I know. That's why I bought two."

He had to reach out and touch her, to feel her soft skin under his. He nibbled her neck and then an ear. "What if we do this. Make love right here and christen the living room. Then we put up the gates."

"Mmm," she said as they slid down into the cushions on the couch. Her hand reaching back to unbutton his jeans. "But we install those things before we go to bed."

"Deal. And then figure out how to sleep late in the morning."

She snickered and ran a hand across his ribs. "Sleep late? What a newbie. You gave that up the second you became a daddy."

They didn't get to sleep late.

Jayden and Delaney seemed to be on the same schedule, waking up around six-fifteen.

And Jayden was pounding on their bedroom door.

Simon rolled over and grunted. But it wasn't until the boy made his big announcement that Simon got moving.

"'Laney's pooped. She smells bad," Jayden informed everyone, making sure the neighbors probably heard.

"Oh great," Simon groaned, tossing back the covers. "I've got this."

Just as bleary-eyed, Gilly offered, "I'll get coffee started."

She also scrambled eggs, but the kids protested. She didn't feel like arguing and dug out cereal from the box that had yet to be unpacked, labeled "Pantry."

"I guess I need to spend the day and unpack. But I also need to make a supply run. I need groceries and a long list of other stuff I held off buying until after the move. I thought I'd stock up on diapers and baby wipes. You want me to pick up anything?"

She looked at him adoringly. "You're gonna do the shopping?"

He gave her a peck on the cheek. "I'm gonna try...before you head to work. I could take either Jayden or Delaney with me. You pick."

"I need to buy Jayden a pair of shoes. He's outgrown the ones he's wearing. So..."

"Okay, I'll take Delaney and Merlin with me and meet you back here or at your house around noon. I'll pick up something for lunch while I'm out."

"Want me to stop at Ferguson's to see about a doggie door? I think they have one that's simple enough to install." But after she'd made the offer, an idea hit her. "You know what, why don't I pick up the groceries with Delaney and you take Jayden to get his shoes, then stop by the hardware store to pick out which prefab doggie door you want. That makes more sense because I'd hate to buy the wrong kind."

Since a simple gesture seemed to be taking a lengthy time for them to decide, he countered, "We could just do everything together."

"But is there time to get it all done before I go to work? That's the thing. I don't think there is."

"I see your point. Where do I get the shoes?"

"Sadie Dawson opened up a kid's boutique across from Drea's Flowers called Crimson & Clover. I don't know what size he wears, so you'll have to measure him. He's probably in an eight by now."

"An eight? For a three-year-old?"

"I know, the sizes are crazy. Can you handle that?"

Even if he couldn't, he didn't intend to admit it now. "I got it covered."

They split up, dividing the errands like a tactical field operation. Gilly even gave him a list.

After buying the shoes, he and Jayden got sidetracked in the train store next door.

"Maybe I should think about getting him a train set," Simon told Cooper Richmond. "He loves anything with wheels."

"He might not be ready for a regular train, but you could start him off with a wooden one that connects the cars using magnets. Easy for a guy his age to handle and not get frustrated."

"They have one like that at daycare."

Cooper grinned. "I know. I sold it to them. I have one with forty-five pieces in a set, enough where he won't get bored."

That sounded good to Simon. "Do you sell the tables? Because the one he plays with at the church has a really cool table with a layout."

"You bet. The one I sell even has storage to go with it, makes for a great place to keep everything off the floor."

That also sounded like a good idea. "Okay. I'll take both."

After stowing their purchases in the truck, they crossed the street to Ferguson's and picked out Merlin's doggie door. They got sidetracked again when Jayden wanted to head down to the wharf to look at the boats. Always up for checking out watercraft, Simon thought it was a good way to bond.

But he lost track of time. By the time he wheeled Jayden's stroller past the T-shirt shop, Simon decided to do a little detective work. He shot a U-turn, wedging the stroller next to a street lamp and out of the way of the pedestrians.

He picked Jayden up in his arms and walked inside. The shop was narrow and full of every color shirt he could imagine, some on hangers, some neatly folded on display tables. In addition to souvenirs, he found out quickly that Malachi Rafferty sold shorts, sandals, and swimwear marketed to the tourists.

"You looking for anything in particular?" Malachi asked, standing next to the cash register, arms crossed, waiting for some poor shmuck to make an impulse buy.

Simon saw the resemblance right away. "Two words. Moss Radley. No, that won't quite cut it. You were lead singer and guitarist for the grunge band in the 90s. I saw you guys in concert back east. Providence, Rhode Island."

Malachi winced at the recognition. "Don't broadcast it around, okay? I've been trying to live that down for some time."

"Why? You guys were great."

"We were, and those were definitely the heydays. But now I own this shop. I'm widowed, have two teenage girls that I try to keep in line the best I know how, probably doing a crappy job of it. And I don't want reporters nosing around bothering my girls or asking me stupid questions like why I gave up my rock 'n roll days."

"I get it. It's tough doing everything on your own, isn't it?"

"You don't know the half of it. I got fed up with Los Angeles. That's why my wife Melody and I moved out of the big city in the first place. We wanted to give the kids another kind of existence, something more normal than superficial glitz and glamour and traffic congestion. It didn't last long for us as a family though. We moved here after we learned Melody had lymphoma..." His voice broke off. "We thought things would be okay. They weren't."

Listening to his story made Simon open up about his own detour into fatherhood.

Malachi listened and afterward looked Jayden up and down. "You got a good-looking boy there."

"Oh, Jayden's not...uh..." Simon changed his mind about sharing too many details. "Yeah, yeah I do. Jayden's a great kid."

"You won't say anything about my...former life...will you?"

"If that's what you want, sure. I won't say a word to anyone."

Simon had been so involved with shopping, the hours had slipped away. He hadn't paid any mind to his text messages or the phone calls he'd let go to voicemail. When he and Jayden and Merlin walked in the door at twelve forty-five, late and unconcerned about it, Gilly met them in the entryway with her hands on her hips.

"Where have you been? I've been worried sick. Why didn't you answer your phone?"

Jayden put his hands over his ears. "Mama, you're too loud. I want to play with my new twain."

"What new train?"

"I bought him a train set."

"Simon, I sent you out for shoes."

"I got those too." He pointed to the kid's feet. "He wanted to wear them out of the store."

She looked down and saw the pair of Downshifter running shoes. "Those are Nikes."

"Yeah. And he loves them."

"Make me go fast," Jayden said. "Real fast."

She dropped onto the hall bench. "You bought my kid a train and an expensive pair of shoes."

"They weren't all that expensive and Cooper gave me a deal on the train because I bought the table to go with it. I figure Jayden needs something to play with here. Where's Delaney?"

"She fell asleep after lunch. I put her down for a nap."

Simon snapped his fingers. "Oops. I forgot about picking up lunch. Sorry."

She pulled him down beside her on the bench. "You're the best, you know that?"

"Is Mama mad?" Jayden asked.

"Mama is definitely not mad."

"Twain. Can I play with my twain?"

"Yes, baby. You can play with your train."

"You're gonna love it," Simon began. "It's just like the one at daycare…only better."

Twenty-Eight

For Simon, it had been a long, tedious workday. The tourists he'd taken out had insisted he make two extra trips circling Smuggler's Bay, so they could take more photos, which made him late picking up Delaney and Jayden at daycare.

It was nearing six-thirty when he walked through the double doors of the church and headed straight for their classroom. He was met by two little bundles of energy that seemed happy to see him. He didn't think it was his imagination that when they spotted him, the kids dropped what they were doing and came running up to greet him like he was the king of the world.

Jayden began to chatter and tell him about a dinosaur. That was certainly different since T-rex didn't come with wheels. But it didn't last long before Jayden went to get his stuff.

"He's obviously ready to go," Simon commented. "Sorry I'm late."

Ophelia, who'd stayed behind to accommodate his schedule, waved off the apology. "They've only been here for three hours since Gilly dropped them off. We all understand around here that not all parents have a nine-to-five setup. We don't mind making allowances."

His baby girl toddled over, looking relieved to see him. Lifting her up, he gave her a big raspberry on her belly. "Daddy missed you."

"Da-da," she said, patting his face.

Simon held the baby out away from him and looked in her eyes. "She just called me daddy again. Da-da. Did you hear that?" he said, whirling around to Ophelia. "It's only the fifth time she's said it."

Ophelia smiled. "You're counting. That's adorable and amazing. I might mention that Delaney put up quite a fuss when Gilly dropped her off. She cried for almost twenty minutes afterward."

He nodded at the information. "Gilly texted me about it. Delaney's started to call her Mama."

"Susan and Neenah noticed that, too."

But then he looked down and caught Jayden staring up at him with wide eyes from the floor. "What's wrong, buddy?"

"Are you my daddy?"

Simon squatted down to Jayden's level. With his free arm, he lifted him up to his chest and looked him in the eye. "You want me to be?"

Jayden bobbed his head up and down. "Jes."

He kissed the top of the boy's head. "Then let's talk to your mom about it." And when Jayden threw his arms around his neck, it made him feel ten feet tall.

"Let's get out of Ophelia's hair now and go make us some supper. What do you say to that?"

"Supper!" Jayden yelled.

After getting them fed and tucked in for the night, Simon did the dishes and started the dishwasher. The sofa called his name from the living room. Dead tired, he put his feet up on the coffee table and texted Gilly about Jayden's question.

I told you he was getting attached.

So is Delaney, to you. Look what happened this afternoon.

I hated leaving her bawling like that. Does it freak you out if Jayden wants to start calling you Daddy?

Does it freak you out when Delaney calls you Mama?

It doesn't. It warms my heart.

Same here. We're two only children. If we make a go of this, at least we'll know that Jayden and Delaney won't end up only children.

Amazing that you would even think of that.

I think about a lot of stuff because I'm not going anywhere, Gilly.

Neither am I.

Then what are we so afraid of here?

Don't know. Gotta get back to work now. Looks like a busy night. Car accident out on the 101 and we're the closest hospital!!! Love you.

With the house quiet, he was able to sort things out without having little miniature people underfoot. Merlin trotted over, plopped his butt down on top of Simon's feet.

Simon combed his fingers through his fur thinking about the hundred chores he still had left to get done. He and Gilly had talked about putting up a porch swing. They'd already settled on a spot. He still had to install the doggie door and finish unpacking.

His head fell back on the cushion and soon Simon had drifted off to sleep.

The first time he'd set eyes on Colt Del Rio, he'd been about to drift off then, too. After a long flight he needed shuteye. Nestled in his bunk, a commotion to the right had him opening his eyes to see a man staring at him in the dark.

Unsettled, Simon noted the man looked almost feral with raven-black eyes that matched his hair. Short, at five-feet nine inches, the guy seemed like a ball of muscle and not all there. Simon could see crazy in his huge dark eyes.

He wouldn't find out until later that the lovable wild man was half Apache, born and raised in a New Mexico orphanage located outside Albuquerque on a dirt-poor speck of land where it was impossible to grow anything in the hard, unforgiving dust and drought. Dumped there as a baby, it seemed no one had wanted Colt Del Rio from the moment he'd let out his first war cry, a fact that had the boy growing up not giving a damn about much of anything.

Now, deep in the barren hills near Kandahar province in one-hundred-plus-degree heat, the man was dressed in a pair of cut-off camouflage shorts, an olive-green undershirt, and his trademark bandana wrapped around his head. It wasn't so much his lack of conversation as it was his sing-song approach to any subject matter that caused him to stick out from the rest.

As a twenty-year-old hot-shot marksman, Simon had been anxious to meet his spotter. But he hadn't expected the man who stared at him now. Colt let out an ear-piercing war whoop to get his attention.

It worked.

"Hey, bro. I hear you aced your MOS. That's good. My guess is, getting to 11B you ended up here quick as they could get rid of you. Trust me, this ain't no promotion."

Simon sat up on his elbows to get a better look. "I'm beginning to get that."

"This your first sniper gig?"

"Yep."

"You can handle that M4?"

"Yep."

"Good, cause I been hunting game all my life and hunting humans who want to kill me is just another kind of wild animal, just a helluva lot more dangerous." Colt let out another war whoop, but Simon sensed he wasn't done talking.

Leaning in closer, Colt whispered, "You'd better be a damn good shot cause I'm the best fucking spotter in this whole damn Army and I'm not looking to get my nuts blown off any time soon."

With that, Colt unceremoniously reached over to the bunk bed and flipped it over with Simon in it.

"What the hell is wrong with you?" Simon yelled. "Get away from me!"

But before he could react, Colt had picked him up like a rag doll, set him on his feet, and slapped him on the back. "Welcome to the Army's version of hell, bro. Whatever you did before to get here, ain't nothing like the real thing."

Twenty-Nine

In the heat of a fall Thursday, Simon had started his morning routine by paying off his debt to Neenah Brewer, pushing a mower through thick, ankle-high grass at her house. Next, he'd moved on to the front lawn at Gilly's, which was just as much in need of trimming as his own. It's how he'd ended up in his own yard, clipping hedges and running his Toro through a thick patch of sod.

Three yards in one day reminded him of his teen years, summers spent earning money by cutting grass and doing odd jobs for neighbors.

By now, he could've used a cold beer. Over the engine noise of the Toro, he heard his phone ringing. He let go of the handle and the machine ceased its roar. It was Bradford Radcliff. "You found anything yet?"

"I did, but it's not a minivan."

"That's a plus right there. What is it?"

"Honda Pilot, an SUV. And get this, it only has twenty thousand miles on it."

"Legit?"

"Yep. The owner bought it a year ago from a dealer in San Sebastian and then decided it was just way too big for him. He wants a look at your Sierra. He's specifically looking for a four-door GMC. I figure it might be a win-win for both of you."

"That's great, Brad. When?"

"Will four o'clock work?"

"I'll make it work. Where? Because I have to get cleaned up first."

"Meet us at the lot, bring your paperwork in case it's a go."

"Do you think this guy's serious…about the truck I mean?"

"He is. It's exactly what he's been looking for."

"Brad may have pulled off a miracle," he told Gilly as he walked into the kitchen where she was busy at the stove. He breathed in the aroma. "That smells like spaghetti sauce."

"It's for lasagna."

His mouth drooled. "After mowing three lawns, I'm starving."

She angled toward him, holding up a spoon for him to sample. "Tell me what you think."

He licked it clean. "Delicious and spicy, like you."

She didn't think of herself as either one of those things but let him nuzzle her neck anyway. "I used the Italian sausage your mother recommended."

"Well, it worked. I'm ripe and need a shower. Where are the kids? I don't hear yelling or screaming. Should I be worried?"

"My mother is in the backyard refereeing."

"Connie's here?"

"For almost an hour. She says she's put away all those knickknacks in her house and wants to try Jayden visiting again."

"You're kidding?"

"I'll know when I go over there tomorrow night if it's the right thing to do."

"What's tomorrow night?"

"She wants another chance at babysitting and I have another fundraiser committee meeting. We're getting to the final stages now and everything's clicking into place."

"How do you feel about your mother taking another run at watching Jayden?"

"Mixed. She is my mom, so the door should always remain somewhat open. Don't you think?"

He brushed his lips to hers. "It's your call. I gotta get going. Any last-minute advice on the SUV?"

"It's not a minivan. How long do you think you'll be? Dinner's almost ready."

"If it's not the right vehicle, I'll be back in time to set the table."

He came back driving a silver SUV and carrying a dozen long-stemmed lilies in soft golden orange.

"Those are tiger lilies," Connie pointed out, as she took them from him. "I'll go put these in a vase. Supper's ready."

Simon noted a change in behavior, an almost subdued demeanor emanating from Connie. Could he finally be seeing the version Gilly had been describing all along?

Her mother stayed for dinner and watched Simon take out plates from the cabinet to set the table. She had to admit this one seemed different than Vaughn, this one didn't seem to have a mean bone in his body.

And as she continued to listen to the couple banter, as if they'd known each other for years instead of weeks, Connie became increasingly convinced she'd been wrong about the man. Grudgingly, she even began to see Delaney in a different light.

Simon helped Gilly put the lasagna on the table and then swooped down on each kid, tussling with each one in their own way until he corralled them to the table.

The trio was loud and boisterous, and Gilly loved every second of it.

"I'd like to try looking after Jayden again in a few weeks," Connie announced.

"What about your job at the doctor's office?" Gilly asked. "Ten to three."

Connie shook her head. "I've decided to quit and not go back at all. Quentin's actively looking for someone to replace me."

Gilly almost choked on the bite she'd taken. "When did this happen?"

"I made my decision this morning. My heart's not in it anymore. I don't think it has been since I left San Sebastian General."

"There's no rush for you to babysit, Mrs. Grant," Simon told her. "I'm happy to continue to watch Jayden. He's no more of a handful than Delaney."

Connie thought otherwise, but kept her mouth closed about it. "I'll be honest. What I don't understand is why? The boy isn't even yours."

Simon shrugged and picked up his iced tea. "I'm not sure I can explain it. I love the kid. It's as simple as that. He's a precocious little guy who listens to a story like he's sitting on the edge of his seat. He never fails to blow me away by asking something pertinent that I've just read to him. And when the story ends, he always seems disappointed. At first, I thought it was because he didn't want to go to sleep, but it became obvious he was into the action and didn't want it to end. I find that…amazing…for a kid that size to pick up on what the characters are doing and then ask me about them later…it's phenomenal. He's like a sponge and is sort of a precursor to what Delaney will do."

From the other end of the table, Gilly warmed from the inside out. "I thought it was just me."

"Nope. He is one smart cookie."

"Cookie!" Jayden repeated.

"Not until you eat your supper," Gilly said.

"Cookie," Delaney mimicked.

Gilly tickled Delaney's belly. "Jeez, we suddenly have a lot of parrots in here. But you still need to finish your supper, too."

Later, while Gilly got the kids ready for bed, Simon did the dishes, leaving him alone with Connie in the kitchen.

"You know Gilly's birthday is next week."

"No, I didn't know that. Thanks for the heads up."

"I know what she wants."

Simon turned from the sink and stared at Connie. "Do tell. I'm all ears."

He made a conscious effort to keep everything a surprise. Connie had agreed to babysit at his house for the day, but with a caveat. Simon had hired Faye DeMarco to be on hand in case the older woman became overwhelmed for any reason. He'd given the teenager a complete rundown of any problem she might face with instructions to contact Cord, who was right across the street at the veterinarian clinic, if anything went amiss. In turn, Cord would get in touch with him on his cell phone if there was an emergency. Simon had paid Faye top dollar to make sure she took the job seriously and knew what a huge responsibility it was keeping an eye on Connie and the kids.

Since he wanted Gilly's birthday to come off without a hitch, to be special, he planned the Saturday out in detail.

Right after breakfast, Faye showed up at the door first, followed by Connie fifteen minutes later.

"What's going on?" Gilly wanted to know.

Simon finished wiping messy faces and faced Gilly. "I'm taking the birthday girl out for the day. These ladies have graciously offered to help with the kids, so we get to spend the entire day together."

Gilly looked truly flummoxed. "No joke? That's wonderful, but..." She took Simon into the dining room. "You're leaving Mom with two kids?"

"That's why I hired Faye. She's here to make sure your mother doesn't come unglued the first time one of the kids knocks something over."

"That was clever of you. How did you know it was my birthday?"

"A little bird told me. We'll have cake and ice cream with the kids this afternoon, but until then..." he whisked her out of the room. "I'm getting you on the water. A Pelican Pointe native should know what's right in front of them and appreciate the sights."

"I appreciate the sights just fine, all over town." But she sensed it was pointless to argue. "If we're going, I need to get my bag."

"Everything you need is already on the *Sea Dragon*. I got up before the kids did and hauled everything to the pier. Now move your pretty fanny and let's get going. We're wasting daylight."

Calling to the dog, he gave final instructions to Faye and inched Gilly toward the door and out of the house.

He decided he couldn't have picked a more perfect day for the excursion he had in mind. The conditions were perfect, plenty of sunshine, a moderate swell of two to four feet at most. And winds were easily no more than fifteen knots.

After boarding, Gilly watched Simon get underway. It gave her a little thrill to watch him master the controls at the helm. But she'd be lying if she said she was completely at ease, which is why she held onto Merlin's neck. "I know you've done this before but…"

"No buts. I can handle all types of wind and weather. Been doing this since I was ten and old enough to navigate on my own. Relax. You see where those boulders are in the distance that make up the mouth of the Bay. We're only going that far. There's no fog on the horizon. No twenty to thirty knot winds. Give a guy a little credit."

As he motored out, he avoided the surfers in the lane.

Gilly waved weakly, as her stomach did a slow roll. But soon she got used to the motion and kept her eyes on the prize. The mouth of the Bay had always fascinated her. It formed a horseshoe and those boulders he'd pointed out were part of the pattern.

"Get the binoculars and you might catch a humpback or blue whale on this trip."

That got her up and to the rail. "Really?"

"It's October, the perfect time for mating and calving."

"That would be awesome." She forgot about her stomach long enough to grab the binoculars and scan the water. "I remember one time a whale came in too close and got stuck in shallow waters. I'd forgotten about that," she muttered as her eyes continued to find interesting things that caught her fancy. "What's that? There in the rocks?"

Simon glanced over to see an unusual formation. "Looks like a small natural cavern. That's what I love about the water. You can see things differently each time you go out because of the change in the wind or the weather and the depth of the water."

She switched from the field glasses to her camera, zooming in on the spot. "I can't wait to share these." She ran up to the helm and put her arms around him. "This was a great idea. I love having the wind in my face. And look at Merlin. Now I know how he feels hanging his head out the window whenever he's in the car."

She drew in a deep breath of ocean air. "I've been so stressed lately over this fundraiser. The masquerade ball was my idea, and I've taken heat about it. On top of that, Sydney's making everyone crazy with catering and venue issues."

"It'll work itself out," Simon said, sliding his arms around her waist and bringing her closer. "You'll see. The thing's almost here anyway and then you can put it behind you. Get work out of your head."

"Not hard to do when I'm here with you."

Within view of Treasure Island, he cut the engine. "Let's drift a while and see where the current takes us."

She knew he wasn't talking about the boat when he took her hand and led her into another part of the deck he called the captain's corner.

"It's like a little apartment."

"With a little bed," he added as he spun her into a long, sultry kiss. Sunlight drifted in through the windows as he backed her onto a soft cushion no wider than a bunk. "Remember that first night we made love?"

"I do."

"It's better on the water."

She yanked his shirt up and ran her nails across his chest. "Prove it."

He did. Twice.

By the time they got back to the pier, the sun had dropped low in the fall sky as Simon pulled the boat into its slip. "Kids are waiting for us."

Feeling loose and relaxed, she threw her arms around his neck. "Before we get back to the house, I just want to say three little words. Best. Birthday. Ever."

Thirty

The night of the fundraiser, moonlight slipped onto the agenda as the festive vibe bubbled up across town. The celebratory mood lapped over to the daycare center where most of the attendees planned to drop off their kids for the evening.

The building hopped with activity. With Reverend Larrabee's help, Ophelia was certain she had everything under control for the dozens of kids that would be left in her care.

Neenah Brewer and Susan Hollenbeck had stopped taking reservations two days ago because the facility was at full capacity. It seemed every child in town had been slated to stay here during the event, dubbed officially on engraved invitations as the First Annual Hospital Masquerade Ball and Auction.

Ophelia didn't think she could jam another child into any of the classrooms even if she tried. Although she'd taken on extra help, the ratio of youngster to adult was still too high to suit her. But she told herself it was only for one night. She'd recruited teen sitters, Sonoma and Sonnet, Faye DeMarco, and Beckham Blackwood to help with activities, like keeping the kids busy until they went to sleep on floor mats used for naps or the sleeping bags they'd brought with them.

She opened the doors at six that evening for early arrivals. The only thing on her mind was how to entertain close to fifty children of all ages for five or six hours. She crossed her fingers and hoped most would be snuggled asleep by at least nine o'clock.

As it got closer to seven-thirty, the drop-off line outside grew longer.

Simon and Gilly could attest to that. They were stuck behind Hayden and Ethan Cody, who were dropping off Nate. Each car that pulled up went through a series of rituals. Either Seth Larrabee or one of the other adults came out to the car to collect their charges, then disappeared back inside and performed the same routine with the next car.

It was like dropping off at school, an orderly procedure where you just had to wait until your car moved up in line. Of course, others had decided to simply walk their kids up to the church and then walk over to the venue.

"Why didn't we do that?" Simon asked.

"Because I'm wearing five-inch heels and I'm not prepared to walk three blocks in them."

"Just thought I'd ask," he muttered under his breath.

When it finally came their turn, Ophelia opened the back door and unbelted Jayden first, handing him off to Neenah who was standing to one side. She then reached across and unfastened Delaney out of her carrier. "Come on, baby. Let's go play with some blocks."

Ophelia moved out of the car with Delaney in her arms. "Have a great time," she said cheerily as she waved them off into the night.

"Shouldn't a woman who looks like that be heading to this party herself?" Gilly wondered.

They'd gone to church services the previous Sunday for the first time as a couple where Simon had made another observation that stuck. "The way Seth looks at Ophelia tells me there's chemistry there."

"Absolutely. I'm just surprised you noticed."

"Hey, when our young minister spends most of his time ogling a member of his flock, I notice."

Since parking would be a nightmare with everyone crammed into one small corner of town, Brent had issued an order that everyone should leave their cars at the elementary school and walk across Ocean Street. Simon maneuvered the SUV into an open space and cut the engine.

"How do you like your new wheels so far?"

"At least we're not crammed on top of each other. And I like the overhead video where the kids can watch a movie."

"I am so jealous. My poor Subaru looks like a relic next to this."

"Hey, you can always drive this anytime you want, and I'll go back to riding my motorcycle."

"Simon, I was joking. My car's fine. I could walk to work if I had to. I even walk to the store sometimes."

"Well, the offer's out there. Are we ready for this madhouse?" he asked, opening the door.

She looked over at him dressed all in black, even his dress shirt was made from black silk, and her mouth watered. "Got your mask?"

"You know I do, you're the one who stuck it down in my pocket."

He took her hand and helped her out of the front seat.

"I feel like a princess."

"You look more like a goddess, or should I call you Buttercup tonight?"

She'd worn a gold beaded gown with a matching beaded cap on the crown of her head and a choker around her neck.

"Aw, I love it when you say things like that." Gilly looped her arm around her very own Westley and felt like she was going to the prom again.

They glided through the elegant doors of what was now the library to purple and golden lights pulsing over the crowd from the second-floor balcony. Some were already waltzing across the lobby to strings and brass and woodwinds.

The women were decked out in masks and every color of French gowns they'd been able to find at antique boutiques or thrift shops in and around the area.

While the men were dressed mostly in formal black-tie, there was a handful of guys who'd gone the extra mile and worn outlandish getups. Wally Pierce had on a suit made from gold brocade and a feathery hat sitting on his head.

She elbowed Simon in the ribs. "See, someone got into the spirit of the evening."

"Give me a break. I wouldn't be caught dead wearing a bunch of feathers on my head." But as the words left his mouth, he spotted Caleb Jennings wearing a frilly shirt the color of scarlet that matched his feathery red mask. Even Logan had put on an embroidered jacket in gold, and wore red tights.

Kinsey pulled Gilly deeper into the ballroom to dance to a rousing rendition of "Girls Just Wanna Have Fun."

Left alone, Simon sauntered up to Logan. "Put a crown on your head and you're the spitting image of Humperdink."

Logan looked insulted. "It's Casanova to you, pal." He took a long pull on the beer in his hand. "What we won't do for our women."

Simon glanced over at Gilly kicking up her heels with Kinsey, who'd dressed in an over-the-top purple gown with ruffles. The females had formed a conga line of sorts and began dancing around the room.

"Where do I get one of those?" Simon asked, pointing to the bottle in Logan's hand. "Bar is on the terrace. Steer clear of that ultra-light stuff. Someone ordered a whole case of it. My guess is we'll be stuck with that crap for months."

Simon wandered that way and ran into Nick at the bar dressed in one of his boring black suits. "What, no fancy getup?"

The banker cut his eyes to his wife, who was sporting an audaciously low-cut, strapless red gown with what looked like rubies at her ears. "We spent a fortune on that outfit. There was nothing left in the budget for me to splurge on tights. Did you get a look at Logan?"

"Yeah. But I'm worried we may have to go through this costume thing every year. The invitation said something about this being the 'first' of its kind."

"Yeah, well, if you ask me this is all Gilly's fault. It was her idea."

Simon tried to loosen the top button of his shirt just so he could breathe. "Don't blame me, I tried to talk her out of it."

"Obviously, you didn't try hard enough," Nick grumbled, glancing at his wife again. Jordan was still prancing in the conga line. "She can't even wear that thing for trick or treating. Now Hutton wants a strapless gown to wear for Halloween."

Simon looked shocked. "But she's only seven."

"Exactly. Wait until yours is talking lipstick and makeup."

Simon made a face. "I don't even want to think about that. When's the auction?"

"In about an hour. It can't get here too soon for me."

Inside the Community Church, Ophelia heard glass shatter. "What was that?"

Seth cocked his head, trying to determine where the noise originated. "Sounds like it's coming from the kitchen. I hope one of the older kids didn't break a window."

But when he rounded the corner into the community room, the second largest space only to the auditorium, Seth spotted a man holding an AR-15. The guy wore two extra ammunition belts across his chest and had some type of device wrapped around his middle section.

Robert Ogilvie leveled his weapon at the preacher and yelled, "Get your ass over here while you still have one."

Seth froze in his tracks.

Ogilvie advanced on him, using the butt of his rifle to hit Seth in the stomach, causing him to double over and fall to his knees.

"Next time I say move, preacher man, move or you won't be giving any more of those flowery sermons on Sunday."

The guy quickly secured Seth with zip-tie cuffs around both wrists and forced him to stand up. "Let's go check on all the little kiddies."

"Why are you doing this?" Seth yelled out.

"Shut up! Just shut your mouth or I'll tape it shut."

Ogilvie forced him out into the hallway and down to the first classroom filled with kids. He opened the door and looked around. "Where's Ophelia?"

"Ophelia who?"

He smashed the rifle into the pastor's face, breaking Seth's glasses. "Wrong answer. Let's try this again. Where is Ophelia? Which room is she in?"

"I'm new here. I don't yet know everyone's name."

"Bullshit. I want everyone here to put their backs up against the wall and sit down."

Spotting the rifle and the cuffs around Seth's hands, Susan Hollenbeck shouted, "These are children. They're no threat to you. Why not let them go?"

"No one's going anywhere until I find Ophelia. Sit down and shut up or you'll get what the preacher got."

Ogilvie yelled out for Ophelia, his voice echoing down the hall. "Get out here, Ophelia. I know you're in here somewhere. I'm not leaving without you. You're only pissing me off more by not coming out. Show me your sorry face. Now!"

In the next classroom over, Neenah Brewer heard the commotion and knew something was wrong. She locked the door and shoved a chair under the handle. She gathered her young charges around her and ushered them into the supply closet, shutting the door behind her. Huddling in the dark as the kids started to cry, she took out her cell phone. She had the police department on speed dial and as her hands shook, she punched in the number.

On patrol near the fundraiser, Eastlyn took the call.

"There's a man here yelling and screaming," Neenah began. "I think Seth is hurt."

"Does he have a weapon?" Those words had no sooner left her mouth when Eastlyn heard multiple rounds of gunfire in the background.

"I'm on my way," Eastlyn said. "Don't hang up. Keep this line open. Try to remain calm and stay put where you are. Try to keep the kids as quiet as possible."

Eastlyn pulled up to the library, put the cruiser in Park, left the engine running as she dashed inside to find Brent.

Her eyes frantically scanned the crowd. She zeroed in on her boss deep in conversation with his brother, Ethan. She worked her way over to where they stood and pulled Brent into a corner.

"There's a gunman at the church threatening everyone. Shots fired."

Brent went into cop-mode. "Get on the horn and call in a tactical unit out of Santa Cruz. Also notify the deputy patrolling this area of the county that we'll need backup. Do it now."

Ethan overheard the conversation as did Simon and Cord.

All four men began moving toward the exit. As they circulated through the crowd a buzz rippled through the festivities.

Logan sensed something was wrong and trailed after them. He caught Simon by the arm just as he reached the staircase. "What's happening?"

"Eastlyn just reported there's an active shooter situation at the church. Shots have been fired. Some guy has taken everyone inside hostage. Ethan's gone to the station to get weapons and vests. That's all I know so far. But someone needs to stay here and keep everyone calm. Don't let anyone leave and go running up to the church. The guy starts opening fire on a crowd outside and we've lost control of the situation for good. No need to give him additional targets."

It didn't take long for the murmurs to reach Gilly. Her eyes searched for Simon in the throng of people who'd stopped dancing. In one glimpse she caught sight of him talking to Logan near the front door. She made a mad dash in that direction.

Breathless, she called out, "What's going on?"

Simon cut his eyes to hers. "Stay put. I'm going with Brent and Cord. There's…a situation…at the church."

"What kind of situation? I'm coming with you."

"No, you're not."

"Don't tell me to stay here. My child is in there. Tell me what's happening."

Bluntly, he laid out the dire scenario.

"Oh, my, God. Could the man in there be Ophelia's ex-boyfriend?"

That stopped Brent in his tracks. "Give me a name."

"Oh. Jeez. Let me think. She told me. It's…Robert something. It was on the police report Eastlyn took. Robert…Ogilvie. That's it. He's been physically abusive in the past. Eastlyn persuaded her to take out a restraining order. Maybe that's what set him off."

"Shit," Brent uttered. "I remember that now. This guy is a nutcase, more money than God, and parents who keep bailing him out of trouble. Let's go. Ethan's bringing the firepower. I want everybody to stay here. That's an order. Simon, Ryder, and Cord, you come with me. You all have Army training. I can count on you to keep calm and do what you're told."

Brent jumped in Eastlyn's cruiser, stepped on the gas, and shot off down Cape May. "We'll set up a perimeter at Main Street and cordon off that part of the block."

About that time, Simon spotted a woman shepherding a group of older children away from the church and across Cape May. "That's Ophelia."

Brent brought the cruiser to a stop and Simon got out. "Is everyone here okay?"

Fourteen-year-old Beckham wiped his nose. "Faye's still in there. I couldn't get to her. She's back there with the young toddlers."

Simon's gut clenched with dread.

Ophelia wrapped up Sonnet Rafferty who was still shaking. She took a step toward Simon. "It's him. Robert is in there terrorizing everyone. He has weapons, ammunition and some device strapped to his chest. I got a few of the older kids out the front door and ran. I should go back and try to reason with him."

"Uh-uh. He's beyond reasoning with now. You go back in there and he'll most likely kill you on sight. Take the kids and keep heading toward the library."

Simon watched her take off with the brood before crawling back inside the patrol car. "We know there's only one shooter and he's armed. Ophelia saw an explosive device attached to his chest. This guy's not messing around."

Brent pulled up to the corner of Cape May and Main about the same time Ethan appeared in another patrol car with the weapons.

"I loaded up everything there was out of the cabinets and everything out of the evidence locker," Ethan told Brent. "Even that 30-30 Winchester you confiscated from Rick Riordan for hunting out of season."

Brent took out the bullhorn and called out to Ogilvie. "Robert, so far you haven't done anything that we can't fix. But you need to let every single one of those kids go now. The longer you stretch this out, the more trouble you're in. Are you listening, Robert? Put down your weapon and come out now before you get in so deep that Mommy and Daddy's money can't buy you out of this."

Brent turned to the others. "That should get some kind of reaction."

It wasn't the one Brent wanted. Ogilvie opened the double doors and appeared on the top of the steps, a knife to the reverend's throat.

"My life's over anyway. I've got nothing to lose," Ogilvie shouted. "I came here to kill that lying bitch Ophelia. And I'm not leaving here until I see her blood running down the streets of this bumfuck town. Get her back here or I swear I'll start killing everyone inside, one by one. I'm ready to blow this stinking church sky-high and take everybody with me."

Using the pair of night-vision goggles Ethan had provided, Cord had been watching Ogilvie. "I have eyes on the suspect. In my opinion, you take him out with a headshot and that device won't explode. He's got it rigged all wrong for instant impact. Simon, you take a look; tell me if I'm wrong."

Simon took the binoculars and studied the man, his vest, and the explosive device strapped there. "No, you're right. This isn't rigged like the ones we've seen before."

"You're only gonna get one shot to take him out," Cord muttered to Brent. "You'd better make it count."

"Let's see if we can talk him down first," Brent offered. "We'll take him out as a last resort. But as agitated as he is, this will only get worse when SWAT gets here. Of the men here, who's the best shot if it comes to that?"

"You're kidding, right?" Cord said, getting the nod from Ryder and Ethan. "It has to be Simon."

Ethan pulled Simon over to the cruiser and brought him up to speed on the collection of weapons.

A sick feeling washed over him. "You know what you guys are asking me to do, right?"

"Yeah, we do," Brent returned. "I'm hoping it doesn't come to that. But we need to have the backup plan in place and you in position."

"My kid's in there," Simon stated flatly, almost to himself, as he scanned the pitiful choices. He shouldered out of his suit coat, loosened the top buttons on his shirt, and picked up the Winchester with what looked like an ancient scope on top.

A ball of revulsion roiled in his stomach as he used a weather vane on top of Murphy's Market to sight in the scope. He took a deep breath, whooshed it out. "If this is the best you've got, then this will have to do."

"Get that bastard to come out," Ethan said to his brother. "Now! Nate's still in there."

"Mine, too," Brent huffed out, holding up the bullhorn to his mouth. He tried one more time reasoning with Ogilvie. "Robert, once SWAT gets here, it's out of my hands. I'm giving you one more chance to think this through. It isn't too late to drop the weapon and put this thing to rest."

"I'm done talking. Here's my answer," Ogilvie said, as he ran his knife across Seth's throat in one fluid motion, then kicked him to the bottom of the steps. He retreated back inside, disappearing behind the door.

Cord ducked down and took off toward Seth's crumpled body. "He's still alive," he yelled back to the others. Cord put pressure on the massive wound. "Help me get him out of here."

Ryder dashed toward them and helped the veterinarian drag Seth's body to the curb out of Ogilvie's line of fire.

Brent turned to Simon. "It's gotta be done. I'm not waiting for SWAT."

Simon automatically checked the mechanism on the rifle and began to load shells into the chamber. "I made a promise to myself I wouldn't do this again. But my baby's in there. A lot of babies are in there. I'm about to break that promise for a stupid asshole who should've been locked away a long time ago. You need to keep him talking until I get in position. The best vantage point should be the bank across the street, second story. Do I bust in or…?"

Nick stepped out of what seemed like the shadows. "No need. I'll unlock the back door for you."

Simon angled toward Brent. "Keep him occupied, I don't care how, but keep his attention on you."

"Will do." Brent tossed Nick one of the two-way radios. "If you're going with him, keep me apprised of what Simon needs, and this guy's movements so we'll be able to coordinate."

The two men took off around the side of the bank building to the alleyway where Nick pulled out a set of keys from his pants pocket and unlocked a back door.

Simon started up the steep steps that led to the second floor. Nick forced open a storage room door with rusty hinges that creaked from lack of use.

"We never use this area, never come up here for anything." He reached up and tugged on a rotten piece of string, a hatch opened from the ceiling. He pulled down an old ladder providing access to the roof. "You get out there, don't fall off."

"I've done this before," Simon murmured as he climbed up and out through the space and onto the rooftop. He crawled along the parapet where he could look down directly onto the front of the church.

"Let me know when you're in position," Nick said quietly.

Simon used the ornamental section of the cornice to hide, sticking his head out just above the scrollwork, then used the ledge to position the rifle on his target. Through the scope, he scanned the double front doors where Ogilvie cowered in the foyer. Periodically, the man looked out at the street, checking for any activity from Brent.

Simon also saw that Ogilvie had surrounded himself with at least three adult hostages.

"How's it looking up there?" Nick asked.

"I need Brent to engage him in conversation, get him to stand up. I need a clearer shot."

Nick conveyed that message back to Brent.

Nervous and beginning to sweat, doubts creeping into his brain, Simon's head throbbed. He heard the two-way crackle to life. It was a voice he recognized instantly.

"Sorry I'm late to the party, Simon, old buddy. But you know you can do this, you can do this in your sleep. I hear there's a couple of hot, young things back at the party who want to meet me, so don't mess this up. I got faith in you, bro."

About that time, Brent stepped from behind the police cruiser with his bullhorn and started across the street toward the church. Standing in the middle of Main Street, Brent taunted Ogilvie. "Come on out, you SOB, or I'm coming in there to drag you out myself."

Ogilvie got to his feet to peer out the door again, the AR-15 poised to take Brent out.

Through the scope of the rifle, Simon zeroed in on his target; he could even make out the smirk that formed on Ogilvie's lips. That's the last thing he saw as he squeezed the trigger.

The shot echoed out into the night.

Brent and Eastlyn rushed the church along with dozens of other parents who'd spilled out from the library and gathered at the corner.

Simon slid down and slumped back against the pilaster, resting his head just under the bank's scrollwork. He couldn't move, didn't want to.

Minutes ticked by as Nick waited for Simon to come down from his perch. He was about to go up and get him when Gilly appeared at the bottom of the steps.

"Is he okay?" she called out.

"Maybe you should give him another five minutes or so," Nick suggested.

"SWAT finally showed up along with a bunch of news vans. Why won't he come down?"

"Probably because he doesn't want to deal with…the aftermath. Like I said, he needs time…"

But Gilly flew past Nick, kicked off her heels, and hiked up her ball dress. She started up the rickety rungs of the ladder. Poking her head through the opening, she wasn't sure what she'd find. She breathed a sigh of relief when she caught sight of Simon, dried tears streaking down his sullen face.

"You shouldn't be up here," he said softly.

"You're up here, so this is where I belong."

"Are the kids okay?" he managed, wiping off his face.

Gilly inched closer. "They're fine. Delaney slept through most of it. Not Jayden though. He's wired."

That got a faint smile out of him. "And Seth? How's the minister?"

"In surgery. Gideon and Quentin are…optimistic." Edging closer, she narrowed her eyes and zeroed in on his clothes. "Look at you, your shirt is ruined. You have stucco stuck in the silk."

"Yeah, well, it's not really my kind of shirt, now is it?"

"Maybe not, but you looked so damn sexy in it. I'm so proud of you, Simon," Gilly announced. "Everyone is. It's time for you to come down now."

"You do realize what I just did, right? What I always seemed to have to do? I'm sick of it. I just want to live my life in peace."

"You did what was asked of you, what someone had to do. Our children were in there. God knows for how long if you hadn't taken him out. Everyone knows it. You saved more than fifty people tonight, Simon. Babies. The town's future. People want to tell you how grateful they are for it and shake your hand."

"I don't want that."

"I know you don't. That's the amazing thing about you. It's what I love." Gilly saved her best ammo for last. "But right now, Jayden and Delaney need to see their daddy."

Simon's head snapped up. "I thought you said Delaney was asleep and Jayden was running around as usual." He started to move, to make his way toward her.

"No, I said she slept through the whole ordeal and that Jayden was all worked up. Now, they're asking for you. Give me that gun and I'll hand it down to Nick."

"I've got it," Simon assured her, suddenly feeling much better. "I'm okay now. I'm fine."

"You sure?"

"I've got you. I've got Delaney and Jayden. That's all I ever really needed."

Epilogue

Four days later
Halloween

The gifts came. The town wanted to thank their hero. Every morning since that night at the church, Simon would walk out on his front porch to find little gifts, note cards attached, some hand-drawn by children, thanking him for what he'd done. Neighbors left food of all kinds, balloons, flowers, jars filled with coins, even cash stuffed down in envelopes.

News outlets kept calling, national and local, trying to get the elusive ex-Army Ranger who'd taken out the man threatening kids to give them an interview.

Simon refused.

Or rather Gilly did. He wouldn't answer the phone, which was even now ringing off the hook.

"That's it, we're changing numbers, home, mobile, the works."

"It'll die down," Gilly promised. "You just have to give it time."

"The phones are bothering the kids."

Gilly hid a laugh while folding a stack of clean towels she'd taken out of the dryer. The kids were oblivious. Mostly. But she knew the constant calling was driving Simon nuts. She couldn't blame him for wanting to put an end to it all.

"At least Seth is healing nicely. His vocal cords will eventually get back to normal. Quentin says he'll probably be able to give a sermon in four weeks or so."

Simon ran a hand through his hair. "It's a good thing Cord and Ryder didn't waste any time getting him to the hospital."

He couldn't see, she thought, his role in the way things turned out. She tried to get his mind on something else and held up two costumes for the kids. "What do you think? Delaney in pink as a little princess and Jayden in a silvery metallic ninja outfit."

"We're taking them trick-or-treating?"

"Of course. And I suggest if you don't want to be mobbed by your adoring fans, you find a suitable disguise to wear. You can't hide in the house forever, Simon. Tonight, we go door-to-door with the kids before heading out to half a dozen parties we've been invited to attend. Faye has offered to babysit. For free. I think she has a crush on you now."

Simon groaned. "This is getting way out of hand. How about we just take the boat out and anchor it in the middle of the harbor until all this nonsense ends?"

Shifting topics yet again, Gilly handed him the dishtowels to put away. "Has Brent found anything out about Del Rio?"

"Only that he's homeless and living out of an old RV in the desert, miles from town or any cell phone service."

"He wasn't drunk or stoned when he called you?" Gilly asked.

"Nope. He's just broken, lost, and not doing very well." Simon began to pace. "No Apache warrior should be homeless."

"When are you leaving to bring him back?"

"I'm thinking of moving up my ticket to this afternoon."

"Oh, no you don't, mister. You're getting out there tonight and facing your neighbors like a man."

"Your Nurse Ratched side is showing, Gilly."

She rolled her eyes. "It's just an evening out with friends. And this is Delaney's first Halloween, your first holiday of any kind with her. Don't let anything or anyone spoil it for you. We'll get dressed and take lots of pics documenting the night to show her later."

"Are you wearing your ball gown?"

She made a face. "No way, I took that back. Too many bad memories. I think most of us plan to get rid of whatever we had on that awful night." She went into the utility room and brought out a large bag, held up a simple shirt and captain's hat. "This is your skipper outfit. I'm going as Mary Ann."

He grabbed her around the waist and nibbled her ear. The stack of towels she'd been neatly folding, toppled over and fell to the floor. "I've always thought Mary Ann was a whole lot sexier than Ginger."

"Good because I want you to go get dressed."

"But it's only four-thirty."

"Rookie. These days kids start trick-or-treating at five o'clock before it even gets dark. I'm feeding them hot dogs and then we'll take off."

They made the rounds, going from house to house on Tradewinds and then hitting most of the shops along Main Street. They walked until the kids were too tired to go on. Even Jayden had tuckered out by seven-fifteen and forced Simon to carry him.

Faye was waiting for them on the porch when they reached the house. She took one of the bags out of Gilly's hand and looked inside. "Wow, you guys really cleaned up. There's enough candy here to last till Christmas."

"Take it," Gilly offered. "All of it. I don't think I can look at another Tootsie Roll Pop or candy bar."

"That's okay. The kids might want…"

Gilly shook her head. "I'm putting Delaney down. She conked out thirty minutes ago and I need to get her pajamas on."

Simon followed her inside. "There's not much to do since both kids are completely wiped. We won't be gone long, probably back around nine-thirty."

"Take your time. I have homework to do. Uh, what do you want me to do with this?"

Simon started up the stairs with Jayden and stopped. "With what?"

"This note I found with the candy."

"I don't remember anyone adding a note to either kid's bag. Let me see that." With his free hand he flipped the folded piece of paper open.

You were here for a reason, the best reason of all. No one could've taken that shot but you. No one could've saved the future but you. Keeping that summer on the Cape alive in your heart was your ticket here, Delaney's ticket to a new life. And now you have a brand-new family to help you through the tough times. Try not to blow it. You'll be tempted to take people for granted. Don't. Take it from me, life is too short to leave things unsaid. Seize the small moments. They might not come around again.

It was signed by Scott.

How could a ghost put his name on anything? Simon wondered.

He turned to Faye and took out his wallet from his back pocket and handed her a twenty. "Sorry, Faye. But we've decided to stay in the rest of the evening. Wait for me to put Jayden down and I'll walk you home."

"That's okay. I just live on Cape May."

"Doesn't matter. I'd feel better if you waited."

"I'll call Beckham. He'll do it." The girl took out her cell phone.

"Okay. But I want to see him show up. Don't take off without him getting here." He needed to explain the change of plans to Gilly anyway, so he climbed the stairs to Jayden's room and started getting the boy undressed, trading the costume for Batman PJs.

Gilly tiptoed into the room behind him. "Delaney's sacked out."

"I told Faye she should go home."

"Why? Simon, you have to get out and mingle some time."

"It's not about that. I…want to be alone with you tonight."

"That's sweet. Fine, I'll go call Kinsey and tell her we won't be coming."

"Gilly?"

"What?"

"You're the one for me, Gilly. The one I need. I want to make Jayden mine, give him my last name, the whole bit."

Sensing the seriousness of what he'd just said, she slid down onto Jayden's bed. "For real?"

"For real. This may not be the perfect moment to ask, but…I want you to marry me."

She opened her mouth but found she couldn't form the words. Her mouth had gone dry. Maybe she was dreaming. "Is this real?"

"It is to me. Will you marry me?"

"Yes, yes I will because I want it all. You. I want so badly for Delaney to be mine. I want us to be a real family."

"That's what I want, to make a life together for the four of us. I know now that's all that matters. It's all that ever mattered."

She held his face in her hands. "I love you, Simon Bremmer, my reluctant hero." When he started to speak, she pressed a finger to his lips. "No argument. You are to me. You're everything to me."

"I can handle that. I'll go run Faye home and when I get back…"

"Beckham showed up to walk her home."

"Already? Then want to go make out under the stars?"

"Absolutely. Every night for the rest of our lives."

Pelican Pointe
Cast of Characters

Promise Cove - Book One

Jordan Phillips—The widow of Scott Phillips living on the outskirts of Pelican Pointe in a huge Victorian with her baby daughter. She's trying to fix the house up to open as a bed and breakfast.

Nick Harris—A former member of the California Guard who served with Scott in Iraq. Nick suffers from PTSD. He tries to adjust back to civilian life after Iraq but finds that he can't ignore a promise he made during the heat of battle.

Scott Phillips—Died in Iraq while serving with the California Guard. In life, Scott was best friends with Nick Harris. Scott doesn't let death stop him from returning to his wife and child and the town he loves. He appears throughout the series as a benevolent ghost helping new arrivals settle in and overcome their problems.

Patrick Murphy—The mayor who owns the only market in town.

Lilly Seybold—Another newcomer with two children living alone on the other side of town, isolated and struggling to get by. Lilly is recently out of an abusive marriage. Lilly and Jordan form a bond.

Wally Pierce—Owner of the gas station and the best mechanic around. He's instantly attracted to Lilly. Their relationship blossoms throughout the series.

Carla Vargas—County social worker and Murphy's longtime girlfriend.

Flynn McCready—Owner of McCready's, a mix between an Irish Pub and a pool hall.

Sissy Carr—Spoiled daughter of the town's banker. Sissy is having an ongoing affair with local developer and shady con man Kent Springer. Sissy went to school with Scott and gives Jordan a hard time at every chance she gets.

Kent Springer—Local developer and sleaze, always working on his next scam. He wants the property owned by Jordan Phillips and will do whatever it takes to get it.

Joe Ferguson—Owner of Ferguson Hardware. Grouch. Complainer.

Jack "Doc" Prescott—Former ER surgeon from San Francisco. Retired. But actively providing medical care for residents.

Belle Prescott—Doc's wife who wants him to retire.

Reverend Whitcomb—Pastor of the Community Church. Wife is Dottie.

Hidden Moon Bay - Book Two

Emile Reed/Hayden Ryan—Arrives in Pelican Pointe during a storm, stranded at the side of the road. She's on the run from a mobster who has defrauded people out of millions of dollars.

Ethan Cody—Native American. Works as a deputy sheriff but longs to be a writer.

Brent Cody—Sheriff of Santa Cruz County and Ethan's older brother.

Marcus Cody—Father of Ethan and Brent. Marcus possesses psychic ability.

Lindeen Cody—Mother to Ethan and Brent.

Margie Rosterman—Owner of the Hilltop Diner, a 1950s throwback to a malt shop.

Max Bingham—Cook at the Hilltop Diner and Margie's boyfriend.

Julianne Dickinson—First-grade teacher who lives in Santa Cruz in the same neighborhood as Marcus and Lindeen Cody. Lindeen often invites Julianne to supper, hoping Brent will take an interest in her.

Janie Pointer—Owner and stylist at the Snip N Curl and best friend to Sissy Carr.

Abby Pointer—Janie's younger sister. Her boyfriend Paul Bonner is serving in Afghanistan

Dancing Tides - Book Three

Keegan Fanning—Marine biologist running the Fanning Marine Rescue Center her grandparents founded.
Cord Bennett—Former army soldier and California guardsman who served with Nick and Scott in Iraq. Because Cord feels guilty about his fiancée dying in a spree shooting, he wants to end it all.
Pete Alden—Keegan's right-hand man at the Fanning Rescue Center.
Drea Jennings—Owner of the flower shop. Her family owns the Plant Habitat, a landscape nursery in town.
Abby Anderson—Works at the Fanning Rescue Center.
Ricky Oden—Founder and lead singer of the local band, Blue Skies. Married to Donna Oden.

Lighthouse Reef - Book Four

Kinsey Wyatt—An up-and-coming lawyer who comes to Pelican Pointe to prove she's the real deal.
Logan Donnelly—Sculptor and artist who relocates to Pelican Pointe with an agenda.
Perry Altman—A five-star chef from L.A. who opened The Pointe, the fanciest place in town to eat.
Troy Dayton—A young carpenter who works hard at surviving everything life's thrown at him.
Mona Bingham—Max's daughter from Texas.
Carl Knudsen—Owns the pharmacy in town he inherited from his family. Married, but not happy. In his younger days ran with Kent Springer.
Jolene Sanders—Hostess at The Pointe. Works part-time as a clerk at Knudsen's Pharmacy.

Megan Donnelly—Logan's sister.

Starlight Dunes - Book Five

River Amandez—Thirty-three-year old archaeologist who arrives in Pelican Pointe harboring a secret. She's in town to excavate the Chumash encampment uncovered during a mudslide.

Brent Cody—Forty-year old sheriff of Santa Cruz County with a bad marriage under his belt and a not-so-stellar record of dating. Brent has someone in his past who wants him dead.

Zach Dennison—Picks up odd jobs around town, trying to make ends meet. Zach lives with his sister, Bree Dennison.

Bree Dennison—Goes to community college in San Sebastian and works as a waitress at McCready's.

Ryder MacLachlan—Cord's buddy from the army. New in Pelican Pointe from Philadelphia and looking to make a fresh start.

Ross Campbell—Pharmacist from Portland, relocates and buys the local pharmacy. Renames it Coastal Pharmacy.

Jill Campbell—Ross's wife.

Last Chance Harbor - Book Six

Julianne Dickinson—First-grade teacher, slated to be the principal of the newly, renovated Pelican Pointe Elementary.

Ryder MacLachlan—Cord's buddy from the Army. New in Pelican Pointe from Philadelphia and looking to make a fresh start.

John Dickinson—Julianne's dad.

Bree Dennison—Goes to community college in San Sebastian and works as a waitress at McCready's.

Malachi Rafferty—Owner of the T-Shirt Shop and single father with two teen girls, Sonnet and Sonoma.
Cleef Atkins—Lives south of town in an old farmhouse. His barn is stuffed with things he's collected over the years.
Drea Jennings—Cooper's sister.
Caleb Jennings—Cooper's brother.
Landon Jennings—Cooper's uncle and adopted father.
Shelby Jennings—Cooper's aunt and adopted mother.
Layne Richmond—Father of Cooper, Caleb, and Drea.
Eleanor Jennings Richmond—Mother of Cooper, Caleb, and Drea.

Sea Glass Cottage - Book Seven

Isabella Rialto—Logan's mysterious renter who shows up in town and starts people talking about her past.
Thane Delacourt—Ex NFL linebacker who comes back to Pelican Pointe to raise his son.
Jonah Delacourt—Thane's six-year-old son.
Fischer Robbins—Thane's best friend from New York and a chef who helps Thane open Longboard Pizza.
Sydney Reed—An ER nurse in St. Louis and Hayden Cody's sister. Sydney relocates to become Doc's nurse.

Lavender Beach - Book Eight

Eastlyn Parker—Ex-army helicopter pilot, crashed her chopper in Iraq and lost the bottom part of her leg. She hasn't adjusted to civilian life very well.
Cooper Jennings Richmond—Son of Layne Richmond and Eleanor Jennings. Photographer who traveled the world but now owns Layne's Trains.
Drea Jennings—Cooper's sister.
Caleb Jennings—Cooper's brother.

Landon Jennings—Cooper's uncle and adopted father.
Shelby Jennings—Cooper's aunt and adopted mother.
Eleanor Jennings Richmond—Mother of Cooper, Caleb, and Drea.
Jonathan Matthews—Eleanor's son.

Sandcastles Under the Christmas Moon - Book Nine

Quentin Blackwood—Doctor replacing Jack Prescott.
Sydney Reed—Sister of Hayden and Jack Prescott's nurse.
Beckham Dowling—Teenage boy, resourceful, savvy, and smart, worried about his grandmother's health.
Charlotte Dowling—Beckham's grandmother who's lived in town for years.
Faye DeMarco—Beckham's girlfriend.
Andy DeMarco—Faye's older brother, who takes care of her after their parents die in a car crash.
Winona Blackwood—Quentin's grandmother, also known as Nonnie.
Stone Graylander—Miwok tribal medicine man. Boyfriend of Quentin's grandmother, Nonnie.
Douglas Bradford—Former professor, moved to Pelican Pointe and became its mayor before Murphy. Owner of Bradford House.
John David Whitcomb—Pastor at the Community Church.
Dottie Whitcomb—John's wife.

Beneath Winter Sand – Book Ten

Caleb Jennings—Brother of Cooper and Drea. Works at The Plant Habitat with his parents, Landon and Shelby.
Hannah Summers—Owns a cleaning service. Picks up

extra money on the weekends working as a waitress at The Shipwreck.

Micah Lambert—Hannah's little brother.

Cora Bigelow—Postmistress.

Lilly Pearce—Wally's wife, who helps him run the gas station and auto repair shop.

Jessica St. John—Works for Cord at the animal clinic.

Jonathan Matthews—Eleanor's son.

Tahoe Jones—Caretaker of the Jennings' cabin.

Delbert Delashaw—Boyfriend of Eleanor Richmond.

Barton Pearson—Funeral director.

Keeping Cape Summer – Book Eleven

Simon Bremmer—Ex-Army Ranger. Sniper. Twelve years in the military.

Amelia Langston—Woman Simon met on Cape Cod.

Gilly Grant—Nurse at Charlotte Dowling Memorial Hospital.

Delaney Bremmer—Simon's daughter.

Jayden Grant—Gilly's son.

Connie Grant—Gilly's mother.

Gretchen Bremmer—Simon's mother.

John Dickinson—Julianne's dad.

Gideon Nighthawk—The new surgeon from Chicago.

Ophelia Moore—Daycare director at the Community Church.

Aubree Wright—Nurse.

Sheena Howser—Nurse.

Seth Larrabee—New minister at the Community Church.

Dear Reader:

If you enjoyed *Keeping Cape Summer*, please take the time to leave a review.
A review shows others how you feel about my work.
By recommending it to your friends and family it helps spread the word.
If you have the time let me know via Facebook or my website.
I'd love to hear from you!

For a complete list of my other books visit my website.
www.vickiemckeehan.com

Want to connect with me to leave a comment?
Go to Facebook
www.facebook.com/VickieMcKeehan

Don't miss these other exciting titles by bestselling
author

Vickie McKeehan

The Pelican Pointe Series
PROMISE COVE
HIDDEN MOON BAY
DANCING TIDES
LIGHTHOUSE REEF
STARLIGHT DUNES
LAST CHANCE HARBOR
SEA GLASS COTTAGE
LAVENDER BEACH
SANDCASTLES UNDER THE CHRISTMAS
MOON
BENEATH WINTER SAND
KEEPING CAPE SUMMER

The Evil Secrets Trilogy
JUST EVIL Book One
DEEPER EVIL Book Two
ENDING EVIL Book Three
EVIL SECRETS TRILOGY BOXED SET

The Skye Cree Novels
THE BONES OF OTHERS
THE BONES WILL TELL
THE BOX OF BONES
HIS GARDEN OF BONES

TRUTH IN THE BONES
SEA OF BONES (2018)

The Indigo Brothers Trilogy
INDIGO FIRE
INDIGO HEAT
INDIGO JUSTICE
INDIGO BROTHERS TRILOGY BOXED SET

Coyote Wells Mysteries
MYSTIC FALLS
SHADOW CANYON
SPIRIT LAKE (2018)

ABOUT THE AUTHOR

Vickie McKeehan's novels have consistently appeared on Amazon's Top 100 lists in Contemporary Romance, Romantic Suspense and Mystery / Thriller. She writes what she loves to read—heartwarming romance laced with suspense, heart-pounding thrillers, and riveting mysteries. Vickie loves to write about compelling and down-to-earth characters in settings that stay with her readers long after they've finished her books. She makes her home in Southern California.

Find Vickie online at
https://www.facebook.com/VickieMcKeehan
http://www.vickiemckeehan.com/
https://vickiemckeehan.wordpress.com

Made in the USA
Monee, IL
24 August 2020

39519321R00226